THE CASKET
cypher

THE CASKET
cypher

BECKY MOREL

To order additional copies of this book, contact:
Xlibris Corporation
1-888-795-4274
www.Xlibris.com
Orders@Xlibris.com
41747

For Claude

Chapter One

Valéry sat stiffly on the stone window seat in her uncle's small chamber. Behind her the last of the day's light filtered through the double lancet window, casting gray shadows of dusk across the floor and walls. In the fireplace, only cold cinders remained from the fire, which must have burned brightly the night before. Of course, under the circumstances, starting a new fire was out of the question. The room had to remain cold because of its only other occupant. Valéry drew her woolen shawl more closely about her small frame and slowly raised her eyes to the bed in the corner. Tallow candles burned at the head and foot of the coffin. Inside its narrow confines lay the body of her Uncle Jacques Lefèvre d'Etaples. Valéry spoke his name in a whisper, wiping away the tears that once again began to blur her eyesight.

He had been so animated at dinner just yesterday. In the company of Queen Marguerite of Navarre and others of her royal court and patronage at Nérac, noted divines as well as men of letters and the arts, he had given thanks for the years of his long life, during which he could pursue his scholarly interests. And ever the priest, he spoke of the great hope which had inspired the difficult and often tedious task of recovering a better translation of the Holy Scriptures, long corrupted by the errors which had crept in over centuries of copying the texts by hand.

"My vision is that of a reformed church which has been given new life and greater purity through a clearer and deeper knowledge of the Word of God," he had declared with an intensity which was rare for this normally soft-spoken and gentle man.

At the end of the meal, he had excused himself early, saying he was quite fatigued. No one was alarmed as he was of very great years and often in the past had retired right after dinner, albeit reluctantly, for he knew he would be missing the lively and learned discussions that inevitably took place then among such an august assembly. This time, however, he turned before ascending the stairs and, with a face aglow, spoke what must have been his last words. "I pray that my work with the Holy Scriptures might lead some to Christ."

Valéry began to sob now, with the poignant memory of her uncle's last hours on earth so fresh in her mind. Toward midday, when he had failed to appear, a servant tapped on his door and, when there was no answer, entered the chamber and found him dead. Word was carried immediately to the queen, who in turn summoned Valéry, and the two hastened to Lefèvre's bedside where they found the great man lying as if asleep, but with the stillness only death can bring. Marguerite summoned several of her maidservants, and together with Valéry, they prepared his body for the coffin. By his own instructions, given several years earlier, they dressed him in the heavy black robe he wore when he taught at the college of Cardinal Lemoine in Paris and added over it the stole given to him at his ordination. Valéry herself placed upon his head the black bonnet signifying his rank of master. She also had tucked a small block of wood under his chin to keep his jaw closed but was gratified to see that his mouth still had its characteristic determined set, and his face its firmness of features. When their task was finished, she had turned to Marguerite and said, "These are the remains of a saint, my queen. How sad that they show only his diminutive stature and the vestiges of his office but nothing of the largess of his mind and spirit."

"My little Valy," her patroness had replied, "What will remain is the memory of his generous nature, his judicious and compassionate spirit, and the multitude of his scholarly renderings, both of the great literature of the past and of the Christian faith. The latter will live well beyond the life spans of those fortunate enough to have known him."

Valéry looked up at the angular face of Marguerite and gave her a little smile, comforted by the truth of her eloquent tribute and by the use of the endearing nickname her patroness often used to address her. Long ago when she first met Marguerite, the great lady had asked her name. Just a child at that time and overawed by the tall and stately woman with the kind eyes, she had replied, "*Je m'appelle Valy*" hardly able to pronounce her own name. And so "Valy" it had remained for Marguerite even now that she was a young woman.

"I will send someone to St. Nicolas to bring the priest, now that we are finished with our work," Marguerite said with a tone of authority. "Please do sit down, my child, and hold vigil until he arrives." With that, Marguerite turned toward the door and disappeared down the stone arcade that ran the length of the upstairs chambers.

In the fading light of day, Valéry seated herself in front of the mullioned window and thought again of her uncle's life. Once he had talked to her of a quibble he'd had with Erasmus of Rotterdam. "He is a brilliant scholar," Lefèvre said earnestly, "but he is wrong on this matter."

"What is that?" the young Valéry asked with honest curiosity, feeling sure that her uncle could not possibly be wrong about anything.

Lefèvre replied by opening his Bible to the psalms. "Look where it speaks of man's nature, just here," said her uncle, pointing to the verse in question. "Erasmus says that the correct translation is 'Thou hast made him a little lower than the angels.'"

"And what do you say, my uncle?" Valéry asked, hardly able to contain her curiosity.

"The truer translation is "Thou hast created him a little less than God."

"Is there a big difference then between angels and God?" Valéry looked inquiringly at her uncle and waited for an answer.

"One must always be sure the Holy Word of God is translated accurately, Valéry," her uncle replied with great seriousness. "Misunderstanding what God is saying to us has eternal consequences."

Valéry was never sure if her question was really answered, but now in recalling this time, she was convinced that Erasmus might have been created a little less than the angels, but her uncle most surely had been created a little less than God. The latter was definitely, she decided, the superior state of creation.

The sound of muffled voices came from outside the window, and soon they grew louder as their source entered the chateau. Soon there was a light tap on the door, followed directly by the entrance of monsieur *le curé* and two deacons.

"*Mon Dieu, mon Dieu*", the priest blurted out, his hand swinging a censer emitting vaporous clouds of incense over the corpse. One deacon carried a cross that he held fast to his face, splaying his rather bulbous nose. The other deacon dispensed little droplets of holy water over the black robe of the dead man. Valéry stood to one side, watching the obviously distraught *curé* fumble with his missal until he reached the right office. Glancing up as Marguerite entered the room, he mumbled, "He was so dear to me, so dear . . . truly a priest to this humble *curé* and an example of Christ's own life to us all."

The deacons nodded their heads in acquiescence as the priest began to intone the antiphon. "*Si iniquitatis observaveris Domine: Domine quis sustenebit?*" Then, looking briefly toward his deacons to be sure they were ready to respond, he continued with the *De profundis*. Valéry closed her eyes as the voices continued on in hushed tones. Was it so long ago, ten years now, that her uncle had recited the same words of Psalm 129 over the body of her beloved mother? Upon receiving word of his sister-in-law's death, Lefèvre had journeyed from the chateau in Blois where he was serving as royal librarian and tutor to the children of King François, back to Meaux where Valéry and her mother were still living even though Lefèvre was no longer vicar general there. After officiating at the funeral mass and burial of his sister-in-law, Lefèvre had asked permission of François I, King of France, to bring his eleven-year-old niece, now an orphan, back with him to Blois. When the answer came in the affirmative, her uncle told her he was sure that it was due in no small measure to the advocacy of the king's sister Marguerite who, with her mother, Louise of Savoy, had first met Valéry when they wintered in Meaux when Valéry was only six. Loving children but having none of her own from her marriage to the Duke of Alençon, Marguerite had taken an instant liking to the little girl when Lefèvre, the scholarly priest and friend of her brother, François I, had introduced them. Wanting to have more contact with the priest's niece, she had spent considerable time helping her learn to read and teaching her some simple lessons from history, French literature, and Latin grammar. "You are so like myself when I was a child," Marguerite told her one day. "You show the same kind of inquisitive mind my tutor, François of St. Mesmin, said I had when my brother and I were brought to Amboise by King Louis after our father died. You are studious, little one, and that is very good and deserves to be rewarded."

When the time came for Marguerite to leave, Valéry, already quite attached to her benevolent teacher, went to her mother in tears. "*Maman*, I don't want the great lady to go. Can you and Uncle Jacques tell her so for me? *S'il te plaît, Maman.*" Her mother simply scooped her up and, holding her close to her ample bosom, said, "I will talk to your uncle, *ma petite,* but the Duchess of Alençon has other things she must be about, for she is a very important lady—the daughter of Louise of Savoy and Charles d'Orleans, who is the Count of Angoulême; the wife of Charles, who is the Duke of Alençon; and the sister of François Premier, who is the King of France." Valéry looked up from the folds of her mother's dress and said solemnly, "But she is also the tutor of Valéry Lefèvre d'Etaples! Surely, *Maman,* that is very important too!" Maddy had laughed delightedly, giving the little girl a hug before setting her down. "You are indeed a treasure to your uncle and me," she said with a chuckle, "but I think the gracious Duchess of Alençon has others who have higher claims on her attentions."

It was only later that Valéry learned of Marguerite's arrangement with her uncle to continue the studies she herself had begun. To this end, she asked him to appoint another teacher from within the circle of scholars at Meaux whom Bishop Briçonnet had gathered around himself in hopes of bringing about some badly needed church reforms within his diocese. Leaving a generous allowance as payment for the tutorage, she had promised to continue her patronage of Lefèvre's niece as long as it was needed.

A loud noise startled Valéry out of her reveries. Opening her eyes, she saw that one of the deacons had secured the coffin lid in place and was holding out to her one of the lighted candles. In surprise, she looked over at Marguerite, who hastened to her side.

"I have given instructions that the Office of the Dead be said tonight, Valy. You will need your warm cloak for the processional to the church. Hurry, child, and join us as soon as you have fetched it from your chamber."

Puzzled at this news since it went against the usual custom, which allowed time for the deceased to lie in state, Valéry hurried down the arcade to her own room and reached in the armoire for the long cloak hanging inside. Made of fine woolen cloth, it was lined in lambskin and trimmed about the collar with vair. It was just one of Marguerite's extravagant gifts to her, and Valéry, always overwhelmed by the generosity of her patroness, had protested the cape at first but nonetheless accepted it gratefully, for the winters were often bitterly cold and damp. Hastily she put it around her shoulders and hurried back down the hall, catching up with the procession just as they reached the door of the chateau. Monsieur *le curé* was in the lead, flanked by his deacons, who responsively intoned the appropriate psalms. Marguerite, holding Valéry by the hand, followed two of the queen's secretaries—Clément Marot, the poet; and Peter Le Maçon, translator of Boccaccio's *Decameron*—as they shouldered the coffin along with Marguerite's valet, Bonaventure Despériers, and several men of letters: John Frotté, John de la Haye, and Gabriel Chapuis, who were also among the queen's retainers. Valéry glanced behind her at other cloaked figures, a curious gathering of the chateau servants as well as distinguished guests, some with candles, others huddling together for warmth as they picked their way carefully over the cobblestone pavement. Valéry could not make out the faces most distant from them but thought wryly that such a mixing of stations—servant and master, erudite and ignorant, exalted and humble—was somehow appropriate for this occasion. After all, death is no respecter of humanly constructed merit. It sweeps from this earthly existence the rich and the poor, the learned and the uneducated, cutting across all the boundaries by which people separate themselves from others. Her Uncle Jacques would have appreciated this tribute from his mourners.

Once inside the church, the coffin was placed on a bier near the chancel and the lid removed. As was befitting a priest, the venerable occupant was placed with his head facing the congregation, and then lighted tapers were set around the bier. Since it was late evening, Vespers for the Dead and then matins came before the Mass. During the rites, Valéry tried to fight back the tears that kept tracing a warm path down her cold cheeks. Marguerite, sensing her struggle, placed an arm around her shoulders, drawing her close. As the priest and deacons droned on, Valéry's head began to hurt, and her feet felt like they had frozen onto the stone beneath. *If eternal is defined as something without end,* Valéry thought, *then this ritual surely qualifies.* The rites dragged on, and then, mercifully, the Mass was ended at last. Valéry watched the priest, now vested in a black cope, go to the foot of the bier for the absolution. The cross bearer stood at the head of the coffin between two acolytes, each holding a lighted candle.

"Non intres in judicium cum servo tuo Domine . . ." intoned the *curé.* After the responsory, he placed incense into the thurible, blessed it, and began incensing the corpse and sprinkling him again with holy water as he silently mouthed the *Pater Noster.* Then it was all over, and as the gathering began to make its way outside into the dark, Valéry went over to the coffin of her beloved uncle, reluctant to leave him. Marguerite came to stand beside her and, after a little while, took Valéry's face between her two hands.

"Valy," she said simply. The young woman, seeing the seriousness in her eyes, looked back questioningly.

When the queen did not say anything, Valéry asked aloud the question which was foremost in her own mind.

"Will he be buried tomorrow then, my queen? St. Nicolas Church here in Nérac has an adequate cemetery, and I suppose it is as appropriate a final resting place for my uncle as any, and certainly convenient."

Marguerite smiled. "You wonder why we did not wait the three days; why I was in such a rush to have the Mass of the Dead so soon after he died, don't you, Valéry?"

The use of her full name came so rarely it made Valéry uncomfortable—as though something unpleasant was about to be revealed.

"Do not be alarmed," Marguerite read her reaction immediately. "I am simply trying to avert any adverse reactions which might take place when the news spreads that your uncle is dead. I gave him refuge from those in powerful positions in Paris who saw heresy in his work and wished to condemn him to death. But I am afraid that even though I have sought to protect many whose vision is a reformed church, I cannot protect them all. Your uncle believed that change within the church could be achieved peacefully. But I fear that news of his death could fan the fires of violence that are burning already between those who think Rome does not need to change and the protestors who are convinced that it must."

"But the news *will* spread, my queen, and I still do not quite understand why he could not lie in state before his funeral and burial."

"Because, child, I am afraid that there would be those on both sides who would make of his death an occasion to come to Nérac and use this sad event as an opportunity to clash. That would not be a fitting way to give final honors to such a man of God as your uncle."

"Then, what *would* be?"

"I have felt it only right that such a great and accomplished man as your uncle and my beloved mentor be buried in the tomb I have prepared for myself."

Valéry was stunned. "And where is that, my lady?"

"It is in the crypt of the Cathedral of Lescar, my child, the place near our chateau at Pau designated for all the kings and queens of Navarre. Already François Faber lies there along with his son Jean d'Albret and wife, Catherine de Foix, who are my husband's parents. There are others of the d'Albret family there too, and one day, Henri and I will add to this number."

"You are a blessed angel, my queen," Valéry managed to respond brokenly, her voice showing the emotion she was feeling. "It is a great honor that you do for my Uncle Jacques, and for myself also."

"Your uncle honored me for many years, little Valy. He counseled me through the deaths of my first husband, my mother, and my little son. He rejoiced with me when I married again. He gave me praise and helpful criticism in my literary efforts, and above all, his scholarly work with the scriptures has deepened my understanding of God's Word and strengthened my faith. How does one return thanks which even approaches adequate for a friend such as that? I shall myself be honored one day to be laid to rest by his side."

Valéry found herself speechless—an unusual state for her, she thought with a slight smile. For a few moments, the two women stood by the coffin and looked in silence at the remains of the great man inside. Then Marguerite leaned toward her protégée and whispered, "Say goodbye to him now, child. At dawn tomorrow, I will dispatch six guards on horseback to accompany the remains via cart to our chateau in Pau. My husband, the king of Navarre, is in residence there now and himself will ensure your uncle's proper burial in the crypt of his family."

"Might we accompany the entourage to Pau, madame?"

Marguerite was firm in her answer. "No, Valéry, no. At best, this journey takes three long days by fast horse. With the cart and the deplorable state of the roads and weather this time of year, the trip will take longer. If we were to go with them, I fear the conditions would be quite adverse to our health, as well as adding to the responsibility of the guards to take care of us."

Valéry felt keenly the disappointment but recognized the wisdom in Marguerite's decision. Turning her gaze toward the still figure in the coffin, she murmured, almost inaudibly, "Then I shall keep vigil over my uncle until the time for departure."

Chapter Two

"Spring seems quite delayed this year," Valéry said to Marguerite as the two women sat by the fire in the queen's large chamber. During the weeks immediately following Lefèvre's death, the queen of Navarre had noticed her protégée's despondency and had seen to it that she was summoned frequently to her side. Here, by the large marble fireplace, Marguerite, who had long practiced the art of writing, liked to dictate to her secretaries various verses or other literary works she loved to compose. Valéry herself helped sometimes with these transcriptions although she also often read to the queen from the wide variety of books at her disposal. Today, however, Marguerite was applying herself to a piece of needlework. Valéry watched the careful embroidery stitches that outlined another device the queen was so fond of designing. Already a number of them had been placed on books or furniture and even given as gifts to royal personages. This one depicted a marigold facing the sun's rays with the motto underneath, "*non inferiora secutus.*" Noticing Valéry's interest, she held it up, saying that because of the influence of the saintly Lefèvre, she was more determined than ever not to follow the lower way in life. "Indeed, child, like this flower, I will strive to turn all of my acts, thoughts, will, and affections towards the great Sun of Justice who is God." Valéry liked to keep her company on such days, for Marguerite, needle in hand, would engage her in lively conversation on a wide range of topics.

"This March *has* been cold and sunless," the queen replied, rethreading her needle with a bright orange *fil.* "I will have to content myself with this embroidered flower while wishing for a gentle rain and warm sun to encourage my garden to grow once again." Valéry recalled how beautiful the chateau grounds had been last summer. Winding about the preexisting oak and chestnut trees, Marguerite had designed paths bordered by violets and primroses, impatiens and pansies. *Pruniers* and *pommiers* were added, making a small orchard along with the addition of several *noisetiers* and *noyers*, for the queen loved fruits and nuts. At that, Valéry thought, Marguerite enjoyed the whole out-of-doors, often riding her horse through the surrounding countryside, which afforded her a chance to stop and talk with her subjects as they labored in the fields. Walking was also a joy for her, and frequently, Valéry would notice her strolling through the chateau grounds, gathering various flowers and herbs that had been planted there by her order and according to her design. Sometimes she would sit down under one of the large shade trees, writing a poem or little story, just to lay down her pen and the ivory of her tablets, seemingly lost in contemplation.

Valéry tried to stifle a cough, turning her head away from Marguerite and pulling out a *mouchoir* to cover her mouth. Marguerite looked at her in concern.

"You are *enrhumée*, my poor little lamb. I have noticed that you do not eat well and that you are unusually pale."

"Ah, madame, please do not worry yourself over me. I have never eaten heartily, and with my dark hair and white skin, I fear I must always look a bit wan. No, I have just a little tickle in my throat and will be quite all right, I assure you."

Marguerite paid no attention. "Child, I will call for my chambermaid and order an infusion straightaway." With that, she pulled the bell cord by the fireplace wall, and soon her servant appeared. "Mademoiselle is ill, Josette. She is in need of a *tisane d'osier*, which I will prepare for her if you will bring the infusion pot filled with boiling water, a *petite cuillère*, and a little honey."

The girl disappeared immediately and returned shortly bearing a tray. While she was gone, Marguerite had gotten a jar from inside her armoire. Valéry watched as she undid the lid and sniffed the contents.

"These are the pulverised and dried pieces from water-willow bark, child. Years ago, an apothecary who also fancied himself a thaumaturge prescribed this to relieve my pain over a cold. Thinking it a nostrum, at first I was reluctant to try it, but as I grew worse, I changed my mind. To my great surprise, the aches disappeared, and I felt so much better. You will profit from it too, my Valy." With that she put a soupçon of the substance into the pot's strainer and then added the hot water. After a few minutes, she removed the top portion of the pot and poured the liquid, now tinctured, into a cup and handed it to Valéry.

"Put a little honey in it, Valy, as you will find the mixture quite bitter to the taste." Valéry did as she was told and then put the cup to her lips. The drink was hot and felt good on her throat as she swallowed, but then she made a face for the medicine was indeed acrid. Marguerite laughed.

"You will be feeling much improved shortly," she assured her protégée. "Do you wish to lie down for awhile?"

Valéry shook her head, finishing the last of the infusion and placing the cup on the tray.

"I wish to remain here with you, talking of warmer weather and cheery gardens, my lady." She looked over at Marguerite, who had again seated herself by the fire and taken up her needlework. She had the long face of a Valois, with its characteristic large nose and mouth, but one did not notice these features as much as one saw the kindly eyes, so often crinkled up at the corners when she smiled, and the sweetness of expression which dominated her face. The poet Marot, whom she had called into her service, exalted her beauty in verse written to honor her. Well that he had also praised her dignity, affability, and talent, which could not be disputed by anyone. Valéry did not much care for Clément Marot. He was a hanger-on in the courts of the king of France as well as in the circles of Marguerite. His dalliances with women, along with his insincerities aimed at soliciting royal favors, made her uneasy in his presence. She avoided him whenever possible while not denying that he had talent as a versifier.

Valéry settled back against the tapestry of her tall-backed chair, enjoying the comfortable silence between the older woman and herself. The warm fire, coupled with the infusion, began to take away the chill and aches she had felt earlier.

"You seem better now," Marguerite observed as she leaned forward, fire iron in hand, to stoke the burning logs. Valéry nodded, much to the queen's satisfaction. She continued, "It takes time, my little Valy, to be able to move on with one's life after the loss of a beloved. You will recover both your health and joie de vivre, given time. I know this because I have experienced such over the course of my own years." Marguerite fell silent for the moment, setting to one side her embroidery in order to lay a comforting hand on Valéry's arm. "It will mark twelve years this coming summer that my little niece Charlotte died. She was so young and such a favorite daughter of my brother, the king. At first I thought that I could not bear the sorrow, having sat by her sickbed for thirty days, hoping and praying she would recover, and her own mother, Queen Claude, so recently dead. Afterwards, I imagined in a poem I wrote that while I was sleeping, I cried out to the soul of my little niece, asking her to speak to her aunt whom she'd left behind. 'Are you happy in the triumphant court of our King and Father? Answer so that the intense sorrow I feel will be lightened.'" Valéry saw tears in the eyes of her patroness and this time it was her turn to gently touch the arm of her patroness. The two sat in silence for a few minutes, watching the fire as a log burned through and fell to one side. Outside, rain began to pelt the large windows of the queen's chamber. Finally, Marguerite broke the silence.

"I have had much sadness in these last years, child, for in addition to burying my first husband, the Duke of Alençon, I lost two baby girls before having my daughter Jeanne, and a year later, after the joy of giving birth to my son, Jean, he died at five months, on the very day we celebrate the birth of God's son. Not all sorrow is brought by death, either." Marguerite paused for a moment, a sigh escaping her lips. "There is the matter of my brother, the king, taking away from us our only living child to be raised at the Chateau du Plessis. You see, he was concerned that her father and I might wish to marry her one day to someone other than his own choosing." Marguerite covered her face with her hands and remained so for what seemed like a long time. Eventually, she raised herself and, looking over at the young woman beside her, commented on their rather gloomy conversation fitting in with the dismal state of the weather. The two women laughed a little at that observation.

"Come, let us talk of happier things. We shall look to the future, Valy. First, I have been meaning to share with you my plans once the weather improves. I will be leaving soon for a visit to the court of my brother."

"You will be going to Fontainebleau?" Valéry tried to sound enthusiastic at this piece of news.

"François is anxious that I come to him, in whatever chateau he is residing. As you know, he does not like to be separated from me for very long! Neither, apparently, does my husband. Henri repeatedly has sent messages asking that I join him in Pau, that we might enjoy the hot summer months nestled in the shadow of the beautiful Pyrenees."

"You are much in demand from your strong men, madame! However will you please them both?"

Marguerite smiled. "It is easily done, little Valy. I shall leave here the first of May to make the journey up north where Paris and the environs will be warm and pleasant. Then when the summer heat begins, I shall go south to the realm of my husband and enjoy the cool of the mountains and streams in the rolling hills of the Béarn."

"Would you like me to accompany you, my queen? I should be glad to do so, if that is your wish."

Marguerite looked down at her needlework and after a minute asked, "Is that what you want to do?"

"I am not sure," Valéry replied simply. She pictured the long days on horseback and the rough roads over which they would be traveling. Then too, the court of the king of France, with its glittering array of nobility, resplendently dressed, playing at this intrigue or that amour, was not to her taste or within her own station in life. The minor court of Marguerite in Nérac was much less pretentious. Here she was familiar with her surroundings and had made the acquaintance of some of the townspeople as well as those servants and guests who would remain in the chateau. As for the d'Albret chateau in Pau, other than being able to visit her uncle's crypt, there were no guarantees that her life in the southern limits of the Kingdom of Navarre would hold much for a woman of her station.

Marguerite, as though she read her thoughts, continued with a note of firmness in her voice. "I think, Valéry, that it would be best for you to remain here in Nérac, at least for a little while. Here you will have a chance to grieve the loss of your precious uncle in the environment he so enjoyed during his last days, and you will continue to be in the company of some of my other retainers and protégés who choose not to go with me to Paris. For instance, my secretary, John de la Hayne, will remain as he prepares several of my manuscripts for publication. In addition, Clément Marot wishes to stay, along with his collaborator Goudimel, until the psalms they are translating and setting to music are finished. Then Marot at least will join me in my brother's court, a life to which he is admirably suited."

Valéry shuddered at the thought of the company of Marot but did not say anything. There would be others around to whom she could talk and plenty of solitude when she wished to be alone with her grief.

"I have an assignment for you during the months I am gone," Marguerite said.

Valéry brightened at the thought, for Marguerite's "assignments" were always stimulating.

"It is time, I think, for you to be about sorting through the contents of your uncle's chamber. I know it will be hard, child, but it must be done. He has left some belongings which will not be difficult to dispose of, but it is his sizeable collection of manuscripts and publications which is valuable. As you know, right now they are stacked up in cupboards and corners as well as on his écritoire and commode. When I used to visit him in his chamber, it was hard to find a place to sit, and I was forced, as you were, to perch myself on the window ledge. In retrospect, I am amazed that he didn't use that place for some of his literature and writings."

"I think he feared the rain and damp might seep through the window and ruin the paper," Valéry laughed in spite of herself. "But I am ready to face the task, and I thank you for the privilege of this undertaking."

"There is one more thing," Marguerite added with some gravity in her tone. "I am asking you to think about your own future, Valéry. You are not of the noble class and thus cannot hope to make the kind of marriage alliance that I would wish for you. But you are exceptionally well-educated and quick of mind. That must not go to waste as it would if you were to accept a marriage below your level."

Valéry gave the queen a puzzled look, to which Marguerite reacted immediately.

"It is true that you are my protégée and as such extremely well brought-up, but Valéry, I cannot arrange for your marriage into a class to which you have not been born. What I can do, though, is to see to it that you find a meaningful living which makes use of your learning and abilities. Think, then, of what would satisfy you, and we shall work toward realizing that."

That evening, as Valéry lay in bed, she realized more clearly than ever since the death of her uncle that she was not a child any longer. The last of her family was gone, and her patroness would be leaving for other responsibilities incumbent with her rank and station. Marguerite was right. She needed to move on. But where? The thought brought with it some anxiety and yet, in some strange way, she felt exhilarated. Instead of lying awake for hours, Valéry fell asleep without difficulty. Tomorrow she would apply herself to sorting out the contents of her uncle's room as well as begin to sift through her own hopes and dreams for the future.

Chapter Three

May was fast approaching, and with it came a flurry of activity about the chateau in preparation for the queen of Navarre's departure. Stable hands and valets readied the horses and mules, along with cleaning and repairing the litters for their trip northward. In the kitchens, foodstuffs, including dried fruits and smoked meats, were assembled and bundled for the journey, and within each bedchamber, the clatter and chatter of the various chambermaids packing up belongings filled the normally quiet hallways. Marguerite herself chose the guardsmen and personal servants she wished to accompany her. Those of noble title in her court, as well as the literati she'd played hostess to, decided whether or not they wished to join the more exalted court of King François I in the newly completed and certainly resplendent chateau of Fontainebleau. Most of them fancied the opportunity which infused the atmosphere around them with a lively excitement. Others decided to return to their various home territories.

There were also in residence some divines to whom Marguerite had given refuge from the accusatory theologians of the Sorbonne who saw in the proclamations of these religious men heresies against the church and were seeking to condemn them. Her uncle had been among those accused and at one time had even been forced to flee to Switzerland to escape punishment. King François himself had called him back into his service and protected him until he retired and went to Nérac at the invitation and under the protection of the king's sister. Others on the run from the Sorbonne's persecution pursued different agendas, and Valéry had often sat among the refugees at the queen's chateau, listening to their animated discussions on the reforms needed in the church and how to achieve them. Valery remembered that Marguerite, who sympathized with them, had often told her that the only crime of these religious men had been to point out the fallacies of thought and practice seen in those who held exalted ecclesiastical positions and to call for much-needed changes. They had hopes much like her uncle's, Valéry thought—that such a reformation of the church would take place without violence. But the Sorbonne had begun to react in ways which were very threatening. The divines who were presently residing at the chateau would have to find refuge elsewhere now that Marguerite was leaving. Some had already fled to Switzerland where John Calvin and others were preaching reform. She remembered well when the latter had sought out her uncle a few years earlier. He was young and brilliant and certainly committed to his vision of a purified church.

In the midst of such activity, Valéry had decided to leave her work with the contents of her uncle's room until after the bulk of the chateau's population had left. It would be easier then to concentrate on what she needed to do, and besides, she wanted to be with her benefactress as much as possible. She had grown much closer to the great lady during the time she and her uncle lived at Nérac. Valéry realized that those precious days now hung on memory's wall, and although she was ready to move on to new ventures, the love she felt for the queen of Navarre would make their separation difficult for her.

Making her way to the queen's chamber, she was surprised to find the door wide open and an array of maids sorting through her possessions. Josette looked up and smiled as Valéry entered the room.

"The queen has gone to the kitchens, mademoiselle. Fancy that—*she* in the kitchens and *I* sorting through her wardrobe. It should be the other way round, but madame insisted that I choose the garments and jewels she will carry to the court of her brother, and she will pick the food to accompany her on the way there!" The young servant did not look all that distressed, Valéry observed with some amusement. In fact, she surmised that little Josette was reveling over the honor of being chosen for this task and joyous at the opportunity to handle such treasures.

"I shall seek her out then, in the kitchens. Thank you, Josette." Valéry found Marguerite some minutes later, just as Josette had said, talking with the chief cook as they lifted jars and boxes off the storage shelves in the pantry.

"You found me out, Valy," Marguerite remarked as the young woman made her way around the large oak table in the center of the room. "Come here, child, and help us with these condiments." Onto the table they placed the various containers, opening them and sprinkling the contents out. *Raisins secs,* along with dried *pommes* and *poires,* were mixed with *noisettes* still in the shell. "These will travel nicely with us," Marguerite commented as the three of them scooped up the various fruits and nuts, depositing them into several sacks.

"I have seen to it that the harvest from my orchards, vineyards, and nut groves last fall were not all lost to the birds and other wildlife," Marguerite remarked. "As you can see, the fruits have been dried and stored in jars. The nuts I gathered myself. They have not been shelled yet, for they store better this way, but that is no matter. Cracking them will provide an amusing pastime for my entourage when we are hungry enough!"

A young lad who served as turnspit in the chateau's kitchens helped carry the sacks up to Marguerite's chamber. "I prefer keeping these edibles with my things," Marguerite commented on the way. "Put with the general baggage, they have a way of disappearing as if by magic, with nary a soul able to account for what happened to them."

Valéry smiled. "Are the fruits hard to dry? I remember my mother slicing apricots and prunes and placing them on a tray in a sunny window before closing them in tight-lidded jars. That way we always had fruit clear through the cold winter days." It seemed so long ago now although the memory of her dear mother, plump and tender like the fruit she picked to dry, always seemed fresh in her mind.

"It is really quite an easy thing to do," Marguerite replied. "All one needs is the fruit, a knife to prepare it, and the heat of the sun's rays." They had reached the queen's chamber where Marguerite directed the turnspit to deposit the several bulging sacks in a corner with other baggage now assembled and ready to go.

"We shall we ready to depart in the morning," the queen said as she looked about the room in satisfaction that most of her belongings were packed and ready to be loaded onto the pack mules. Turning to Valéry, she asked,

"Will you come to the farewell banquet this evening, Valy? It will not be grand because most of the preparations the servants have made leave little time for cooking a splendid meal, but it will bring together this special group for one last time of fellowship before we leave."

Valéry tried to hide the growing sadness she was feeling. "It will be such a pleasure, my lady, to be included."

Valéry rose early the next morning, dressing in a hurry so as not to miss the grand departure. The chateau courtyard was crowded with an array of those who would be making the journey—servants, guards, men of letters and titles, horses, mules loaded down with baggage, and litters filled with noble ladies who did not wish to ride by horseback. Marguerite herself preferred her own horse and stood now by the dappled steed surveying the scene.

Spotting Valéry in the crowd, she hurried over to her, enveloping the petite young woman in her arms and giving her a kiss on the top of her head. Then, stepping back, she scrutinized her comely features, skin white as porcelain, nose as small as hers was large, lips and cheeks the hue of a spring sunrise, and especially the large blue eyes, now filling with tears. "Your best feature are those eyes, child," the queen said softly, wiping with her gloved hand the droplets which fell from Valéry's black lashes. "Remember what we talked about, Valéry. I have treated you as a young girl because you are like my own little daughter to me, but you are grown now and ready for another kind of life. We will talk of this when I return in the fall. I shall miss you, my Valy."

After a kiss on each check and one again added to that, the stately Marguerite mounted her horse, and the procession was off. Valéry stood in the courtyard, looking after them until the last horse in the *arrière garde* disappeared from view. Slowly she turned toward the chateau with a heavy heart. Her beloved Marguerite was gone. Her uncle did not wait for her in the chateau. In all her years, she had never felt so alone. As the heavy portcullis clanked down behind her and the massive oak doors of the chateau opened to let her through, she was overwhelmed by another emotion. For the first time in her life, she felt fear. Decidedly, it was a sensation she did not like.

Chapter Four

For the next several days, Valéry kept to her room, asking that meals be brought to her there. Certainly she would find solace in the company of those who had chosen to remain at the chateau, but that would have to wait. First, she needed to sort out the emotions that kept overwhelming her usually outgoing and enthusiastic nature. When Marguerite had first told her she would be leaving Nérac for visits to her brother as well as with her husband in his chateau in Pau, she had rejoiced, for she knew that these journeys would be pleasant for her benefactress. Even then, when Marguerite expressed concern for the welfare of her protégée, Valéry had been excited, for it meant the possibility of new venues for her own life. But after Marguerite left, the reality of what that meant began to sink in, and doubts about her future crept into her thoughts. Perhaps it was because, for the first time in her life, she was truly alone. For some years, she had always had her mother, Maddy, and her Uncle Jacques. The gracious queen of Navarre took her under wing when she was barely six and provided for her education and the welfare not only of herself but of her uncle as well. As a child, she had taken it all for granted, as children do, for she lived in the moment, not given to thinking much of the past or worrying about the future as long as the "right now" was secure.

Valéry walked over to the one window the room provided and looked out. The beautiful gardens of the chateau lay below her, greening now with newly unfolding leaves and brightened by the profusion of daffodils rivaling the yellow of the sun. She looked away as the tears began to fall, as they had so often since the loss of her beloved uncle. On the far shelf she saw one of the books he had given her after it had been published. It was a translation of the psalms, printed in five parallel columns, each in a different language, which Lefèvre had compared and then rendered his own translation as the best text. This she would treasure, along with all his other materials, but right now it simply served to remind her of her loss. Loneliness must go along with feelings of loss, she thought, although she could not remember being quite as devastated when her mother died, for her uncle had been there. Equally as overpowering, though, was the new sensation of being afraid. She should be grateful that her protector and patroness had promised to support her. But there were no guarantees about the future—not for her, not for Marguerite, not for anybody, she thought with some degree of cynicism.

Walking over to the large armoire set against one of the walls, Valéry pulled out a metal key she kept in the pocket of her skirt and opened the door. Above her, on the top shelf, sat one of the most tangible reminders she had of her mother. Reaching up, she grasped the small chest and then sat down with it on her bed. Memories came flooding back as her fingers traced a path over the exquisite casket. Made of jasper, the dark green of the stone contrasted beautifully with the ornate gold mount of the ovolo moldings. Figures of Roman soldiers blowing trumpets stood guard at each corner, with tiny tortoises beneath their feet to support the coffer. Carved into the middle of the left side of the jasper-faced stone lid was her name. Her fingers traced the elegant letters Valéry, which were followed by a complex of gold filigree covering the rest of the lid. Her very earliest memories were of this box. She was about four at the time. They were living in Paris, her mother and herself, in a house on Rue de l'Echaudé, provided for them by the Abbey Church of Saint Germain-des-Prés where her Uncle Jacques was a priest in residence. One day, as she was eating her *petit déjeuner*, her mother smiled at her from across the little table in their kitchen.

"Do you know why this is a special day for you, *ma petite?*"

"It is the day you will take me to the fair of St. Germain?" Valéry answered hopefully, a note of excitement in her voice. She had watched the preparations for this great event as merchants from many trades and businesses set up their stalls on the grounds of the abbey. Every day the marketplace was crowded with people, laughing, eating *friandises,* and having fun as they wound their way around the grounds. Valéry had begged her mother to take her, but with each plea, her mother shook her head, saying it would be way too hard for her to walk that far and definitely too expensive if one succumbed to all the temptations to buy.

"Please, *Maman,* can we go today?"

"No, Valéry. The fair is for those who have money and can help benefit the finances of the abbey by spending their coins. But," she quickly added as she saw her daughter's face fall, "this day is special because it is your saint's day, and in honor of that, I have a great treasure to show you, which will one day be yours when you are old enough." With this she went to the armoire, and reaching high up, she withdrew an object which she set down gently on the table before her daughter. Valéry forgot immediately her disappointment at not going to the fair as she looked at the beautiful little box. She had never seen anything quite as exquisite.

"What is this, *Maman?*" she had asked excitedly as she ran her finger over the shiny green side of the casket.

"That is a precious stone called jasper, child, and it is held in place all around by real gold, with fancy gold scrollwork on the lid next to these letters. See, they spell your name, carved right here on the top."

Maddy took the little girl's finger and had her trace the grooves of the letters that spelled out Valéry. Valéry remembered now that this was how she had learned to write her own name. But it was what came next that had made the greatest impression. After wiping her hands on her apron, her mother slowly opened the lid to reveal a fold of plush green velvet, which she carefully withdrew. Placing it on the table, she unwrapped it to reveal the contents. It was the most beautiful necklace Valéry had ever seen. She gasped in awe and amazement as she looked at the exquisite piece of jewelry hanging from her mother's hand. "Look, *Maman,*" she'd exclaimed. "Those are tiny gold hands, each holding a jewel the size of a grape and the color of wine! And see, they are connected to each other all the way around, with such a big hand and stone hanging in the middle. It is almost as big as my fist!" Her mother had smiled at that.

"I don't think it is nearly as large as that, child, but certainly larger than the other hands and stones." Then, sitting down on the bench beside her daughter, she continued, "Valéry, I am going to tell you a story about this box with the pretty necklace." Valéry remembered her mother's face then, for much to her surprise, the look of contentment that usually characterized her features had disappeared. In its place was another expression that Valéry could not quite understand.

"Are you sad, *Maman?*" Valéry queried. Once she had seen her mother cry and had never forgotten it. She was afraid that might be about to happen again. Maddy was quick to reassure her that she was only trying to recall something that had happened in the past, and that she was all right. Valéry remained puzzled, however, as she watched her mother's mouth twitch and her chin tremble. Then, too, there was something to her downcast eyes which bothered Valéry, for her mother always looked into her face whenever she talked to her.

"When your father, Etienne, and I were first married, we lived in a little seaport town called Etaples, far to the north of us. Etienne's older brother was your Uncle Jacques, and he had already left to join other students from Picardy in Paris where he was pursuing his studies. Soon after that, we found out that you were coming, and we were overjoyed." Maddy's voice broke here, and Valéry sat patiently, waiting for her to continue.

"Not long after your arrival, your father went to fight for our King François in the battle of Marignano. It was a great victory for our king, but when other men of our village who had fought in this battle returned, your father was not among them. They told me the sad news that I had been widowed. You were so little, and I was so young." Maddy's voice trailed off, and she fell into silence for a moment.

"Didn't I make you happy, *Maman?*"

The older woman looked lovingly at her little daughter. "You are the most precious thing in my whole life, *mon trésor*. I think I could not have gone on living if it hadn't been for you." Tears now filled her eyes, and Valéry threw her little arms around her mother's plump neck.

"Please, *Maman*, don't cry, for see, I am here still to make you happy."

Maddy quickly recovered her composure, wiping her eyes with the corner of her *tablier*.

"The story gets happier now," she said, holding her daughter close for a minute. "When word was sent to your Uncle Jacques, my *beau frère*, that his brother was dead, he left for Etaples immediately, insisting after he arrived that I take you and return with him to Paris. By that time, he was teaching and able to offer us a modest place to live near the University of Paris. And that's what we did, my little one."

"But what about the beautiful box and the necklace, *Maman?* I thought this was a story about that!"

"And so it is, child, but just be patient a little, and you will hear how this came into our possession. Before your father left for battle, he gave me the casket with the necklace in it and had your name etched on the lid. He said that it was a treasure for his little treasure, which was you, Valéry. Perhaps he had a premonition that he would not return to see his little daughter grow up."

"What is a premonition, *Maman?*"

"It is when you have a feeling that something might happen, even though it hasn't happened yet or might not ever happen." Valéry wrinkled up her face, trying to think of a time when she had had that kind of feeling. Nothing came to mind. Her mother continued.

"I have saved this story to tell you until I thought you were old enough to hear it, Valéry. Someday you will be old enough to keep the casket and to wear the beautiful necklace, but for now, we need to put it away where it is safe."

"But I wish to wear it now and to keep the beautiful box by my bed," Valéry had blurted out.

"It is far too valuable to treat like that, child. Come now, help me to put it back where it will be safe."

"May I kiss the big stone first, *Maman*? Surely Papa would like me to do that, wouldn't he?"

"That would be a lovely thing to do, and yes, it would make your father very happy to see how you value his gift."

Shaking herself out of her remembrance, Valéry lifted the lovely piece of jewelry to her mouth and once again kissed the larger claret-colored gem. Garnets were not as valuable as rubies, but Valéry loved the deep red color of these cabochons better than the pinkish red of the more valuable gem. The former showed off much better the richness of their tone against the delicately cast gold of the hands which clasped them, and the larger hand and garnet which dangled from the middle of the necklace was surely the pièce de résistance. Even now, Valéry felt awed at its magnificence. She held the necklace against her chest for a long moment before putting it back in the casket, closing the lid, and replacing it as her mother had done so many times before, far back on the highest shelf of the armoire. On very special occasions when Valéry had worn the necklace here at the chateau, Marguerite herself had praised this precious piece of jewelry, saying it was worthy of gracing the necks of the highest-born women of the land but could not possibly have looked as beautiful on any of them as it did on Valéry.

How many were the times her mother had repeated this little ritual, she thought. Each year, on Saint Valéry's day, the casket would come down, the necklace held up in wonder, and the story retold. Always, her mother seemed to struggle as she recounted the tale. It must have been hard for her to think back to that difficult time.

She too must have gone through the same feelings of loss and lonliness which Valéry herself was feeling now. No doubt, there was also fear of the future as she wondered how she would be able to earn a living as a widow with a baby to care for. Valéry felt a strangely comforting bond with her beloved mother which she hadn't felt before. While she had missed her and for many years, longed to have her loving presence with her once again, she had never thought much about her mother's feelings. Yet look at how well she took hold of her new life, sewing to bring in some income in addition to what her brother-in-law could provide and raising her little daughter with love and devotion.

Her death, which came some years after they had moved from Paris to Meaux to be with her Uncle Jacques, who was serving as vicar general there, had not been entirely unexpected, for Maddy had grown quite heavy and was warned to be careful. It did not seem to make a difference, though, until her heart was unable to support the extra strain. She died quickly, and her uncle, who was then in Blois, working as librarian and tutor to the king's children, came immediately. The move with him to the grand chateau on the Loire had been exciting, for she could sit with the children of the king and learn along with them the lessons her uncle taught. He also enlisted her help with the cataloging of the wealth of manuscripts and printed books the king had collected, and she was fascinated with the beautiful writing and the information which they contained.

As Valéry prepared herself for bed that evening, she felt a new sense of hope. She had been loved. She had been educated. She was young, with her whole life ahead of her. She would not give in to her feelings of loneliness and grief. Neither would she let fear of the future dominate her life. Her own mother had not buckled; her uncle, who had invested so much in his niece, would expect courage from her. Marguerite was asking her to think about her future and was prepared to help her realize it. She was indeed undergirded by arms now felt but not seen anymore. She was blest by the continuing patronage of Marguerite. *Today is gone*, she thought as she nestled down under the sheets of her feather bed, *and tomorrow will see a new Valéry Lefèvre d'Etaples*. With that resolution, she felt a peace which had eluded her during the past weeks. She closed her eyes, a smile still on her face as she fell asleep.

Chapter Five

When Valéry opened her eyes, the sun had just begun to cast pale yellow rays through her window, creating a pathway across the floor right to her bed. *It is a good omen for the day*, Valéry thought, *and certainly a call for me not to faire la grasse matinée!* She arose with enthusiasm for what the new day might bring and was dressed by the time the knock on her door came and Josette entered the room with her *petit déjeuner.*

"Put it down just there, Josette," Valéry said, indicating the small round table by her bedside. "Oh, and Josette, beginning today, I will be taking the big meal of the day with the others."

"Very good, mademoiselle." The young chambermaid smiled in approval. "We have only a small number of guests now since *madame la reine* left. You know most of them, I think, and certainly you'll enjoy their company, for they all seem to have animated discussions with each other during the meal. And I do believe that sometime today, there will be the arrival of another guest whom Queen Marguerite told us about before her departure."

Valéry finished her breakfast and then made her way down the arcade to her uncle's chamber. She had not been in his room since his death and at first felt sad as she surveyed his belongings. Once he had told her that when he died, he would leave his body to the soil, his soul to God, and all his goods to the poor. *The first two are already accomplished*, she thought. Now she would address herself to the last task. Just as Marguerite had said, at first glance, the room was littered with manuscripts and printed books which had been collected, edited, translated, or even written by her uncle over his lifetime. These would be hers now to sort through, and that would take an appreciable amount of time and effort. Opening the armoire, she took out the clothes, folding the priestly garments into a neat pile: surplice, stoles, chasuble, and one black *soudane*, with its long row of buttons clear down to the hem. These might be appreciated by monsieur *le curé*, who while not as

31

slender as her uncle, was of about the same height. The other garments were folded into a separate pile. As for the remainder of his belongings, she would leave be the few pieces of furniture that were his and let the *curé* dispose of the rest since he knew better than she the needs of his village. Wrapping the pile of clerical robes into a length of sheet, she decided to pay the *curé* a visit. The bundle was not very heavy, and besides, the day was sunny and inviting. A walk would do her good. Outside the chateau, Valéry turned down the cobblestone road which wound its way around to the stone bridge arched across the Baïse. Valéry stopped to lay down her bundle for a moment and looked below her at the river. It was not large or impressive as some rivers, but rather lazy, providing a hospitable home for fish and ducks, both of which she could see from her vantage point. The dirt paths by its banks were busy with villagers going here and there as they went about their business of the day. Valéry moved on, arriving at the church just as a group of young boys were exiting. The *curé* stood right behind them in the door, stopping as he spotted Valéry coming towards him.

"*Bonjour,* Mademoiselle Lefèvre. But this is a nice surprise on such a beautiful morning. I am delighted to see you looking so cheerful, for you have suffered a difficult loss in the death of your uncle."

"*Bonjour,* monsieur *le curé.* I am quite well, thank you, and see—I have brought you my uncle's clerical robes, in case you might have need of them." She held up the bundle of clothing with a smile.

"*Eh bien,* indeed I would be most appreciative," the priest replied, motioning her to come inside. "As you can see, I have just dismissed my class for the day, very good lads all, who are anxious to learn their catechism as well as some other simple lessons which I am happy to teach them. They come for an hour each morning of the weekdays, so I guess that I am monsieur *le professeur* as well as monsieur *le curé.*" He chuckled a little as he led Valéry through a side door of the nave and into an anteroom of the rectory apartments.

"We meet here," he said, motioning toward the little row of chairs set facing a lectern.

"What, besides catechism, do the boys learn, *monsieur?*" Valéry felt a growing interest in these classes offered by the village priest.

"I am teaching them a little grammar at the moment," he replied, looking rather proud of himself. "I think it is very important that the young acquire some learning, and I am happy to be the person who can make that possible."

"And where are the young girls?"

The priest looked surprised and then confused. "Why, I imagine they are home where they belong, helping their mothers. It is doubtful," he added with a note of conviction, "that any learning such as I offer would do them much good. After all, where would they use it?"

Valéry did not reply, sensing that the last question was meant rhetorically, stating what the priest judged to be the obvious. *Why argue?* she thought to herself. *His mind is made up and will not be changed by whatever I might say. But I do not agree with him.* She tucked that away in her mind, resolving to think more about what she saw as an opportunity for the future—her future! Instead, she asked the priest if he would be able to help distribute to the needy of Nérac the rest of her uncle's worldly goods.

"I would be most willing to do that," he replied.

"Then, perhaps you might be able to take a look at what my uncle has left and then dine with us at the chateau today?"

"I will be there with gratitude, Mademoiselle Lefèvre," the priest replied. *"A tout à l'heure."* As Valéry returned to the chateau, she felt annoyance that the priest was so sure there was no need to educate the girls of the village. Marguerite would be as incensed at this attitude as she was. She resolved to have a talk with her in the fall after the queen returned.

After stopping by the kitchens to tell those responsible for the main meal of the day that there would be an additional guest, Valéry returned to her uncle's chamber and surveyed the disheveled state of his books. She would need to decide how to organize the materials before she could even begin. Sitting down on the window seat, she thought of the different periods in her uncle's life. There were his years as a professor in Paris where he taught philosophy and mathematics and became the leading Aristotelian authority of his time. In his desire to purge the great writings of the ancients of alien elements, he had sought better texts and applied himself to purer translations of Aristotle's *Physics* and *Metaphysics* and a whole host of other learned writings which would enable him to better teach these subjects. That would be one category of organization. Then came a growing interest in the great mystics and his efforts to recover better texts of Christian literature and holy scripture. Added to this were other materials of the trivium, including some grammars he had used in tutoring the king's own children. As she sat surveying the room, an idea occurred to her which she found exciting. Marguerite had often spoken of the library her first husband established in Alençon and also the one she and her husband, Henri, had amassed at their chateau in Pau, but there was no such library here at Nérac. Because Marguerite was a woman of letters herself, she certainly would approve of the organization of another library here in the northern capital of her Navarrese kingdom.

There came a knock at the door, and Valéry, startled out of her thoughts, found the *curé*, accompanied by two boys, no doubt his pupils.

"Please come in and help me with the clearing-out which must be done," Valéry said as she invited them into the room. "I would ask that you overlook the furniture, the books, and my uncle's writing materials, for they will remain here, but the rest is yours to take if you know of any villagers who would benefit. There are cloaks and shoes in the armoire as well as toiletries and other personal possessions of which I have no need." Valéry smiled at them, noting the wide eyes of the priest's young students. Most probably they had never been inside such a grand domicile as Marguerite's chateau and no doubt had looked upon the outside of this one with curious eyes almost every day of their lives.

"We have brought a cart, which we left at the entrance door, mademoiselle. My students will load it up and take it back to the rectory when we are finished here. I will be happy to remain for the meal." The priest and his two young villagers then went about the room, picking out what would be useful. Before long they had a number of large bundles, which took several trips to the cart in the courtyard. Within the hour, the cart was well loaded and the boys took off, both of them pushing the cart from behind.

A bell within the interior of the chateau announced the main meal of the day, and the priest, following his hostess, sought out the dining hall. One long table with a bench on either side was set for the meal. Among those now seating themselves were three men, two of whom Valéry knew from before Marguerite had left.

"Monsieur *le curé*, I would like for you to meet two of our queen's secretaries—Monsieur John de la Hayne and Monsieur Clément Marot. They both were at the funeral Mass for my uncle." Valéry looked at the other man who accompanied them and added, "I am afraid I have not had the pleasure of meeting you, monsieur." The stranger smiled and introduced himself as Claude Goudimel.

"Monsieur Goudimel and I are collaborating on rhyming the psalms and setting them to music—I on the first task, and he on the second," Marot explained. Valéry noted Marot's light brown eyes set against the bronze tones of his face. His smile, under the well-trimmed moustache and bearded chin, was pleasant enough, but something about the attentiveness of his look made her uneasy. Perhaps she was just imagining things, tainted as he was in her mind by the tales which she had heard of his various amorous pursuits of ladies in the court.

As they were taking their places around the table, two more of Marguerite's guests entered the room. John de la Haye went to greet them and make introductions.

"We are honored to have the seneschal of Poitou and his wife join us tonight," he said with obvious warmth. "They are resting here for a few days before continuing on their journey to Pau where Henri d'Albret awaits them."

The seneschal nodded to the group and helped his wife take her seat before sliding his rather large frame onto the bench beside her. He did not smile but expressed his gratitude for a bit of a rest before they continued their travels.

"I am most happy to be away from my region for a time as there have been numerous disturbances which I find very difficult to control," the official stated with a firmness which conveyed well his displeasure.

"And what is the nature of those disturbances, monsieur?" a voice from the doorway queried.

Valery turned to see an older man dressed in ecclesial robe walk toward the table. Valéry thought he looked familiar, but she could not imagine where she had seen him before. He was at once greeted by Clément Marot, who sprang from the table to approach the newcomer.

"My dear friends," Marot waved his hand theatrically over the gathering, "It is a privilege indeed to have the abbot of the Monastery of Clairac in our midst."

From the exaggerated manner of Marot, Valéry surmised that this must be a distinguished person. She looked at the abbot with interest, still wondering if they had met sometime in the past.

A smile flickered across the older man's face and perhaps just a slight expression of annoyance also.

"Please, please, Monsieur Marot, I am just Gérard Roussel, on my way from my old position as abbot at Clairac to a bishopric in Oloron and quite disappointed that our gracious Queen Marguerite is not presently in residence. Also I had hoped to have seen one last time my beloved colleague Lefèvre, but sadly, he has been taken from me and all those who loved and admired him here on this earth."

As he sat down at the end of the table, Valéry suddenly remembered where she had seen him. Leaning forward, she looked down the table at the speaker.

"Abbot Roussel, although you will not be able to see your dear friend, you can, however, speak with his niece, who remembers you from the days we all lived in Meaux!"

The venerable priest, surprised at this announcement, threw back his head and laughed in delight.

"Truly, it is little Valéry then, grown into a charming young woman and still in the care of her benefactress, I see. It has been so many years, and so much has happened since the days when the circle of Meaux was together. We will talk, mademoiselle, before I leave for my new assignment. Ah, but I am delighted at finding you here."

After the others around the table had introduced themselves, Roussel looked at the seneschal and repeated his question.

"You spoke of disturbances in your area, monsieur seneschal. Just what is the nature of these?"

"The instigators seem to be a rather disorganized group of men," he answered, "who seek to make trouble for the Holy Church and her prelates. Ever since that awful affair of the placards in Paris, two years ago, these rabble-rousers go by night through our towns, breaking statues of the saints, destroying holy relics, and distributing hateful handbills accusing the church of all sorts of abuses against God and the people. I am charged with keeping order, and I am finding it quite difficult."

"Everyone has heard of those broadsheets in Paris," the *curé* of St. Nicolas added. "They were straight off somebody's printing press, nailed to boards, and apparently posted all over the city and beyond. One was put even on the bedchamber door of King François. He was incensed, I hear, wondering who had the audacity to flaunt such hateful venom against the church clear to his residence in Amboise."

"No doubt it was a group of radical dissenters who were intent upon defying the authority both of the church and the kingdom." The seneschal spoke with a rising voice, his face turning an intense shade of pink. "These *loups-garous*, as they are called in my jurisdiction, these despicable werewolves, know full well that the unity of our land is based on one law, one faith, and one king. It is their intent to destroy this for their own nefarious purposes. When they refuse to pay their tithes, when they mock their priests and monks and accuse them of all sorts of unsavory practices, the result is the disruption of the peace and a threat to our land."

The seneschal's wife, a seemingly timid soul, Valéry thought, as she noted the woman's downcast eyes during most of the meal, spoke next, her soft voice belying the feeling behind her words.

"I try to be obedient to the church, and I know that it is not perfect, but when my husband showed me one of those fliers, I could hardly believe my eyes. The fanatics who wrote it were crude and abusive, denouncing the Mass as a horrible and execrable blasphemy, and depicting the pope, cardinals, and priests as vermin, liars, and false antichrists. Their ultimate insult was to call for everyone to reject the church and all its practices."

John de la Haye, who had been silent during this exchange, laid down his knife and cleared his throat loudly enough to draw attention to himself.

"I was in Paris during the aftermath of that, for I was seeking a publishing house courageous enough to put into print a collection of Queen Marguerite's poetry I had compiled."

"Courageous enough, Monsieur de la Haye? Why do you say that?" Valéry, who had spent hours at Marguerite's side while she composed her beautiful verse, could not help but express her surprise.

The queen's loyal secretary hastened to explain. "Perhaps you did not know that after the distinguished Parisian printer Antoine Augereau published our queen's poem, "*Miroir de l'âme Pécheresse,*" he was condemned for heresy, hanged, and then burnt at the stake, mademoiselle. It was only at the intervention of her brother, the king, that Marguerite herself escaped the cruel and bigoted censure of the Sorbonne."

"But I still do not understand what there was to condemn in her moving confession of a sinner's soul," Valéry said.

"In my opinion, it had little to do with the contents of the poem, mademoiselle. It had everything to do with power and control. The Sorbonne was not consulted first as to the contents. They had not given their official permission that there was nothing objectionable contained in the work."

Valéry looked incredulous at this piece of news. She could not help but feel anger towards the men who had the temerity to pass judgment like that on her beloved patroness. No doubt her brother, the king, felt his own authority challenged by the theologians of the Sorbonne and refused to concede to them, especially when it involved his own sister!

"At any rate," de la Haye continued, "a year later, after the affair of the placards rocked Paris, the theologians of the Sorbonne condemned the placard, and the Parliament ordered a search for the unknown bill-posters. Suspects were tortured, their tongues torn out, their hands cut off, and some of them were even burned."

Valéry shuddered, looking to her uncle's dearest friend for some sort of reply. Roussel got up from his place and began to pace back and forth as he spoke. He commanded the attention of all present, Valéry noted with some pleasure, for her uncle had often talked of his friend's eloquence when preaching.

"My dear friends," he began, "I would ask that you keep in mind two things. First, the actions of those horned theologians of the Sorbonne show that they regard any departure, real or contrived, from their own teachings as heresy, and they look to the Parliament of Paris to enforce obedience to their doctrinal pronouncements, even to the point of punishment by death. But in addition, one must take a good look at those whom these two bodies condemn and not judge them all by the same measuring stick. The queen of Navarre and her publisher are not at all in the same category as the fanatical perpetrators of the broadsheets. The latter's stupid and utterly mindless actions have done great damage to the cause of those who work peacefully for a church purged of its errors."

"But there seems to be a confusing variety of people who call for reform, Abbot Roussel," Goudimel observed, his face reflecting the perplexity he felt. "The venerable Lefèvre worked to give to the world better translations of the Holy Scriptures, even putting them in the French vernacular so that all would have access to the pure Word of God. You, abbot, preach the Word eloquently. I was one who listened to you in awe three years ago when, under the sponsorship of Marguerite and Henri, you preached in Paris during Lent. Marot here is working on rhyming the psalms in our language, and I, setting them to music, with the hope that they may be sung even by people in the streets! But there are also those who have broken with the Church of Rome and are teaching their own version of the one true faith. Some have fled persecution in France, but there are others who remain, and it seems many have become militant in their protests. Furthermore, how does the Sorbonne make distinctions between them all?"

"There is a simple answer to your last question," Roussel replied. "They do not even try. As for the divisions we see developing among those who protest the present state of the church, I believe that, unlike the Sorbonne, we m*ust* differentiate between them." Then, looking directly at Marot, Goudimel and de la Haye, he continued, "We are not breaking with the Church of Rome, and we are not violent. It is much to my sorrow that we are being persecuted and that this movement appears to be taking on a hateful face. I fear that the conflict between those who have an investment in the status quo of the church and those who seek to change it will only grow more intense."

"You and I have had to flee outside France, Abbot Roussel, as did Lefèvre," Marot interjected. "We joined others in exile, but unlike us, many of them remained there to be able to more freely pursue reforms apart from the Church of Rome."

Gérard Roussel nodded. "I myself have met with one such when he came to the Abbey of Clairac. His name was John Calvin, and I did not much care for his doctrine or his methods. However, he also met with Lefévre here at Nérac, and I think my gentler friend got along with him better than I!"

The room was silent for a few minutes as those gathered at the table tried to swallow both their food and the content of the discussion they were having..

After Valéry had finished eating, she offered the last reflection of the evening. "I agree with you, my uncle's dear friend, Abbot Roussel. One must make the effort to distinguish between those whose actions result in harm and those whose work results in blessing. My uncle used to talk about priests whose vocation calls them to lovingly shepherd their sheep but whose main goal was to fleece the flock instead. 'By their fruits ye shall know them,' he would tell me, pointing to the passage in St. Matthew's gospel. I think that is the best measure we can use!"

Roussel glanced appreciatively at her and smiled. So did Marot, much to her displeasure. The latter reached over to touch her hand, letting it linger longer than Valéry deemed appropriate. Hastily, she rose from the table and hurried from the dining hall, fearful that if she tarried, Marot would corner her with unwanted advances. Back in her room, she barred the door and prepared for bed. The presence of her uncle's friend was tremendously comforting to her. She would look forward to the meeting he had promised her before he left.

That came sooner than expected. Early the next morning, Valéry decided to take a walk in the orchard. All about her, the fruit trees were heavy with blossoms, a fragrant harbinger of the fruit to come. It was here that Gérard Roussel met her.

"*Bonjour ma petite* Mademoiselle Lefèvre." Valéry greeted him in return, relieved to see him looking quite refreshed and obviously as pleased at their chance meeting as she was. Seating themselves on a marble bench placed under the white blossoms of an apple tree, Valéry smiled over at him.

"It was a lively conversation we were having yesterday at dinner, if not a bit disturbing," Valéry began. "I have a feeling that much more could have been said, but wasn't. Perhaps that was just as well."

"Yes, it was wise to stop where we did, child. For one thing, there were too many knives available on the table if the talk escalated into argument!"

Valéry looked startled but then realized that the abbot was chuckling as he spoke. She felt more relaxed at this bit of humor, especially since it came from one who was so intimately involved in the turbulence of the times. She was curious about his present situation, but also she wanted to take advantage of the wisdom of this man who had meant so much to her uncle. Perhaps he could help her now as she faced the challenge of her own future.

"Did you enjoy your abbatial at Clairac? Will you be sorry those days are over?" Valéry wondered if her uncle's dearest colleague and friend was finding such a move difficult.

"I enjoyed Clairac, especially because of the abbey's principal means of support. Years ago, the monks had decided that a good source of income for the abbey would be the planting and cultivation of plum trees!"

"How unique," Valéry observed. "Were there already such trees in the region?"

"There were some which grew well but haphazardly all over the territory of the abbey domain. Then, years ago, a monk brought back a special kind of plum he'd found on the crusades and crossed it with this local species of plum. It had produced beyond anyone's imagination. Thus, the monks of Clairac decided to lay out orchards, harvest the produce, and surprise of all surprises, dry some of the crop to make a new fruit, which kept well for a whole year!"

"I have never seen such a fruit. How is it called?"

"They named it *pruneau*. It turns black and all wrinkled up as it dries. The townsfolk of Clairac loved it and helped in the process of growing, harvesting, drying, and marketing. Of course, the biggest need at first was for enough land. Here a local seigneur, Charles de Clairac, was a real boon. Interested in an additional source of income himself, he donated a sizeable portion of his domain to the abbey and even helped in the planting and eventual harvesting of the crop. In addition, he decided he would try to ferment the juice of the plum. The first batch, which he called *pruneau d'Agen* after a nearby large town, was a huge success both with the abbey and the townspeople. He was still at it when I left!"

"I will try to harvest those plums when they are ripe," Valéry said, pointing to an adjacent plum tree, "and then dry them as you say! It is always wonderful to have fruit all during the winter months. As for fermenting the juice, I will just take your word for it that *pruneau d'Agen* is as good as you say!"

The abbot laughed right along with Valéry, and then turning to the young woman, he asked, "And what else will you be doing, niece of my dearest colleague? Both your uncle and your benefactress have seen to it that you received a most excellent education. Surely, your ambitions go far beyond that of picking fruit."

Valéry sighed and then took a deep breath as if first trying to rid herself of the old life and then attempting to inhale the air of new possibilities.

"My patroness has rightly pointed out that I need to be thinking beyond my present situation, *mon père*. When she returns this fall, she has promised me that we will talk about it, but I am sure that she means for me to move beyond where I am now. She does not want me to marry below my educational level, but neither can she arrange for my marriage to someone in a higher station than mine."

The abbot frowned. "Is marriage the only hope for an educated young woman like yourself, Valéry?"

There was silence between the two as Valéry pondered his question.

"Abbot Roussel, since you were so close to my uncle, I hope I can be honest with you. I know that my beloved Queen Marguerite has a husband who does not always treat her well. It is even common knowledge that he has built a home for his mistress right here in Nérac. I would rather never marry than to have a marriage like that."

The priest reached over to pat her head. "Valéry, I did not mean that you should give up the idea of ever marrying, and if a good marriage is one of your hopes, I shall keep that intention in my prayers for you before God. But, my child, God calls each of us to serve Him in ways that suit our uniqueness. Your education, for which both Marguerite d'Anglouême and your uncle sacrificed their time and energies, surely is one of the ways you can return honor to them both as well as to God."

Valéry's eyes filled with tears, which she hastily sought to wipe away before the abbot saw them, but to no avail. The priest reached into his robe and withdrew a large *mouchoir*, which he silently handed to her. When she had recovered her composure, she attempted a reply.

"My uncle has left a formidable amount of materials, *Père* Roussel. They would make an outstanding collection for a library here in the chateau, one I feel sure Marguerite would appreciate. Since I helped my uncle with King François's own library at Blois, I am sure I could organize one at Nérac also." Valéry looked to the abbot, hoping for some kind of validation for her idea. After a few minutes, he replied.

"And what else did your uncle do when he was at the chateau of Blois?"

"Why, he taught the king's children. He was a wonderful teacher, *mon père*, so learned and knowledgeable but also patient and very kind. I think the children loved him like a grandfather, and benefited, as did I, from his lessons."

"Are men the only ones who are able to teach, Valéry?" Roussel leaned over to look at Valéry full in the face. Valéry's large eyes opened even wider at this, her hand flying to cover the smile on her lips.

"Of course not, Abbot Roussel. I could teach, and very well too, I think. Do you know that the *curé* here in Nérac offers classes to the boys of the village but thinks that girls have no need of his lessons? I wonder what he would make of the education that I have had?"

"If you do not use it, Valéry, then our monsieur *le curé* and others who hold his bias will continue to be certain they are right."

Valéry lay awake far into the night, going over and over the conversation she had had with the abbot of Clairac. He had given her a great gift—of that she was certain. She felt the presence of her beloved uncle lending support to his friend's idea. She had not gotten validation for setting up a library at the chateau, but she did receive something even better. Teaching was an honorable calling, and one for which she knew she was suited. When sleep finally came, she dreamed of a classroom filled with girls, and herself conducting the lessons.

Chapter Six

Valéry was seated unceremoniously in the middle of the floor in her uncle's room, surrounded by stacks of books, manuscripts, and other papers. Gérard Roussel had just left that morning, anxious to take up his new benefice as Bishop of Oloron. As he bade farewell to his best friend's niece, he again reminded her of the importance of honoring her uncle as well as her benefactress by making use of the education they had invested in her. He, in turn, promised to continue the vision which her uncle and he had shared, by preaching the restored Word of God. So with the abbot's voice still fresh in her mind and a renewed sense of purpose, she sought to apply herself once again to the task Marguerite had given her.

A voice from the doorway broke her concentration.

"My child, why have you done this to us? Monsieur de la Haye, Goudimel, and I have been worried, searching for you everywhere." Valéry looked up into the solemn face of Clément Marot, who apparently had been studying her intently before she was aware of his presence.

"Did you not know that I must be about my uncle's business?" Valéry replied, then playfully added, "May we be forgiven for the liberties we have just taken with those verses in the Bible!"

Marot looked amused.

"You would, of course, know your Bible well as I imagine you have availed yourself of your uncle's translation of it into French."

Valéry fumbled around in the books before her, finally laying her hands upon the very Bible to which he referred.

"When Queen Marguerite asked my uncle to recover a better text of the Bible, he set to work believing that if he translated it into the vernacular, he would be putting the treasures of the faith into the hands of all the people. Of course, his work was condemned by the Sorbonne, so it had to be published out of the country in Antwerp. We are fortunate, indeed, that copies have been smuggled back into France, but they have to be carefully concealed."

"Blessed are they who are persecuted for my sake, for great will be their reward in heaven."

"I would like my rewards here and now, thank you. At least I wish that the work of my uncle's life might bring some spiritual blessings into the lives of others, and to this end, I am trying to put some order into the material he has left us."

Marot cleared off a stack of papers on one of the chairs and sat down.

"And do you have, somewhere in this mess, a copy of your uncle's translation of the Psalms?"

Valéry searched further and held up a copy of the *Psalterium Quincuplex,* handing it to Marot, who was obviously interested.

"It is indeed an impressive work, and one which Theodore Béda was glad to use in his translation of the psalms into French. And it is Béda's work which I have made use of to put the psalms into rhyme so that Goudimel might set them to music."

"I have heard you singing some of them here at the chateau, monsieur."

"Ah, not me, mademoiselle. I sing like a *grenouille* attempting to attract flies for supper! No, it is my collaborator who has the voice. When we finish, we will be gratified if others avail themselves of our work and begin to sing the psalms, for they were *meant* to be sung."

"I imagine that they would be especially popular among those who are protesting the abuses of a clergy who sees such liberties with the scriptures as heretical."

"So I would hope, Mademoiselle Valéry. You know that our Marguerite was the one who commissioned me to do this work with the psalms in the first place. To this end, Goudimel and I have remained behind here at Nérac to complete several more, which we intend to present to her in Paris and, of course, to our patron King François."

"In spite of your not having a good voice, monsieur, I would like to hear the results of your recent labors."

Marot stood up from his seat, tossed his head back, and sung a few verses.

Valéry listened with interest and applauded sincerely after he had finished. "You are quite modest about your voice, Monsieur Marot. It is much better than you would allow."

"And, you, mademoiselle, are much warmer on the inside than you let on with your cool behavior."

Marot left his chair and came to stand over her. Valéry began to feel uncomfortable once again. Something in his manner was disarming and felt dangerous. Yet it was hard to keep up her guard with such a congenial and talented protegé of both the king and his sister, Marguerite.

Rising to her feet, Valéry picked up a small stack of books and placed them on one of the shelves of the armoire.

"These are some of the little texts which my uncle used in tutoring the king's children. Several are on grammar, a few more on languages other than Latin—see: here is one of Spanish, another on Italian, and two additional books on Hebrew as well as Greek. Of course, it is wise to study French also. My uncle was so gratified when two of the king's sons, François and Henri, showed a special interest in literature written in this language of ours. My own favorite volumes are the ones from literature."

Marot came to stand beside her, ostensibly to examine at closer range the books, but also, Valéry feared, to be closer to her. Quickly, she stepped back and returned to her place on the floor.

Marot turned lazily and sauntered back over to his chair.

"You would make a good teacher, mademoiselle."

There again was the charm of the man, Valéry thought to herself.

"Monsieur *le curé* says it is a waste of time to educate girls," she replied. "He holds classes for the young boys of his parish after their catechism is finished."

"Well then, there is precisely where he is shortsighted. This is the dawn of a new age, and with it comes a realization that women have much to contribute to the new learning. Look at our Marguerite, for she is a fine example of this. There are others also. In Lyon, where I have spent much time, I can think of more ladies who are well educated and sharing this knowledge as they are able."

"Lyon!" Valéry exclaimed. "Marguerite once said that this was her favorite city. That surprised me since I know her first husband, Charles, Duke of Alençon, died there under her care. I would have thought that the memories would be hard for her to bear."

Marot waved his hand in dismissal of this idea.

"That was an alliance not of the heart but of convenience. She, no doubt, was glad to be rid of him."

"Monsieur!" Valéry could not hide her astonishment at such callousness.

"*N'importe quoi,*" Marot was impatient at her reaction. "What I mean to point out to you, mademoiselle, is that I know personally some ladies who are making good use of their talents in ways other than for the satisfaction and amusement of men." His voice sounded earnest, but his eyes, traveling slowly over her petite frame, put Valéry once again on her guard.

"I would be interested in hearing about such women, Monsieur Marot, if you would stop your veiled insinuations."

Marot's eyes brightened at this observation. "You are indeed a fruit ready to be plucked and enjoyed, and I savor that thought, in spite of the prickly exterior I see. No, no, mademoiselle, put your sword away for the moment at least," he added hastily as Valéry began to get to her feet, anger motivating her movement. "I will tell you about a woman who gladly received from the city the use of a priory disgraced for its abuses. Here she is running a home for girls, teaching them the art of sewing and spinning, and even how to read. Then there is a great hospital, truly a model of its kind, managed, if you will, by women!"

Somewhat mollified, Valéry sat back down but remained on edge.

"You will be particularly interested," Marot continued, "in Pernette de Guillet, who is an expert in tongues both dead and living, a graceful musician, poet, and renowned for her knowledge. She is indeed an accomplished spinster, who has the good and bad fortune to live during these days when the new learning is changing our world. She is leaving her mark, for she and other like-minded ladies have gathered around themselves others who wish to learn to assert their minds and become equal companions of men. Some have begun schools of their own. Others are exploring the publication of the volumes they are producing, feeling it right to avail themselves of the great print houses of Lyon."

"They must have the backing of some who are wealthy," observed Valéry. Marot nodded in agreement.

"True, there is the need of a living for these women. But, Valéry, you have the support of Marguerite, as do I!"

"You have the added advantage of the king's favor, monsieur, and the revenues from the royal house because of your writings."

There was silence for a few moments. Then Marot spoke. "I have two advantages over you, mademoiselle: I am talented, and I am a man." Valéry stifled an urge to chastise his arrogance and let him continue.

"But you have two advantages over me."

"Surely, you are straining yourself to think of them, Monsieur Marot."

"Not at all," he replied evenly. "First, you have a formal education while I am self-taught. Second, you have beauty to use to your advantage with men—the right men, of course."

"I intend to take advantage of the former, Monsieur Marot. As to the latter, the very thought sickens me. I have seen too much of where that leads for ladies of the court, and I want no part of that kind of life. Now, if you please, I must ask you to leave me to my present pursuits."

Marot stood up. As he strolled towards the door, he stopped briefly, and over his shoulder, he got in the parting quip.

"You speak bravely now, but you are not so impervious to corruption as you seem to think. We shall see just how immune to male guiles you really are. I shall look upon it as a challenge."

Chapter Seven

Summer finally spread its gracious panoply over the countryside, and Valéry found it impossible to stay inside with her books and manuscripts all day. At first, since she was an early riser, she would begin each morning by taking a walk. Sometimes it was through Nérac, stopping to talk with the villagers who she was getting to know. Some of them she had seen at Mass. Others were the families of the young boys the *curé* taught each day, the latter of whom she now knew by name since she often visited the priest before or after his lessons, bringing him bits and pieces of materials which her uncle had used in his own tutoring. Always she made note of the young girls of the village, not yet old enough to be carrying a significant load of work around the house yet not so young as to be tethered to their mothers' *tabliers*. The very idea of the priest that these girls would be a waste of time to teach still annoyed her, a feeling she did not want to lose as it was giving her the resolve to prove him wrong.

On other days, when she just wanted to enjoy the quiet of the countryside, she would cross the arched stone bridge and follow the path along the banks of the Baïse, flanked on both sides by the open pastures and fields of grain which so characterized the Néracais landscape. Willows dangled their slender leafy arms into the tranquilly-flowing waters. Little groups of ducklings paddled their tiny webbed feet as fast as they could to keep up with their mothers. Fish jumped to catch the bugs flying close to the surface of the river. Here Valéry could let her mind run freely, imagining herself in a classroom filled with attentive girls of the village, who were becoming much better at their grammar lessons than the *curé's* class of boys. Inspiration, she thought, could be found if one was clever enough to be able to infuse some fantasy into the reality of the moment.

On those days when she slept later than usual, she would seek out the beauty of Marguerite's gardens, sometimes gathering flowers to put in the great hall where all could enjoy them, other times sitting with her back against a tree, reading from the various books in her uncle's collection. At first when she chose the chateau gardens she was left to her own amusements. It was not long though before Marot, noticing her habit, would find her there, and although he was certainly charming and often complementary, his real motives were not above suspicion. He made Valéry uneasy, and as he got more forward in his manner towards her, she resolved to avoid him whenever possible.

In the afternoons, when the intense heat of the day made it unpleasant to be outside, she was grateful for the coolness of her uncle's room where she could devote herself in comfort to the sorting and cataloging of his literature. By midsummer she had finally finished her work, but much to her dismay, the room still looked disheveled. The problem was that other than the storage room she had found on the shelves of the armoire, there was nowhere else to display the various sorted manuscripts and books which she had placed in little piles all over the floor. A solution came to her one day as she sat by the banks of the Baïse, throwing some dried crumbs from her morning's bread to a noisy family of ducks floating by. Shelving needed to be built along the walls to hold upright the collection of printed books. For the larger and bulkier manuscripts, slanted racks could be fashioned from sturdy oak, with strips of birch attached along the front to keep the material from sliding and enabling one to attach a chain, binding manuscripts to rungs so that they would not be stolen. After all, it was wise to exercise precautions. Marguerite had often told her of the disappearance of some very valuable, hand-illumined manuscripts, which were found missing from both her library at Alençon as well as that of her husband in Pau.

Excited about her idea, Valéry hurried back into town, stopping at the atelier of the local *menuisier*. Monsieur Jallais was at work when she arrived and looked up, smiling.

"*Bonjour,* Mademoiselle Lefèvre. If you seek my son Michel, he is off helping my brother with a load of wood we have purchased for my carpentry."

"*Bonjour,* Monsieur Jallais. No, I seek you, for I am hoping you might be interested in a project at the chateau."

"Are the king and queen in need of more furniture, then?"

Valéry laughed. "I believe there is quite enough of that as it is, Monsieur Jallais. Instead, what I have in mind is the construction of some pieces to hold books and manuscripts for a *bibliothèque*. It will be to honor the memory and the life's work of my uncle. I would be able to offer you a reasonable amount of money as I have a modest allowance which our good queen has seen fit to give me. I cannot think of a more worthy way of using it than to invest it in shelves and racks to contain my uncle's materials."

Monsieur Jallais laid down his lathe, obviously attracted by such an offer of income and by the prospect of contributing some of his handiwork to the benefit of the royal house of d'Albret. "Would you like for me to see the room? Before I can begin such work, I will need to measure and then discuss with you just what you want me to make."

"Could you come tomorrow afternoon, Monsieur Jallais?" Valéry was excited now over her plans and just a little apprehensive at what she was about to undertake. The *menuisier* assured her that he would come then and thanked her for her confidence in his skills.

"I have seen some of the pieces which you have fashioned, Monsieur Jallais, and I am certain I will not regret my choice of you as the craftsman."

Valéry returned to the chateau just in time for dinner. She found de la Haye, Goudimel, and Marot waiting for her as she entered the great hall.

"You are quite flushed, mademoiselle. It becomes you." Marot walked over to take her hand and usher her to the table where he took a place beside her on the bench.

"I have just returned from the atelier of Monsieur Jallais, and the afternoon is hot," Valéry replied, trying not to let her annoyance show in her voice.

"Is he the local carpenter?" Monsieur de la Haye spoke from across the table. "Our gracious queen, I seem to recall, commissioned a writing desk from him for my use in preparing several of her poems for publication. You have seen me at work on it, no doubt, as it sits just there." Monsieur de la Haye pointed to a far corner of the room where a small escritoire and chair stood by one of the large windows.

"I imagine he is the one who made it, yes, and now I have asked that he help me set up my uncle's former room as the chateau library." Valéry looked across at Marguerite's secretary and smiled. He was not a young man, as his gray hair would attest, but he was a conscientious worker, quiet and gentlemanly in his manner. Valéry felt comfortable in his presence, unlike that of Marot, around whom she could never relax.

"What a wonderful idea, mademoiselle," said de la Haye. "I will enjoy seeing the transformation from bedroom to library as it takes shape. You will make room for additional volumes, I trust, for our gracious Queen Marguerite will surely want to add to the collection?"

"I will make that a requirement of Monsieur Jallais's construction—that he provide plenty of shelf space for future additions! To that end, Monsieur de la Haye, would you be able to add any of the writings of our queen to what we presently have?"

"Perhaps Marguerite will want to do this, but I myself will surely ask if some of the things which I will be responsible for getting into print may find their way into this new library. You value books as I do, mademoiselle, which is much to your credit and deserving of encouragement and praise."

Valéry felt herself blush as she murmured, "*Grand merci,* monsieur." She felt Marot's arm press against hers as he whispered next to her ear. "You are once again red in the face, my little mademoiselle. Flattery must be the key to your emotions, I surmise. I will remember to use it often with you."

The meal ended, and Valéry hurried off to her room, looking over her shoulder to be sure Marot was not following. Once there, she shut the door and did something she had never felt necessary to do before. Grabbing the iron bar which stood by the doorframe, she slid it into place between the metal brackets on each side of the door. No one would be entering her room uninvited, she thought, realizing that she had only one person in mind who might even try. Thank goodness there were other guests who were trustworthy. The thought comforted her as she sat on her bed, a prisoner by her own doing in her own chamber.

Chapter Eight

Monsieur Jallais appeared promptly at the chateau the next afternoon. Together with Valéry and Jean de la Haye, who had taken an interest in the library project, he discussed plans for transforming the bedroom into a *bibliotèque.* The fireplace stood in the middle of one wall, but shelving could be installed on either side with no problem, Jallais said. The opposite wall had a window flanked by a commode to the left and two chairs to the right. If the furniture were removed, ceiling-to-floor shelves could be fit there instead.

"Is there a problem with keeping the chairs in front of the bookshelves?" Valéry asked, thinking that those who would use the library needed a place to sit down to read. It was discussed and then decided that both the commode and the chairs could be pulled out far enough to allow access to the bookshelves as well as a place to put some candles on top the commode and chairs next to it.

"The armoire is a beautiful piece of furniture, but it takes up an entire wall," observed Jean de la Haye.

"It is beautiful because I made it myself out of the finest oak, monsieur," the carpenter replied with a twinkle in his eye. "But I agree that the wall space is far too valuable to lose, for the armoire cannot hold nearly as many books and manuscripts as shelving across the wall would hold. If you think you might need some cabinets, I can surely build them below the shelving and have the *serrurier* install locks on the doors. Perhaps this would be a better idea for storing very valuable manuscripts than your idea, mademoiselle, of slanted racks, and it would also keep the dust off them."

"Then let us move the armoire to another room—perhaps the apartments of Marguerite, which are quite large," Valéry suggested, "and the bookshelves with the cabinets beneath them sound like the best plan."

"There remains only the problem of the bed, then," the carpenter said as he went over to measure its length as it stood out from the wall adjacent to the door. "This, too, will have to be moved from the room if you want more bookshelves."

Valéry frowned. "I wish to use it as a couch, monsieur. It is a very short and narrow bed. Could we not turn it so that one side lies against the wall by the door? I could cover the mattress with some fabric and sew pillows to lean upon. Think what a comfortable place that would be to spend long hours reading long books!" Jean de la Haye laughed. "Or to fall asleep on when thoroughly bored!"

"Then, it is set, I believe," said Monsieur Jallais. "I shall enlist the help of my brother. It would be best if we built the units in our atelier since it will make quite a mess, and then we shall install them in this room. It should take us the rest of the summer. Let us say, three weeks for the making but then only one day for the installing."

Valéry was excited. "I will have time to fashion my chaise longue and some pillows in that time."

Monsieur de la Haye added, "And I shall have time to finish my work for Marguerite, but before I leave the chateau to find a publisher, I would like to help with the installation and placing the books and manuscripts where they belong."

That evening, after dining with de la Haye, Marot, and Goudimel, Valéry decided to return to her uncle's chamber before the daylight had totally disappeared. Dark green velour draperies hung to each side of the lancet window. Her uncle used to draw them closed at night, hoping to keep out any cold drafts as well as preventing the rising sun from waking him too early. They would not be needed now that the chamber was no longer a bedroom, Valéry thought as she fingered the thick soft fabric. *What an excellent cover these will make for the feather mattress and several big back pillows!* She pulled over one of the wooden chairs and, standing upon it, tried to reach the bar holding the curtains in place. She was too short. Just then a voice came from behind her.

"You are in need of some assistance, I see, mademoiselle. Permit one taller than yourself to help." It was Marot, who came swiftly across the room as Valéry vacated the chair. It was no problem for him to reach up and remove the heavy fabric.

"Where would you like me to put these?"

Valéry had intended to carry the material back to her own chamber where she kept her sewing supplies, but the thought of letting Marot deposit the curtains in her bedroom was not wise.

"Please put them on the bed, Monsieur."

Marot did as he was directed, then walked over to Valéry and, taking her by the elbow, said, "Come, let us sit on this bed and see if it will be comfortable enough to use as a couch."

Valéry tried to free her elbow and hold back, but it was to no avail. She was pushed, gently but firmly, onto the bed, and Marot took his place close beside her. His hand moved to behind her back and then up to her neck, restraining her when she tried to stand up again.

"You are a very beautiful woman, Valéry, and I believe you find me attractive, too, in spite of your attempts to avoid me."

His face was very close to hers now. She could feel his breath on her cheek and the warmth of his hand placed around her neck. She would not be able to get away from his hold.

"You are presumptuous, monsieur, and your attentions are neither pleasing to me nor those of a gentleman. Please remove your hand and let me get up."

"I will soon change your mind, *ma petite*." To her horror, he forced her back on the bed and bent down, kissing her lips while slipping a hand inside the top of her bodice.

Valéry's heart began to pound in fear of what might happen next. The sound of steps coming down the arcade made Marot draw back and walk toward the door, which no doubt he fully intended to close. But just then, Goudimel appeared in the growing dusk, and a voice queried, "Is that you, Marot? I heard voices and have come to ask if you would like to join de la Haye and myself in the great hall for a round of wine and a game." Then, seeing Valéry, he added, "And you, too, are invited, mademoiselle, if you wish, although it will be a decidedly masculine game, I am afraid."

Valéry was all too glad to decline, slipping past the two men and almost running down the long stone hall until she reached her own chamber. Closing and bolting the door, she leaned against the smooth wood, trembling all over and very close to tears. But to her surprise, tears did not come. Instead she felt outrage. The man was despicable. How did he think he could get away with his insulting actions when Marguerite found out? Perhaps the queen would cut him off from her patronage. It would serve him right. But then she had a sobering thought. Marguerite was not due to return right away. Added to that, Jean de la Haye would be leaving in a matter of weeks. Valéry felt helpless and very frightened. There appeared to be no one to whom she could go for protection.

It was a long time before she slept as she kept going over and over her dilemma. She had thought that by careful planning, she could avoid any meetings with the lothario. As it turned out, she was like a hunted prey, with no hiding place which was safe. When she did fall asleep, her dreams were of being pursued by a wild beast, and although she had a head start, the animal could run faster and was stronger than she. It was only a matter of time, she knew, before the chase would be over and the battle lost.

Valéry woke to the sound of rain pelting against her window. This day's weather matched her stormy mood, she thought, as she dressed and made her toilette. The events of the previous evening weighed heavily on her mind, putting a damper on the enthusiasm she had felt for the library project. Nonetheless, she was determined to move ahead in her plans to fashion a couch out of her uncle's former bed. Stepping into the hall, she heard Marot and Goudimel singing as they worked on the psalms. Good, she would not have to contend with Marot. She moved quickly down the arcade, descended the stairs, making her way to the kitchens, which were toward the back of the chateau. She found the cook haggling with the egg and milk vendor and Josette taking directions from the woman who Marguerite had left in charge of housekeeping. They turned at her entrance, somewhat surprised to see her in this section of the chateau.

"I have managed to oversleep today. Would I be able to get a morsel of bread with butter and something hot to drink?" Valéry looked imploringly from Josette to the housekeeper and then back.

"Surely, Mademoiselle Lefèvre," the housekeeper replied. "On a day such as this, it is nice to be able to sleep late. Would you like to sit at the table to eat?" She motioned towards the thick slab of oak set on large barrels in the middle of the main kitchen. Here the cook and his helpers would cut large slices of beef and ham or lay out the carcass of a goat after it had been turned on the spit in the large fireplace. It was wiped clean now, and Valéry sat down on the bench, grateful for the food put before her. *I need some sustenance for the battle which surely lies ahead of me*, she thought to herself. Josette, noticing Valéry's downcast eyes, asked if she was feeling poorly.

"No, no, Josette. I did not rest well last night, that is all."

"I imagine it was the storm, Mademoiselle Lefèvre. There was quite a lot of thunder, and the rain was noisy on the roof above me." She motioned toward the hallway leading from the kitchens. "My room is just a small nook built onto the side of the chateau. It used to be a larder, but when Marguerite invited me to work at the chateau, she said it would be turned into a place for me."

"You have no family then, Josette?" Valéry knew that most of those employed at the chateau had homes either in the village or in the adjacent countryside.

"I am an orphan, Mademoiselle Lefevre. Marguerite found me living with a farmer's family, who did not want an extra mouth to feed as they had plenty of their own. She was like an angel, taking me to this grand house and letting me be one of her chambermaids. When she is gone, I help wherever I can, sometimes aiding the laundress or the housekeeper, or even doing errands. I am glad to do whatever I can in exchange for my keep."

Valéry studied the ruddy face of the servant girl. *She must be in her teens now*, she thought, *and although she is not comely of looks, she is sweet in disposition and of positive outlook on her life. She would make a wonderful pupil, for I am sure that she would like to learn even more skills than she has already acquired doing chateau work.* Valéry brightened at the thought, thinking that the girl would also made a good assistant in the classroom, somebody the younger children could relate to as one of their own and yet old enough to elicit respect and cooperation.

"Josette, if you are free for a few minutes, I could use your help upstairs," Valéry said. The girl turned a questioning glance toward the housekeeper, who nodded her approval, and the two set off for the library. The draperies still lay on the bed where Marot had put them the night before. Valéry and Josette divided the panels between themselves and carried them along the arcade to Valéry's room.

"I will be sewing a coverlet and some pillows for the bed in my uncle's room," Valéry explained. "The room will be made into a library, complete with bookshelves. It is planned as a surprise for the queen and as a tribute to the memory of my uncle."

Josette's face registered her interest in such a project. "I would be so happy to help with anything, mademoiselle. And how grand the library will be. If I could only read, I would like to use this room myself whenever I have a break in my duties. Marguerite would let me, I know, since she has great faith in the intelligence of women and likes to encourage their learning. She told me so one day when I asked her about what she had been writing. She read to me some of her poetry. I still remember how beautiful it was, all about the marguerites which fill her garden. She even laughed as she read the poem, saying she was sometimes called 'the Marguerite of marguerites.'"

Josette stopped short, looking a little embarrassed. "Oh, Mademoiselle Lefévre, I am being far too forward and out of place. Please do forgive my audacity."

Valéry gave the servant girl a hug, which surprised her even more. "You are not being too forward, Josette. You are delightful and have brightened this dismal day considerably for me."

As Josette left, Valéry realized how much she missed the company of other women. Her life since the death of her mother had been largely centered upon her uncle and his colleagues. Marguerite had filled that void since she and her uncle had come to stay at Nerac, but now that the queen was gone, her life again was filled with males—the *curé* and the boys he taught, M. Jallais, John de la Haye, Marot, Goudimel. *I shall change this with my own school,* Valéry thought to herself, *for I will surround myself with those of my own gender, and together we shall show the men in our lives that they are not the only ones worth educating. We have minds also.*

Valéry bolted her door and busied herself with the sewing she needed to do. She spread out the draperies lengthwise across the stone floor, and with the sewing implements her mother had used to supplement her income, she measured, pinned, and then cut the heavy fabric according to the size pieces she would need. From the armoire, she withdrew a large-eyed needle and some dark green thread and was just beginning to sew when there came a tap at the door. Valéry froze, her hand holding the needle and thread in midair. The knock came again, this time louder. Valéry held her breath, afraid that any sound from within the room might tip off her presence. She was sure it was Marot. The knocking stopped, but to her horror, she saw the long metal handle of her door slowly turn downward. The bar was in place, so when the person on the other side pushed, the door did not move. Whoever it was, they would now know that she was inside. Still, she waited, not moving and scarcely daring to breathe. Nothing. Then she heard footsteps retreating down the stone floor of the arcade.

If it had been de la Haye or even one of the chateau servants, they would have identified themselves, stating their purpose in coming. No doubt, it had been Marot, who knew that he had behaved badly the night before and who would not be repentant, only persistent. He would hardly wish to yell the purpose of his visit through the thickness of the door separating them. Once again, Valéry felt anxious. To whom could she appeal for help? The *curé* would be embarrassed and reluctant to get involved, feeling it was none of his business. Goudimel was Marot's close friend and collaborator. He certainly would not risk taking Valéry's side against his colleague. As for John de la Haye, he had been polite enough in his dealings with her, but as a fellow secretary with Marot to the queen, they would need to work companionably together, and taking her side might well be viewed as driving a wedge between the two secretaries. Valéry did not wish to risk confiding her fears concerning Marot to any of these men. As for the chateau staff, little Josette would hardly be of any help, and the rest of the chateau servants would be equally as helpless against a man of the stature of Clement Marot, protegé of the king of France, confidant and secretary to his sister, the queen of Navarre, and a recognized man of letters among the circles where the new learning was taking hold. *No, she thought to herself. If I am to escape unscathed from this, I must trust in my own abilities to outwit him in his nefarious plans. I will begin by redoubling my efforts to keep out of his way, to lock my door whenever I am in my room, and to avoid being alone with him. Ever.*

In the days ahead, Valéry stayed in her room, sewing. When it came time for dinner, she was careful to arrive in the great hall after the men did and to sit at the opposite end of the table from Marot. She would eat quickly and excuse herself, returning to her room. After the weather cleared, she walked early in the morning before Marot was awake, returning to the chateau just as Goudimel and Marot were beginning their day's work with the psalms.

Several weeks went by, and Valéry, finished with her sewing, decided to go into the village and pay a visit to M. Jallais. She found him in the atelier just putting stain over a large section of the cabinetry he'd designed for the library. The *serrurier* was there also, installing the locks on the cabinet doors after the stain dried.

"Mademoiselle Lefèvre, *bonjour*. We are just about done with our project, as you can see." Monsieur Jallais pointed to a row of impressive shelving along one wall of the atelier. "Within a day or so, we will load all this up in our cart and bring it to the chateau. Are you ready for us?"

Valéry beamed in approval. "I will notify Monsieur de la Haye, who will, I am sure, be happy to assist you. I have already instructed two servants of the chateau to move the armoire into the queen's apartments. Before you arrive, I will have the chaise longue in place also. Then we will settle up our accounts, for I am sure you have more than earned what we agreed upon as payment."

"We are grateful for this honor bestowed upon us, mademoiselle," the carpenter replied simply.

"I am in need of one other service besides yours, messieurs. Perhaps you could direct me to a farm where there are many geese? The mattress is already stuffed with down, but the pillows remain flat as crepes in the pan. Surely there would be feathers available for me to buy, if only I knew where to go to get them!"

The locksmith looked up from his work. "That would be the business of my brother-in-law and his family, mademoiselle. He is quite poor and has a large family to feed along with a sick wife to nurse, but they are raising geese in hopes that they will bring in some badly-needed money. Their farm is located just next to the mill. Do you know where that is?"

Valéry nodded her head yes, thanking the two men for their assistance. She found the goose farm with no trouble, purchased enough down feathers to stuff the three pillows she'd made, and arranged for them to be delivered to the chateau that afternoon. Feeling in a generous mood, she handed the farmer five gold *écus*, leaving him dumbfounded as this amount could have bought his entire flock of geese. She was not entirely sure that such extravagance was wise, but it would surely help ease the poverty of this family, and that alone, she rationalized, justified the generous gesture.

Back at the chateau, she stopped by the kitchens again, looking for Josette. The turnspit, a lad of perhaps twelve, was tending to the roasting of a pig for the dinner. "She is in her room there, mademoiselle." The boy directed her to the small chamber adjacent to the kitchen. Josette, busy with mending some sheets, greeted her with warmth. "I have been thinking about your library and how beautiful it will be, mademoiselle. Are you finished yet with your sewing?"

"I have done everything that needs doing, Josette, but would like for you to help me put the cover on the mattress and stuff the pillows with goose down. In a few days, the cabinets and shelving will be installed, and then the books and manuscripts can be placed where they belong."

Josette dropped her mending and sprang to her feet. "How fun that will be to stuff the pillows. I shall ask the housekeeper for the time to assist you."

"Good," replied Valéry. "The feathers will be delivered this afternoon. Could you watch for them, Josette? I think we should do this in the garden as no doubt we will have the down flying all over the room if we try to do the task there." Both young women laughed at the thought and agreed to the garden as the logical place.

Several hours later, Valéry and Josette stood in the middle of the orchard, pillow casing in hand. Valéry held them open, and Josette took handfuls of the soft feathers and stuffed them in. Valéry was right. The fluffy down flew everywhere, carried by the light breezes into branches of the nearby apple and apricot trees making it seem as though they were covered with their spring blossoms once again. Into this scene strolled Marot, who stood looking at the activity, an amused expression on his face.

"Do you wish some help?" Without looking in his direction, Valéry replied in the negative. She felt somewhat protected in the company of Josette. At least he could not make any unwanted advances or pay her unseemly compliments in the presence of the servant girl.

"No matter," he remarked. "I will seek to help you later when you cover the mattress and prop the pillows up. It will make for a very comfortable, um, resting and reading place." He studied Valéry's expression as he spoke, knowing his remarks would make her uncomfortable.

Much to her embarrassment and Marot's satisfaction, Valéry blushed.

"Josette and I will handle that task, Monsieur Marot. I would not dream of letting someone of your high station help with such menial labor. It would damage your, um, unblemished reputation, which you certainly would not want sullied by doing women's work, now, would you?"

Her sarcasm was not lost on Marot, but he remained unaffected. "Oh, I will help you in other ways, then, mademoiselle. The time and opportunity will come, I am sure."

The two women carried the pillows, now plump with feathers, up to the library and sat down on the bed to sew the casings closed at the ends. Then they went to Valéry's room to retrieve the duvet she had sewn, returning once again to the library where it slipped over the mattress without difficulty. After the pillows were propped up along the couch wall, the two stood back to view the results. Valéry was satisfied. It would make a fine chaise longue for the library. Once again, she was excited about the project and anxious that the shelving be installed and the books put into place.

Josette left for the kitchens to help prepare the day's big meal, and Valéry returned to her room, barring the door until the dinner bell rang. The end of her library project was in sight. It would correspond to the end of summer when surely the three men would have left, and she could turn her attentions to devising a curriculum for the classes she wished to start and also a compelling argument for them to present to Marguerite.

Two days later, the carpenter and his assistants arrived with a large cart, filled to overflowing with shelves and cabinets. John de la Haye joined them in the installation while Valéry stood out of their way. "You need someone to supervise," she told the men laughingly. When they had completely finished, the room was indeed transformed. Valéry withdrew from her armoire a pouch filled with *sols*, *deniers*, and a few *écus*, giving *Monsieur* Jallais half again as much as they had agreed upon originally. It was money well spent, and certainly Marguerite would approve this use of the benevolence she had bestowed on her protégée. She was gratified that she still had some money remaining, which she hoped to use in setting up her school for girls. They would need reading material, which she might possibly get printed if she could locate a printer to do such a small job. Perhaps de la Haye would know of someone. Also, the goodwill of the carpenter no doubt would be an asset when she requested some chairs and tables for her classroom. Then a new thought occurred to her. Maybe, just maybe, her classes could meet in this very room!

For the next few days, Valéry, de la Haye, and Josette placed the well-sorted books on the shelving, with the more valuable manuscripts put into the cabinets where they were locked up for safety as the library had no lock on the door.

"Where shall we put the keys?" Valéry asked the secretary.

"I would imagine they could be hidden in the commode drawer," he replied, walking across the room to pull out the one compartment of the stand. "Anyone who uses the library on a regular basis will know where they are, but someone who has no business here will not even know there are manuscripts hidden away, and if they try to open the cabinets, they will not succeed."

Much to Valéry's relief, Marot was nowhere to be seen. The library organization was finally complete, and the effect was most satisfying.

"You had a good idea, here," de la Haye said to Valéry. "Marguerite should be both amazed and gratified when she returns."

"Have you had any word from her, monsieur?"

"I have not, but she will surely return before the weather changes. And speaking of that, I shall be leaving soon, for I will need to find my friends in the publishing world as I have promised Marguerite that I will put to print her latest poetry. This will take me to Lyon and perhaps to Paris also, and I wish to make those journeys before the inclement weather sets in and many of the roads become veritable quagmires. I understand that Goudimel wishes to accompany me with the completed psalms over which he and Marot have labored."

Valéry's heart sank, and she suddenly felt weak.

"You are pale, mademoiselle," de la Haye observed. "This has been hard work for you, placing all these books. Please try to rest a bit before your next project." He smiled down on her, stating that knowing her, he was sure there would be a next project.

Valéry tried to smile back, but her mouth quivered. "And Monsieur Marot, will he be going with you?"

The secretary walked toward the door. "He has told me that he wishes to remain here until the queen returns and he can talk with her about another commission after that of the psalms."

As de la Haye left the room, Valéry tried to stave off a sense of panic. In just a few days, she would be left alone with Marot. There was no guarantee as to when Marguerite and her entourage would return. She certainly had known fear when Marguerite first left on her journey, but it was nothing to what she felt now. She still had some money left. Perhaps she could flee. There were other small villages close to Nérac, but she knew no one there, and a woman traveling alone would not be safe. If she tried to stay in Nérac, Marot would seek her out. This must be how a *sanglier* felt as he was hunted by the nobility, who were well armed and on horseback. However, the boar did not fully realize what was about to happen to him when he was cornered. Valéry did, and she was terrified.

Two days later, de la Haye and Goudimel left, their horses loaded down with leather satchels filled with manuscripts ready for publication. Valéry had said her goodbyes at dinner the day before and stood watching their departure now from her bedroom window, which overlooked the courtyard of the chateau. Marot, who had accompanied them to the courtyard, turned when he could no longer see them and disappeared into the grand hallway. Valéry waited behind her bolted door, thinking that he might come directly to her chamber. After a considerable time, she decided that he had other plans for the moment. She withdrew the iron bar and walked down the stairs, seeking out the kitchen staff. Josette met her on the way, which was convenient. She requested that her meals be brought once again to her chamber, and that when they were, she would have her door barred so that Josette needed to identify herself after knocking. Josette looked puzzled but was agreeable to the plan.

It was still quite early in the day and Valéry, noting the sunshine and blue sky, sought out the chateau gardens. There was plenty of activity around the chateau as the servants had begun preparing for the anticipated return of their mistress and her court. Valéry thought that surely during the daylight hours she would be safe in such a busy place. The day turned out to be a little chilly. *Fall is just around the corner*, she thought, and looking at the orchard trees, laden with fruit almost ready for the picking, she resolved to bring a basket some morning soon and gather up the riper fruits for meals or for drying. Sitting down on a stone bench placed amidst a flower bed, she studied a butterfly winging its way from petal to petal. A voice by her side said, "It flits from flower to flower, savoring the sweetness of each blossom."

Without turning, Valéry replied to Marot, who came to sit down beside her. "It is much like you, *Monsieur Papillon*, except that you flit from place to place, from verse to verse, from patron to patroness, from woman to woman, unable to alight anywhere for very long and looking only for what is fleetingly satisfying."

"I must say that I agree with your assessment of me, mademoiselle, and you, at least right now, are the blossom whose fragrance I desire and whose sweetness I would taste before I fly to another temptation."

"And have you no conscience over what you do to those flowers you destroy in the process, monsieur? I understand from the queen of Navarre that you have left to her care an illegitimate daughter in addition to discarding the woman you married in favor of the dalliances to be found at court."

"That is of no concern to me now, mademoiselle. If I am *un papillon*, you are certainly *une prude*. It is unbecoming of one so beautiful as you and quite a waste of your charms, which are meant for a man's pleasure." He paused for a moment, then added, "For my pleasure, *ma petite fleur*."

"*Ta gueule!*" Valéry spat out. "Your mouth is vile and your heart eaten away by vermin. You turn my stomach and fill me with contempt."

Marot rose from the bench and looked down on her. "I will soon fill you with something else, and you will like it." With that, he left her. Valéry sat for a long time, all the pleasure of the mature garden's fruition drained from her senses. She felt numb, not able to move, her eyes fixed on a point somewhere in the distance but not seeing anything. As the day grew cooler, she arose and found her way back to her room. Closing the door, she reached for the bar to go across the door. It was not there.

Josette brought her dinner, which she could barely eat. Setting the tray aside, she looked about the room for something she could use in place of the bar. There was nothing. Perhaps another of the rooms which was adjacent to hers would have a bar. She explored each one. No bars were to be found. Returning to her chamber, she decided to push her commode against the inside of the door. It was heavy, but she was driven by fright. It finally stood in place and might hold against an intruder. Going over to the table by the side of her bed, she lit the lone candle on her bedside table and readied herself for bed, but sleep refused to come. All night, she imagined she could hear soft footsteps in the hall outside. When dawn finally came, she arose exhausted. The commode would need to be pushed back into place in order for her to open the door when Josette brought her morning's meal. It was barely done when the servant girl knocked and then announced herself.

"You do not look well this morning, Mademoiselle Lefèvre. Should I send for the *medecin* who treats our queen?"

"Gracious, no, Josette." Valéry tried to look more alert. "However, the bar for my door seems to be missing. Do you know where we might find another one?"

"I will look, mademoiselle. Is there anything else you might need?"

"I was wondering if you had access to our queen's apartments, Josette. She has a remedy in one of her armoires for a headache. I would greatly benefit from a dosage right now."

"I am sorry, but I would rather not enter her rooms when she is not present, mademoiselle. But if I go to the pharmacist, surely he will have the same remedy."

"Yes, please, Josette. See what you can find for me—the bar as well as the medicine." As the servant left, Valéry once again moved the commode against the door and then lay back down on her bed. She awoke sometime later to a light tapping on her door, with Josette calling to her.

"I have found another bar, mademoiselle, and the willow bark which will relieve your headache. And I have made a tisane just like our queen made for you some months back."

Valéry slid the commode back once again and gratefully drank the infusion, noticing Josette's perplexed look, for she certainly had heard the piece of furniture being moved. Soon Valéry began to feel better. The infusion had helped, but so had the receipt of the new bar for her door. She would sleep much better this evening than she had the night before.

"Monsieur Marot has already taken his dinner, and I believe has gone into the village for the evening. There is a tavern which he and Goudimel went to sometimes. Perhaps he seeks some diversion since his companions have now left."

"In that case, Josette, and to save you some trouble, I will come to the kitchens to take a warm meal before retiring for the night."

Valéry followed the servant girl into the warmth of the room where most of the meals were cooked. A large fire still burned in the fireplace, casting a pleasant orange glow over the oak table and bench. She felt better from the nap she had had, and the meal took away the faintness she was experiencing. Before she left to go back to her room, she thanked Josette for her trouble, and as it was getting quite dark, she borrowed from the table a candle stuck in a heavy brass holder and returned up the stairs and down the long arcade to her room. Once inside, she turned to bar the door, and walking over to light her own candle from the flame she held, she heard a noise. There in the corner stood Marot.

"We are now alone, and there is no easy escape for you." His smile revealed a row of even teeth underneath his moustache. As he stepped toward her, Valéry blew out the candle, leaving the room in darkness. She could hear him breathing as he drew closer to her, but as she attempted to back away, he pinned her against the barred door. His hands ripped away her bodice and chemise and then grabbed at her skirts, lifting them above her waist as she struggled ineffectively to free herself. When his lips sought the soft flesh of her breast, Valéry raised the heavy candlestick holder still in her hand and hit his lowered head as hard as she could. He crumpled to the floor. Removing the bar with trembling hands, Valéry ran down the hall, clutching the torn garments against her chest and stopping only momentarily to look behind her into the darkness when she reached the stairs. There was no sound. Fleeing down the winding stone steps, she found herself once again in the kitchens. It was deserted by this time, but the embers of the fire still burned brightly enough for her to find the door which led to Josette's room. Tapping lightly, she called out her name. After a moment, a startled Josette opened it, and Valéry, glancing back again and seeing nobody, pushed past her, closing the door behind her.

"Is there a way to secure this door, Josette? We are in danger unless we can do so." The alarmed girl pulled out a key from a small drawer in the one table in the room. "I can lock us in from both sides, mademoiselle, as this room used to be storage for food supplies and had to be kept locked so as not to be looted." When the key was turned, Valéry tried the door handle. The door held fast. She then turned to Josette, whose eyes were wide as she looked at the torn garments of her visitor.

"Josette, Monsieur Marot has tried to do me harm. In order to get away from him, I had to hit him hard on the head with the candlestick I borrowed from the kitchens. I left him lying on the floor, but I fear he will come looking for me. Does he know where your room is?" Josette replied that she didn't think so. He had never been in the kitchens or any part of this section of the chateau, as far as she knew, and so probably thought that all the servants went to their homes for the night. Valéry relaxed a little. She was not sure how badly she had wounded him, but at the moment, she did not care.

"Mademoiselle, you are shaking. Please, you must get into my bed and cover up." Valéry tried to protest.

"But where will *you* sleep, Josette?"

"I will take a counterpane from my cupboard, mademoiselle, and sleep quite comfortably in that."

Valéry was too tired to argue. Curling up under the covers, she soon fell into a deep sleep. Her last thought was that come morning, she would be in danger once again, and perhaps doubly so, as Marot would undoubtedly add anger to his lust, seeking to get revenge.

But when she opened her eyes again, Josette was gone, and all sorts of commotion came from within the chateau kitchens. Trying to tidy her hair, Valéry opened the door and peered out. Josette, seeing her, came running over with an excited look on her face.

"Oh, mademoiselle, Queen Marguerite has returned and with her King Henri d'Albret and a whole bevy of others. We are having to scramble to feed and accommodate them all."

"Have you seen Marot, Josette?"

"Yes, mademoiselle. He is in the great hall, a wide swatch of sheeting wrapped around his head, explaining to everybody that he fell in the night, having tripped over a wardrobe trunk he did not see. You are safe, Mademoiselle Valéry, but I would hope that you would talk to Marguerite as soon as possible."

"Thank you, *ma chère* Josette. I will do just that at the earliest convenience." Valéry quickly made her way back to her chamber. She stripped off her torn clothing, then washed and redressed in a fresh gown. Marguerite was back, and all would be well. She did not have to be frightened anymore. The relief she felt was almost indescribable.

Marot left that afternoon with no explanation and no goodbyes. He rode away on a horse laden down with satchels stuffed to overflowing. On his head was a jaunty black beret, pulled down to try and cover a strip of sheet which still bandaged the wound made by the candlestick. Valéry watched him go from her window and whispered an unkind farewell. "Go with the devil, and may we never meet again." Then she turned to join the others in the great hall and to greet her beloved Queen Marguerite.

Chapter Nine

While Marguerite's greeting had been warm, the usual animation which so characterized her was missing. "My little Valy, you see I have returned to you, and I trust you have kept yourself well-occupied in my absence." Valéry assured her that this was the case, mentioning that she had been thinking about her future and also that she had proof to show Marguerite that she had not wasted her time.

"I will be glad to see what that is," Marguerite had replied. "I will be wanting to talk with you, but at the moment, as you can see, my husband, Henri d'Albret, is here, wanting to attend to some business connected with this part of his kingdom of Navarre. It should not take him long, and then he will be returning without me to our chateau in Pau, which he much prefers to Nérac. After that, I shall send for you."

Valéry felt a sense of impatience, for she was proud of the library she had created and wanted to share her enthusiasm with Marguerite. Also, she was excited about her plans for starting a school for the young girls of the village and anxious to begin implementing her plans now that summer was at a close and fall definitely in the air. No matter. She would have to practice patience as it would be unthinkable to argue with the queen. Marguerite was kind and loving, but she also had regal ways about her and a sense of the proper place for those who touched her life. A protégée with little social status certainly could not dictate to her queen and protector what she was to do and when she was to do it!

The weeks of September dragged by, and Valéry tried to fill her time with projects which kept her busy. She enlisted the help of Josette to go into the orchard and pick the ripened fruit. Her mother had taught her how to cook, and Valéry, although it was not her station, sought the kitchens to do some baking. Apricot, plum, and peach *tartelettes* all made their appearance on the tables of the court gathered around the king and queen of Navarre. The cook, fortunately, was glad of the extra help. He and his assistants could concentrate on the *viandes* and *poissons* so important to a proper royal meal. Josette was willing to help, also, and seemed to especially enjoy the process of drying the fruit, which inevitably became an overabundance during the height of the season. Soon the grape harvest would begin, and already the fields of grain were being harvested, the *batteurs en grange* hard at work with their threshing and hay being cut and rolled into bundles, ready to feed the cattle and sheep so abundant in this area. The hot, lazy days of summer were at an end, and there was work to be done. Valéry was happy to be part of this.

Early in October, Henri d'Albret readied himself for his journey to the southern part of his kingdom. Marguerite was occupied in helping with the preparations. Henri, considerably younger than Marguerite, treated his wife, it seemed to Valéry, with ambivalence. At times he appeared interested in her, listening intently as she spoke, answering her kindly, and was solicitous in his actions. At other times he was curt and impatient. Certainly he did not try to hide his attraction to some of the more comely ladies of the court, and it was common knowledge that he had a mistress living in the village of Nérac. Such romantic adventures seemed to be a usual practice among the highest ranks of nobility where marriages were made for political alliances and advantage and not for love or even attraction. Perhaps everybody involved accepted this as the way it should be, but Valéry couldn't help wondering if it wasn't hard on Marguerite to see her husband's dalliances right under her own nose. It also made her glad she was not a part of that milieu. But then she thought of Marot and shuddered. To be the shallow romantic interest of someone of higher station than her own, used but not given the dignity of a marriage bond, would not be the kind of life she herself would settle for under any circumstance.

Henri d'Albret finally departed, along with some of the court, leaving Marguerite freer of responsibility. However, several days passed before she summoned Valéry to her apartments. During that time, Valéry went over and over what she would say to her. Certainly, she would relate the visit of Gérard Roussel, who admonished her to make good use of her education. She thought also of de la Haye, who encouraged her in setting up the library so that it could be used, rather than packed away somewhere. Even the *curé* had played a part in her determination to live a useful life, for the idea that only boys were worth educating had stuck in her craw and rallied her motivation to prove him wrong. Then there was Marot, who although of contemptible motivations toward her was able to give examples of women who were developing skills beyond their home front duties—those remarkable women of Lyon. She resolved to tell Marguerite of all these influences in her life, paying high tribute to the queen herself, whose caring patronage was a primary factor in shaping her life up to this point and in encouraging her to move on. Finally, she was the most enthusiastic over showing Marguerite the library and presenting her plans for gathering the young village girls together so that they too could learn to read and write, be exposed to figures and language, and even to the fine literature being recovered from antiquity as well as Marguerite's own poems and stories.

The day the queen's summons finally came, Valéry entered her patroness's apartments full of excitement and hopes for the future. She found Marguerite standing by the expanse of windows on one side of her antechamber, looking out at the vibrant hues of fall's foliage in her gardens. Turning to Valéry as she came in, she hurried towards her, taking both her hands in her own, and then motioned for her to sit in one of the tapestry-covered chairs next to a writing table. As the queen sat down next to her, she reached for a heavy fold of paper which lay on top of the desk, holding it up for her protégée to see. Valéry looked with interest at the broken wax seal, bearing the head of a fox, which adorned the letter paper, but before she could speak, the queen leaned over toward her and said, "You may be wondering, Valéry, why it has taken me so long to summon you to my side. The truth is, I was waiting for this letter before I took any action." The young woman's train of thought came to a complete stop as she looked over at Marguerite. The queen's eyes, usually sparkling with humor, were dull this morning and her eyelids droopy. Had she been crying, Valéry wondered? Perhaps she wished to accompany her husband to Pau but he had refused to let her come. She dared not ask but knew that something was amiss. She waited for Marguerite to continue.

"While I was at court in Fontainebleau, I met a certain baron, Paul de Renard, from our lands in Gascony. He was most interested in hearing about the royal library collections at Blois as well as King François's patronage of those scholars and printers who were working to recover and make available the great literary treasures from antiquity. He told me that for many generations, the de Renard barons had collected an impressive number of manuscripts which lay helter-skelter now in his chateau. Something needed to be done to organize and preserve this collection, and since his father had just recently died, he himself now felt a responsibility in the care and use of such a valuable mass of materials. To this end, he was looking to employ a knowledgeable librarian who could help in this endeavor. In addition, he was to be leaving the next day for Lyon where he would search for a journeyman printer willing to set up a small printing establishment on his chateau grounds, in order that many of the valuable volumes might be made available to a wider group of people through putting them into print. The sale of such books in the Armagnac region, which had no printing facilities as yet, might become an additional source of income for his estate, as well as a source of learning for many."

Valéry expressed interest in what Marguerite was telling her but privately wondered about her point. Sensing this, the queen continued. "I told him that I had a protégée whose uncle was tutor to my brother's children at Blois, who had been formally educated, and in addition, had helped with the cataloguing and inventory of the king's own extensive library." Marguerite paused, casting a glance at the young woman next to her. When Valéry said nothing, the queen continued. "The baron was interested in retaining someone of your qualifications, Valéry. You would have lodging and a pension at the Chateau de Renard and would be doing what you have had experience and training to do."

When Valéry still did not respond, the queen picked up the folded piece of paper on her lap, opened it, and began to read:

My esteemed Queen,

I have just arrived back from my trip to Lyon and am happy to report that I found a very suitable journeyman printer, a Monsieur Arsène Faguet, who had been working for one of the most prestigious printing houses there. He was, at first, hoping that the master printer for whom he worked would hire him as head of the printing shop after he retired since he was quite advanced in years. Instead, he appointed two of his nephews, leaving Monsieur Faguet without a promotion and still a journeyman. Thus, he was most interested in my proposition, and since I was able to offer him more than he was presently getting paid, he has accepted my offer and will arrive at Chateau de Renard, along with an assistant named Bruno, within the week. Thus, I am now ready to take on a librarian and hasten to let you know that the one of whom you spoke, Valéry Lefèvre d'Etaples, would do nicely. Thank you for your assistance, and I will be expecting the arrival of your protégé just as soon as possible.

Your obedient and humble servant,
Baron Paul de Renard

Valéry sat in stunned silence. How could she refuse such an opportunity? She realized right away that she really had no choice, yet what about her own plans? She had done all the preparation to stay in Nérac, completed the library which would serve as a textual base, made the acquaintance of most of the families in the village who had children, both boys and girls, and already had someone in mind who would be able to help her—namely, Josette. All this, and it was not to be? Tears came to her eyes, and Marguerite, thinking she was overcome with gratitude, rose from her chair and drew Valéry up also.

"Come, child, you will need to prepare. Chateau de Renard is a two days' trip south of here, along the same road which leads to my chateau in Pau. Of course I will accompany you, but I wish to leave by the end of the week, for the weather might turn at any moment, and as you know, I do not relish the cold." As Valéry walked toward the door, the queen called after her.

"I have seen the transformation of your uncle's chamber, Valy. I understand you did all this with the small allowance I have given you. It is most appreciated and beautifully done. It will be a treasured addition to this chateau, and it will always remind me both of your uncle and of you. However, Valéry, I think that those materials rightfully belong to you now and would make a valued addition to the baron's own library. I would like to ask you to pick from those well-arranged shelves anything you think might be useful to the baron in his own plans. The rest can be left here, and I surely will want to add to the collection over time."

Valéry could not reply due to the tears which were flowing freely now. She left the room quickly for her own *chambre à coucher* where she could give free reign to her emotions. After a time, her crying abated, and she began to think more rationally. She would have to leave her dreams behind and begin preparations for a new life. Thanks to the queen's endeavors on her behalf, there was no other recourse.

Chapter Ten

The week of preparations for the trip kept Valéry so busy she did not have much time to reflect on her feelings. When the day of departure arrived, she looked one last time at her uncle's room, now transformed into a library, and whispered a goodbye to the books and manuscripts which were now the only tangible reminders of the venerable priest. It had been difficult for her to decide which materials to take along with her, but in the end, she'd settled upon one copy each of her uncle's printed works as well as the various materials he had used in tutoring the king's children at Blois. The latter held a special place in her heart for she, too, had been part of those classroom experiences. She was gratified to see that what she had removed from the shelving and cupboards was barely discernible.

Marguerite greeted her in the courtyard, suggesting that they both ride by horseback since the October morning had dawned clear and sunny. Besides the five pack mules loaded down with their baggage, two horses drew a litter that would offer some shelter if the weather became bad. Marguerite had chosen six burly men from the guards her husband employed at the chateau whom she separated equally between the posts of *avant*—and *arrière garde*. In addition, two lads of about sixteen years were hired from neighboring farms to tend the animals and take care of other minor chores.

The chill of autumn evenings had begun to have an effect on the leaves. Valéry kept turning her head in all directions, scarcely able to get her fill of the glorious golds, oranges, and reds which graced the tree branches as well as lined the hard-baked dirt of the road underneath. The air was filled with the scents of harvest: newly cut hay, grain winnowed from wheat stalks, grapes in fat bunches on the autumn-hued vines. Marguerite too seemed to be enjoying the surrounding beauty of the countryside, humming one of Goudimel's tunes or pointing out the colorful birds nesting in the willow trees which grew in profusion along the banks of the Baïse river.

"We shall look for a nice patch of grass under the shade of a tree, for our meal. The horses will be able to rest a bit and drink from the river before we must leave its banks and head west," Marguerite commented as they rode along. After several hours, they found the perfect spot and dismounted. The guardsmen separated themselves from the women, finding a secluded spot downstream where they could enjoy some camaraderie and eat from their own food supplies. The two lads led the horses and mules down to the water and then tethered them to several nearby trees. Then they removed from one of the mules' saddlebags some smoked ham, bread baked just that morning at the chateau, a round of hard cheese, and a bottle of wine. Valéry withdrew from her own pack some of the fruit she and Josette had dried the month before. After the boys spread a *couverture de voyage* over the grass and laid out the food on it, they went to join the guards, and Marguerite and Valéry sat down to eat.

"Will the journey this afternoon be a long one?" Valéry asked. Marguerite had told her nothing about their route, nor where they would stay for the night, only that it would be a two-day trip if all went well.

"This is the same road I travel when I go to Pau, Valy. The first night will be spent at the Prieuré de Notre Dame du Calvaire. The prioress there is a dear friend who has been most hospitable to me in the past and who will welcome us graciously."

"And tomorrow, will it take long to reach the Chateau de Renard?"

"I have never been there, Valy, but the Baron de Renard assures me that if the weather is favorable, the journey should be scarcely a half-day. His lands lie among the rolling hills of the Gascogne countryside, with the chateau located quite near the village of Eauze. Shortly we must leave the banks of the Baïse and turn west. We will be crossing the Osse and Auzoue rivers before we enter the fertile land lying between the waters of the Gélise and the Izaute. As long as the weather remains dry, the river crossings should not be difficult."

The two women finished their repast and called to the boys to clean up the remains. Before long they were back on the road, but the weather had begun to turn. Within an hour, storm clouds overhead produced some rain, light at first, but within minutes, it began to pour. The little band of travelers stopped under a large oak tree, and the women got into the litter, leaving their horses to be led by the two youths, who themselves were handling the mules also. Valéry was surprised to see them laughing, obviously enjoying the challenge. She, however, was very happy not to be one of them.

Marguerite spoke. "I have not dictated to you in quite some time, Valy. Here, take my tablet and pen, and see if you can write down some of my words."

Valéry grasped the *stilo* tightly and tried to record what Marguerite was saying. It was difficult as the litter lurched and bumped over the rutty roads, now turning muddy with the rainfall. Marguerite seemed oblivious to it all, lost in one of her stories of highborn ladies and gentlemen on which she had been working for some time. It was all about how the rain had swollen the rivers in the land of the Pyrenees, forcing a group of nobility to accept the fact that they could not continue their journey until the rain stopped and they could ford the river. They decided to pass the time by telling each other tales which were true, and then the rest of the group would critique each story. In the past, Valéry had enjoyed writing down such fanciful tales as Marguerite dictated to her, but that was under different circumstances, when they were in a comfortable room in the queen's chateau apartments. This was entirely different. Marguerite spoke just as rapidly in the litter as she did in her rooms, and Valéry was having great difficulty keeping up.

Finally, the light of day began to fade, making it impossible for Valéry to see what she was writing. Her hands were cold and stiff from grasping the *stilo* so tightly, and her body ached from sitting hunched over her tablets for such a long time.

"We will need to stop now, I think." The queen's words were most welcome to Valéry's ears. She tucked her writing implements away, drew the fur-lined cape around her shoulders, and tucked her frozen fingers into its folds. A glance at Marguerite revealed that she was dozing, her capped head gently nodding to one side as the litter slowed its pace. The horses were no doubt trying to retain their footing as the road became muddier. As it grew darker, the *avante garde* lit the enclosed lanterns they carried on posts attached to the horses' tackle. Valéry began to worry that they might not be able to continue. What would happen then? She and Marguerite would, of course, remain in the litter, which could be placed under the shelter of some trees. The guards would have to brave the elements as best they could.

The horses' hooves suddenly made a hollow sound, followed by the exuberant voice of one of the forward guardsmen. "Water's high, but we have crossed the bridge. Won't be long now, for I see the lights of the convent in the distance." Marguerite roused herself, straightened her cap, and smiled.

"God is with us, my little Valy. There is more than one reason why He created religious houses!"

The prioress was there to greet them as they entered the courtyard of the convent buildings. The guardsmen and the two lads were directed to an outbuilding on the grounds, which had a stable for the horses and mules, along with quarters for the men upstairs. Valéry followed Marguerite into the priory hall where they were able to remove their cloaks, hanging them on hooks affixed to the stone wall. Hopefully, by morning, they would be free of the dampness which had penetrated the wool in spite of the protection of the litter.

They went next to the refectory, which was empty of the nuns. Valéry heard them singing vespers in the chapel, which must be close by as the office came through clearly. The prioress invited them to sit on a narrow bench at one of the long wooden tables and then disappeared through a door. She reappeared presently, followed by one of the sisters, who laid before them two steaming bowls of potage, along with some slices of bread spread thickly with butter.

"The fruits of God's garden this summer," said the prioress, pointing to the legumes in the soup. "The butter we churn each day after milking our cows. You are tired from the journey, I can see. If God wills, this will nourish your body, and a good evening's rest will restore your soul!"

Both women nodded their gratitude, and after eating, Marguerite went over to join the prioress by the fire. Valéry, sensing that they wished to talk privately, filled her cup with a little wine left in the carafe and drank it slowly, savoring the warmth it brought to her insides. She glanced from time to time at the queen and the prioress, noting the pain on Marguerite's face as well as the tears running down her cheeks. She was sure now that something was troubling the great lady, but in the weeks since her return at the end of the summer, she had not confided anything to Valéry. The prioress had taken the queen's hands in both of hers, an expression of loving concern on her face. Their voices were low, but Valéry could not help but catch snatches of words, especially from the queen, whose voice became rather high-pitched when choked by emotion.

"*Ma petite Jeanne,*" she heard. "*Elle était si malade.*" Then, "*Elle me manque énormement.*"

Valéry knew the queen was speaking of her only living child, Jeanne. Marguerite had often talked to her about how King François took little Jeanne when she was barely two and had her raised by people of his own choosing. He told his sister that he did not trust Henri or her to raise their daughter in a way that would please his purposes for her once she came of age. Of course the king had political reasons, but how cruel for the parents. *It is a wonder that Marguerite continues to adore her only brother*, Valéry thought. As the conversation continued, Valéry learned that apparently the little girl, now about eight, had been quite ill, and Marguerite rushed immediately to her side but then was not allowed to take her daughter back with her to either of her chateaux.

The snatches of conversation continued. "*Le dauphin est mort . . .* poisoned, some say. The king is in mourning for his oldest son." The prioress said something in return, her tones soft and soothing. Then Marguerite's voice, "My brother now knows the sorrow of a lost son.

Valéry thought about the little boy born to the king and queen of Navarre, who lived only five months. And now came the surprising news that François's eldest son, the dauphin, also named François, had died recently. What awful news. In addition, Valéry wondered if the king of Navarre had added to Marguerite's sadness. She would probably never know, but she began to feel a deep sympathy for Marguerite's sufferings.

Silence fell over the room. Eventually, the two women arose, and the prioress beckoned to Valéry.

"Come, I will show you both to your rooms so that you might rest for the night." She led them from the refectory and into the entrance hall. From there, a large wooden door led to the halls of the hostelry. Marguerite's room was just inside the door, off the hallway. The queen kissed Valéry on both cheeks, whispering, "*A demain mon enfant et dors bien,*" and then disappeared into her room. The prioress led Valéry farther down the hall, opened a much smaller door, and standing aside, let Valéry enter. Then, bidding her goodnight, she disappeared noiselessly into the darkness. The cell was small, with no fireplace to keep off the chill and no window to let in light during the day. There was barely enough room for a narrow bed along the wall, over which hung a crucifix with a sprig of *bruyère* tucked behind the head of the Christ. A small stand by the bed, holding a bowl and a pitcher of water, completed the furnishings. No matter, it was enough for her needs, Valéry thought. She undressed quickly and slipped beneath the coarse sheets, thinking that sleep might be a long time in coming, but the fatigue of the journey overpowered her almost immediately, and she slept.

Somewhere in the depths of the priory, a bell was ringing. Valéry opened her eyes. The room was dark, and Valéry wondered if the bell was a summons to vigils or perhaps lauds. She had no way of knowing what time it was, but she felt quite rested. A thin covering of ice lay on top the water in the pitcher, but it was easily broken when Valéry poured it into the bowl. Washing hurriedly and dressing in the same clothes she had worn the day before, she thought of what the day would bring—a new position in a new place with new people. While it was somewhat intimidating, she felt a sense of happy anticipation. Marguerite would be with her, introducing her to the baron with high praise for her abilities. That would make a big difference in how she would be received and treated. Tucking her long dark hair into her white cap, she opened the cell door and, treading lightly down the hall, paused at the queen's door and knocked. There was no response. Again, she knocked; this time a little more forcefully. Still no answer. Slowly she lifted the long handle and pushed open the door. Kneeling by the fireplace was a novice, setting a nice fire for the day.

"I am searching for Queen Marguerite," Valéry stated.

"Mademoiselle, you might find her in the refectory, taking the morning meal," the novice replied, giving Valéry a smile.

Again, the dining hall was empty of all save Marguerite, who looked up as she entered and then motioned to Valéry to take a place beside her at the table. The same nun who had served them the evening before appeared, placing a large bowl of steaming milk before Valéry and then motioning toward the loaf of bread, which Marguerite was now cutting. Valéry was hungrier than she had realized at first rising. She finished the bowl of milk and every morsel of several thick slices of bread.

Marguerite looked at her protégée with amusement. "I can see that you have resurrected overnight and are ready for the adventure which lies ahead."

Valéry smiled at the queen, noticing that although she appeared rested, the sad look had not left her eyes.

"I am indeed ready, my queen, and rejoice that you will be with me to give me courage and support. Will we be leaving soon? The day is overcast and drizzly, so the journey may take longer than just a few hours."

Marguerite followed Valéry's gaze out the window, looked down for a moment, and then rose from the bench. Drawing Valéry up by the hand, the queen led her to the seats recessed on either side of the large brick fireplace. Seated there in the warm alcove of the hearth, Valéry looked expectantly at her patroness.

"Child, I have not been as open with you as I should have been." Marguerite paused for a moment, then continued. "You will be leaving with my guard and my litter, but I shall remain here."

Valéry's heart began pound. She could not believe what she had just heard. Casting an imploring look at her queen, she tried hard to mask the terror she felt at the prospect of arriving at the chateau without the help of Marguerite. The queen, sensing the tension and having anticipated the reaction, hardened her expression and with a note of finality in her voice, said, "Valéry, my dear, you will be fine. There is nothing to fear, for I have arranged for your reception and your position. Your talents are perfect for the tasks which lie ahead of you, and you are much needed. I can assure you that you will be made welcome at Chateau de Renard, just as though they were receiving me." Marguerite searched her charge's face for some flicker of acceptance. It was not there. The queen arose from her seat and walked past the long refectory tables toward the large windows at the other end of the room. There was silence for a few moments. When she returned to Valéry, she had softened some, her eyes again filled with sadness and a hint of tears.

"My original intention was to come with you, *ma petite* Valy. I would have liked to renew my friendship and acquaintance with the baron. But child, my heart needs healing. I must seek the face of God and the solace only He can provide. This is where I must be, for a time, at least. I hope to be able to do some writing along with praying with the good sisters and seeking the counsel of the prioress. It is she who has urged me to stay on retreat for a while. I hope that you will understand . . ." Her voice trailed away.

When Valéry did not respond, Marguerite turned her gaze to some undefined image far away from the present time and setting. Valéry sat silently for what seemed like a long time, and then, with a quiet voice which she herself could scarcely hear, said, "Of course, my beloved queen. You must do this, and I . . ." There was a pause and then a quiver in her voice as she continued, "and I will meet my new opportunity with the strength and courage you expect of me." Valéry rose and then bent to kiss her benefactress on the cheek. "And you will always, every day and forevermore, be in my heart and my prayers."

Chapter Eleven

What should have been a journey of only a few hours took far longer due to several unfortunate happenings. To begin with, although Marguerite's baggage had been unloaded from the pack mules the night before, it was left in the courtyard until morning when the guardsmen had to carry it into the priory. The queen liked to bring along with her everything she thought she might need, and thus there were books and writing materials, in addition to an extensive wardrobe to cover any type of weather. Next, Marguerite's horse and mules needed to be taken out to pasture. Marguerite supervised it all, making sure that Valéry's horse would be ridden by one of the boys while the mules, loaded down with her belongings as well as the manuscripts and books, would be tended by the other lad. Valéry herself was to ride in the litter since the day was rainy and cool. The six guardsmen were to accompany Valéry to Chateau de Renard for her own protection as there could be brigands along the route. Then they were to return to the chateau at Nérac until Marguerite summoned them to come get her, for she was not certain about how long she would remain at the priory.

When the party finally got under way, the roads had become even more precarious than the day before. They made slow progress but were able to cross the Gélise river without incident, which had been a major concern of the head guardsman, who feared a flood. By late afternoon, the horses and the men were tired, so shortly before they reached the village of Eauze, one of the guards informed Valéry that they would be stopping at an inn for a little rest and refreshment. Valéry was ushered into a small side room off the main hall where there were several other ladies present. She was glad to be separated from the men, who were enjoying their ale in the larger room. While Valéry sipped cider and ate some of the dried fruit she had brought along with her, she watched the guardsmen and the two lads from her vantage point by the fireplace but grew concerned when the two youths downed several more tankards of ale than they could apparently hold. Their behavior turned loud and argumentative, and soon they were involved in a brawl, which had to be broken up by the innkeeper and several of his strapping sons. The boys, angry and drunk, put up a protest at first but were taken to task by Marguerite's guardsmen, who yanked them outside by the scruff their necks and gave them a good scolding accompanied by a warning that if they ever did that again, they would be dismissed from the service of King Henri of Navarre and booted off his lands.

The youths, considerably subdued by this warning, went back to their duties with the animals, and the journey resumed, but valuable daylight time had been lost. Before long, it began to grow dark, and the drizzle that had kept up most of the day further obscured the route. The entourage picked its way slowly the last leg of the trip, found the small road which turned off from the main one, and with a sense of relief, stopped at the gatehouse leading to the Chateau de Renard. The gatekeeper motioned them on through the stone portals bearing matching foxes carved from the limestone of the region. In the fading light, they looked menacing to Valéry, and she hoped that was not a precursor of what lay in wait for her.

Valéry leaned out of the cover of the litter to catch a glimpse of the chateau. Lining both sides of the road were large sycamore trees, their falling leaves making a soft path beneath them. Ahead, Valéry could barely make out the outlines of the chateau. It appeared to have two keeps. Valéry saw a candle burning in a window of the south keep while the north tower had a light illuminating the windows at each level, all the way up to the belfry. In between the keeps was the main body of the chateau, four levels high and fronted by rows of windows, which overlooked the courtyard they were now entering. Encircled by a stone balustrade, it was covered in fine gravel, making the area free from mud when it rained. Valéry was helped from the litter by the head guardsman just as the front entrance to the chateau opened, bathing the courtyard in light which emanated from the interior hallway. Standing in the doorway was the gaunt figure of a man. Valéry was filled with excited anticipation. There would be a welcome from the baron and others, followed by a warm meal which would soothe her hunger pangs. She pictured being shown to her fire lit chamber, which would certainly include a feathered bed made warm by the ministrations of a chambermaid with a charcoal-filled bed warmer.

As she drew closer to the figure standing in the doorway, she smiled and introduced herself. "Monsieur, I am Valéry Lefèvre d'Etaples, hired to be the new librarian at Chateau de Renard."

The expression of the man in the doorway did not register any greeting. Instead he stood staring at her, his mouth forming a straight line across his face. Valéry felt awkward, not knowing what to do next as she had not been invited to enter.

"Is there a place where my guardsmen can put up the horses and then receive lodging and a meal for the night?" Still the man did not move although his eyes traveled past her to the men standing at a little distance in the background.

Valéry was taken aback at first but then became a little angry at the cool reception.

"You are rude, monsieur, to keep us standing outside in the rain and cold. I have been sent by the queen of Navarre and at the request of the Baron de Renard, to take up a position here, and I must insist that if you will not show common courtesy, you call the baron himself. In the meantime, I would like my guardsmen to deliver my baggage inside. I will have need of it tonight."

At this, the manservant cast her an unfriendly look but motioned for her to step into the hallway and then turned his attention to the guardsmen. "If you will wait here, messieurs, I will summon some stable hands to show you the livery stable and lodgings where you and your horses can be accommodated." With that he left Valéry standing alone in the foyer while he disappeared into the darkness of the courtyard. The two youths, who had been quite on their best behavior since the incident at the inn, brought in her baggage, depositing it on the stone floor in the middle of the foyer. Soon the manservant returned with several stable hands, who helped with the horses and gave instructions to the guardsmen as to where they were to go. Seeing this accomplished, the manservant reentered the chateau and, without looking at Valéry, opened a massive oak door to the right of the foyer and pointed to the room inside.

"You will wait here." Valéry barely entered the room when, without another word, he closed the door behind her, his footsteps fading away down the hall. Valéry was stunned. She looked around the room, uncertain as to what to do next. A fire burned brightly in the large fireplace that took up most of one wall. It was flanked by high-backed wooden chairs covered with exquisite tapestry. A man's chairs, Valéry thought, but nonetheless inviting, for she was shivering from the wet, cold weather, and perhaps also from the frosty reception. She seated herself in one, letting her frozen feet dangle over the edge without worrying about not being able to touch the floor. No doubt the manservant who so coldly received her had gone to locate the baron, who would give her a proper greeting, and all would be well. As the moments passed and no footsteps were heard outside the door, Valéry's fatigue got the better of her. The large logs in the fireplace were burning well, sending heat to relax her stiff limbs. Soon she closed her eyes, drowsy from the warmth that enveloped her aching body. No sounds other than the crackling fire interrupted her dozing. She would rest thus for just a moment, she thought to herself, but be ready to stand when the baron made his entry.

How long she slept, she could not tell, nor could she put her finger on what roused her from her somnolent state. Gradually, though, the sense that something had changed reached her conscious mind. Opening her eyes, she saw that the fire still burned well, but she felt a slight cold draft of air intruding on the enveloping warmth she had been enjoying. In addition, the fresh air carried with it a distinct smell of the forest, a musty odor of damp leaves and pungent pine, and something else as well. What was it? Valéry rubbed her eyes and stretched her arms toward the fire. As her fully-awake state returned, she realized that it was the scent of leather. With that came the feeling that she was no longer alone in the room. Looking up over her left shoulder, she was startled to see the figure of a man standing in the shadows by the doorway, absolutely motionless, his eyes fixed unblinkingly upon her. They were luminous, very like the cold gray steel of the knife he wore at his side, catching the reflection of the flames in the fireplace.

Valéry got out of her chair much more quickly than she would have thought possible, turning to fully face the figure in the corner. For a moment, he did not move as he continued to stare at her, almost as if he were a beast of prey, Valéry thought, and she the intended victim. She stood rooted to the spot for what seemed like an interminable time. Then, ever so slowly, the man in the shadows moved across the room toward her, his steps measured and timed. His eyes never left her face. Muscles around his square jaw flinched slightly, and his clenched mouth bore no smile. All Valéry could think of at that moment was that it was no wonder she had smelled leather. He was dressed in high-topped leather boots, leggings, and a leather jerkin held in at the waist by a thick leather belt, into which the knife had been tucked. *He must be one of the groundskeepers, and a formidable one at that,* Valéry surmised, for his appearance was quite rugged. Stopping just the other side of her chair, he spoke, his voice so soft that Valéry had to strain to hear it.

"If you are Valéry Lefèvre d'Etaples, then I have been deceived."

"*Pardonnez-moi,* monsieur?" Valéry managed to ask, incredulous at his words.

The slate-gray eyes never left her face. "I said that this is surely some sort of trick."

Valéry hardly knew how to reply. "I am that person, monsieur, and I assure you that there has been no deception. I do not understand why you say such a thing,"

"I expected a man, not a slip of a girl, barely out of the nursery," he replied curtly.

Valéry drew herself up to her full height. "I assure you, monsieur, that I am much older than a nursery child, and very much more educated. Who do you think you are to insinuate that the queen of the kingdom of Navarre, and also these lands of Gascony, deceived you? I demand to see the Baron de Renard immediately."

"You are looking at him, mademoiselle."

Valéry drew in her breath, scarcely able to accept that the roughly dressed figure before her was anyone other than one of the baron's grounds—or gamekeepers. She opened her mouth to speak, but nothing came out. The baron, however, was not finished.

"There has been a misunderstanding, then, between the queen and myself. In deference to her wishes, I will keep you on, at least for a while. Then, because you will certainly prove yourself unequal to the skill required in the position, you will be returned to the queen, whom I greatly admire . . . and," he added after a short pause, "would not want to offend in any way. It will be done of course with my deepest regrets." Valéry did not miss the sarcasm in his voice.

With that, he turned abruptly and exited the room. Valéry stood, shaking with the aftermath of the encounter. "You arrogant ass," she said aloud as the door closed behind him. She would prove him to be wrong if it meant working herself to death in the process. His library would be the boast of the entire region, far excelling the one she had set up in the chateau in Nérac. Marguerite and her husband, King Henri d'Albret, would visit and pronounce it a remarkable piece of work, greatly to the chagrin of the baron. With that thought, she regained her composure, and just in time too, as the door opened again, and the baron reappeared, this time with a large-boned woman, whose expression was hardly friendly.

"My housekeeper, Madame Thibault," the baron said. "She will show you to your room." With that, he left again, leaving Valéry at the mercy of the formidable woman.

"Follow me," she snapped as she led the way back into the hall. Motioning toward the baggage, which lay in a pile on the floor, she remarked, "This will wait until morning."

"No, it will not, Madame Thibault. I have need of my bags tonight. Please find someone to carry them to my chamber, if you will." Valéry was amazed at her own temerity but then even more amazed at the reaction it brought.

"Very well, you may carry them up yourself!" Her words were clipped, but Valéry was not to be cowed.

"Then I will have to ask you to wait here, madame, while I fetch my guardsmen to help me with the task."

This seemed to persuade the housekeeper to change tactics. Calling for her husband, who turned out to be the manservant who had met Valéry when she first arrived, she instructed him to get some help to bring the luggage up to Valéry's room. Next, she led the way up an expanse of winding marble stairs until they reached the second landing where to the left there was a long hallway leading across the middle portion of the chateau, and to her right a pair of massive oak doors reaching almost to the ceiling. Yanking them open, the housekeeper entered a wide passageway illuminated by a sole candle set into the window ledge. *This must be the south keep*, Valéry thought, remembering the light she had seen in this tower when she first arrived. A few paces beyond the window, the housekeeper pointed to some beautifully carved doors. "The library is in there, mademoiselle." When Valéry tried to catch a glimpse inside, the housekeeper grabbed her away by the elbow.

"You will have time enough to explore tomorrow. Please have the courtesy to follow me, mademoiselle. It is late, and I will tolerate no delays."

What a charming woman, Valéry thought sarcastically. No wonder her poor husband had such a sour disposition. She could not imagine that Madame Thibault would dare adopt the same acerbic manner with the baron. But then the baron himself had not been at all gracious toward his new librarian. Perhaps the whole atmosphere of the chateau was toxic to its occupants. She hoped it was not catching!

The housekeeper stopped abruptly in front of a small white door adjacent to the library, took out a key from the pocket of her *tablier*, which she fit into the lock, and then pushed the door open.

"You will stay here, mademoiselle. This is the chamber which Baron Guillaume de Renard favored in his last years, until he died several months ago. It was furnished according to his taste and needs, which may not suit you, *mais tant pis*, you will have to accept the room as it is." Having so spoken, she stepped aside to let Valéry enter, followed by Monsieur Thibault and several other men who had caught up with them, carrying the baggage. After they deposited their load in the middle of the floor, they left immediately, with the housekeeper slamming the door behind them.

Valéry stood alone in the middle of the chamber and looked around her. Someone had anticipated her arrival as a fire burned in the large green marble fireplace dominating the middle of one wall. Since the library was on the other side of the wall, Valéry surmised that it contained a matching fireplace, which shared the same flue. A black marble mantel ran the full length of the fireplace, above which there was a mirror held in a heavy gold frame. On the hearth sat a wrought-iron pot, its handle resting to one side. In addition, she noted a *cremaillère* with several hooks within the fireplace itself, from which hung a larger black pot filled with gently bubbling water. *The pots with their pot hanger will come in handy*, Valéry thought to herself, *beginning tonight, for I will have hot water to wash off the grime of the trip.* She imagined the aged Baron Guillaume sitting in the overstuffed chair placed just by the hearth, a potage heating over the fire, ready for him to sip as he wished.

To the right of the fireplace, Valéry noticed a set of shelves, which held jars filled with various dried foodstuffs and leaves—*morilles* from the forest, *feuilles seche de mente*, sprigs of *romarin* and *basilic,* even some herbs for medicinal purposes. She smiled at the willow bark she remembered so well from Marguerite's ministrations. She would add to this her own dried fruits, and when warmer weather came, she would collect chamomile petals and the leaves of the *tilleul* and *verveine* to make tisanes. If company at the Chateau de Renard became too unbearable, she could always take a meal in her room and do very nicely with such a larder at her disposal.

Attached to the upper wall on the left of the fireplace, an empty bookshelf rose to the ceiling. What a perfect place for her to arrange her uncle's books, Valéry observed with satisfaction. Underneath were several enclosed cabinets, their doors artfully carved with scenes from mythological literature. Opening one, she found to her delight piles of manuscripts and books, many beautifully bound in leather, their covers bearing various hand-tooled emblems, devices, and blazons. She remembered Marguerite telling her how the line of Barons de Renard had collected manuscripts over many centuries, resulting now in an impressive amount of material. Valéry could imagine the aged Baron Guillaume, sitting by the fire and reading with pleasure from this collection. What a pity he was gone now, for she would have loved getting to know him. Already she was convinced that, unlike his son, he had been a kindly man, like her Uncle Jacques. She imagined she could feel the spirits of both men with her now.

Next to the one window in her room, now shuttered and covered with heavy blue draperies, stood a small writing desk and chair flanked by a massive armoire. Against the wall, directly opposite the fireplace, a feather bed rested on a raised platform, its four posts supporting bed curtains, which matched the draperies and could be closed all around to keep out the cold at night. Adjacent to the bed there was a small table, and next to it a sizeable niche carved into the wall which held a toilette seat and a porcelain basin. Touching the bowl, Valéry was surprised to find it on hinges, so that when one wanted to empty the water, all one had to do was to tip the bowl, and the liquid would fall down a shaft, probably to the ground outside the chateau. She would have to write about this to Marguerite, whose chateau in Nérac did not have such a convenience.

Valéry began to feel more optimistic. As she unpacked a few of her toiletries, she nibbled on some dried fruit, and taking a cup off the baron's shelf, filled it with hot water and dropped in some mint leaves. The hot drink and fruit began to revive her. She washed in the basin and listened to the water travel down the chute after she was done with her ablutions. She would unpack the rest of her belongings in the morning, after a good night's rest. Climbing into bed, she pulled a large down coverlet over herself and closed her eyes. In spite of the cold welcome she'd received, life here would be good. The baron would get over his disappointment at her gender, she would be efficient at her work, and all would be well, just as Marguerite had promised. With those comforting thoughts, she fell asleep.

Chapter Twelve

Valéry woke to a light tapping on her door. Opening her eyes, it took a minute to realize where she was. The tapping came again. Getting out of bed, she called out, "*Un moment, s'il vous plait*," and went to her bags, which lay in a pile in the middle of the room. Pulling out a woolen robe, she went over to the door and opened it to find a young girl standing in the hallway, holding a tray with *petit déjeuner*.

"Mademoiselle Lefèvre," the girl said pleasantly, "*je m'appelle Lisette Maguis*. Madame Thibault wished me to bring you something to eat. May I place it in your room?"

"How kind, Lisette. Yes, please come in, for I am indeed famished." Valéry could scarcely believe that the formidable housekeeper from the evening before would spare a thought for her welfare. Perhaps the woman had some modicum of mercy in her after all.

The girl set the tray on the small table by the bedside and turned toward Valéry. "I will be your maidservant, mademoiselle, so if there is anything that you need, I will be happy to help you." Smiling up at Valéry, her warm brown eyes twinkled.

"You are very young to be a chambermaid, Lisette. I shall be delighted to have your help, but you must tell me if I ever ask too much."

"Oh, Mademoiselle Lefèvre, I am nearly twelve years old and am able to do a whole lot of things around the chateau. I am sure you will not be any burden to me at all."

Valéry laughed at the forthrightness of her answer. She liked the girl, perhaps because she was the first one to be nice to her since her arrival, but also because she reminded her of Josette.

"Lisette, do you know if the guardsmen who brought me here have departed yet?"

"I think they are eating just now, mademoiselle. My brother Lucien is helping get their horses ready at the moment."

"Good, then I will have a little time to eat, unpack my belongings, and get myself dressed before they leave. I would like to speak with the head guardsman before they go."

"I will tell Lucien to pass that word on then, mademoiselle. Here, if we open your shutters you can look out over the courtyard and see the stables up the road apace." The girl opened the window, unhooked the heavy shutters, and pushed them back against the outside wall until they snapped into their latches.

Valéry peered over the girl's shoulder, impressed with the view. Sunshine bathed the surrounding land with its warm yellow tones. Below them in the courtyard, both men and women, no doubt servants of the baron, went about their morning chores. Beyond the stone balustrade encircling the front of the chateau, there was a road lined by various outbuildings. One of them had a row of high-arched doorways marking it as the stables. A youth was leading horses, one by one, from inside, tethering them to the metal posts in front of the building.

"That is my brother, Mademoiselle Lefèvre," the young maidservant said, pointing toward the boy with the horses. "He helps with many things here, as do I, since our father, Régis Maguis, is the baron's steward, the *régisseur* of the estate." The girl beamed as she spoke, obviously proud of her father's position as well as the place of responsibility given to his two children.

"I am sure the baron is very fortunate to have all three of you in his employ, Lisette, and please, you may call me Mademoiselle Valéry, for I hope that soon we shall be good friends."

The girl looked appreciatively at Valéry. "I have been instructed to bring your *petit déjeuner* each morning, along with water so that you might wash, Mademoiselle Valéry, and to make sure that you have a nice fire for the evenings. Lucien will see to it that you always have a good supply of firewood, for the weather is turning now, and the evenings can be quite chilly."

"You have anticipated my needs very well, Lisette. *Merci!*"

The girl looked pleased. "Is there anything more, Mademoiselle Valéry?"

"I have just two concerns right now, Lisette. First, since you have not been told to bring me my main meal of the day, I assume that I am to take it with the baron and his household. Do you know at what time that is and where?"

"Oh yes, Mademoiselle Valéry. I quite forgot. Madame Thibault told me to let you know that dinner is served in the great hall, which is just off the main foyer, to the right of the stairs as you descend. Someone from the kitchen always rings a bell, which can be heard throughout the chateau, so you can listen for that summons."

"And here is my second concern. I noticed that Madame Thibault used a key to open the door of this room. I am wondering if I should have it, now that this is my room. If it has been the custom to keep this room locked when no one is in it, then whenever I am not in my room, I also would like to keep it locked."

"I am not sure about the key, mademoiselle, but perhaps you could ask Madame Thibault." The girl looked like she wanted to add "and good luck in that" but then thought better of it and kept still.

Valéry smiled and tilted her head to one side. "I can well anticipate what her answer will be! Keys are a symbol of position, and I expect Madame Thibault values her place as housekeeper of this chateau. She will hold tightly to all the privileges inherent in it, which undoubtedly include possession of that key!"

Privately, Valéry made a mental note that there had to be other ways to lock her room besides begging the housekeeper for a key she was sure the woman would never give to her. She would have to think about that. To Lisette, she said, "Regardless of the key, I notice that there are brackets to hold a metal rod on each side of the door in my room but no bar to put in them."

"That is easily explained, Mademoiselle Valéry. You see, the old baron's son was afraid that his father might bar the door to his room from the inside, and then if anything happened to him during the night, nobody would be able to enter, so Baron Paul had the bar removed. I do not know where it was put, but I will ask my father. Surely, nobody could object to your having the bar since you are of sound health and a clear mind and certainly don't want anyone to come charging in upon you in the middle of the night!"

Valéry laughed. "You are very observant, Lisette, and have a delightful way of expressing yourself. Have you ever wished that you could write?"

"Write, mademoiselle? I do not even know how to read."

"Would you like to learn, Lisette?"

The chambermaid looked surprised. "How could that be possible, mademoiselle? There is at present no parish school in our village of Eauze like we had before the old priest died. My father himself went to this school when he was a young boy, and so he learned how to read and even write a little."

"You do not have a priest now?"

"We just got a new one, mademoiselle. His name is Pierre Pénicaut. My father hopes that he will begin another parish school so that Lucien can be part of it, but the priest is quite young and new, so that might take some time to happen."

"If you and your brother wish to learn how to read, then so you shall, and to write also, even though it has not been the custom to teach the two together. I will speak to your new priest, but in the meantime, I will make sure that you do not have to wait to begin your learning. If the baron will give me permission, and your father agrees to let me teach you, we can begin classes right away."

"You can teach *me* reading and writing, mademoiselle, not just my brother? I never even dared hope that such classes could be offered to a girl! It would be so wonderful, I can scarcely believe it could be true."

"I will speak to your father as soon as possible. Do you live in the village?"

"We have a cottage in Eauze, yes. It is not large, but it is comfortable for the three of us."

"That would be your father, your brother, and yourself?" When the girl nodded, Valéry queried, "Then you have no mother, Lisette?"

"No, mademoiselle, not anymore. Our mother died about five years ago now. It has been a sad time for us all, but for Papa especially. He still cries sometimes when he thinks we are not looking, and he can be very moody too, but we are all grateful for each other and for the work we have here at the chateau."

"I am sorry for your loss, Lisette. I am sure you and your brother are a great source of comfort and happiness to your father."

"He's very happy with his duties as *régisseur* too, Mademoiselle Valéry. He has been so helpful to Baron de Renard that he has been given many other duties as well, including overseeing the grape harvest and the Armagnac distillery. He even constructed this room!"

When Valéry looked surprised, the girl continued. "The original library was one big room. But when Baron Guillaume de Renard grew too old and infirm to walk between his apartments in the north keep to his library in the south keep, he asked my father to partition off this portion of the library to make a bedchamber for him. He could be right next door to his beloved *bibliothèque* and yet be warm and comfortable in his new chamber."

"Ah, that would explain this door with its lock, then. It used to be the library door, right?"

"Yes. It had a lock originally to keep the contents of the library safe when the English were fighting us and taking over our lands. Thank goodness, they were too busy trying to conquer territory belonging to the counts of Armagnac to bother with this chateau although some of our barons in the past helped the counts fight against the English. After the English went back to their island, there was no need to lock the library door anymore, and then, when my father built this bedchamber, he had to construct a new set of doors for the library. You will notice that there is no lock."

"That is an interesting history, Lisette. Your father must have built the common wall of the library and this room using wood, then, and not stone and mortar."

"I believe so, mademoiselle, and he also put in two back-to-back fireplaces, one for each room, so his father could keep warm, and he added shelving with cupboards below, just like on the opposite side of the wall in the library."

"He is a carpenter of great skill, I can see. When I have a chance to unpack the books my uncle gave to me, I shall take great delight in displaying them on these beautiful shelves."

Lisette was beaming with pride as she turned to go, and Valéry reassured her that she would try to arrange for classes at her earliest opportunity. "Tell your father that I will talk to him soon, for I wish to meet him and to sound him out on the education of his children."

After the girl had gone, Valéry sat down to eat. The simple repast seemed like a banquet after the long hours she had gone without a proper meal. Next she began to unpack her valises, hanging up her dresses in the armoire and neatly folding other clothing on its shelves. The baggage which contained her uncle's various books and manuscripts would have to wait until she had time to arrange them on the shelves. The precious casket with its valuable necklace would add a visible touch of herself to the chamber, so she placed it on the mantel over the fireplace. Embers still burned from last night's fire, keeping the water in the kettle warm. Valéry poured it into her porcelain bowl, pleased to be able to wash in comfort and to dispose of the water by tipping the bowl on its hinges. Dressing quickly, she hurried into the hall, passing up the temptation to open the library doors and instead taking the winding stairway to the *rez de chaussée*. The double doors of the chateau stood wide open, letting in fresh air and sunshine as one of the servants swept out the dirt, no doubt tracked in when she arrived the night before. Valéry crossed the courtyard in the direction of the stables, meeting the head guardsman just as he emerged from his quarters there.

"*Bonjour*, Mademoiselle Lefèvre." He looked no worse for wear from the journey, and for that, she was glad as he had worked hard to deliver both his charges safely to their destinations.

Valéry wished him good morning in return. "Will you be leaving soon, monsieur?"

"Certainly within the hour," he replied. "We will attempt to make the entire trip back to Nérac without stopping except to rest the animals and take refreshment ourselves. Without Queen Marguerite and yourself, we can make better time."

Valéry nodded with a smile, thinking to herself that it would also help if the two youths did not stop to drink too much at any *auberge* along the way. "God grant you fair weather and a safe journey, then. As for the horses, I understand that Queen Marguerite wished the horse I rode to remain here with me. I plan to arrange with the stable hands for his care."

"We will leave your horse, Mademoiselle Lefèvre, as those were our instructions from the queen."

Valéry thanked him and returned to the chateau. She would be glad to have a horse at her disposal. It would give her a bit more freedom to come and go when she wished to journey into Eauze or ride into the surrounding countryside. She would need the permission of the baron to stable her horse, but given his promise to let her remain, at least for a while, she felt sure that the care of her horse would meet with his approval.

Back inside, she decided it would be the perfect time to explore the library, where the majority of her days would be spent. She was tempted to take the marble stairs two at a time, so great was her anticipation, but decided not to risk criticism of being unladylike, in case somebody was watching her. Gripping the ornate wrought-iron railing which wound its way up one side of the wide marble stairway, she noticed on the opposite wall the entwined letters *RR* embedded in the stone every so often. Perhaps they were the initials of the first Baron de Renard, placed there when he built his chateau. Opening one of the massive pair of doors into the south keep, she went directly to the elaborately carved library doors, turned the long handle on one of the panels, and stepped inside. A gasp escaped her lips. Before her was a room which could only be described as magnificent. An enormous mullioned window rose twice as high as the window in her own room, and although the view was the same, the scene was certainly much more elegantly framed by heavy burgundy-colored velour draperies, richly embroidered with gold thread.

Turning her back to the window, Valéry looked around the room in sheer amazement. On all four walls, finely crafted shelving laden with books and manuscripts rose up almost to the coffered ceiling. Valéry tilted her head back as far as she could to see the elaborate decorations, fleurs de lis painted in red, gold, blue, and green, interspersed every so often with the gold lettering of the entwined *RR*. Just under the ceiling, a brass railing ran the length of the tops of the bookcases. Hanging from this was a ladder which one could slide to whatever wall one wished in order to access the books on the higher shelves. Lowering her gaze, she noticed that from about waist-high to the floor, there were a series of cabinets, their doors carved with scenes from mythology, just like the cabinets in her own room. Opening one on the common wall with her chamber, she found that the interior was piled high with manuscripts, just like in her own room. It would be a task indeed to sort through, but necessary as no doubt they were all a valuable part of the Barons de Renard's collection over the ages. There would be a physical challenge also when it came to accessing the materials high up on the shelving. She tried to picture herself balanced precariously at the top of the ladder, removing one of the heavy books, tucking it under her arm, and carefully descending the ladder with her precious burden. How many times would she have to repeat this? She felt apprehensive just thinking about it!

Over the fireplace mantle hung a large blazon depicting a fox *statant* against a diagonal panel of *gueules* placed on an *écu d'argent*. Underneath was the motto *Immobiliter intueri,* fixed gaze. It certainly suited the present Baron de Renard. Valéry was familiar with the coat of arms of King François, which boasted a large salamander. She had seen one of them carved in the stone fireplace of the library at Blois. Somehow a fox seemed to be a more dignified symbol than a lizard, she thought, laughing out loud at the animal the king of France had chosen.

"You are amused by the de Renard coat of arms, Mademoiselle Lefèvre?" Valéry turned to find Baron Paul de Renard standing in the doorway, surprised that she had not heard him enter the room.

"Not at all," Valéry replied. "It is most impressive. I was just thinking about King François's choice of the salamander for his coat of arms. I like your fox much better!"

"The king's device resembles a dragon, mademoiselle, engulfed in flames but not consumed by them. I think he chose this as a symbol of his strength, and not as an object to be ridiculed."

"I certainly did not mean any disrespect, Baron. The king is brave on the battlefield as well as a generous patron of the arts and has a sister who I love very dearly." Valéry felt thoroughly chastised at the baron's remark, not knowing how to redeem herself in the eyes of this prickly man. She decided to change the subject.

"I am truly overwhelmed by this library, Monsieur le Baron. I know well the king's *bibliothèque* at Blois, but this one, although not as large, surely rivals it both in magnificence and perhaps even the wealth of its contents."

"Then we had best not tell the king of France that, mademoiselle, for I have heard that he is not above requisitioning from his nobility that which he covets."

Valéry was not at all sure whether he was serious or joking, but she decided to reply in the same vein. "Nor will we invite him to visit, and if his sister Marguerite comes, I think we will need to swear her to secrecy!"

Valéry was amazed to see a slight smile on the baron's face and imagined that his eyes were not quite as steely gray as they had appeared the night before. Perhaps he could be persuaded eventually to soften his position against being sent a woman librarian. Right now, however, those eyes still held no warmth in spite of his smile. Valéry harbored no illusion that she would not have to prove her worth, and at the moment, that challenge appeared quite formidable.

"Surely no one person was responsible for acquiring all of the books I see before me," Valéry said, anxious to continue the conversation on a positive note.

"The de Renard family's interest in collecting manuscripts goes back to Richard de Renard, who was made a baron by King Charles V of France after exemplary military service under the king's commander, Bertrand du Guesclin."

"He fought the English then?"

"Yes, for most of his life, as did his son and grandson after him. Richard's reward was this barony and the friendship of the king, who not only lent his royal patronage to literature and learning but also collected manuscripts, some of which he would give as gifts to favored nobility. My *arrière arrière grandpère* was one of them."

"Then it was Baron Richard de Renard who built this chateau? I have seen the entwined *RR* initials on the stairway walls and painted on this coffered ceiling." Valéry pointed above her as she spoke.

The baron nodded his head. "You are observant, mademoiselle."

"Do you mean to compliment me on something, Baron de Renard?"

"Very rarely do I hand out praise, Mademoiselle Lefèvre, and when I do, it has to be well-deserved. I was simply making an observation." The hard line of his mouth and the cold look in his eyes was enough to convince Valéry that he did not appreciate her attempt at being coy.

The baron continued. "Richard de Renard acquired the title and land from the king along with a royal pension, which enabled him to build this chateau, and although he managed tenants who raised cattle and planted *blé* on estate lands, he never lost interest in finding new manuscripts for his own collection. King Charles V was his inspiration."

"My Uncle Jacques Lefèvre d'Etaples used to speak of this king. I remember him saying that Charles had amassed a library of nearly one thousand volumes which contained important works on the Holy Scriptures, theology, philosophy, and the sciences. Uncle Jacques showed me some of them which were part of the Blois collection."

"And some of them you will undoubtedly find in the de Renard collection also, Mademoiselle Lefèvre."

He paused for a moment, and then added, "That is, if I retain you that long."

"I fully intend to discover those manuscripts and more in the course of my inventory, Baron de Renard."

The baron cast her a quick glance but said nothing.

"I imagine that what I see before me is the result of acquisitions made by several generations of Barons de Renard after Richard." When the baron nodded, she continued. "But wouldn't that be a great expense, especially in the midst of the century-long fight with the English on French soil? It is my understanding that during this period, subsequent French kings did not have the money, as did Charles V, to continue patronizing the arts."

"It is true that the war made it difficult for these kings to give much financial support to the work of the copyists, and for three generations, my own forebears had to fight for their lands and their country against the English kings. Even my grandfather, Jean de Renard, was part of an alliance with the powerful counts of Armagnac to drive the usurpers out of our territory. Obviously, these ancestors of mine did not have much time to devote to such things as building up this library, but still made acquisitions as they were able. In the end, they were proud to have retained their rightful domain here in the Bas Armagnac and to have added to this library."

"Then it must have been your father, Baron Guillaume, who did not have to contend with the English, and who could devote more of his energies to the collection of books."

"My father enjoyed a period of prosperity, adding vineyards to the grazing land and the grain-cultivated fields. Then came a summons from King François to fight with him in his Italian campaigns. My father was there at the Battle of Marignano, and although the victory was ours, my father, who was forty at the time, was severely wounded. He spent a time convalescing in Lyon and then returned to this chateau. However, he never completely recovered from his wounds. The library gave him great pleasure, especially as he aged and had to hand over the management of the estate to me. He actively continued to seek out new materials, both handwritten and printed, and then spent hours pouring over their contents. I think you know the room you occupy was his."

Valéry, sensing the emotion the baron felt as he talked about his father, only so recently dead, answered softly. "I am honored to be the room's next resident. I sense all around me the presence of Baron Guillaume, and it is my hope that my work will do justice to the collection which meant so much to so many generations of barons."

The baron gave her a look which could only be described as enigmatic. He was certainly not in the early years of adulthood as the graying hair at his temples would testify to, but neither was he at all old. Valéry would have liked to ask him more about his own life. He did not mention his mother, nor whether he himself had seen any military service to the king. In addition, there had been no sign of a baroness at the chateau. At his age, this was contrary to the ordinary practice although given the way he was treating her, it might be no wonder that he was unmarried. This baron did not seem to value women very highly. No matter, she thought to herself. It was enough that he had shared something of his family history with her. He obviously cherished the de Renard tradition, and this insight might prove useful to her in the days ahead when she was on trial.

"I trust that you have settled in, then?" The baron seemed to have shaken himself out of his previous mood and into more practical matters. "The room was set up for the convenience and comfort of my father, but you may make the changes necessary to suit your needs."

"I have started to unpack, and the little Lisette brought me my breakfast this morning, which was most appreciated as I had not had a meal since yesterday morning at the priory."

The baron frowned. "You received no food last night after your arrival?"

"I did not, Baron de Renard."

"Then I must apologize for the oversight, Mademoiselle Lefèvre. I will speak to Marthe Thibault, who surely should have seen to it that you were fed." The latter was said without emotion, but nevertheless, it gave Valéry hope that the man was able to show some consideration for her needs, and this, in turn, gave her the courage to ask her next two questions.

"Speaking of feeding, Baron de Renard, is it be possible for my horse to be cared for in your stables and put to pasture with your other horses?"

"Of course, of course." The baron sounded slightly impatient, but Valéry continued. "I have another request, Baron de Renard. Would you have any objection to me teaching Lisette and Lucien to read and write?"

For a moment, it appeared that he had not comprehended her question. His mouth opened as if he thought he could answer immediately, but then he said nothing. Valéry was just about to repeat her question when the baron recovered himself sufficiently to reply.

"If you do not neglect the work you have been brought here to do, mademoiselle, and if it meets with their father's approval, you may teach Lisette and Lucien whatever you want. In the meantime, I have made a listing of your responsibilities." Withdrawing a slip of paper from inside his leather jerkin, he handed it to Valéry.

As she bent to read it, he added somewhat curtly, "Please read it *after* I have left, mademoiselle, and make special note of your first assignment, which needs to be addressed before you do anything else. You will note that I have written down the title of a book which my father and I read together shortly before he died, but which now seems to have disappeared somewhere in this profusion of unorganized materials. The author intended it to be a textbook for schools, but Baron Guillaume and I agreed that in its present form it would be both expensive as well as difficult for students to use. It was my father's last request of me that I apply my education at the university by making changes to the materials, using the book as a guide."

"Did you make notes in the margins, then?"

"No, I wrote my own changes on separate sheets of paper but then gave the original book back to my father. I have no idea what he did with it, but before I can have the reworked material printed by Monsieur Faguet, I will need to show him the original text."

"Could you give me a description of the book I am to find? It might be of great help if in my search I knew what it looked like."

"My only recollection is that it was printed in quarto, mademoiselle, and that the title was on the cover. I will expect you to find it within the next fortnight as that is when my print shop should be ready, and I intend to have Monsieur Faguet run off the revised text as a first test of the press."

Valéry was flabbergasted. *He expects me to find in two weeks one specific book out of the thousands in this room? No, this is not as much a test of how well the press will work as it is to show how incompetent I am when I cannot locate quickly the material in question. It will provide a perfect excuse on his part to dismiss me.*

"You are challenging me to locate the proverbial *aiguille dans une botte de foin,* monsieur. I think you are hoping to set me up for failure."

The baron was already in the hallway but called back over his shoulder. "Think what you will, mademoiselle. If you are as qualified a librarian as you purport to be, then I am sure you will accomplish this one simple request with ease. During the next few weeks, I will be involved with the grape harvest, but *if* you locate the book, I want to know immediately,"

Valéry stood in the middle of the library, holding the piece of paper before her. It read *In linguam gallicam Isagoge* and bore the author's name, Jacques Du Bois. Of course she would find the book. By the time the baron's footsteps faded away down the hall, she had resolved to make this task the driving force of her life in the days ahead. Not to find it was simply unthinkable, for she knew it was crucial to her own future here at the Chateau de Renard.

Chapter Thirteen

Valéry sat in Baron Guillaume's large tapestry-backed chair by the fireplace and began to form her plan of action. Since Baron Paul would be occupied with the grape harvest for the next few weeks, he would not be watching her. This was good because she would have the freedom to organize her time and work the way she wanted to without having to answer to him. She would begin by seeking out Monsieur Arsène Faguet to see how he was progressing on setting up the *imprimerie.* Obviously, no books could be printed until the printer's atelier was ready. Finding out his exact timetable would give her an idea of how much time she really had to locate the specific book the baron requested. Next, after reading the list the baron had given her of her responsibilities as librarian, she knew he expected her to have an overall plan for the inventory and organization of his library collection. When the press became fully operational, if he wished to have Monsieur Faguet print a certain work by Aristotle, for instance, he would need to be able to find it without searching through everything in the room. The actual sorting and cataloguing would require time, and in this matter she had no illusions that the baron would be lenient with her. He might, however, respect a well-thought-out scheme for the accomplishment of his wishes, and when he did have the time to look into what she had been working on, she wanted to be able to point to something substantial.

Since it was early in the day, Valéry decided first to make arrangements with Lisette to have all her meals brought to her room, thus saving the time which would ordinarily be spent eating in the dining hall. To further extend the hours she could spend working, she would request an extra supply of candles, so that when darkness fell, she would not have to wait until the next day to continue her labors.

She found Lisette down in the kitchens, helping to prepare the main meal of the day. Two scullery maids were there also, along with a man who must have been the head cook. All four of them were listening to Marthe Thibault give instructions. She stopped as soon as Valéry entered the room, staring at her for a moment, and then asking, "Mademoiselle, these are the kitchens. What business could you possibly have here?"

Ignoring her blunt greeting, Valéry replied, "I wish to request that Lisette bring all my meals to my chamber, Madame Thibault. Baron de Renard has asked that I begin my work as librarian by locating a particular volume just as soon as possible. I will be needing to spend as much time as I can on this endeavor."

"You are here but one short day, and already you are making personal demands which require extra work for the staff." The housekeeper made a disparaging sound but turned to Lisette, saying, *"Fille,* you will do as this woman requests until further notice."

Valéry caught Lisette's eye and winked. She suspected that the little domestic, although intimidated by the formidable housekeeper, would welcome the chance to see Valéry each day. They would be able to get better acquainted, and Valéry could speak more about the possibility of school lessons for her.

"I have another request, Madame Thibault." The housekeeper looked horrified, but Valéry didn't much care. "I will need a supply of candles, or perhaps a lamp, so that I may continue my library work into the evenings."

The housekeeper pounced on that one immediately. With a tone of authority, at which she obviously was quite good, she pointed her finger close to Valéry's face. "You will do nothing of the sort. The baron has forbidden both candles and lamps in the library. In fact, he will not even permit the use of the fireplace. You are stupid, mademoiselle, to think that you could bring flame into a room whose entire treasure could be destroyed if it caught fire."

Valéry had to admit that her point was a good one, although how she got it across was deplorable. No doubt she ran the chateau efficiently, and that was all that mattered to the baron, who had many more important responsibilities than overseeing the mundane affairs of housekeeping. She probably kept Monsieur Thibault in line also. He would obey his strong-willed and controlling wife just to keep the peace. Poor man, she thought. It must not be a very happy life for him.

Exiting the kitchens, Valéry went in search of Lucien Maguis, finding him cleaning out the stables.

"I am afraid my entourage, with all their horses and mules, created much more work than usual for you, Lucien."

The youth looked up at her and smiled. He was probably about fourteen or fifteen years of age, and his resemblance to his sister was marked.

"Mademoiselle Lefèvre, Lisette has told me of your arrival." Wiping a hand on his leggings, he extended it to Valéry. "It was extra work, yes, but I enjoyed it, for I love animals, especially horses."

"Speaking of horses, do you know where mine is?"

"Yes, Mademoiselle Lefèvre. The baron has just spoken to me about your horse, and he says it is all right to stable him and put him to pasture with his own horses. It will be a pleasure to tend him equally with the others."

"*Merci,* Lucien, and please call me Mademoiselle Valéry. I will be wishing to ride him from time to time. Where exactly is this pasture?"

"It lies behind these stables," replied Lucien, pointing towards the back wall of the room. "You will see it when you leave here. Oh, and the tack room is through that archway over there, right next to this room. If you let me know in advance, I will be glad to catch your horse and saddle him when you want to ride."

"Then I will surely ask for your help. Thank you, Lucien. And now I must find the *imprimerie.* Do you know where that is?"

Lucien looked puzzled. "*L'imprimerie?*"

"Yes, the printing shop that the baron hired Monsieur Arsène Faguet and his assistant Bruno to set up in one of the outbuildings."

"I have not yet met Monsieur Faguet as he arrived only a short time ago, but I imagine you will find him in the old winery building, which is just down the road from these stables as you head towards the chateau. A week ago, before the grape harvesting began, the baron asked Papa to pick out several of the best wine presses since none of them are being used anymore, so that this Monsieur Faguet could begin working to convert at least one into a printing press. I am not sure just what a printing press is, but Papa says that the baron is quite excited about having this done."

"I myself have never seen a printing press, either, Lucien, but I have heard of Monsieur Gutenberg's invention, and I have marveled at what it is able to do. Furthermore, my uncle, who was a tutor to King Francois's own children, used a few printed texts in his teaching, and most of the books he wrote or recovered during the course of his lifetime were published by this method."

Lucien's eyes grew quite wide as Valéry talked. "Do you think that I might be able to see one of these printed books, Mademoiselle Valéry? Of course, I cannot read them, but just to see what such an invention could do would be very exciting."

"I promise that you will see a book which has been printed, Lucien. And since you are so interested, I would like to speak to your father as soon as possible about teaching you to read, if you should so wish. Then you would be able to enjoy what you are looking at."

"I could learn to read, mademoiselle?" Lucien looked as incredulous as had his sister at this news.

"Of course you could learn, Lucien—that is, if you want to."

"I am not sure I could get enough time off from my duties for such a thing, but perhaps if you talked to my father, he would allow it. He knows how to read and once told me he hoped the new priest might start a parish school like he had attended when he was young."

Valéry left the youth sweeping out the stables with much more energy than when she found him. How she would find time herself to offer reading lessons to Lisette and Lucien, she did not yet know, but she was certain of one thing: If she remained in the employ of the baron, she would find a way. Her dream of starting classes for the girls in the village of Nérac would not be all in vain. She would just transfer her plans to the village of Eauze, extend the gender qualifications, and her first pupils would be Lisette and Lucien Maguis.

Going directly to the building adjacent to the stables, she found the high wooden doors wide open. Stepping inside, a strong smell of wine permeated the room, probably coming from the long row of oak barrels stacked on top of each other against the far wall. Out of the dark corner to her left came the sound of a grunt, followed by a thud. Valéry turned to see the burly figure of a man bent over the staves of a large barrel tub surrounding a wine press, pulling apart the planks one by one and throwing them roughly onto the hardened dirt floor.

"*Excusez-moi*, monsieur. *Je cherche* Monsieur Arsène Faguet."

The man went right on with his work, appearing not to have heard her. Valéry moved closer to him, noticing his massive shoulders and muscled arms. Beads of perspiration ran down the laborer's forehead. Valéry tried again. "Pardon me, monsieur. I am the new librarian at Chateau de Renard, hired by Baron Paul de Renard. It is necessary that I find Monsieur Faguet before I can begin my work. Do you know where I might find him?"

At this, the man stopped his work and slowly raised his head to look at her. His black hair was disheveled, and the black eyes which now regarded her held no sign of respect. Opening his mouth, the sounds which came out were not intelligible, but with one arm, he gestured toward a flight of stairs rising from a far corner of the room.

Deciding that she would not return his rudeness, she thanked him and began the ascent up the narrow wooden steps. At the top, she came upon a smaller room which, unlike the one below, was flooded with sunshine from the numerous windows all around. At first glance, the space appeared empty except for one long table with drawers underneath it. Scattered across the top were various-sized vials and bottles such as one would see in an apothecary.

"Monsieur Faguet" Valéry called out, hoping that he was somewhere within earshot. With this, a bald head, round as a full moon, popped up from behind the table, followed by a torso equally as rotund. Wiping his hands on his *blouson*, which left black smears on an already splotched garment, he came out from behind the table to greet her.

"You are, of course, Mademoiselle Lefèvre. The baron has told me of your arrival and the duties that will be yours as librarian here." He grasped her hand and shook it vigorously, giving her a rather lopsided smile. His light blue eyes, exactly on her level since he was no taller than she, seemed to hold a genuine greeting, and for that, she was grateful.

"I apologize for my soiled hands and smock, mademoiselle," continued the *imprimeur*, "but I am in the process of trying to find just the right mixture of ink we will use for printing. If it is too thick, it will leave blobs on the paper. If it is too thin, it will run right off. If there is not just the right admixture of ingredients, it will not dry properly, nor will it be permanent. I do have several formulas which I obtained from the printing house in Lyons where I used to work, but never before did I have to mix my own ink." Shrugging his shoulders, which seemed to require that he gesture with his hands also, he gave her another asymmetric grin. Valéry was finding him quite endearing, and certainly a welcome contrast to his assistant in the room below.

"You are undertaking a formidable job, Monsieur Faguet. My own has its challenges, but yours will be far greater, and I certainly wish you every success. You seem to have a strong assistant who can handle the heavier work of dismantling the wine press. Can he also help with the construction of what is needed to transform it from a grape crusher to a book printer?"

"You have met Bruno, then?"

"If you are referring to the giant of a man downstairs who grunts but does not speak, then yes, I have met him, if you can call it that. He seems gruff and certainly quite unfriendly."

"Perhaps that is because he has lost part of his tongue and cannot speak anymore, Mademoiselle Lefèvre. I first met him in Lyon, soon after I arrived there. He was working as a press operator in the same printing establishment as I. When Baron de Renard offered me this position, I asked Bruno if he would be willing to come here with me. He has the strength to tear down the old grape press to the actual screw itself as well as the skill to reconstruct it into a printing press. He agreed immediately, especially when he heard that there would be a place for him to live right on the premises. I know only a little about his background. The master printer we both worked for said that Bruno had been involved in the placard affair in Paris and that he was caught and punished by having his tongue cut out. He was supposed to be imprisoned but managed somehow to escape to Lyon. I surmise that he is very much dedicated to the cause of the so-called Huguenots, but he has had to suffer for acting on his convictions."

"How horrible for that poor man." Valéry found herself much more forgiving of the pressman's gruffness at this new information. "He certainly is working very hard," she commented. "Just how long do you think it will take before you are ready to start printing?"

"Bruno should have the wine press stripped to the giant screw by the end of this afternoon. Next will come the construction of the component parts of the printing press, along with building the trays and drawers to hold the metal letters, paper, and ink. In addition, space must be set up for binding the books, as well as two other screw presses readied, one to keep the unprinted sheets flat and another to hold the books tight after they are bound so they do not warp. We will need to put up lines on which the printed sheets can be hung up to dry and to arrange for a source of water since the sheets of paper to be printed must be wet down first and also the metal type will need washing after use. There are many details, mademoiselle, but I estimate that by the time the *vendange* is over, we also will have our press complete."

Counting the days ahead on her fingers, she asked her next question. "If you are to do a test printing first, when would you need to have the material the baron wishes to be printed?"

"Ah, mademoiselle, I already have in hand the manuscript written by the baron and his father. Now I will expect from you the original textbook, which the baron wishes to show me as he says it is an unusually handsome quarto, which uses a special font cut with accents and small superimposed letters which convey the author's phonetic ideas. Of course, the fonts I have brought with me from Lyons will not be the same as this, but the baron hopes I might be able to utilize something from the original work. As for the timetable on this . . ." the printer tilted his head to one side and thought for a minute. "I would like to be familiar with the printed book before I meet with the baron, which means that if you can bring it to me any time before the next two weeks are up, that would be ideal I am very anxious that we do the job well and that the baron will be pleased."

Valéry's heart sank. She had been hoping for much more leeway, but now it would seem that there would be little time to concentrate on much else other than look for the material in question.

"I think I shall need every bit of those weeks, monsieur. Apparently, no inventory has ever been made of the contents of the library, let alone any organization, so I have no recourse but to hunt through the entire contents of the library. Of course there is always the chance that I will come across the manuscript early."

The printer gave Valéry a curious look. "There is no master listing of the contents of such a valuable collection? That is hard to believe. My dear mademoiselle, you do indeed have a formidable task in front of you! I wish you *bonne chance* in the weeks ahead."

Chapter Fourteen

For the next half-dozen days, Valéry rose with the first light of morning and worked until the last rays of the sun disappeared below the winter horizon. She began first with the contents of the cupboards in her own room, thinking that the old baron might have kept the textbook he and his son had worked on in his room and not in the larger library. It helped to know that the book was bound, titled, and printed in quarto, for it enabled her to discard rather quickly all the handwritten materials as well as the books that had been printed in folio or in octavo. She had taken from her uncle's valise some paper and a stylus, and although it slowed her down in her search, she listed the materials she went through as a start on the inventory. Sometimes it was hard not to pause when she came across a particularly beautiful piece of work. One such was a 1486 edition of *Cent Nouvelles Nouvelles,* copiously illustrated, and with a frontispiece showing Louis XI and the Duke of Burgundy together with their courtiers. This would have provided hours of delightful reading for an aged baron, Valéry thought, making a note that she too would like to read it. By the same publisher was a 1492 edition of *Art de bien vivre et de bien mourir* with lovely woodcuts to illustrate the author's idea of the art of living and dying well. Valéry hoped that in reading it, Baron Guillaume had the satisfaction of knowing his life was exemplary and the hope that his passing would be equally as commendable.

However, the work in question was not to be found in the old baron's cupboards, so Valéry moved her base of operation into the library. First she cleared the ledges which separated the bookshelves above from the cupboards below, placing the often heavy volumes on to the library table in the center of the room and carefully recording the titles on her inventory sheet. When the table could hold no more, she began to lift the materials off the shelving and, after making note of them, stacked them according to their subjects on the floor against the walls. Again and again, she marveled at the sheer variety the library collection contained. So far, more than half of the materials seemed to be religious in nature and included magnificently illuminated books of hours, Bibles, various breviaries, missals, Psalters, and the Church Fathers. Another category was that of law, both civil and canon, and yet another the *belles lettres*, which included not only works by the ancients such as Ovid, Cicero, Virgil, and Homer but also of contemporary poetry and literature. For future acquisitions, which the present baron would surely want to make, she would recommend the writings of Queen Marguerite, Rabelais, and even Clément Marot although just thinking of the latter man made her shudder. Additional piles for the arts and sciences began filling up a great deal of the floor space, for there were sizeable volumes on astronomy, mathematics, and medicine, and Valéry felt sure there would be many more subjects to add under this category. As she continued to uncover more and more new material, including maps and geographies along with histories and various school texts of grammar and rhetoric, Valéry feared she would run out of places to pile them and knew that soon she would need to begin labeling the various shelves and placing the sorted materials on them accordingly. But this would have to wait until she found the elusive *Isagoge* text.

At the end of each day, when the fading light made it impossible to continue work in the library, Valéry would carry load after load of material into her room, continuing to search for the baron's book. Here Madame Thibault could not see her work by the light of candles and the blazing logs in her fireplace. Of course, in the morning, she would have to carry all the books back. Before long, her back and arms ached and she began to feel both exhausted and discouraged, for in spite of all her effort, it seemed she was no closer to locating what she needed to find. On the evening of the sixth day, as she sat by the fire, sipping a steaming cup of willow tisane, the thought came to her that there must be a way she could make the search easier on her physically.

A tap on the door announced the arrival of Lisette with her dinner.

"Mademoiselle, you are looking very sad. Have you had no luck yet? I wish I could help, but Madame Thibault would never tolerate that."

Valéry gave her a hug. "You are a lovely help to me just in what you do already, Lisette. Please do not concern yourself on my behalf. I am a bit disappointed that the book for which I am looking has not turned up yet, but there is still time. From my window at night, I can see light burning in the *imprimerie*, so I am guessing that Monsieur Faguet and Bruno also are working late into the evenings, trying to set up the printing press atelier, and this means that I still have time for my search."

"Papa tells me that the harvest may be more drawn out this year as the crop of grapes is quite plentiful. Maybe that will be a good thing for you too, Mademoiselle Valéry. If the baron is overseeing the harvest, he will not be thinking too much about anything else."

"What a happy observation, Lisette. You always seem to brighten my day in some way. However, following the harvest, I am afraid that he still will expect me to have found the book and his printer to be ready to print up the new text."

"Perhaps so, but after the harvest and the grapes are sold, my father and the baron will concentrate next on the distillery they have built in one of the smaller outbuildings. You see, some years ago, when the old Baron Guillaume became too feeble to manage the estate anymore, his son decided not to continue making wine. My father thinks that this was because Baron Paul always seems to like new challenges. He began selling the grapes from his vineyards to other wine producers and then using the past vintages from this estate to distill a very fine brandy called Armagnac."

"I have seen barrels along the back wall of the print shop, which I gather used to be the winery. Do they contain the remaining wine from the estate, or are they aging the Armagnac?"

"Those barrels are the remaining wine vintages from the estate, Mademoiselle Valéry. Papa says they will have to move them soon into the outbuilding, which contains the distillery plus the barrels aging the Armagnac. My father would be so happy to show you how it all operates when the harvesting is over and the work at the distillery begins. You should see the baron and my papa working together there. They are almost like two children playing with their favorite toy!"

Valéry could not imagine the baron enjoying anything with the enthusiasm and abandon of a child, but she did make a mental note to avail herself of a tour of the distillery when the opportunity presented itself. She harbored no illusions, however, that the work in the distillery would distract the baron from his expectations either of her or his journeyman printer. She was beginning to realize that he was indeed a man who liked the risks of new enterprises and had the energy to keep them all spinning like so many plates on top of the sticks of street entertainers.

Turning her attention to the agenda she had set for herself, Valéry asked Lisette if Lucien was helping with the harvest.

"He would like to, but my father wants him to take care of many of the grounds keeping chores which must be done but Papa cannot do during this busy season."

"In that case, I would like to ask a favor of you and Lucien."

"Anything, Mademoiselle Valéry. You are so good to me, and Lucien says you are the most beautiful woman he has ever seen." Lisette blushed, looking a little embarrassed by this revelation.

Valéry laughed. "Then I am flattered at such extravagant praise, and you do not have to tell your brother that you shared his appraisal with me. What I need you to do, Lisette, is to let Lucien know that I would like to have my horse ready for riding early tomorrow morning as I think a little fresh air in this delightfully vibrant season will do me good Do you think this would be convenient for him?"

"Early tomorrow will be an especially good time, Mademoiselle Valéry, as Lucien will be able to get your horse ready before he and I leave for the day." When Valéry looked puzzled, the girl continued. "You see, it is Thursday, and the baron insists that the Thibaults and myself, as well as all the others who work in the chateau, take that day off of their duties to do what they would like. He has included my brother, too, so that we can be together."

"How thoughtful of the baron," Valéry replied.

"Yes, he is a kind man, always thinking of ways to benefit those who depend upon him for their daily bread. He lets Monsieur and Madame Thibault go all the way to the city of Condom to visit relatives, and he tells Lucien and myself that we are still children and must have fun together, especially now that our mother is gone." Lisette paused for a minute as though pulled toward memories of the past, but then she brightened. "Mademoiselle, if you come to the stables right after *petit dejeuner,* you will be able to meet Papa. He will be working with Lucien to make sure that all the duties are completed before he goes back to the vineyards and we leave for the day."

"I will look forward to that, Lisette. Perhaps then I can ask him about your reading lessons!"

Morning dawned crisp and sunny. Valéry hurried toward the stables, anxious to begin on her plans for the day. She had lain awake well into the night, excited by the thoughts which were forming in light of Lisette's revelation that Thursday would be a day off for the formidable and seemingly omnipresent housekeeper and her oppressed husband. With them out of the way, there were several things she would be able to accomplish without their knowledge, and which she deemed absolutely necessary before she could devote any more time to her search.

She found Régis Maguis helping Lucien pitch bundles of hay into the *grenier* above the horses' stalls.

"You are wise to store feed for the winter months, Monsieur Maguis." When the man turned, she smiled and held out her hand. "I am Valéry Lefèvre d'Etaples, Monsieur Maguis. You have delightful children, and I am so happy to finally meet their father."

Régis extended his hand in return. It was rough from all the labors which were his responsibility, but his grasp was firm as he leaned forward in greeting. "Mademoiselle Lefévre, my son and daughter talk much about you. I understand that you have offered them classes so that they might learn to read, *n'est-ce-pas*?"

"Lisette and Lucien are eager to learn, monsieur, and assure me that you might wish for them that skill, which you have acquired yourself. I hope that is so. I have already spoken to the baron about this matter, and he has given his permission. Now I will need yours if we are to commence."

The *régisseur* did not smile, and his eyes held a brooding look to them as though he was preoccupied with weightier concerns, but he nodded at her. "*Mes poulets* wish to peck at seeds outside the farmyard, I see. I was in hopes that the new priest would start some sort of parish school. We have been without a priest here since the old one died, but now that we have Monsieur *l'abbé* Pénicaut, I would prefer to wait on classes to see if he will offer some. Lisette and Lucien have their duties to perform, and they cannot be let off for too much time just to learn to read."

Valéry had a hard time keeping from arguing with him. She would succeed with her plan by remaining pleasantly persuasive. "I will talk to Father Pénicaut today, Monsieur Maguis, to see what his plans are. Would you be agreeable if the priest and I divided the time in classes so that your children could learn both their catechism and to read in the same hour?"

Régis glanced at his son, who implored him to consider the proposal.

"I would give my permission to that, Mademoiselle Lefèvre."

Outside the stables, Valéry mounted her saddled horse, held by Lucien, feeling that she had begun the day and its agenda on an encouraging note. After riding through the chateau gate, the church of St. Luperc was just to her right, by the side of the road leading into the village. A young man in a black soutane stood in the doorway, looking at her.

"*Etes-vous le Père Pénicaut?*" Valéry called to him.

The young priest smiled as he came down the church steps toward her horse. "*A votre service*, mademoiselle. Here, let me help you down from your mount. I am so new here, I do not know many people. Are you from the chateau?"

Valéry dismounted with his help and introduced herself. The priest looked impressed. "You are young indeed to be a librarian. I have heard that Baron de Renard has an impressive collection in his *bibliothèque.* You must share his love of books, mademoiselle, and have good credentials for the work which lies before you."

"I was educated through the generosity of Queen Marguerite of Navarre, *mon père.* Later, when my Uncle Jacques Lefèvre d'Etaples, a scholar and priest, became for a time the librarian at Blois for King François, he tutored me there along with the royal children."

The young priest looked dumbfounded. "We are fortunate to have you in the village, mademoiselle. I think you might teach us all something!"

"I would like to share some of my learning in a way which would be of benefit to the children of your parish, *mon père.* Do you have plans to begin a parish school? If so, I would count it a privilege to help teach in it, especially the skill of reading and perhaps even writing, for those who are interested."

The priest smiled. "My plan is to begin very soon some catechism classes for an hour on an afternoon of the week when it suits the villagers. I am thinking now that winter is approaching, there is less work to be done in the fields, and the children will have a bit more leisure from their usual duties. I, of course, have my own catechism materials, but for you, perhaps with your access to the library, there will be a simple grammar you could use as a teaching tool. If you could find one, I would be happy to have you supplement the catechism learning with other lessons."

Valéry's heart began to beat a bit more rapidly. This was almost too good to be true. What a contrast this young priest was to the elderly one in Nérac. "I will look through the materials I have inherited from my uncle for anything he might have used with the king's children. Also, did you know that the baron has hired a Monsieur Faguet to set up a printing press in one of the chateau outbuildings? Perhaps there would be a possibility of supplying the students with printed lessons from the baron's press."

Valéry amazed herself at the liberty she was taking with the baron's possible generosity, but she didn't care. It was a good idea, and one which she decided she'd pursue with the baron at a later date.

When the priest expressed enthusiasm at this idea, Valéry continued. "Thursday is the day the baron gives off to those who work at the chateau. These include two young people who are eager to begin both catechism and reading lessons. They are Lisette and Lucien Maguis, whose father, Régis, is the *régisseur* for the estate. Would it be possible to begin classes next Thursday, starting with them?"

"Consider it settled, mademoiselle. I shall set up a room in the church, perhaps the sacristy since it has a fireplace and can be kept warm during the winter. If you will bring Lisette and Lucien, I will see what I can do to gather up other children in Eauze."

As Valéry remounted her horse, the priest added, "*A jeudi prochain, vers deux heures l'après-midi*, Mademoiselle Lefévre, *et merci!*"

Two successes so far, and it is still early morning, Valéry thought as she rode towards the village. *That is a good omen for my other business, which I hope will go as well!* It was slightly troubling to her that the new classes would take time from her pressing search for the right manuscript, but perhaps by then she would have found it, and besides, the thought that these classes were about to begin boosted her morale and reenergized her motivation.

The village of Eauze lay several kilometers down the road from the church. Valéry made note of its narrow side streets bordered by cottages, many of which must be inhabited by those who worked in some way for the baron, either in the fields, which grew grain or grazed livestock, or in the vineyards. Although the town was of modest population, it appeared to be prosperous, for on each side of the main road there were shops which testified to an array of services. Boards that hung over entrances boasted various trades: butcher, rope maker, barber, carpenter, saddler, mercer, baker, cooper, and even seamstress. Valéry was impressed with the sheer number of trades operating in the town. There must be many smaller hamlets in the vicinity which utilized the skills offered by this one. A sign toward the edge of the village caught her eye. Hanging from a wrought-iron frame hung a board which bore a large gilded key in the middle surrounded by the various hardware of a blacksmith's shop. *This is exactly what I was looking for,* Valéry thought to herself—*a place where locks and keys could be made as well as a forge.* Stopping here, Valéry entered the large open door of the atelier. Sounds of metal striking metal came from deep within, but Valéry could not locate the source. All around her were piles of ironwork, some twisted into fancy gates and railings, others shaped into horseshoes, sickles, plowshares, and a seemingly infinite variety of other farm implements. Propped up against the walls and placed on rough shelving were various saws and hammers, pokers, tongs, and fire backs, plus keys and locks of all descriptions. Clear in the back stood a huge furnace, its fire door open, making quite a roar as it burned. Then to one side, Valéry saw the blacksmith, bending over an anvil on which he was pummeling a piece of red-hot metal. As she moved toward him, he looked up, beads of perspiration rolling down the sides of his face.

"I will help you in just a minute, mademoiselle. I must work with this metal while it is hot, or I cannot fashion it like I need to."

"Please, monsieur. I am in no hurry and will gladly wait." Valéry found a seat on a rough wooden bench near the blacksmith and watched in fascination. Soon the long piece of metal was entirely flat but still hot. The blacksmith took a pair of tongs and curled the metal around until it formed a circle, not quite closed. Satisfied, he dipped it into a tub of water and then placed the sizzling metal on the anvil again before he turned towards her.

"I am making truss hoops which our village cooper will use to band his barrels, mademoiselle. He does a lively business with the winemakers this time of year and also with Baron de Renard, who likes the Limousin oak for his *tonneaux* in which to age his Armagnac."

Valéry introduced herself, and the blacksmith did likewise, saying he was André Guyot, and that the Guyot family had been both blacksmiths and locksmiths for the chateau and village for many generations.

"Then you must have had an ancestor who made the lock for the chateau's library door, Monsieur Guyot. I understand it was necessary to protect the precious collection of manuscripts during the hundred years when we were fighting the English."

"Ah, yes, Mademoiselle Lefèvre. My grandfather it was who fashioned that lock for Baron Paul de Renard's grandfather, Baron Jean de Renard."

"It is a handsome lock indeed, Monsieur Guyot, but perhaps you did not know that when the aging Baron Guillaume had the library partitioned off to make an adjacent chamber for himself, the door with the lock became the entrance to his bedroom, and new library doors had to be installed which do not have a lock. Perhaps the present baron will wish to have a lock installed in the library doors, but in the meantime, as librarian, I have been given Baron Guillaume's room, and I am afraid that I do not have the key for the lock on my own door. Is it possible that you might be able to install a new lock, with a new set of keys?"

Valéry hoped she looked quite innocent of any questionable scheme, but just in case, she added, "The baron has given me permission to change the room in any way which would make it more suitable for me, and I will feel more secure if I am able to lock my room when I am not in it. After all, there are some who work in the chateau who should not have access to my private chamber."

Much to her relief, the blacksmith nodded his head, saying that he understood completely, and since he was not pressed for the completion of any other job at the moment, he would be glad to return to the chateau with her right away to do the work.

Valéry could hardly contain herself at this piece of good news. Not only would she have a new lock and set of keys for her room, but the work could be done while the housekeeper and other staff were not present.

"I most gratefully accept your offer, Monsieur Guyot, but before we leave, I wonder if you could tell me where I might purchase a supply of candles for my room. I do not like to ask Madame Thibault for anything as she can be so difficult."

The blacksmith tilted his head back and rolled his eyes. "That woman is a terror, Mademoiselle Lefèvre. I do not blame you for not wanting to approach her with any request, even for candles! Here, my wife makes candles for the village, and so you may help yourself to my supply." When Valéry protested, the blacksmith paid no attention but rolled up a big pile of tapers in a bit of sacking and tucked them under his arm.

As they prepared to leave, Valéry selected a small saw from the ones the blacksmith had for sale and also a simple iron bar for the inside of her door. No doubt Lisette had forgotten about her request for the latter, so it made sense to purchase the bar now and not have to ask Lisette again.

After the blacksmith had selected a lock and set of keys from his shelf, Valéry reached into the pocket of her skirt and withdrew a small pile of gold coins, holding them out to the blacksmith.

"Perhaps this will cover the initial cost, and I will pay anything else which is owed after you have completed your work." She smiled up at the blacksmith, who was looking at the gold pieces in disbelief.

"Is there something wrong, Monsieur Guyot? I can assure you they are good tender. You work with metals. Here, please examine them."

The blacksmith grasped the coins between his thumb and forefinger, holding them up before very wide eyes.

"I have never before seen coins of such great value, mademoiselle, and I can see they are quite real. I am always paid in *sols* and *deniers*, which are much more common than these gold *écus*. With these, you could buy a dozen locks and as many keys as you would like!"

Valéry laughed and assured him it was a fair price for his supplies and labor.

It took only a short time to ride back to the chateau. All the while, Valéry could not believe how well her day had been going. She was to start classes the next week, and the lock on her room would be changed without the knowledge of the insufferable Madame Thibault. In addition, she had purchased a bar to secure her chamber when she was in it, a supply of candles for her night work, and a saw which she hoped to use in a way that would relieve the hard physical labor of carrying materials back and forth between the library and her bedroom.

Once in the chateau, Valéry and Monsieur Guyot entered the south keep without a soul seeing them. The servants of course had the afternoon free, and the baron and Régis were overseeing the grape harvest. Thomas and Marthe Thibault would not be back until evening. Things could not have been more perfect for the task to be accomplished without being observed. Valéry did not feel any guilt, for after all, the baron had told her to do what she needed to do to make the room more to her liking. To feel secure in it was definitely to her liking. If Marthe Thibault tried to use her own key on the door, she would get a big surprise, perhaps thinking the lock was broken. Valéry smiled at the thought.

It took Monsieur Guyot about an hour to remove the old lock and to install the new one. After he had finished, he gave Valéry two keys, thanking her again for the gold *écus*, which no doubt would carry him and his wife handsomely through the month. The generous allowance Marguerite had given her before they left the chateau at Nérac was serving her needs very well. She said a silent prayer for the queen as she placed the keys in the jewelry casket atop the fireplace mantel.

The iron bar fit perfectly into the slots on each side of her door. She kept it in place as she proceeded to the next task she wished to accomplish before anyone returned to the chateau. Bending to open the cupboard doors which shared a common wall with the cupboards in the library, she removed the materials which lay on its shelves and was relieved to find the wall in back was of wood. There were no manuscripts on the library side of the cupboards as she had removed them the day before in preparation for the task now at hand. Taking the saw, she tipped it up at an angle and tried to begin sawing through the back wall. When that didn't work, she went over to the armoire where she kept her mother's knife. Holding it in her hand, she took a moment to appreciate its gilded iron blade and the ebony handle carved with arrows which pierced tiny hearts. How well she remembered her mother using it to peel the fruit she loved to preserve for wintertime eating, and which so much later she herself had used for the same purpose when she lived in Nérac. It was somewhat smaller than an eating knife but much sharper and with a good point, which Valéry hoped would not be damaged when she tried to begin a hole in the wood big enough for the tip of the saw to fit through. Grabbing the handle, she sat down on the floor and stuck the point into the wood at the back of the cupboard. Fortunately, it was soft enough for Valéry to cut out a chunk into which she could then insert the saw. After some effort, she was able to saw around the entire square of the backing and to remove it entirely. Bending down, she looked through the hole into the library and felt sure that manuscripts could pass through from one room to the other with no problem. Then she replaced the piece of wood she had just cut out, thinking that if anyone were to look into either cupboard, they would not be able to detect anything amiss if she piled both sides high enough with books to hide the cut edges of the back. For now, however, she would be able to place a stack of manuscripts from the library through the hole to her room for her night work and then shove them back into the library for the day. There would be no more aching arms and back, and her work would be greatly facilitated.

Since it was not yet late in the afternoon, Valéry decided to take a walk around the grounds. Going through the kitchens, she found a service entrance leading into a work shed whose door, barely hanging onto its hinges, opened to the orchards. Rows of apple and pear trees were laden with fruit ready to be harvested. Adjacent to them stood nut trees, their produce already beginning to cover the ground below. Selecting a basket from the work shed, she climbed one of the ladders propped up against an apple tree and picked until the basket was half full. Then she moved on to a pear tree, selecting the plumpest yellow fruit until the basket could hold no more. Setting her heavy load down, she reentered the shed, taking one of the hemp bags hanging on a peg in which to gather the nuts. It did not take long before the sack bulged with its load, and Valéry, realizing she was hungry, found a hammer in the shed to crack and eat some on the spot, interspersing the tasty morsels with bites from an overripe pear. The juice ran down her chin and covered her fingers, and Valéry savored every delicious moment. Then, wiping her hands on the cloth of the sack, she emptied the fruit into it, right on top the rest of the nuts, and replaced the basket on a hook next to a row of blousons and culottes, which no doubt were worn by servants when they worked in the chateau gardens.

Shouldering the bag, Valéry made her way into the kitchens proper, taking from one of the tables a loaf of bread and some cheese, which she would use for her dinner since none of the servants was there to prepare a meal that day. As she stuffed the food into the sack, which by now was growing very heavy, it occurred to Valéry that there must be a shortcut the kitchen staff could use to reach the dining hall, which lay clear at the other end of the chateau. She remembered the back hallway at the chateau in Nérac which enabled servants to go directly from one end of the chateau to the other without having to go through the large reception rooms of the castle. Sure enough, after a little exploration, she came upon a long passageway, and within a few minutes, she saw the dining hall just ahead and, to her left, a narrow staircase leading to the upper floors of the chateau.

Valéry began to climb the steps until she reached the second level door and, pushing it open, was overjoyed to see she had entered the south keep just opposite the library. Once inside her room, Valéry washed her knife and began to peel the apples and pears, laying out the pieces carefully on a serviette she had spread on her window ledge. The sun would soon dry them, and they could be stored in the empty jars on her shelving. She enjoyed a meal of bread and cheese, apples and nuts, and then made herself a tisane from some dried mint leaves in one of the jars. It had been a wonderful day, with much accomplished. Perhaps she would add one more task for good measure since there was still sunlight.

Going to the large valise which stood in the corner of her room, she began to remove the books and manuscripts her uncle had given her. Perhaps in the jumble she might come across some instruction materials she could use in her classes. One by one, she placed the volumes in the empty bookshelves. There was her uncle's *Psalterium Quincuplex* as well as the Bible he had translated into French, along with many volumes recovered from the works of Aristotle and other ancients. She remembered two books: a Latin commentary on the Gospels, which had been published by Simon de Colines when they were living in Meaux, and another from a couple of years after that, which he had called a "sacred hymnology"—his French translation of the psalms. Tucked between its pages was a listing of explanations he had made for the royal children along with a Latin-French book of vocabulary for the Psalter. Many other volumes filled up the empty shelving very nicely. Then, from the very bottom of the valise, she withdrew two small printed works, which at first glance looked like textbooks her uncle might have used in his tutoring of the king's children and herself. The first one was printed by Etienne Dolet in Paris and entitled *Brefve doctrine pour deuement escripre selon la propriete du language francoys*. The second work appeared to be a Latin-French grammar, printed in 1531 by Etienne Dolet in Paris. The author was Jacobus Sylvius. Thinking this might be helpful material for her classes, she opened the cover and froze, barely able to believe her eyes. The title page read *In linguam gallicam Isagoge* by Jacques du Bois. It was the same title for which she had been searching without luck in the baron's library. She had just found a copy in her uncle's collection.

It was impossible to sleep that night. Valéry turned and tossed and finally rose to open her shutters and look out on the fields beyond her window. The moon was full, casting over the landscape a warm amber glow which only a harvest moon could achieve. She had found the book. Soon she would take it to Arsène Faguet and also inform the baron, who would be at the very least nonplused. She decided that neither man needed to know that it was not the library copy she had located. And as for her position as librarian, which she now felt would be assured, she had time to make more progress on her inventory of the library as well as to prepare a curriculum for her classes.

Somewhere an owl's hoot pierced the still night. *I am not the only one awake*, Valéry thought, *but the owl could not possibly be as happy as I am. This day has been a gift from the Almighty. It has made up for the loneliness I felt after I was separated from Marguerite. It has assuaged my feelings of rejection when I arrived here. I have bested the mean housekeeper although she does not know that yet! Soon I will earn the respect of the baron. My future is secure, and all will be well.* With that thought, she climbed back into bed and fell into a peaceful slumber. Her last thought was of Marguerite, who would be so glad to hear how her hopes for her protégée were being realized. She would write to Marguerite soon and tell her the good news.

Chapter Fifteen

Valéry spent Friday and Saturday applying herself to the first lessons she would be giving in the new parish school. Work on the library inventory could wait until next week, she reasoned, since there appeared to be no rush now that the *Isagoge* text had been found. The baron was still occupied with the grape harvest, and Arsène Faguet and Bruno had not yet completed the print shop setup. She would look for an opportunity to tell the baron about finding his book and then take it to the printer so he could have a chance to familiarize himself with its format and contents before he met with his employer.

Laying out a sheet of paper on her little desk, she began to outline her class sessions. Initially, she would have the children begin by deciphering single letters and then move on to reading syllables, then words, and finally a whole passage. By then, she hoped she could put into their hands a modest printed text. For those who showed special promise, the next step would be learning to write. Most probably the process would take at least several years, but in the end, the next generation of villagers in Eauze would have the rudiments of an education, greatly facilitated by the availability of inexpensive printed materials. She wondered if this might be the baron's motivation in rewriting an elementary text and then having it printed up in simple form on his new press. She reflected on the value of the education she had gotten as a child and realized how it had enlarged her understanding of the world and her appreciation of the difference knowledge can make. It was wrong to have such learning available only to the elite. Her uncle had often talked about his vision of putting the best translation of the Holy Scriptures into the hands of the common people. But the common people needed to know how to read first. Gérard Roussel had reminded her of the importance of investing in the lives of others the education she had received so gratuitously. As Valéry put her lesson plans on paper, she renewed her resolve to do just that.

On Sunday morning, Valéry woke to the sound of church bells. She welcomed the chance to go to Mass at St. Luperc, support the new village priest, and meet some of the villagers whose children they both would be teaching. Upon first entering, the sanctuary appeared dark, but as her eyes adjusted, she saw the sun's rays filtering through the chancel's stained glass windows, leaving bright splotches of blues and reds, yellows and greens across the wooden benches and stone floor. The marble altar was beautifully carved with scenes from the life of Jesus, which included the Last Supper in the center. Father Pénicaut nodded to her as she took a seat near the chancel. Only after she sat down did she realize she was directly behind the baron and right next to Thomas and Marthe Thibault. It was too late to move, but it would be hard not to feel uncomfortable in such company. After the Mass ended, she started down the aisle, and spotting the Maguis family in the narthex, waved to them as they smiled at her. A voice came from behind her.

"You have a pretty singing voice, Mademoiselle Lefèvre. I think I shall want to sit near you in future masses."

Valery turned to see Paul de Renard following her down the aisle.

"You flatter me, Monsieur le Baron, but thank you for the compliment, which," she paused here for effect, "I know you give only when it has been earned." When the baron looked amused, she continued. "Queen Marguerite used to tell me the same thing about my voice—although I always thought that it was because her voice, may God forgive my frankness, was always a little off key, and I think she knew it!"

To Valéry's surprise, the baron laughed. At the church door, the priest greeted them both and then, turning to Valéry, remarked that there were several more village youth who would be joining Lisette and Lucien for Thursday catechism and lessons. Valéry was grateful for the chance to meet some of them as well as their parents, expressing her excitement over the opportunity to offer the lessons.

Once inside the chateau gate, the baron took Valéry by the elbow and turned her to walk along the stone wall separating the church from the chateau grounds. "I assume, since you have arranged for classes, that you have completed the first assignment I gave you?"

"Yes, I have found the book and await your permission to give it to Arsène Faguet, who tells me you and he will need to go over it before the new text is printed." The baron stopped in his tracks and looked astonished. "And just where, exactly, did you find it, mademoiselle?"

"It was in my room," Valéry replied truthfully, hoping that the baron would think his father had placed it among the books he kept on his own bookshelf and not ask any more details from her.

The baron commenced walking again. "That is most interesting, mademoiselle, most interesting."

"Why is that so interesting?" Valéry queried and then regretted that she could not curb her curiosity.

"I am afraid my answer to that might be misconstrued, but I will think about telling you why at some future date. As for now, there is something I wish to show you."

He pointed to a thick rectangular slab of limestone lying on the ground close to the wall.

"The stone is about as long as I am tall," Valéry observed, "and it must be very heavy. What is it for?"

The baron bent down and with some effort slid both hands under an edge of the stone. To Valéry's surprise, he was able to lift it up and lay it to one side, revealing a set of steep, narrow steps leading down into a dark underground space.

"Do you like to explore the unknown?" the baron asked her, his expression very serious.

"I have never passed up a challenge, if that is what you mean," Valéry replied, thinking she would not let the baron see that she could be intimidated.

"Good, then gather your skirts and follow me, but take care. These steps are often slippery as this underground passageway remains damp most of the time."

The baron entered first, turning to lend a hand to Valéry as they descended. At the bottom it was still light enough to see a narrow barrel-vaulted tunnel, beautifully constructed of brick, through which there ran a muddy path that disappeared into the dark. The baron reached on top of a corbel attached to one wall and drew down a fat candle, which he lit and held before him. Turning to Valéry, he again took her hand, leading her into the depths of the *souterrain*. Corbels lined the walls at even intervals, each supporting a candle, which the baron left unlit, choosing to use only the single candle he had in his hand. Here and there, Valéry spotted a bat attached to the ceiling, and underfoot there were little brown frogs and slithering lizards, which scurried out of their way before they could be trodden under foot.

"You are not squeamish, Mademoiselle Valéry. That is most unladylike, I think."

"Do you wish me to scream and throw up my hands in horror, monsieur?"

"Somehow it would not suit you," the baron replied. "Your appearance is delicate, but underneath that, you are as tough as any man."

"I am sure there are men who would not like this tunnel, with its low ceiling, narrow walls, and slimy floor. As for what lives in this dank, dark underground, if it is to their liking, let them remain. They do not frighten me."

"What *does* frighten you, Valéry?" The baron turned to look down at her, his steel-gray eyes reflecting the flame from the candle he held, giving them a slightly sinister but curiously warm cast.

"If you blew out the candle you hold, the darkness in here would not scare me," Valéry replied. "What I do fear is that which might extinguish the light that burns within me, for this is what illumines my path and gives my life direction."

"And from where do you think this threat comes, my brave little librarian?"

Valéry's mouth began to tremble, much against her will, for the baron was studying her intently now.

"I think you already know the answer to that, monsieur. Please do not taunt me although you obviously enjoy doing so."

There was silence, but then, as if the muses had decided to bless the moment, the baron raised his hand and gently pushed back a strand of hair that had fallen over her cheek. "I have no wish, Valéry, to extinguish that light. Will you believe that?"

"I may stay in my post, then, Baron de Renard?"

Immediately the baron's expression hardened. "That remains to be seen, mademoiselle."

The magic moment was over as the baron turned abruptly and holding the candle high, led the way down the brick-lined tunnel until it terminated.

"My father had this underground passageway built in order to facilitate him in his old age as he went from the chateau to the church and back when the weather was bad. The doors at both ends have been bricked over since his death, and now the only way in and out of here is the stairway by which we entered. The large stone covering the steps stands halfway between the chateau and the church and was originally used in case there was need to come out of the tunnel before reaching either the chateau or the church. Régis and I have chosen to keep this center part of the passageway open as it seems to serve a purpose. Do you see that opening?" The baron pointed above him to a large round hole in the wall just below the ceiling at the end of the tunnel.

"That," continued the baron, "is the entrance to an underground drainage channel, through which the water empties when it rises high enough down here. The chateau grounds are between two rivers, the Gélise and the Izaute, and the water table here is quite high, especially when we have heavy rains. When this happens, this *souterrain* completely floods, so we installed a large clay-lined pipe through which the water can empty into the large basin which you may have seen on the grounds outside the south keep. Before we had this runoff pipe, the ground-level rooms of the chateau would also flood. The drainage channel protects the chateau from this now. Unfortunately, though, the print shop building still fills with water when the underground passage is inundated. I have warned Monsieur Faguet about this problem, and he assures me that they will put nothing which could be ruined close to the ground in the print shop."

As they retraced their steps back through the *souterrain*, Valéry wondered privately why the baron had shown her this vault. Did he want to further test her mettle to see if he could unnerve her? Instead she remarked that she was glad to get acquainted with places other than the library and her own room. Once aboveground, the baron suggested that she also might like a tour of the north keep, which was the oldest section of the chateau, built some two hundred and fifty years before the rest of the castle. Valéry looked up at the imposing donjon, with its cupola on top. "If you have the time to show me, I would be very happy to make its acquaintance, Baron de Renard."

"My Christian name is Paul, Valéry. You do not need to be so formal when we are alone." Valéry cast him a questioning glance, but he had already walked past her toward the double doors which gave entry into the north keep. Pulling on a rope attached to a small bronze bell, the doors were opened by one of the servants from the kitchens, and the baron ushered Valéry into a small anteroom and then through a wooden door so low that Valéry herself had to bend her head to get through it. On the other side rose an impressive set of stairs curving around a newel post which ascended up the north keep. The baron began to climb, and Valéry followed, thankful for the slit windows every so often on the outside walls letting in enough light so she could see where she was going. These must be the lit windows she noticed when she first arrived, Valéry thought. After several turns, they reached a small platform with another low door. Pausing, the baron told Valéry that this entered into the apartments where he lived, as had his father when he was younger and all the barons before him.

"You are not going to show me this section?"

"No," came the firm answer. "You will be much more interested in what lies above them." Valéry followed him as he continued up the spiral staircase.

"To your right, you will notice a rope which runs the entire height of the donjon," the baron said. "Pull on it, Valéry."

She did so and after several tugs heard the bell in the cupola ring. "We do not use the bell much anymore, but for many decades, it served as a good warning to the village when the English were about to attack," the baron explained.

They continued on until they reached the third landing, and opening another small door like the one below it, the baron motioned for Valéry to step through. On her right, a massive oak door stood open, revealing a truly magnificent room, with furnishings which took her breath away.

"This room has a history of which we are quite proud," the baron explained. "Come in, and I will tell you the story."

Once inside, Valéry noticed that there were several servants cleaning windows, sweeping the floors, and making up the huge four-poster bed.

"Right now, we are readying these chambers for guests, but I will tell you about that after I relate my tale."

Valéry looked around her, noting the claret-colored velour draperies over mullioned windows fronted by window seats of white marble. An enormous fireplace, big enough to walk into, took up most of one wall. A coat of arms she did not recognize hung over the mantle. The fire back sported the same blazon, with huge logs stacked on the hearth, ready to be lit. The counterpane on the bed itself was embroidered with gold-threaded fleurs-de-lis, as was the drapery hung from the four bedposts. Marble-topped commodes and several enormous armoires, all exquisitely carved, made up part of the other furnishings of the room. On one wall hung a portrait of a man with a crown on his head, long wavy hair, and flowing beard. Around his neck was a collar of ermine. The picture was set in an ornate gilded frame.

"That is King Jean II *dit* le Bon," said the baron, following Valéry's gaze, "and this was his room. In early September of the year 1356, the king and his son, who would be the future Charles V, stayed here in preparation for the battle of Nouaille-Maupertuis."

"That was with the English then?"

"It was, and unfortunately for the king, he was defeated and taken captive to England, to be held for ransom until it was paid in 1360."

"Then it was your great-great-grandfather, the Baron Richard de Renard, who made him welcome just days before the fateful battle?"

The baron nodded. "Ever since then, the room has been given over to guests of distinction, as it will be again in a few days. My father's old friend, Viscount Charles de Clairac, who fought with him for King François in the Batttle of Marignano, will be coming for an extended stay, along with his wife, Odile, and her son, Jules Machet. The viscount has an extensive domain around the town of Clairac, which is north of us. He has established large prune orchards on his land, and his estate makes an excellent *pruneau* liqueur. All through the years, the viscount has treated me like a nephew, and I regard him as my uncle, and even though my father is gone now, the viscount remains like a member of the family and still wishes to come for his annual visit. He will be very interested in how we distill our grapes into Armagnac and has timed his visit to us during this particular season so he can enjoy the process."

"I will look forward to the visit," replied Valéry simply.

The baron regarded her for a moment and then said, "When they arrive, I would like you to take your main meal with us in the great hall. Up to now, you have kept quite to yourself. I think it will be good for you to have some other contacts besides that of Lisette."

The baron ushered her out of the king's chambers and down the hall that lay before them.

"This is the central part of the chateau, now that we are out of the north keep. To your right, the rooms you see are for other guests. Jules Machet will stay in the large chamber adjacent to the king's rooms, and then in the central part of this hallway are several smaller rooms for the servants of the de Clairac family. The Viscountess Odile de Clairac has a chambermaid named Sidonie Soulard, I believe, and of course there is the old retainer, who has been in the de Clairac family for many, many years, Philibert Favard."

They reached the tall double doors at the end of the hallway that opened onto the landing of the main staircase. From there, they walked through the doors which took them into the south keep where the library and Valéry's room were located. The baron left her outside her door, saying that he hoped she had enjoyed the little tour. He had again become abrupt and distant, his gray eyes cold as he bid her *bonsoir*. *What an enigmatic man*, Valéry thought. Perhaps he felt he had been a little too familiar with her earlier; or then again, he might have been absorbed in the forthcoming visit of his father's old friend. Regardless of his behavior, though, she looked forward to continuing her work in the library and starting her new classes. Added to this, there would be the arrival of the viscount and his family. Certainly their presence would change the atmosphere of the chateau and bring into her life some new and, she hoped, interesting contacts.

For the next several days, there was great activity as preparations were underway for the arrival of the de Clairac family. Marthe Thibault was in her element, seemingly everywhere at once, directing the preparation of the various rooms to be occupied by the guests and their servants, ordering about the servants who were cleaning every floor of the chateau, and seeing to it that enough food would be on hand to feed the de Clairacs in the manner in which such nobility was certainly accustomed. Lisette was all a dither as she described to Valéry how much work this involved.

"Mademoiselle Valéry, do you know that there are over fifty rooms to be readied? Of course, not all of them will be occupied or even used, but Madame Thibault insists that they be cleaned anyway. My father has had to go from hard work overseeing the *vendange*, which is thankfully finished, to making sure the baron's laborers chop enough wood to keep the fireplaces ablaze, and the grounds—and gamekeepers are prepared to supply the tables in the great hall with enough meat and fish. In addition, he and the baron will be starting to distill the estate wine to make Armagnac. Lucien must have the stables ready for the extra horses. We will come to the catechism class this week for our first lesson in reading, but we must not stay too long."

"I understand, Lisette, and I am sure both Father Pénicaut as well as I do not wish to add any extra burden on you and your brother."

Lisette still looked anxious. Guessing what might be upsetting her, Valéry asked, "Are the viscount and his wife very difficult guests, Lisette?"

"The viscount is a wonderfully kind man, but the Viscountess Odile is very demanding. Last year, she complained about the slowness of the servants when they did not do her bidding as fast as she would have liked, and her poor chambermaid, Sidonie, was always in tears. She is much older than I and quite pretty, and I liked her very much, but I felt sorry that her mistress treated her so badly."

"I understand the viscountess has a son, who must be from a previous marriage as he has a different last name from the Viscount de Clairac. Is he like his mother?"

"Monsieur Machet is too often controlled by his mother, I think. She orders him around and tells him what to do and how to do it, much like she does the servants. He must be about your age, Mademoiselle Valéry, and is quite a handsome young man. My brother teased me about my staring at him, but it is hard not to." The girl paused here and blushed beet red, turning her head so that Valéry would not see her embarrassment.

"I think there is nothing wrong with wanting to look at someone so good-looking, Lisette. Shame on Lucien for teasing you about that. I imagine that he would do the same if there were a pretty young girl around."

Lisette giggled and nodded her head. "He does that all the time now with the girls of the village, and I tease him about that!"

"Good for you, Lisette. We shall see who the others are in the catechism classes! Maybe both of you will spend so much time staring that *Père* Pénicaut and I will have to work hard to keep your attention!"

Lisette giggled again. As she turned to go, Valéry informed her that when the viscount arrived, she would be dining in the great hall instead of in her room. "That should help you a little to have more time for your added duties. Also, Lisette, I can prepare my own fires as long as Lucien will provide the chopped wood."

"You are most thoughtful, Mademoiselle Valéry, and I promise that you will have my undivided attention in classes, even if there are handsome boys my age present."

When Thursday arrived, Valéry gathered her class materials together and walked over to the church. Father Pénicaut was just finishing up his religious instruction and greeted her when she entered the room. Besides Lucien and Lisette, there were six other young people, several quite young, and a couple about the same ages as the Maguis children. The priest introduced her, and Valéry told the class that each one of them could learn to read if they really wanted to, and she showed them some printed books from the library, complete with pictures to illustrate the text. Next, she began to read to them from one of the collections of fables she had found in the library and promised them a little more of the story each week, which she hoped would bring them back.

"When you can read," she told her class, "you will be able to enjoy many more tales such as this one and learn lots of other new things from books that you read for yourselves."

"But where will we get these books, Mademoiselle Lefèvre?" The little girl who asked the question gave her teacher a skeptical look.

"That is a good thing to ask," Valéry replied, "and I want to promise you that the Baron de Renard is setting up a special machine called a press which will be able to print many books that I am sure he will let you use after you have learned to read."

Valéry realized she was volunteering the baron to do something he had in no way told her he planned to do. She, however, was determined to persuade him that it was part of his duty as a good seigneur to share the contents of his valuable collection of books in this way.

"Both *Père* Pénicaut and I will quiz you on what you have learned, and those who study with diligence will be rewarded."

"How will we be rewarded?" asked one of the students.

"I will let that be a surprise," Valéry replied, thinking that the baron's printing press might supply the best students with their own book to keep on a subject in which they had expressed an interest. Even beyond that, perhaps he might be willing to send the most brilliant ones to university in Montpelier or Toulouse or even Paris. She realized her temerity, but nothing of much worth was ever accomplished if one did not think ahead to new possibilities. The students seemed excited, and Valéry certainly was encouraged by their expressions of eagerness to learn.

That evening she sat in her room and thought of her Uncle Jacques and Queen Marguerite and felt for the first time that she might be able to give to others what her mentors had given to her, namely a love of learning and a good education. She was surprised at the tears which came so easily at the remembrance of two of the people she loved the most. As she gathered up the dried apples and pears she'd placed on the windowsill and began putting them in jars, she thought also of her mother. Going over to the mantel, she picked up the jade casket, running her fingers over her name engraved on the lid and then tracing the gold scrollwork next to it. She remembered the little ritual of the necklace which lay inside, and especially the affection with which her mother had tenderly cared for them both. Her life would be made worthwhile only if she could share what she had been given. That chance was now before her, and she resolved to persevere no matter what challenges she had to face. Of course, much depended on the good graces of the baron, who was hard to figure out. He seemed to have ambivalent feelings towards her, and she certainly did not know how to understand his behavior. Still, she felt she had made progress, for after all, she had found a copy of the *Isagoge* book he requested, and he had made no objection to her beginning reading lessons for the village children. Furthermore, she had begun to compile an inventory of the contents of the library and to organize the various materials. Next, if she could persuade him to let Arsène Faguet print some inexpensive tracts she could use with her beginning students, she would be making some headway toward eventually providing them with whole books. Her dreams that night were peppered with scenes of excited children, exclaiming over the little books they were learning to read, hardly able to put them down in their quest to devour the contents.

She was awakened the next morning by the sounds of a great commotion in the courtyard below. Opening the window and pushing back the shutters, she looked down to see the courtyard filled with activity. Servants scurried to unload a half-dozen pack mules of their baggage and then disappear with their bundles through the doors of the north keep. The muleteers of the party, along with the baron's own stable hands, including Lucien, were leading the unloaded mules toward the stables where the animals could be fed and cared for. The baron himself was greeting a tall man with silver hair and a black cape as he dismounted his steed. This must be the Viscount de Clairac, Valéry thought, noting that the distinguished-looking nobleman went immediately to help an elderly man dismount from his horse, then said something to him while pointing toward the north keep. The elderly man looked like he was protesting at first but then nodded and walked a mite unsteadily toward the tower door. Perhaps that was the viscount's aged manservant, Philibert. It spoke well of the viscount that he had such regard for his longtime family retainer. As Régis Maguis led the men's two horses towards the stable yard, the baron and the viscount went over to the litter and gave assistance to a lady as she, followed by a young man, climbed out of the vehicle. That, Valery thought, must be the Viscountess Odile de Clairac and her son, Jules Machet. The lady immediately summoned a young woman, no doubt her serving maid, Sidonie, pointed to the litter, and the maidservant hastened to withdraw several small leather boxes, stacked one on top of the other. The viscountess, whose voice was shrill enough for Valéry to hear, ordered her to take the boxes immediately to her chambers. Then she turned to her son, straightening the cap on his head and the mantle about his shoulders before they began to walk toward the chateau. The viscountess held her head so high Valéry drew back from the window, afraid that the woman might spot her looking down on them. She certainly did not want to do anything to draw the viscountess's attention to herself. She would make the acquaintance of the de Clairac family soon enough, and from what Lisette had told her, Odile de Clairac might not be that pleasant to get to know.

It was not long afterwards that someone rapped loudly on her door, which was then opened before she could do that herself, to reveal Marthe Thibault.

"Mademoiselle Lefèvre, the baron has summoned you to come to the great hall immediately. You are to meet the Viscount and Viscountess de Clairac. Hurry up, will you. It is rude to keep people of such distinction waiting."

"I will be down shortly, Madame Thibault," Valéry replied evenly.

"You will follow me now," the housekeeper replied bluntly.

"I repeat, Madame Thibault, I will be down shortly. There are things I must finish up here first."

"You are an unwelcome person, and now you dare to be impertinent too. Very well, I will tell the baron what you have just said. You had best use the time to change into something more suitable than that drab garment, mademoiselle," the housekeeper retorted, frowning as she looked Valéry up and down. "Highborn people dress for supper, something that their inferiors do not seem to know." With that, the housekeeper left the room, slamming the door behind her.

As Valéry looked in her armoire for an appropriate dress, she resolved to keep her door locked and barred from then on. Marthe Thibault would never again be able to barge into her chamber like she had just done. If anybody had lowborn manners, it was surely Marthe Thibault. Valéry chose a soft-flowing gown of deep blue velvet, and as she dressed, she decided not to let the housekeeper upset her. It was simply not worth the energy.

Following the directions Lisette had given her earlier, Valéry found the great hall without difficulty. The room was indeed magnificent, with beamed ceilings, walls hung with exquisite tapestries, and enormous fireplaces at each end. A long oak table ran the length of one wall, set with fine linen, pewter plates, and candelabra while servants brought in various dishes for the main meal. In front of the near fireplace, the baron stood talking with the viscount. The viscountess and her son held a separate conversation over by the table. As Valery approached the group, the baron motioned to her.

"Viscount Charles de Clairac, permit me to introduce to you my new librarian. This is Valéry Lefèvre d'Etaples, a protégée of our Queen Marguerite de Navarre, and highly recommended to me by her majesty."

The viscount took both her hands in his own and bowed to her, a smile hovering around his mouth.

"I am delighted to make your acquaintance, Mademoiselle Valéry Lefèvre. Your first name is a favorite of mine, as is the great lady of letters and state, our gracious Marguerite d'Angoulême."

"It is an honor and privilege to meet you, my lord, and to find that immediately we have something in common, namely our esteem of my patroness."

"Yours is a formidable task here, I surmise, for Baron Guillaume prized his library more than almost anything else, but unfortunately, he did not spend time bringing it into order. I know you have only just arrived, but soon I would be interested in seeing the transformation you will be bringing about in the b*ibliothèque*."

Valéry replied that she would be most happy to share her progress with him. He was indeed kindly, just as Lisette had said, and also tall and distinguished looking, with silver hair at his temples and a gracious manner about him. Something about his eyes and his smile reminded her of someone, but she could not think who at the moment.

"I wish for you to meet my wife and my stepson," said the viscount, drawing her past the fireplace to the two who stood talking by the table.

"The Viscountess Odile de Clairac and Monsieur Jules Machet," he said by way of introductions. Then, turning to his wife, he continued, "My dear, you will want to make the acquaintance of the baron's new librarian, Mademoiselle Valéry Lefèvre d'Etaples." With that, he left them and returned once again to the baron.

Valéry gave the tall woman a small curtsey. "*Enchantée*, Viscountess de Clairac *et* Monsieur Machet." The woman looked down at Valéry and said nothing. Her son, who was every bit as handsome as Lisette had described him, gave her a smile as he took her hand and bent to kiss it lightly. Straightening up again, he told her that it was indeed a great pleasure to meet such a lovely young woman, one he hoped to get better acquainted with during his stay at Chateau de Renard. Valéry started to reply when the viscountess interrupted.

"You are the person who was spying on us from an upper window when we arrived, *n'est-ce pas*? The baron has hired a librarian with no breeding, I see, as well as no taste in fashion, either. We wore dresses like that last year, but of course they are hopelessly outdated now."

Valéry looked quickly at the folds of her blue velvet skirt and then up at the viscountess. "This was a gift of Queen Marguerite of Navarre, whose dressmaker made it for me just before I came to my position here, Madame de Clairac. She will be most interested to hear that you felt it was outdated." Valéry gave the woman a sweet smile and waited.

The viscountess snorted as she raised her chin another notch. "I imagine with such a tongue as yours, you will not last long in your position here, mademoiselle. I can recognize a liar as well as a lie. *Tu me fais marcher, bibliothécaire.*"

Valéry tried to look calm in spite of the woman's sheer gall. Using the "*tu*" form was meant to be an insult. Accusing her of lying was blatantly rude. What a pair Marthe Thibault and the viscountess would make, she thought to herself, secretly amused at the prospect of any interaction between the two difficult women.

Jules Machet stepped towards her and, placing a hand on her back, turned her towards the table as the baron called out, *"A table, tout le monde."* The baron seemed in high spirits as he took his place at the head of the table, with the viscount to his left and the viscountess in the place of honor on his right. Jules sat next to his mother and Valéry across from him, next to the viscount. The servants set before them a dizzying number of resplendent dishes, and the wine was poured liberally. Soon Odile de Clairac, who was drinking way too much, began to talk loudly, dominating the conversation. Her husband looked uncomfortable and the baron embarrassed at the display. Jules, however, had a wry smile on his face, glancing often at Valéry across the table while piling his plate liberally with the abundance of food and motioning for a servant to keep filling his chalice with the fine wine from the baron's cave.

After the meal, the baron invited everybody to stay for a *digestif* while the servants arranged chairs around the nice fire, which was warming the room well. The viscountess, wobbly on her feet, announced that she was fatigued and wished to go to her chambers. The viscount, looking relieved, instructed his stepson to aid his mother in climbing the stairs and getting her settled.

"Sidonie can do that," Jules replied, but the viscount shook his head, replying that Sidonie could use the help of a stronger person, and for Jules to render aid. The young man obeyed but looked quite annoyed at the order. Obviously, he wished to stay and talk with Valéry, who he couldn't keep his eyes off of all during the meal.

Once the two had disappeared, the ambiance of the great hall took on a more congenial tone. The baron motioned for his manservant, Thomas Thibault, to bring a bottle of Armagnac and some glasses and the manservant of the viscount, Philibert Favard, in turn, produced a flacon of *pruneau* d'Agen.

"Mademoiselle, you can see that there is to be a contest here between the baron and myself, as to who produces the better *digestif*," the viscount said with a chuckle.

"Ah, my good man," replied the baron, "there is certainly no contest between the two as it is my Armagnac which is the vastly superior product!"

The two men laughed, and Valéry could not help but sense the affection between them.

"We will let our little librarian make the call, then. Which would you like to try, mademoiselle?"

Valéry smiled at the viscount, replying that she would have a small taste of both and then render her decision.

"We have a diplomat in our midst," observed the viscount, smiling at Valéry as Thomas Thibault poured a small amount of Armagnac into her glass. "Sniff it first," counseled the baron, "and then take a small sip, for you will find it quite strong." Valéry did as she was told and then gave a slight gasp. It burned all the way down her throat and brought tears to her eyes. The two men, who were watching her closely, began to laugh again. "It is not exactly a ladies' drink, as you will not doubt agree!" said the viscount. "But now, try my *pruneau* d'Agen." Valéry found that much more to her suiting and said so, to the great pleasure of the viscount, who announced to the baron that he had won the contest. "You are herewith invited to the Chateau de Clairac where you may tour my plum orchards, observe the distillation of my liqueur, and drink all of it that you may wish, mademoiselle of my favorite name."

"Just where is your chateau located, Viscount de Clairac?" Valéry queried.

"About two days' ride north of here, in the village of Clairac. You may not have heard of it, but perhaps you know of the large abbey located there," the viscount answered.

"Of course," Valery replied, real enthusiasm in her voice. "My Uncle Jacques had a dear friend who was abbot there not long ago. Do you know Gérard Roussel?"

The viscount looked astounded and then, leaning towards her, replied with equal enthusiasm. "Know him? Why, he has been a true friend to me, even to the point of enlisting his monks to help with the orchards and production of the *pruneau*. I am delighted to hear of this connection, mademoiselle. Now I can place your uncle, of whom Gérard talked so often. Jacques Lefèvre d'Etaples was a brilliant scholar, and now his own niece is my adopted nephew's librarian. This is truly a wonderful surprise. I am sure that you share with Abbot Roussel, myself, and the baron your uncle's love of books and the new learning. How fortunate we are to have you here."

At this, Valéry sneaked a look at the baron, but he registered no outward reaction. Nonetheless, Valéry drank in the viscount's words and felt the pain of her earlier encounters with Marthe Thibault and Odile de Clairac melt away with the warmth of the affirmation she was receiving from Charles de Clairac. The rest of the evening was spent talking of the great literature of the past and the hopes of the baron to be able to print up relatively inexpensively some of the valuable manuscripts in the library along with some new literature reflecting scholarship of the present day. The sale of such affordable printings would help to spread the love of learning way beyond a small circle of wealthy elite and go a long way toward transforming an illiterate world into a much better-informed one. In part, that had been the vision of her uncle, and it was certainly the vision of the baron and the viscount. Most assuredly now, it was her vision also.

Valéry went to bed that night, warmed both by the fire in the fireplace and the company of Paul and Charles. She felt privileged to have been included in an after-dinner ritual that usually was reserved for the men, and even more special because of the esteem the viscount held for her uncle and, by virtue of that, for herself. She could take the insults of Marthe and Odile when she had the support of those who really counted. It was as though Marguerite herself was present between the three of them, beaming with pride at her protégée and saying, "Valy, I told you that you were the right person for the task. Now, do you believe me?"

Chapter Sixteen

While the baron and Régis were occupied with marketing the grapes they had just harvested, and Arsène and Bruno completed the necessary work for the *imprimerie* to be operational, Valéry began to place the already-sorted stacks of books back on the lower shelving of the library. As she did so, she double-checked her inventory listing, which now amounted to several closely-written pages. Much more needed to be done, of course, and she looked with some degree of anxiety at all the higher shelves, which were crammed with as-yet-untouched materials. Reaching for the ladder, she was just about to begin to climb it when Jules Machet entered the room.

"You have already made a huge difference in here," he observed, looking around the room with interest. "I remember what it used to look like, you know."

"I appreciate the observation, Monsieur Machet," Valéry replied. "I fear, though, that the most difficult task lies ahead of me and not behind."

"How is that, Mademoiselle Lefèvre?"

"Look up, monsieur," Valéry said, pointing to the overhead bookshelves.

"The greatest number of volumes still await my attention, and I have a feeling that they make up both the oldest as well as the most valuable contents of this library."

"Most of them look to be manuscripts, and very sizeable ones at that," Jules commented, having climbed the ladder to inspect some of the materials. He selected one of the smaller books and handed it down to Valéry. It was bound in boards and tucked in a scarlet and silver slipcase, which Valéry opened to reveal a handsome codex on vellum, which no doubt a scribe had labored over in order to render some moral tracts of Aeneas Sylvius.

Valéry made a note of it on her inventory sheet. "By the end of today, I think I will have replaced enough of the sorted books onto shelves that

I will be ready to begin on these," Valéry said, pointing to the overhead manuscripts.

"Then you will be needing the help of some very strong men, I think. Let me be the first to volunteer, and I will see who else I can recruit. Would tomorrow morning be agreeable?"

"That would be perfect, Monsieur Machet, as I wish to begin just as soon as possible. Right now, however, I am going to seat myself at this table and count the books I have already placed on my inventory. It will be a chance to rest as well as to compile some figures I can present to the baron to prove that I have made some progress."

"Would you mind if I stayed and watched?" It was put as a question, but Jules had already seated himself beside her and was looking over her shoulder at the inventory sheets. "I could help you count," he suggested with a smile.

Valéry laughed. "I'm afraid that is a job for only one person, monsieur, but I would be glad of your company and could postpone my numbering for a few minutes. Who were you thinking of trying to recruit?"

"I know that both Arsène and Bruno, whom I have been watching work, are far too busy with the print shop, and of course the baron and Régis are finding buyers for their grapes. Philibert is too feeble for the task, but perhaps I can enlist my stepfather and Thomas Thibault."

When Valéry winced, Jules asked why.

"The viscount, if he is willing, would be a wonderful help, but I do not much care for the baron's manservant. He seems surly and a mere pawn in the hands of his overbearing wife."

"I know about overbearing people, mademoiselle." Jules paused for a moment and bit his lip. "They can be most, um, unpleasant, but perhaps Monsieur Thibault will not behave so badly in the presence of the viscount and myself."

"Very well, I will be appreciative of whomever you bring tomorrow morning, monsieur. It is too bad, though, that Monsieur Faguet cannot be a part of this as I do not think he has had a chance to acquaint himself with this library. The baron certainly must have selected him as a man well-educated in the art of printing, who has handled many manuscripts during his years in Lyon. I imagine our printer might have valuable suggestions as to what materials here could be profitably printed and perhaps even the know-how to market them."

"Is that how Paul plans to make use of his library and the new print shop?"

"Beyond my assignment from him to compile a master list of the contents and to organize the materials, I have not been given any detailed outline of his plans," Valéry replied truthfully. "As to the reason he is starting a print shop, I only know that he has selected for the first pressrun a simple grammar he and his father wrote, using a printed textbook from the library as a guide."

"Arsène told me he hopes that the baron might be interested in printing books on various subjects, some at the request of wealthy patrons, and others which could be sold to students and for use in the universities," Jules added. "The former would fetch a good price, and as for the latter, he thinks that this might prove to be a lucrative venture if the number of copies run off is large enough. What seems to disturb him is that the baron has requested only a few dozen copies of the initial grammar and did not seem at all interested in talking about printing up any of the library manuscripts for profit."

"That does seem strange, for my uncle once told me that printing can be a very expensive undertaking. Apparently it is not so much the cost of setting up a print shop, especially if you already have the pressing screw and a ready supply of seasoned wood. But acquiring a variety of fonts, along with paper and bookbinding materials, can be very dear and easily amount to the greater part of a printer's expenses."

"Arsene has said the same to me, mademoiselle, and that is why he is worried about the future of what he views as a business venture. I think he is a very ambitious man, hoping to make a name for himself in the printing business and highly motivated to work hard to bring that about."

"Perhaps the baron is beginning cautiously with his initial pressrun, not wanting to invest too much at first until the press has been perfected and he can think ahead to larger undertakings." Valéry was as puzzled as Jules but expressed confidence that the baron was aware of all this and, in addition, would be seeking the advice from his journeyman printer in the matter.

Jules rose from his chair and walked over to the window, running his hand through his hair several times before he spoke again.

"I have been helping Arsène and Bruno complete their work and am finding the whole process fascinating. Arsène tells me that every basic print shop needs at least a typesetter, a pressman, and an inker. He is an expert compositor, and Bruno's experience is that of a press operator. He has asked if I would be interested in becoming the inker."

Valéry turned around in her chair to look at him. "But Monsieur Machet, you are the stepson of a viscount, and surely you will be inheriting that title and a vast estate to run. Doesn't Monsieur Faguet want someone more permanent than you would be?"

"I am the son of a mere foot-soldier who was killed in a battle while serving under the command of the man who is now my stepfather, mademoiselle.

I always thought that the viscount married my mother because he felt responsible for her state of widowhood. After the marriage, my mother and I came to live in his manor house near St. Germain-des-Prés in Paris. I think that for some time my mother hoped for children of her own from this marriage, but they never had any."

It was hard for Valéry to believe that Charles de Clairac would have chosen to marry a woman such as Odile, let alone want to have children with her, but she did not say so.

Jules continued. "Then came the Battle of Marignano when both Charles and his older brother, who was the Viscount de Clairac, went to fight for King François. It was a great and glorious victory for the king, but unfortunately, the viscount was killed. It was thus that the patrimony, along with the title, passed to his younger brother, my stepfather. We moved to the chateau in Clairac then, and for many years, my mother has been pressuring her husband to agree to adopt me so that I can inherit the title and domain, but he has been steadfast in his refusal."

Valéry noted the hard tone of Jules's voice and the way he clenched his jaw as he spoke.

He turned toward Valéry and said with a note of resignation in his voice, "I do not much blame him. The marriage has not been a happy one, and I think this has affected the viscount's relationship with me."

Valéry walked over to the window and looked earnestly at the young man. "Monsieur Machet, after the viscount dies, who then *will* inherit the viscount's title and land?"

"If my mother survives her husband, she can remain as viscountess on her husband's land, but she cannot pass on the inheritance to me. The fact remains that with no blood heir, the viscount's title and land will be confiscated eventually by the king, and he will bestow it on whoever will bring political advantage to the throne of France. It is hard for me to know that the viscount would prefer this to handing over his noble title and possessions to me."

Valéry did not know how to respond but couldn't help feeling sorry for Jules. He was showing signs of anger and resentment now, but justifiably so, she thought. Still, the viscount had appeared to be a true gentleman, and it was difficult for her to believe that he would deny the estate and title to his stepson unless he had very good reasons to do so. Just the same though, to hold a troubled marriage against an innocent child did not seem worthy of such an honorable man.

Jules turned to walk toward the door but stopped long enough to impart one last thought before leaving. "You can see why I am trying to think ahead with respect to my own welfare, Mademoiselle Lefèvre. Arsène Faguet has been very persuasive in his offer to take me on as an apprentice, beginning with training me to be an inker. He says that the printing profession is spreading all over the country and has proven to be most lucrative, if one knows the market and is willing to compete."

After he had left, Valéry watched him through the window as he walked toward the *imprimerie*, where no doubt he would continue to collaborate with Arsène in the preparations for the first printing of the baron's grammar book. Apart from his domineering mother, he seemed quite nice. Certainly, he'd expressed enthusiastic interest in the inventory she'd begun as well as willingness to organize help for her with accessing the heavier manuscripts which lay out of her reach. He would make a good printer's assistant, she thought, and she wondered if his mother knew anything about his latest plans. The formidable Odile would surely not take with good grace her son's intention to be apprenticed to Arsène Faguet, not when her own ambitions for her son were to inherit the title Viscount de Clairac and the accompanying estate.

Early in the afternoon, Valéry bundled up in her woolen cloak and headed for her class at the church. The weather was definitely turning from the crisp sunny days of fall to the chilly drizzle of winter. The damp wind whipped at tendrils of dark hair which had escaped from her bonnet, leaving her cheeks wet and her skin tingly. She inhaled the musty pungent smell of dead leaves under her feet and felt invigorated. A cough from somewhere ahead of her made her raise her head. It was Sidonie, wrapped in a light shawl, walking very rapidly.

"You look frozen, Sidonie. It is too cold for you to be out and about with such a flimsy wrap," Valéry told the maidservant.

"Oh, mademoiselle, I thought I would take advantage of the viscountess being gone today and try to take a little walk. I am afraid that this is the warmest cloak I have, and you are right, it is no help against the wind."

"Come here then, and I will share my mantle with you." Valéry wrapped part of her cape around the woman's shoulders, and they continued to walk.

"I was not aware that your mistress had gone someplace, Sidonie, although I am glad for you. She does not seem to regard as important anyone else's feelings."

"She is not a kind woman, Mademoiselle Lefèvre, but also I am very sensitive and cannot seem to find how to get along with her without evoking her ire. As for where she has gone, she and the viscount have chosen to accompany

Thomas and Marthe Thibault to Condom where my mistress hopes to do some shopping. She is always so concerned about how she looks."

"I cannot imagine that the housekeeper and your mistress would get along, Sidonie. They are both so outspoken and sharply critical. Why would the viscountess want to do anything with Marthe Thibault?"

The chambermaid let out a sigh. "I have heard them talking, Mademoiselle Lefèvre, and I hope I am not too bold in saying this, but they agree very forcefully on their dislike of you, and they seem to enjoy talking about it."

Valéry laughed. "Of course, that would be what bonds them for now, at least. I hate to think what would happen if I were out of the picture, though. The two would surely destroy each other!"

It was Sidonie's turn to laugh. "You are good for me, Mademoiselle Lefèvre. I am so glad we ran into each other."

"And I am, also, Sidonie, and since I am on my way to the church where I have started to hold reading classes, would you like to come and watch?"

"If it is warm there, then I would be most happy to join you," Sidonie replied.

Entering the sacristy, the two women found Régis bent over a fledgling fire in the room's fireplace. He straightened up when Valéry and Sidonie entered.

"Father Pénicaut is ill today but has sent word that he would like me to see that a fire is set so the students will be comfortable for their classes. Lucien and Lisette are rounding up the other children and will be here shortly." He looked at Sidonie and held out his hand. "I am Régis Maguis, *régisseur* of the estate, mademoiselle, and I do not believe we have formally met, but Lisette has told me that you are Sidonie Soulard, the maidservant of the Viscountess de Clairac."

Sidonie gave him a wan smile, still shivering from the chill of the outdoors.

"Your hand is like ice, mademoiselle. Here, step closer to the fire. Your shawl is not adequate for the weather we are now having."

"I am afraid it is the only one I have, Monsieur Maguis. Perhaps if I can persuade my mistress to buy me some yarn, I can knit myself a cape before I have to go outside again!"

Régis's face registered concern. "Mademoiselle Sidonie, if you would not take offence at this, I have a very warm cloak which belonged to my late wife. It might as well be used as it has just lain in a cupboard for the last five years."

"You would offer that to me, monsieur? I am touched and would be ever so grateful. I assure you I will take very good care of it." Sidonie gave Régis a look of appreciation and moved closer to warm her hands before the blaze.

"If you are staying with Mademoiselle Valéry for the class, I will fetch it right away and be back before you go home," Régis told the shivering maid.

"Have you and the baron successfully marketed the fruits of your harvest, then?" Valéry asked.

"The sales are going very well, and soon, the baron and I will turn our attentions to the distillery. Right now, though, I plan to get caught up with my other estate work, and within a day or so, the baron too will have time to concentrate on his new printing press."

Just then, Lucien and Lisette entered the room, along with the other class members, and lessons began. It was wonderful to have the entire time to devote to her own teaching and not have to share it with the priest, although she hoped he would recover before too long as both she and the children missed him.

True to his promise, Régis reappeared toward the end of the session with his wife's coat over his arm. As he wrapped it around Sidonie's shoulders, Valéry saw tears in the maid's eyes. It was a generous gesture on the part of Régis, Valéry thought, and one which perhaps signaled that he had made peace with the death of his wife and was ready to move on. Certainly, it was the first time she had seen him look happy.

Régis insisted on walking Sidonie back to the chateau, and Valéry headed for the print shop, anxious to see what progress had been made. She found Arsène and Jules deep in conversation over the type case, but they looked up as she entered.

"I am explaining to Jules the arrangement of the type," Arsène told her. "A good man learns by touch where the letters are in the case and can set up to 1500 letters in an hour. See here," he motioned for Valéry to come closer, "the upper line is for the capital letters, and the lower for small, and these large compartments are for the most frequently used letters."

"What is the small box you are holding in your hand?" Valéry asked the printer.

"It is called a composing stick, and I hold it in my left hand like so and pick out the letters I need from the case to set the copy using this reading galley as a guide." Here he pointed to a stand containing text mounted before him in the case. He picked out some letters then and continued to explain. "When a line is completed and justified, it is placed in this long, narrow tray, and we can run off a preliminary proof, from which we can make corrections. Next comes the imposition of the pages so that when the paper is printed and folded, the sequence will be correct."

When Jules and Valéry looked puzzled, the printer asked Bruno to demonstrate how the press worked. He took a sheet of paper, wet it down, and placed it on a hinged wooden frame attached to the press. Next, he grabbed two ink balls, rubbing them over the letters that had been placed in an adjacent wooden frame. Folding down the paper over the type, he slid the whole case under the platen, gripped the long handle attached to the press, and lowered it to onto the plate by means of the giant screw. Then he slid the plate out again, opened the frame, and lifted up the printed sheet for them to inspect.

"This is just a simple one-sheet tract we are using as a test of the press, but I have a meeting set for tomorrow with the baron, and then I will begin in earnest to format the pages and run them off." Arsène's voice conveyed his excitement, and even Bruno looked pleased.

"Perhaps Jules has told you that he is interested in becoming an apprentice," Arsène said. "Right now I am training him to be an inker, which involves mixing the ink, using these wooden spheres with handles to ink the letters, and then washing up afterwards."

Jules held up one of the inkers for Valéry's inspection. "It is covered with *peau de chien,*" he explained, pointing to the leather covering over the ink bulb.

"The poor dog!" exclaimed Valéry.

Jules looked amused. "Nevertheless, dog's skin seems to work better than any other covering to hold the ink."

"I shall have to keep a careful eye on the dogs Régis uses when he hunts," Valéry said with some feeling. "Right now there are six of them, and the disappearance of even one will be noticed, messieurs!"

To Valéry's surprise, all three men chuckled. "I will buy the inkers along with other supplies we need from outside sources, mademoiselle," Arsène said, giving her one of his lopsided smiles. "You needn't worry that I will deplete the baron's kennels!"

"Will you be able to obtain new supplies fairly easily?" Valéry asked.

"I will have no trouble purchasing what I need," Arsène answered, "but it will necessitate a trip to Lyon after we have finished the first pressrun. I have a feeling that the baron will want a variety of fonts as well as different qualities of paper, which we do not have on hand now. I will know better what I must purchase after we have met."

Before Valéry returned to the chateau, Jules told her that he had arranged for his stepfather and Thomas Thibault to help her in the library the next morning. As she returned to the chateau, she was already planning how she would put the three men to work.

Chapter Seventeen

The team showed up promptly right after breakfast, and Valéry assigned them to their stations. Thomas Thibault climbed the ladder to the top, handing down all materials within reach to Jules, who stood several rungs up on the ladder. He in turn gave the books to Charles, who walked over to place them on the library table as Valéry sat at one end, recording them on her inventory list. It wasn't long before she fell hopelessly behind and decided that there was no hurry as she would be able to continue her work after the men had completed theirs.

Every so often, Thomas and Jules would move the ladder to a new section of the shelving and begin their operations all over again. By the end of the morning, the last shelf had almost been cleared when Thomas let out an exclamation.

"Look at this!" He handed down a large package, which upon closer inspection had been tightly sewn up in a piece of linen.

As the men stood looking at it, Valéry said she would be right back and left for her own room where she found her mother's paring knife.

"I can carefully cut the threads holding the wrapping together, and we shall see what our mystery bundle contains," she told her crew. The linen covering was opened to reveal a large folio, perhaps eleven by sixteen *pouces* in size, bound in blind-stamped brown calf stretched over strong boards and reinforced by brass corner pieces. The cover bore the title *Biblia Sancti*. Valéry ran her hand over the four octagonal brass plaques with protruding iron bolts which dominated the front and then reached over to unlock the single brass clasp holding the manuscript closed. The pages were written in a fine Gothic book hand, magnificently rubricated and illuminated. As Valéry turned the vellum sheets, both she and the viscount exclaimed over the many small and large initials, some beautifully painted in red and blue, filled with exquisitely designed floral scrollwork in green and yellow on red and purple grounds. There were floral borders and foliation on the middle of the lateral margins. Interspersed on some pages were artistically drawn scenes illustrating various Bible passages.

"This is the finest manuscript Bible I have ever seen," the viscount said in a hushed voice, "and easily the most rare and valuable manuscript of the entire library, I would judge. My old friend Baron Guillaume once told me of its existence, saying that any library worth the name had to have such a Bible as its cornerstone. But he never showed it to me, and I wondered if he had lost track of where it was."

Valéry turned to the last leaf where a scribe, without name, had written the words Brothers of the Common Life, and below it this simple sentence:

Having labored many years on this book, may this scribe earn
the reward of being inscribed into the Book of Life
by the grace of God.

The viscount, excited over the valuable find, left immediately to inform the baron, who he felt sure would want to see such a treasure.

As Valéry sat with Jules at the table, turning page after page of the precious Bible, the library doors opened, and Odile swept into the room, her head held high and her expression haunty.

"Jules, you are to come to the *imprimerie* at once. I have been searching all over for you and finally went to the print shop where you have been spending so much of your time. Arsène said I might find you here, wasting your time no doubt in this depressingly musty room. He is in need of your help right away."

Her son jerked slightly, his mouth twitching as he closed the cover and turned the Bible so Odile could see it more easily.

"Look, mother, at what we have found. This is an uncommon manuscript Bible of exquisite quality, which has just been discovered, or might I say *rediscovered* in the baron's collection."

Odile glanced briefly down her nose at the ornate cover, opened it somewhere in the middle, and then closed it so carelessly that Valéry reached to grab the book away from her. This did not sit well at all with the viscountess, who raised her voice to an almost screeching pitch.

"*Tu est mal élevée, fille.* The baron shall hear of your rudeness, I assure you."

A voice came from the doorway.

"I shall hear of what, my dear Odile?" It was the baron, minus the viscount, who entered the room smiling at the viscountess. The woman immediately turned to him and, with a manner completely changed, answered that she was impressed with the work her son had done today in the library and especially with the magnificent manuscript which he had just discovered.

Valéry felt sick to her stomach at the audacious lie but said nothing. Jules looked quite uncomfortable, stepping into the background as though trying to detach himself from the scene.

Odile stooped to pick up the Bible from the table, holding it out for the baron's inspection.

"I wondered where this was, as my father used to talk of its existence, but this is the first time I have actually seen it," said the baron, taking the book from Odile's hands and holding it out before him.

"We have only just discovered it in a high corner of the shelving," Valéry said. "It was sewn into this linen covering, which I carefully undid with my mother's knife. I could sew it back again into its shroud, but, Baron, I would entreat you to consider displaying it somewhere in the library. Perhaps Régis would be willing to build a special stand where it could be chained for security but admired and read by anyone who can appreciate such a work of art."

The baron continued to look at the book, turning the pages one by one. Finally, he laid it down on the table and said to Odile, "Perhaps you might have a good suggestion. We shall talk about that, shall we not, madame?"

Odile tilted her head to the side in a gesture meant to be coquettish, Valéry thought, but which did not suit the middle-aged woman.

"I shall be thinking of some solutions to this problem, Paul. Perhaps we could confer over a glass of your excellent Armagnac?"

The baron took her hand and kissed it lightly, replying that it would be a pleasure. After he had left the room, Odile gave Valéry a truly malicious look of triumph and then grabbing Jules by the arm, told him again that he was to go immediately to the print shop. The two disappeared, followed by Thomas Thibault, who closed the door on her without so much as a parting glance.

Valéry stood alone in the fading light of day, surveying the empty shelving overhead and the new pile of unsorted materials all around her. She rewrapped the precious Bible in its linen covering and placed it on one of the ledges with several other books on top of it so that it would not be knocked off accidentally onto the floor. Then she returned to her chamber where she began dressing for dinner. The day had been a curious mixture of accomplishment and discovery. The men had lent their valuable assistance to clearing the upper bookshelves and in doing so had found the valuable Bible. But the more troubling discoveries were the behavior of the baron, who had given his attentions to Odile and ignored her, as well as the pitifully subservient behavior of her son, who obviously shrank before the vituperative tongue of his mother.

She dreaded the thought of dinner that evening, but it turned out to be much more pleasant than she had anticipated. Odile positively basked in the attentions of the baron, who seemed fascinated with her every utterance. Jules, the viscountess explained, was lending his valuable assistance to Arsène and Bruno, and since she went on and on in her bragging, this left Valéry free to enjoy conversing with the viscount, who was both charming and interesting.

"You will appreciate the weeks ahead," the viscount was saying to her. "The festivities during Christmastide are always sumptuous at the chateau, but the best is to come at the end."

"You must be referring to the Twelfth Night celebration," was Valéry's animated response. Marguerite and Henri de Navarre had always made much of this fête, and she herself loved it.

"Does the baron observe the *étrennes*?" she asked.

"Yes, and I am sure that Paul will be extremely generous in his gift-giving, just as his father was before him, seeing to it that he rewards all those who have been in his service over the past year. There will be a magnificent banquet in the great hall, where almost the entire village will be present for the feasting. Tables laden with food the likes of which the villagers have seldom been able to enjoy will be accompanied by the finest of wines from the baron's own cave. You will enjoy yourself, I am sure!"

The evening ended on a positive note, and Valéry returned to her chamber feeling much better about the encounter with Odile earlier in the day. When she reached her door, she was surprised to see the baron waiting for her. Taking her hand, he looked down on her with an expression of concern in his gray eyes.

"I want to make sure that you are all right, Valéry. The viscountess can be quite hurtful. I hope that her acerbic tongue has not cut you too severely."

He must have overheard Odile's remarks to her before he entered the library this morning, Valéry thought with satisfaction. To the baron, she replied,

"Yes, it cuts, Paul, but I have a tough hide—perhaps as tough as the leather which covers the beautiful Bible we just discovered. But it is kind of you to inquire, and I want to assure you that I do not wound easily."

Valéry was far from feeling unscathed, but under the baron's scrutiny, she did not want to show her vulnerability.

The baron stood for a moment longer, looking at her intently.

"I am not sure that I believe you, but you put on a very brave front, my little librarian."

With that, he gave her hand a slight squeeze before disappearing through the doors of the south keep and down the long hallway. Valéry took out the key to her door and let herself in to her room, glad that there was no one who could see her face at that moment. She felt quite flushed from the encounter and just a little light-headed. The baron, though older in years than she, was undeniably attractive. Increasingly, she found herself looking forward to seeing him and resented the recent attention he had paid to the viscountess. What was happening to her, she wondered? It was an entirely new feeling, and although somewhat bewildering, she was enjoying it. Perhaps she needed to be more careful with her emotions. After all, the baron was of the nobility, and she had no rank at all. Marguerite had reminded her of this when speaking of her prospects for the future. Nonetheless, she went to bed happy, looking forward to what the days ahead would bring.

Chapter Eighteen

Midway into the year's last month, winter had definitely established itself, almost as though the season possessed fingers of ice which curled around the brilliant hues of autumn, leaving silvery-white marks on all of nature. Dead leaves from the giant sycamore and oak stands on the chateau grounds crunched underfoot as they were pressed against the hard-frozen earth beneath. Water in the large basin to the chateau's south side had a thin layer of ice covering the summer's accumulation of plants and leaves.

Valery shivered as she headed toward the *imprimerie*, her steps more hurried than when she had visited the outbuilding housing the printing shop during previous weeks. Arsène met her as she entered, shutting in a hurry the heavy wooden door before too much cold air got inside. Bruno, as usual, did not look up but remained working at a corner sink where he and Jules appeared to be washing ink from various metal type.

"You have been working late into the evenings, Monsieur Arsène," Valerie said to the rotund printer as he returned to his work. "Every so often when I cannot sleep, I have seen your lights from my chamber window burn until early morning."

"Indeed, Mademoiselle Valéry. Both Jules and I, along with Bruno, are progressing very well on the task of our first printing. I am not sure that you know of the baron's directions to run off only a very limited number of copies of the work he commissioned, but we are quite pleased with our endeavors, and the baron has praised us, which makes us glow with pleasure."

As he spoke, he brought forth a stack of completed sheets of printing which were ready to be folded and bound. Valery looked appreciatively at the pages and smiled her approval.

"By the end of the week, I will have bound all these pages into small books," he said, indicating the rows of paper drying on the hanging lines, "and then I shall see to it that you get a copy for the library."

"Has the baron said anything about the disposal of the rest of the copies?" Valery queried.

Arsène gave her that curious lopsided smile of his and said that he knew nothing of the baron's plans for the books after their first assignment had come to completion. Valéry thought to herself that perhaps, then, there was hope that they could be used in the classes she and Father Pénicaut had started. The thought excited her.

Jules, who had been listening to the conversation, pointed to a small packet of papers Valéry had tucked into the pocket of her cloak. "You have brought us something, Mademoiselle Valéry. Perhaps it is a new manuscript from the library which the baron has selected as our next endeavor?"

Valéry looked at the young man with an appreciative expression on her face. He was obviously working hard to be of help to Arsène and hopefully learning something of the trade which might be a good future for him.

"Yes, I have brought you something of great value and which represents much work on my part, so you are partly right," Valery replied. "However, this is not something to be printed, but a partial listing of the contents of the library. Much more work needs to be done before there is a master list of all the library contains, but monsieur, I thought that you might be interested in looking over what I have done so far. No doubt, you will be taking some subsequent assignments for printing from this list."

Arsène almost jumped toward the papers Valéry held out to him. As he scrutinized the inventory before him, she noted the intensity with which he read over what she had recorded. Certainly, the baron's journeyman printer was enthusiastically dedicated to the job entrusted to him, for there was no mistaking the excitement he exhibited.

"I will want to look the listing over very carefully, mademoiselle. What a superb labor of love and devotion to your assignment here at Chateau de Renard . . . to have produced this inventory out of the chaos you no doubt found waiting for you!" Arsène impulsively grabbed her hands in his pudgy ones, pumping her arms up and down in his state of exhuberance.

"You flatter me, Monsieur Faguet," Valérie laughed, "but I thank you for what you have said. It helps make me feel even more satisfied that I have accomplished some of what I was assigned to do."

"Ah, my dear mademoiselle," Arsène could hardly contain his enthusiasm, "I am so grateful, and I would like to ask your permission to keep these pages for a few days in order to better digest their contents and familiarize myself with the various categories of materials."

"By all means," Valérie replied, gratified that someone had taken such an interest in the results of her long hours of work. "But I wish them back as soon as possible since I want to share the results of this inventory with the baron."

"I will return them, of course, before I leave. As soon as this task of printing is completed, I will be departing for an extended trip to Lyon where I hope to purchase more supplies and perhaps find a market for the books we will be issuing in the future. If my journey is successful, I should return by mid-January, when I hope to begin the next printing assignment from the baron."

"It seems a wretched time to travel, monsieur, as the weather will be bitterly cold and the roads in deplorable state, but I wish you Godspeed, much success in your endeavors, and a safe return to us." Valery smiled at the portly little printer, noting how he rubbed his hands together in sheer delight over the list Valéry had brought him and no doubt in joyful anticipation of the trip which would enable him to expand the printing operations he'd worked so hard to establish. Before she left, the printer asked her when she thought she would have the entire master list done, and Valéry replied that she had barely begun on it and that she couldn't imagine completing it until early spring.

Valéry walked briskly back to the chateau, hastened in the short walk by a biting wind to her back. Entering the library, she was pleasantly surprised to find the viscount Charles and his manservant Philibert Favard waiting for her. The viscount rose to greet her.

"Your cheeks are the color of holly berries, my child, and your eyes glisten with what surely must be something of great pleasure. Come, take off your cloak and tell us what you have been up to!"

"I am so glad to find you here," Valery replied, "for I have much I wish to share with you. First, I've just returned from the print shop where I gave Monsieur Faguet my preliminary library inventory. And, oh, it is so marvelous that he, with the help of Jules and Bruno, has just about finished the first printing off the new press and is about to bind the pages into books. It is no wonder that my eyes glow, for I am happy that all our hard work has turned out so well!"

The viscount threw back his head and laughed. "You are a delight, my little Valéry, and especially so when you are excited. I admire that quality in you which combines determination in spite of adversities with a joie de vivre which energizes you and those around you. It is quite catching, you know!" The viscount looked down at her with kindly eyes and a tender smile on his face.

Again, Valérie noticed something about the viscount which was vaguely familiar and yet totally elusive to identification. But she basked in the compliment, feeling that Charles was much like her beloved Queen Marguerite in the way in which they both exhibited an almost parental concern for her. She was deeply moved.

"And now, what else, mademoiselle librarian, do you have to share with us?" He glanced then at Philibert, who was seated over in a corner of the library but had been regarding Valery with some intensity. "You do not have any qualms about Philibert being here also, do you?"

"Oh my, no," Valery was quick to reply. "Please, Monsieur Philibert, do come over here because I have a great treasure which I do not think you have seen yet."

When the manservant did not respond, the viscount said that she would have to speak up as Philibert was becoming somewhat deaf in his older years. Valéry repeated more loudly her initial invitation, and with that, the old retainer drew closer as Valéry removed the books on top of the cloth-wrapped Bible she had placed on the ledge. Setting the latter down on the library table, both men bent over the finely crafted pages of sacred text, pointing out one exquisite illumination after another. When they finally closed the cover, Philibert commented that his father had been an artist in his own right, albeit with precious metals, but he would have been appreciative of the fine brass work on the cover, which was not only decorative but served the purpose of safely enclosing its precious contents.

"The monks who produced this have given to us a masterpiece. The baron will need to decide how best to preserve it and yet make it accessible to those who can appreciate such a work of art." The viscount was as serious now as Valéry had ever seen him.

"Until that time," Valéry replied, "I will wrap it back up and return it safely to this ledge, securing it under several books so it won't fall." The viscount helped her with the task and then noticed the little knife Valéry had used when she first cut the stitches away from the linen.

"This also is a work of art, but along a much different vein," Charles observed as he held it up for inspection. "The carved ebony handle contrasts well with the finely crafted steel of the blade and it is also well-balanced."

"My mother used to peel fruit with it, my lord, and now so do I. But I have found that it is a knife capable of many uses."

Philibert, who again seemed to be studying her, broke his silence. "Your mother, Mademoiselle Lefèvre, has she been gone for a long time?"

"Yes, for many years now, Monsieur Favard. While she was alive, we lived in Paris, close to my Uncle Jacques Lefèvre d'Etables, who was my mother's brother-in-law and a priest at Saint Germain-des-Prés in Paris and then later in Meaux. After *Maman* died, it was my uncle who undertook to raise me. He is gone now, too." Valéry's voice trailed off as she finished the sentence, thinking that already nine months had passed since her uncle's death.

"You have tears in those beautiful blue eyes, Valéry. Well-loved family whom one has lost will always tug at the heartstrings, child. I know." The viscount put a comforting hand on her shoulder and Philibert, pulling out a chair for her at the table, added, "And I too know this, Mademoiselle Lefèvre. I have lost my beloved wife, Delphine, who was so long by my side in service to the first Viscount de Clairac and his wife Marie, and then, when he was killed at battle, to Viscount Charles." Valéry noted that he did not add the Viscountess Odile. No wonder. From what she had observed, there was no love lost between the two, but his devotion to his master was quite evident.

"Many years ago Philibert's father, who was a goldsmith of some renown in Paris, made this *chevalière* for my brother." The viscount pointed to the gold signet ring he wore on the little finger of his left hand. "After he was killed in battle, the ring passed to me as the next Viscount de Clairac. I have always cherished it, first because it belonged to my brother, but also because it is truly a fine piece of work by Philibert's father."

The viscount looked over at his loyal manservant and smiled. "It is a wonder that you did not follow in your father's trade, Philibert, but I know that your older brothers also were skilled in the craft."

"And I was not at all," Philibert said, shaking his head. "It was so fortunate that when the first viscount commissioned his signet ring from my father, he also expressed an interest in a manservant who my father might recommend, and knowing that I did not want to carry on the trade, he suggested his youngest son!"

"Now there is a tribute to the value of family, Philibert. Come, then, and let us talk of family," the viscount said cheerily. "It is a subject on which I never tire!"

"I have noticed the *chevalière* you are wearing, Viscount Charles. Is that the de Clairac blazon?" Valery bent over to get a closer look at the signet ring. Made of *or massif*, it was stamped with a shield, in the center of which was a detailed etching of the palm of an open left hand. Underneath was the name de Clairac.

"It is a simple coat of arms, to be sure," the Viscount said. But *la main sinistre* brings out a distinguishing characteristic of the de Clairac viscounts: We were all left-handed!"

"That is curious indeed," Valery observed. "What are the colors?"

"Ah, that is a good question, mademoiselle. The official description is *d'azur à une main appaumée d'argent á la bordure de gueules.* I have brought along with me an ivory which has been painted with the de Clairac blazon. It adorns a small book containing the de Clairac line, which I have in my chambers. The next time you are in the north keep, please feel free to come into the room and take a look. There is the family motto, in Latin, of course, carved underneath it. Translated, it means Strong and Distinguished.

"And that is surely what you are, my lord!"

Philibert agreed, saying what a privilege it had been to be in service to such a family for so many years.

"And in turn, what a privilege it has been for the de Clairac family to have you, Philibert." As the two men left the library, the viscount's hand rested under the old manservant's elbow, a touching gesture of support and aid on the part of the viscount, Valery thought, and certainly symbolic of the love the viscount had for his faithful retainer.

Chapter Nineteen

Thursday classes continued in the church despite the chilling weather of winter. The students huddled around the large limestone fireplace in the sacristy but continued to make progress in their studies, which was a great source of satisfaction to Valéry, who had begun to think of them as her children. The priest, whom the students now affectionately called *Père* Pierre, taught his catechism first and then gave over the rest of the time to Valéry, who was working her way through a few simple grammar lessons her uncle had used when he taught the king's children. It was touching to see how some of the older ones helped the younger in the class, and it was a special source of satisfaction to observe the leadership of both Lucien and Lisette, who commanded respect because of their father's position at the chateau. Because the baron had insisted that Sidonie and Philibert be given Thursdays off along with his own staff, Sidonie always accompanied Valéry to the classes, listening as carefully to the lessons as did the children. It amused Valéry to notice how Régis would make an appearance just before class was over, insisting on walking Sidonie back to the chateau. They would huddle close together, talking earnestly, and seemingly oblivious to even the worst of weather.

After her class was over, Valery often enjoyed exploring the extensive wooded grounds of the estate. Sometimes the weather was drizzly and cold, but sometimes too, the pale rays of the winter sun illuminated the frosty trees and underbrush in such a way that the whole world seemed to sparkle. Returning to the chateau as the light began to fade, she would walk past the print shop windows, which revealed Arsène Faguet, Jules Machet, and Bruno hard at work. She would have loved to enter and watch them operate the press but knew she would be an unwelcome distraction for the men.

One afternoon, when her walk was cut short by dark storm clouds and a biting wind, she saw Jules, bundled up in his cape, leave the *imprimerie* and walk rapidly toward the chateau. Returning to the chateau some minutes after him, she had just entered her room and removed her cloak when she heard a noise in the library. When she opened her door to investigate, she saw Jules rushing down the far hallway and disappearing through the door of the circular staircase. Out of curiosity, she went into the library. There, on the table before her, lay a newly printed copy of *In linguam gallicam Isagoge*, with a note attached. Valery bent to read it in the fading light. "We are finished at last with the first printing," it read. "Here is the copy I promised you for the library." It was signed "Arsène." Under the book, Valéry found her preliminary listing of the library's contents. Taking the newly printed work back into her own room, she sat by the fire and read the contents from cover to cover. It was a simple and easily understood grammar, well laid-out on numbered pages, with clear, legible roman characters. It would be a pleasure to use it in her classes, and she hoped the baron would make more copies available for her eager students.

The very next day, Arsène Faguet left for Lyon. He sat astride one of the baron's horses, wrapped in a thick black mantle which also partially covered bulging saddlebags thrown over the animal's haunches. Provisions for the journey, no doubt, thought Valéry, who did not envy him the trip ahead.

In the weeks following Arsène's departure, Bruno virtually disappeared. During the day, the print shop was deserted. At night, Valery would see a light burning in his quarters, but the taciturn pressman gave no indication that he either needed or wanted company. When she expressed concern about him to Régis, he assured her that from time to time he appeared in the village, where he bought food for himself, and that he looked to be in good health.

Jules, freed from any printing duties, was also an enigma. Whereas before he had been affable, at least when away from his mother, he now seemed agitated and somewhat preoccupied and distant, the cause of which eluded Valéry. Often, he would saddle his own horse and ride in the direction of Eauze, where he remained well into the evenings, missing dinner and, of course, Odile's acerbic tongue in the process.

"I think Jules has found some drinking companions," Lisette observed one morning when she brought Valery her *petit déjeuner* tray. Over the weeks since Valéry had arrived, Lisette liked to divulge what was happening behind the scenes at the chateau as well as in the town of Eauze, and Valéry always listened with interest, learning much from the young girl's idle chatter.

"How do you know that, Lisette?" Valery asked, surprised at the revelation from a mere child.

"Well, Papa goes to the *Sanglier Sauvage* in the village every so often, and he says he always sees Jules there, a pint of ale in his hand, talking to acquaintances he has made in the course of the weeks Monsieur Faguet has been gone."

"Do you think he is uncomfortable when he sees your father at the inn, Lisette?" After all, Valéry thought, Jules's behavior would reflect badly on the baron, who was his host, if he got too drunk or unruly, and he would know that Régis would carry that report back to his lord.

"Oh, he never lets on that it bothers him," Lisette replied. "Papa said that he barely gives him a nod when he is there."

More often than not, Jules would be absent for dinner. This did not seem to bother the baron or the viscount, but Odile alternated between fretting that her son was so often gone and making excuses for his absence.

"Jules has important business in Eauze these days," she said one evening as they sat around the immense fireplace, enjoying the warmth coming from the blazing logs. "Monsieur Faguet has found my son's aid invaluable in the print shop and has begged him to make contact with wealthy merchants who pass through Eauze who might spread the word of your new press, Paul, as well as be potential customers."

The baron looked at her somewhat indulgently. "My dear Odile, it is not my intent to become a great printing house in the region. There are other centers, such as Lyon, Paris, and Poitiers, which will continue to far surpass what we will build here."

"But Paul," Odile replied, her voice dripping with honey, "printing is a very costly endeavor and will surely drain your resources if you give no thought to making a profit."

"True, I do not wish to lose money on this new venture of mine. However, I will not overextend myself, gentle lady, but only print that which I deem to be useful and affordable for a wider population. With the rebirth of interest in the masterpieces of antiquity, along with the scholarship and new learning of our times, the printing press has the potential to make a wide range of reading available to a growing number of people. I feel a deep responsibility to my forebears, who have put much devotion into their collections, to make some of the best and most useful in these collections available in print. Let the great houses worry about mass printings. I will be selective and, as far as possible, frugal in what I undertake to publish."

The viscount, who had been listening intently to this exchange, nodded his approval. "Your father, Paul, would heartily concur with your unselfish plans to make some of the contents of the library more available. Certainly, with the income generated from your lands and the sale of Armagnac, there will be money enough to put into a modest printing establishment. *L'imprimerie de Renard* has a certain dignity to the title. I feel certain that this enterprise of yours will eventually establish its own reputation for honesty and value of product."

Odile leaned toward the baron, putting a hand on his arm and smiling rather tightly, Valéry observed. "Surely, your print shop can be all these things and also a great financial success. Think how wonderful it would be to have a reputation for one of the finest printing establishments in the land, and," she added with a rising voice, "boast the very best journeymen and even master printers also."

"If you are speaking of Arsène Faguet," the baron replied, "then I am sure he would agree with such an ambition. As for your son, madame, he shows great interest and motivation to learn the printing business. I will want to encourage excellence, of course, but not an overweening ambition to outdo the leaders in this trade."

The evening ended on an uncomfortable note. Valéry sensed the firmness of Paul's position and also Odile's opposition. Settling into bed that night, Valéry wondered if Odile had finally accepted that her son would not inherit the de Clairac title and estates and now was trying console herself by imagining that Jules would eventually become a widely known, respected, and wealthy printer. When she finally fell asleep, her dreams were a jumble of vignettes—the viscount announcing to his stepson that the estate and title would not be his; Odile shrieking in the background, face contorted with anger; the baron telling his librarian that she was no longer needed now that the inventory was complete; and Arsene and Jules running off pages and pages of print until they completely disappeared, smothered by their own excesses.

Chapter Twenty

As the days grew shorter, Valéry was determined to take advantage of the hours when it was light enough to work in the library. She rose at dawn, and soon after washing, dressing, and eating would go to the library where, much to her satisfaction, her scheme of organization was falling into place very well. Row upon row of manuscripts, along with printed volumes, now lined the shelves, grouped according to their subject matter and labeled accordingly on the front of each section. The valuable Bible, however, remained on its ledge, wrapped in the protective coverlet and topped by several other books. She would leave it there until the baron decided on how best to display it.

One afternoon, there came a tap on the library door, and before she could say *entrez*, the viscount stepped into the room. He had a big smile on his face as he looked appreciatively around at the neat bookshelves, complimenting Valéry on the difference she was making with her work.

"*Vous êtes toujours un gallant homme*, monsieur," Valéry smiled back at him. "I am making progress toward my goal, and it is quite gratifying."

"I have come in the hope that you would be willing to take a little respite from your labors, Valéry, and accompany me to the old barn where Paul and Régis are distilling Armagnac. I know that it is not your preferred *digestif*, but you might find the process interesting, and I would be delighted to have your company."

"How very thoughtful of you, Monsieur Charles. A tour of the distillery would please me immensely and is something I have wanted to do ever since little Lisette told me how much her father and the baron enjoy their new *jouet!*"

The viscount chuckled. "Then fetch your cloak, and we shall avail ourselves of this opportunity."

Valéry followed Charles across the courtyard and up the path lined with outbuildings. She waved at Lucien as they passed the stables and noticed with interest that Bruno appeared to be working in the *imprimerie*.

"I am surprised to see the pressman back in the print shop," she said. "He has been keeping to himself ever since Arsène Faguet left. I wonder what he is doing?"

"Paul talked to him about designing a label for the Armagnac bottles which could be printed up by his press. Much to our surprise, Bruno made a sketch of the chateau and offered to chisel it into a woodblock that should print very nicely. I imagine that is what he is busy with now."

"I had no idea he had any artistic sensibilities," Valéry said. "I have only seen him doing hard physical work—and not looking very happy with it, at that."

"Perhaps this new assignment will give him so much pleasure that he will look for other opportunities to illustrate texts which Paul wishes to publish," said the viscount. "I understand that the poor man has suffered because he was once active in speaking out against the abuses of the church. Now that he can no longer speak, he might find a new sense of satisfaction using his artistic talent."

"I hope so too," Valéry replied. "I do not blame him for his gruff manner and wanting to be alone. It must be hard to be with people and not be able to communicate anymore."

The viscount leaned forward to ask her a question. "And you, Valéry, are you happy with your work, and are you enjoying the company of those around you?"

Valéry was silent for a few minutes, trying to think how to be diplomatic in her answer. "Lisette and Lucien are a godsend to me, as is their father. *Père* Pierre has been most gracious in allowing me to offer reading lessons to the dear children in his parish school. You, as well, are a source of my contentment, and your stepson, until recently at least, has been helpful. And as for Arsène, perhaps you do not know that he was really one of the first to welcome me warmly. There are others, though, with whom I have had some difficulties." Her voice trailed off as she struggled with how much she wanted to reveal.

The viscount patted her arm. "I know that my wife is one of those others, Valéry, but I am at a loss as to who else is making your stay a troubling one. You have said nothing of the baron, child."

Valéry bit her lip but answered as honestly as she could. "He was very upset when I first arrived as he was led to believe that I was a man, monsieur."

"You have a name which is used for both males and females," the viscount observed. "It was probably a lack of clear communication between Marguerite and Paul, I would suspect."

"The truth of the matter can only be brought to light by asking my patroness, and I do not feel it is my place to confront her on this matter."

The viscount nodded. "Of course not, Valéry. But, certainly this no longer needs to be clarified as you are quite obviously equal to the position. Hasn't Paul told you as much?"

"He has indicated that I am still on trial, monsieur. I fear that no matter how well I accomplish my duties, it will not be enough for him to accept me. It is almost as though he does not like women. And then there is Madame Thibault, who is blatant in her dislike of me. I do not understand what I have done to deserve such distrust and hostility."

The viscount stopped walking and turned her around to face him.

"Valéry, I am going to share with you something which needs to be kept between us. Can you promise me that?"

Valéry looked questioningly at him, but nodded.

"When my old friend, Baron Guillaume, lost his wife, his only child Paul was a baby. He hired Marthe Thibault to help raise the child and to take care of the duties involved in housekeeping. At first she seemed quite capable, but before long, it also became apparent that she was bossy and controlling. I tried to talk with Guillaume about this, but he was often too busy with his own affairs to pay much attention. He did adore his son, and the two were always very close. However, the only mother Paul knew was the formidable housekeeper, and she, stuck with a weak husband, developed a strong and I think unhealthy attachment to her little charge."

"But what does that have to do with the baron's mistrust of *me*?" Valéry asked

"First, Valéry, Paul has not had many women in his life. His world has been that of men, with the housekeeper as his closest contact with a female. Can you blame him for being suspicious of you?"

When Valéry did not reply, he continued, "It is obvious to me, child, that Paul is realizing you are not of the same mold as Marthe, and furthermore, that he is attracted to you. If I have noticed this, how much more would Madame Thibault be aware of what is happening. Her whole life has been centered around Paul. You are a threat to her, *ma chère*, and," he paused here for a moment, "you are also a threat to my wife."

Valéry felt the cold wind blowing in her face, but that was not what caused the chill down her back. She was stunned at the viscount's insights, which were beginning to make sense, at least as far as Paul and Marthe were concerned.

They began walking again, and after a few moments, she asked, "I do not understand about your wife, monsieur. She has disliked me from the first moment we met when she didn't even know me."

"I find it hard to talk about my wife, Valéry, but I will say this, and then we must let it drop. Madame de Clairac is a beautiful woman but with a great deal of vanity. I am afraid that she likes to be the center of adoration, and you are a threat to that."

The two walked on in silence until they passed a chicken coop and then entered a rustic old barn. The interior was dark, the floors dirt, and Valéry had to pick up her skirts to avoid the numerous puddles until they reached the back section where Paul and Régis were working. They looked up as the two visitors approached.

"Ah, you have come for your tour," Régis said. "Welcome to the *chai*," he indicated with a sweep of his arm, indicating the rows of barrels lining the back wall as well as the giant copper still in front of them.

"This is called an alembic," he said, indicating the distillation vessel. "If we work hard, it can produce as many as three to four barrels in a twenty-four-hour period. It is heated with wood, as you can see, which keeps me busy making sure the fire always burns at a certain level during the process."

The baron came over to join them. "And I in turn am kept busy feeding wine from past vintages into the wine-warmer where it is heated by the hot upper part of this condensing coil, and from there flows over copper plates, where it continues to get hotter and hotter. Finally, when it reaches this lower boiler, it begins to steam and evaporate. The vapors then rise back through the plates where they are continually forced into contact with the incoming wine. Next the vapors exit through the top of this column and into the condensing coil where they can cool enough to change from steam into a liquid which is called eau-de-vie."

"Is that what I see flowing into that wooden barrel?" Valéry asked. She was not about to admit that the whole explanation needed to be repeated several times before she understood any of it, but she thought her question might give the impression that she was at least listening to what the baron was telling them.

"Yes, that is the end product of the alembic. It needs to age in casks in order to acquire color, tannin, and flavoring as well as permit the spirits to breathe through the wood. After a number of years, it will be ready to be enjoyed as a fine Armagnac."

Valéry made a face, which was duly noted by the baron. "Given your reaction, I'm sure you will have no trouble believing that many years ago this eau-de-vie was distilled only by chemists, who touted it as a medicine for the treatment of various ailments. But my father was convinced that it could be refined enough to become an enjoyable brandy. That was when he had this alembic built. The *digestif* you tasted awhile back came from his first distillation though he really did not pursue it then as he was more interested in wine making. I, on the other hand, would rather concentrate on producing Armagnac."

"Marguerite once told me that an ancestor of her husband's so believed in the medicinal properties of these spirits that he used to soak rags in them and then wrap himself up, thinking that the moistened sheets soothed his body and relieved his pains. Then one night, while he lay thus entwined in his bed, he knocked a candle over and perished in the ensuing blaze!" Valéry finished her story with a smug smile on her face.

The viscount howled in delight, a notable departure from his usual gentle reserve.

"Not that I am happy that a past king of Navarre perished in such an unfortunate way," he hastened to explain, "but I think that our little Valéry will not be persuaded to like anything better than my *pruneau* d'Agen."

Walking back to the chateau, they came across Jules just entering the print shop. He turned to acknowledge them, saying he would not be present for dinner that evening and then disappeared hastily through the doorway.

"My stepson is a handsome young man, Valéry, and if he had more strength of character, I might wish there to be an attraction between you two," the viscount said. "You would be a delightful addition to my family."

Valéry blushed at the compliment. Charles continued. "Over the years, I have noted the difference between how Paul was able to develop a strong character despite the domineering influence of Marthe but how Jules failed to do the same with Odile. I have some guilt about this, and even now, feel I might be partly to blame." Turning toward Valéry, he added, "This also needs to be kept between you and me, Valéry."

"I feel honored, monsieur, at your candor. You may trust me to tuck it all away in my heart where it will find a very private home."

Before they parted, the viscount gave Valéry a little hug. Again, something in his face seemed so familiar, but just what it was continued to remain illusive.

Chapter Twenty-One

With the advent of the Twelve Days of Christmas, the weather grew worse. Each morning, Valéry looked outside her window in the hope that she could continue her practice of walking. It was not the cold and wind which prevented it, but the rain, which thoroughly drenched everyone who ventured outside and which showed no signs of letting up. No matter, she thought to herself, because she had a special project she wished to complete, and it needed to be done indoors.

First, however, she would have to brave the elements and pay a visit to Bruno in the *imprimerie*. Bundling up in her woolen cape and drawing the hood closely around her head, she hurried over the chateau courtyard and burst into the print shop without knocking. Bruno must have been startled, for he jumped from his seat at the worktable, crumbling a sheet of paper he held in his hand.

"*Excusez-moi*, Monsieur Bruno," Valéry said apologetically. "I did not mean to alarm you. I have come in search of a few large sheets of vellum, if you have any here in your paper supplies."

When the pressman did not respond, she continued with a smile.

"Since we are now celebrating the Twelve Days of Christmas, with its custom of gift-giving, I wish to present to the baron my record of the contents of his library as I have compiled it so far. You may remember the listing I gave to Monsieur Faguet to look over. I wish to recopy it as it was very roughly written on quite ordinary paper."

Bruno continued to stare at her with an expression which, curiously enough, looked like fear.

Thinking that she had an opportunity to praise him for something, she glanced at the sheets of printed material drying on the lines overhead.

"These must be the labels you have designed and printed for the baron's Armagnac bottles," Valéry exclaimed enthusiastically. "The viscount told me about the woodblock you made from your sketch of the chateau. It has come out beautifully, Bruno. How proud the baron will be to put these on his brandy bottles."

She smiled at Bruno as she said this, hoping it would make a difference in his attitude toward her. He continued to stand by the table but raised his hand to point to a stack of paper under a press toward the back wall of the print shop. Then he bent to write something on a scrap of paper lying on the table. After a minute, he held it out to Valéry.

"The ordinary paper is in the paper press," it read. "There are a few sheets of vellum next to it, if you want something finer."

Valéry thanked him, but he had already turned his back on her and reseated himself at the table. She located the vellum, rolling several sheets up as quickly as she could and then tucked them under her cloak. Before she stepped back outside into the rain, she thanked Bruno and complimented him again on the Armagnac labels.

"They can be *your* gift to the lord of the chateau, Bruno. You have a great talent, and one that I hope you can put to good use in the future."

As she left, she heard the man grunt and tried to imagine that he was pleased.

Back in her room, she hung up her wet cloak by the fire and went into the library. Her initial listing of books, in which Arsène had been so interested, lay on the table next to the new pages on which she was continuing to record more manuscripts. Since the latter would have by far the most titles, she would not be done with that in time to present it to the baron, so she left this work on the table. The other sheets she carried into her room, placing them on her desk along side the fine vellum and the pen and ink which she had saved from her uncle's materials. Only when she separated the top page of sheepskin from the several sheets which lay beneath did she discover that the one on the bottom contained printing. Her first thought was to return it to Bruno, but then the words on the page caught her attention. Printed in octavo, it was most obviously a strongly worded tract against the abuses of Rome and the church, including the false beliefs, practices, and teachings which the church had promulgated down through the ages. It ended by calling for a rebellion on the part of all true Christians.

Initially, Valéry was flabbergasted, but upon reflection, she concluded that the tract was quite in character with Bruno's background. He had been part of the protest movement in Paris and was punished severely for it. He'd escaped with his life and found refuge in the printing houses of Lyon. She wondered if Arsène had promised him the freedom to continue printing his tracts if he agreed to come with the journeyman printer to Eauze. At any rate, she was now faced with a predicament. She very much doubted that the baron had given his permission for such a printing, but she was not sure. Should she show the tract to Paul, or should she take it back to Bruno and let the pressman handle the matter as he felt best? Either way, she would be involved in a matter that potentially had serious consequences. The temptation was to do nothing and hope that Bruno did not miss it, but she knew that if she took this last option, the matter would weigh heavily on her conscience.

Far into the night, Valéry turned over and over in her mind the possible ramifications of any action she might take. Before going to bed, she looked out her window, noting the oil lamps were still burning both in the print shop and, curiously enough, in the back apartments also. Whatever Bruno was busy with, he must have been anxious to finish it while others slept. By morning, her mind was made up. She would return the propaganda sheet to Bruno, assure him that she did not intend to tell anyone about it, but stress that she trusted that he had gotten the baron's permission for such a printing.

The heavy rainfall continued all morning. Valéry worked for several hours on the pages she would present to the baron, but toward noon, her hand began to cramp. Surely, by now, Bruno would be up, and she could return the tract sheet to him and give her hand a rest at the same time.

As she passed the stables, Régis called out to her. "Do you have time to talk for a minute, Mademoiselle Valéry?"

"With pleasure, Monsieur Maguis," Valéry replied, glad to be able to step out of the rain. "You are done with your distillation, then?"

"We are all done for the year, and now the baron is preparing for his *étrennes*. The custom of giving gifts to all those who have labored for the estate over the year is a very important tradition of the de Renard baronage. He will give gold *écus* to those who have rendered outstanding service, and to others, there will be the customary offerings of chickens, ham, sausage, and other meats, along with fruits, honey, and wine to provide the makings of some fine dinners for those who have labored in the fields and vineyards."

"Lisette and Sidonie have told me that Madame Thibault is making many demands on them now in preparation for the grand Twelfth Night banquet at the chateau."

"Yes, and Lisette returns home each evening very tired from these preparations. You see, the banquet marks the culmination of the festivities of the Twelve Days of Christmas and is meant to extend the baron's charity to everyone in the village. The great hall must be set up with enough tables and benches, and I am already organizing the men who will be given permission to hunt game on the baron's lands to supply the banquet tables."

"I have heard commotion coming from the kitchens already, and Lisette has tried to describe to me what it is like to bake enough Twelfth Night cakes to feed so many people," Valéry commented, laughing. "It may be a tremendous amount of work, but what a time of rejoicing it will be for the entire community. The baron is a most generous gift-giver."

"And that reminds me why I wanted to talk with you, Mademoiselle Valéry. I have just built a stand for displaying the valuable Bible you have discovered. I thought it might be an appropriate way of thanking you for what you have taught my children. Since tomorrow is the eve of the Twelfth Night fête, I would like to deliver it then, if that is convenient for you."

Valéry looked into the earnest face of the *régisseur,* once so sad but now reflecting the joy he obviously felt. She was sure that Sidonie was a big part of his transformation, and she rejoiced.

"I am filled with delight at such a thoughtful gift, Monsieur Maguis, and will look forward to receiving it into the library tomorrow." She stepped back into the rain with a much lighter heart, feeling more confident now to face the intimidating Bruno.

That confidence, however, was short-lived. Bruno's reaction to being given the octavo tracts was one of anger. It was obvious that he had not discovered the sheet missing, and it was equally as obvious that he was now trying to control his rage. He yanked the paper out of Valéry's hands, his eyes wild and a deep growl coming from his throat.

Valéry tried to redeem the moment. "Monsieur Bruno, you can trust me not to tell anyone about this," she repeated again. "It really is a matter between you and the baron, and I have no wish to be involved."

The giant of a man backed away from her, but his eyes never left her face.

"I know you have suffered for your beliefs, Bruno, and I can appreciate any fear and anger you may be feeling. Perhaps you do not know that my uncle himself had to flee the censure of the Sorbonne and the prosecution of the Parliament, after he was condemned for his work. He remained in exile until King François brought him back. Later, the king's own sister gave him protection, along with many others whose lives were in danger due to their stand on the abuses of the church. You see, you have nothing to fear from me, monsieur."

The pressman made no attempt to acknowledge what she had said. After an agonizing minute when they stood face to face, he turned suddenly on his heel and disappeared into his apartments, slamming the door behind him.

Valéry returned to the chateau shaken by the encounter but, nonetheless, relieved that she had done what she felt to be right. She sat down once again at her desk and worked until the book inventory listings were all on the sheets of vellum. She would let them dry overnight and then seek out the baron to deliver her own *étrenne*.

The next morning, she began work again on recording the vast number of manuscripts that had been removed from the higher shelving. It was there in the library that Régis and Jules entered a time later, carrying the oak stand Régis had fashioned to display the exquisite Bible. After setting it in several spots, they finally settled on a corner directly across from the door, where the book could be seen immediately by anyone coming into the room. Jules left then, saying that Bruno needed his assistance, leaving Régis and Valéry to discuss the placement of the book and how it could be secured.

"Let us prop it up on the stand, and then maybe we can tell better whether to chain it or perhaps fix some sort of lock directly from the binding boards into the wood," Régis told Valéry.

Valéry went over to the book ledge and removed the cloth-wrapped Bible. Setting it down on the table, she unfolded the linen and then stared in disbelief. It was not the Bible at all but a roughly bound book of the same dimensions, containing material on astrology and necromancy.

She must have let out a gasp, for Régis came over immediately, asking what was the matter.

"I don't understand. This is not the Bible. What has happened?" Valéry was beside herself and very close to tears.

"Perhaps someone borrowed the book and has simply forgotten to put it back," Régis offered. "Who knew that the Bible was here?"

"The viscount, Jules, and Thomas Thibault were helping me when it was first discovered," Valéry replied. "Then Paul and Odile saw it."

"I also knew about it when the baron came to me about a display stand," Régis said, his voice reflecting his concern. "It is very possible that any of us could have mentioned it to others, and that enlarges the possibilities of who might have it," Régis volunteered on a hopeful note.

"But why then would somebody take the trouble to put another book of the same size in its place unless they were bent on deception?" Valéry was beginning to face the distinct possibility that it had not been borrowed, but stolen.

"It could be that whoever it was knew that the baron would not grant his permission for the Bible to be taken out of the library, yet they wanted a chance to study it in the comfort of their own room and in their own time frame. They would have put the surrogate book in the Bible's place, thinking that no one would be the wiser and that they could return the Bible before it was discovered missing." Régis tried to sound convinced, but somehow it rang hollow.

"Perhaps you are right," Valéry said somewhat hesitantly. "I think that before we inform the baron, we should make sure that it has not just been misplaced. What I will do is to visit the guest rooms and have a look around. If I find it, I will know that it is not really missing, and I can make sure that the person responsible returns it before anyone notices the bare stand you have made."

Régis agreed with the plan and then hurried off to the myriad of Christmastide duties which awaited him. Valéry locked the door of her own room and ventured down the long hallway across the center of the chateau where the bedrooms were located. Tapping lightly on Philibert's door, there was no answer. She found the door unlocked and the room empty. She looked around carefully, but after several minutes, it was obvious that the Bible was not there. The next room was Sidonie's, and she too was gone, no doubt hard at work under the housekeeper's whip or perhaps trying to meet the demands of Odile. There was no Bible in her room either.

Jules's room was in immaculate order, making a search quite easy, but in the end, her search was fruitless. Finally, she approached the de Clairac apartments with some trepidation. When no reply came from her knock, she pushed open the massive oak doors and stepped inside. The armoires and cupboards revealed nothing except clothing and other personal articles. She was just approaching the commode when the door suddenly opened and Odile and Marthe Thibault entered. They did not see her right away but walked directly to the large window overlooking the courtyard. Odile was saying, "The rain has swollen the wood on the window frame, and we cannot get it shut. It was most annoying last night, Marthe, with all that downpour keeping us awake."

"I will notify Thomas right away, of course, and I am sure it will be no problem . . ." the housekeeper replied but then stopped in midsentence as Odile shrieked when she saw Valéry standing across the room.

"How dare you come into my chambers! What do you think you are doing here?" The viscountess was livid with rage.

"I beg your pardon, Madame de Clairac," Valéry answered, her heart pounding so loudly she feared the two women could hear it. "Your husband told me there was a book on the de Clairac lineage that I was welcome to see, and he invited me to come into his room to get it whenever I was free." It was the truth as far as it went, but of course not the real reason she was in the chambers. To tell these two women who hated her so much that she was searching here for the missing Bible would not only be an insult, but it would add fuel to the fire they so obviously wanted to use to destroy her. Besides, they just might be the people who had removed the Bible from the library in the first place, hoping the baron would place the blame on his librarian who, after all, was in charge of the valuable collection.

"You lie, mademoiselle. What are you really searching for? If you have stolen anything, you will suffer for it, I assure you."

"Madame de Clairac, I am telling you the truth, and I would never steal, not from you or from anyone."

"You think you can deceive me that easily? I am a very powerful woman," Odile shouted, pointing her finger at Valéry as she came closer. "When my husband and the baron hear of this, you will be dismissed. I will see to that, I promise you."

"You can try, of course, Madame de Clairac, but both your husband and the baron know you to be quite self-centered and vain, and thus you resent the attention I get from them. I think you will do nothing by your vindictiveness except embarrass yourself."

Valéry could not believe she had said such a thing, but her anger at the unjust accusations brought out a very assertive streak in her. She was tired of working so hard in the library with no recognition or assurance she could stay. She was tired of the meanness shown to her by the housekeeper and the viscountess. She was tired of the rude and hostile Bruno. It all seemed to reach a point where she could no longer take the abuse.

Odile's reaction was interesting. She turned quite pale and stood staring at Valéry as though she were in shock. It did not last long though. Before Valéry could move, she reached out and hit her across the face and then spit on her. The housekeeper stepped between them and, pressing her face quite close to Valéry's, whispered between clenched teeth. "Get out, you crass, ill-mannered scum. And I am warning you, girl, you will pay dearly for this, very dearly."

Back safely in the south keep, Valéry's hand shook so badly that she dropped the key before she could fit it in her lock. Bending down to retrieve it, she noticed a small parcel propped up against the door. When she finally succeeded in entering her room, she sat down by the fire and opened the package. Inside lay a small book, richly bound in plush velvet. An accompanying note read:

Ma Chère Valéry,

Please accept this small volume as a token of my thanks for the long hours of labor you have spent in the library. You may be interested in the book's history. On the eve of Twelfth Night in the year 1430 it was given as a gift to King Charles VII. Later my great-grandfather acquired it for his collection and then gave it to my grandfather, who in turn passed it down to my father. Finally it came to me, again on the eve of Twelfth Night. I can think of no one I would rather give it to now than you, certainly in tribute for what you have done, but even more so in appreciation of who you are.

Paul

She opened the cover and gasped. It was a small book of hours, exquisitely illuminated by a Parisian book painter. A slip of vellum marked a page where a breathtakingly beautiful scene of the Nativity depicted the Virgin, in an intensely blue gown, surrounded by tiny angels in various hues of red, green, gold, and rose. All were adoring the tiny Christ child lying in a bed of straw the color of the sun's rays.

Tears came very easily, and Valéry let them flow. After awhile, she rose, and picking up the inventory list she had completed for the baron, she rolled it up and tied a bit of ribbon from her mother's sewing supplies around the tube. Still holding the book of hours and tucking the inventory scroll under her arm, she walked down the marble staircase to the floor below and headed toward the baron's apartments. Before she had gone very far, though, she heard familiar voices. From the shadows which enveloped her, she watched as Odile and the housekeeper had an animated discussion with the baron outside his door. After they left, the baron stood watching them, and Valéry continued her way down the hall until he saw her. His expression was grim, and there was no welcoming smile.

"I am afraid that the viscountess and the housekeeper have just told you about an unpleasant encounter we had this afternoon, Paul. I would like the chance to tell you about it from my perspective."

"I do not want to stand out in the hall for this discussion, Valéry." He opened the door to his apartments and motioned for her to enter. The antechamber was filled with massive pieces of furniture, and heavy draperies covered the mullioned windows. A fire blazed in the enormous fireplace, which dominated one wall and lent warmth and color to the impressive room. Valéry sat in a high-backed tapestry chair the baron indicated to her, and he sat across from her in a matching one.

"Well?" he said. "I need to hear how you explain your presence in the de Clairac chambers and how you justify what you said to the wife of my father's dearest friend."

"The viscount told me about a book on the de Clairac ancestry which he said I could find in his room whenever I had a moment to look at it. I knocked on the door, but when nobody answered, I thought I would just slip in, find the book, and slip out again. I meant no harm, Paul, but when the viscountess entered, she said she suspected me of stealing and got very violent."

Valéry could not bring herself to look the baron in the eyes, and she felt even more uncomfortable with her explanation, but what could she say? She did not want the baron to know about the missing Bible, at least not yet. Her place as librarian was still under question, and she neither wanted to do anything which would make the baron question her competency at overseeing the library nor add to the concerns he had at this busy season of the year.

"Valéry, do you expect me to believe your story?"

"You can ask the viscount, Paul. He will tell you that he gave me his permission to find the book in his room."

"The viscount is a tenderhearted and generous man, Valéry, and he is fond of you. I have no doubt that he told you what you say he did. However, your breeding should have taught you that it is never appropriate to enter without permission the chambers of someone of his standing in society, and especially without the permission of his wife."

"I realize that now, Paul, and I am so very sorry. My presence upset the viscountess and also the housekeeper, who seems to have a special bond with Madame de Clairac. I did apologize, but it was not accepted. Odile accused me of deceit, and Marthe called me crass and ill-mannered scum."

"As I understand it, Valéry, that was only *after* you said what you said to the viscountess. It was not your place to tell her she was self-centered and vain and to insinuate that she was jealous of the attentions the viscount and I gave to you."

"But that is true, and you know it, monsieur."

"Valéry, I am very disappointed in you. Perhaps Madame Thibault was right when she said you were crass and ill-mannered. I would have thought that you had more character than what you showed."

"Again, I am sorry that I said what I did. It cannot be undone, and now I have to live with the consequences, which your housekeeper assured me would be severe."

"They have asked me to dismiss you, Valéry."

"And are you going to do that?"

The baron got up and walked toward the fireplace where he stood for a few minutes, looking down at the blazing logs. When he turned toward her, he said, "You have given me cause to, Valéry. Perhaps if you tell me the real reason why you were in the de Clairac chambers, I will be persuaded to rethink any such action."

Valéry rose from her chair and came close enough to look the baron full in the face.

"Régis and I discovered that the valuable Bible was missing from the library, monsieur. He had brought up the stand for it, and it was then that we unwrapped what we thought was the Bible and found that a book the same size had been put in its place."

"I should have been notified immediately, mademoiselle. It is my property and my loss, and a valuable one at that."

"I know that, my lord, but Régis and I thought that maybe someone had just borrowed it, and we did not want to bother you until we knew for sure that it was truly missing. That is why I was looking in the viscount's chambers, and I also looked in the other bedrooms along the hall, but with no luck. Surely, you can understand that I was very upset and also afraid, and that my actions can be understood in that light."

Valéry's voice shook, and tears filled her eyes. She had not seen the baron look so formidable since he had first come upon her after her arrival at the chateau.

"What were you afraid of, Valéry?"

"I was afraid of *you*, my lord. You have never given me any assurance that I can remain in my post. You have often reminded me that I am still on trial. Now, I have failed to safeguard the most valuable book in your library."

"To guard the library collection was not part of the duties I gave you, mademoiselle. I do not hold you responsible for the missing manuscript. What I do hold you responsible for is your inexcusable behavior toward the viscountess de Clairac."

"She hates me, my lord." Valéry was both angry and hurt. "Look at my face. It is badly bruised. That is where she hit me and then spit at me. I am not of the nobility, and I have no standing in your world of highborn rank and privilege, but I do have pride, and I will not tolerate being mistreated, not by Odile, not by Marthe, not by Bruno, and not by you, Baron de Renard. I am tired of it all. I will spare you the trouble of trying to decide whether I am worthy of my position here. I will leave."

Before the baron could reply, Valéry took his hand and placed the book of hours in it. "I do not want something I am so clearly unworthy of, so please take your gift back." Handing the scroll to him next, she said that it was the preliminary inventory she had completed and had planned to give him as a gift. As she left the room, she turned to him with one last comment.

"I am sure that you will find a much more acceptable librarian to complete the rest of the library work, Baron. And now, I must write to Marguerite and to pack. I hope you can take your noblesse oblige duties seriously enough to let me stay until Marguerite sends for me."

Valéry ran down the dark hallway and burst into her room, realizing as she did so that she must have forgotten to lock it before she left on her mission to find the baron. She locked and barred the door and then went over to her bed where she intended to curl up under the covers and try to still the shaking of her body. On the bed lay a folded piece of paper. Someone had obviously come into the room in her absence and left a message. The note was printed in large block letters. It read:

"Mademoiselle Valéry, when I was inspecting the underground tunnel to see how badly it was flooding, I saw a large package setting on top of the farthest corbel. I thought of the missing Bible immediately but did not have time to inspect further. However, if it is indeed the hiding place of the missing manuscript, I would recommend that you go there as soon as possible. The tunnel is filling with water very rapidly, and if it is the book, it will be ruined if not removed right away."

The note was signed "Regis."

Valéry rose from her bed and was just reaching for a wrap in her armoire when a tap came on the door. "I know you are there, Valéry, and I am not done talking with you. Please let me in."

Valéry did as she was told, looking at the baron with a tearstained face.

"Are you so distrusting that you needed to have the lock changed on your door and to place a bar across it when you are in the room, Valéry?"

"How did you know about the lock?" Valéry asked.

"My housekeeper was quite upset when she found she could not enter your room. I sought out Monsieur Guyot in Fauze, who confirmed that he had changed the lock at your request. You are upset that the viscountess called you deceitful, but how else would one describe this action?"

"You gave me permission to change anything about the room which did not suit me, my lord," Valéry replied with defiance. "It did not suit me to know your housekeeper, who has treated me with contempt ever since I arrived, had access to my room when I was not in it. Besides, I am very leery of not feeling safe in my own chamber. I once had a very upsetting experience when I was living in the chateau at Nérac."

"And what was that, mademoiselle?"

"Clément Marot tried to rape me."

The baron looked at her in disbelief. "Marot, the poet?"

"The very same," Valéry replied.

The baron looked at her for a very long minute and then said, "And do you think that I too would be capable of such a despicable act, Valéry?"

When she did not answer, the baron put his hand gently on her cheek and, drawing her near, brushed the bruised skin with his lips. "I am sorry that Odile struck you, Valéry. I know how volatile she can be, but striking you was cruel and completely unacceptable." He paused and took a deep breath. "So too were my words to you in the aftermath. You are upset now, so we will talk more about this after the Twelfth Night banquet. I would like for you to be there. Will you promise me that you will come?"

"I do not feel like celebrating, but yes, I will come. After all, it would be abysmally crass and ill-mannered of me if I didn't, wouldn't it? And I am sure it would give you yet one more opportunity to chastise me."

"It would make me quite sad not to have your presence at the fête, Valéry. You may not believe this, but the viscount isn't the only one who has grown very fond of you."

As the baron walked back down the hall, Valéry closed the door and went over to her armoire. She decided to wrap herself in an old thick shawl instead of her good cloak, which she did not want to be ruined by the rain. Then she quietly let herself out of the room and locked the door, dropping the key into her skirt pocket. She descended the dark staircase and left the chateau unobserved, making her way to the underground passage and, she hoped, the Bible inside. Yes, Paul knew now that it was missing, and yes, he *said* that he did not blame her. The fact remained, though, that it had disappeared while she was the librarian. She wanted to do everything she could to make sure that it would be found and placed where it belonged while she was still in charge of the books.

Chapter Twenty-Two

Due to the heavy rain, which obliterated any light from the heavens, Valéry had to navigate the terrain almost from memory. The saturated ground underneath her feet made her progress even more difficult. Once across the courtyard and outside the balustrade, she was grateful for the light coming through the windows of the print shop. Bruno was probably working late again, but at what, she could only guess. His oil lamp, though, shed enough light for her to see the large stone slab partially open over the entrance to the underground tunnel. Squeezing through, she negotiated the slippery stairs, her fingers finding a hold between the cracks of the stones lining the wall.

She descended into what became total darkness and was dismayed when she found that the last stair was totally underwater. With the next step, the water reached her knees, and by the time her hands found the first overhead corbel, she was submerged up to her waist. The fat candle was still on the small shelf, and once lit, she could see ahead to the next corbel, which also held a candle. Because the floor of the passage sloped downward, the water got deeper and deeper as she struggled to reach each successive ledge and light the candle on it. Soon her shawl and skirts were waterlogged and such a drag to her progress that she removed them, continuing in her chemise and light underskirt. By the time she reached the end of the tunnel, the water reached just under her chin, and her feet no longer touched the bottom. Clinging to the ledge of the last corbel, she lifted herself up enough to run her fingers over the surface. It was totally empty. There was no candle. Worse still, there was no book.

She hung tightly to the stone surface projecting from the wall and tried to think through the implications. Perhaps Régis had been able to return and retrieve the package before the major flooding began. If so, the book was safe, but she was not. The water was continuing to rise at an alarming rate, and this meant that she would need to retrace quickly where she had just been and get out of the passageway before it was completely inundated. It was slow going, but she was able to grab at the bricks lining the walls and propel herself forward until her feet touched the stairs. Glancing up at the exit, which lay just above the water level, she let out a cry. Someone had completely closed the stone slab. For a minute or two, Valéry tried to get enough leverage to push up on it, but the limestone did not budge. Just then, the last candle was extinguished by the rising water, leaving Valéry in total darkness, and also, she realized full well, trapped.

Panic threatened to overcome her ability to be rational, but only for a moment. Her way of escape would have to lie at the other end of the *souterrain*. With an intense sense of urgency, she struggled through the rising waters until her hands once again found the last corbel. It was completely underwater, and her head scraped the barrel-vaulted arch of the ceiling. Pulling her body up high enough so that her knees rested on top of the last protruding ledge, she plunged headfirst into the drainage pipe just under the ceiling, which was already beginning to take some of the overflow from the flooding. Lying flat on her stomach, she grabbed the edges of the tiles lining the pipe and pulled herself forward. It was very slow going, but the passage was large enough so that her small frame moved unhindered. Soon, she could not feel her hands or her feet, and before long, the pain she had felt at first turned into numbness. After awhile, she discovered a rhythm whereby her arms pulled her forward while her legs pushed. There was no way of telling how far she had to go, but she knew she could not stop to rest, even for a moment, even when she began to cramp and shiver with the wet and cold. Already water began to flow around her body, and she knew she would have no time to spare in her effort to reach the end of the pipe. Two things occurred to hasten her resolve to press forward. First came the mental picture of herself entombed and not being discovered until someone wondered why the pipe was not draining. Next, when something clawed at her skull, pulling her matted hair, she had felt warm fur pass over her face and realized that there were rats trying to escape the deluge, just like she was. Far from feeling horror, she was encouraged. There must be enough oxygen ahead, and if they could find freedom, so could she.

Suddenly, she heard the sound of rain followed by a cold breeze in her face. One more effort to advance, and her head hung out the end of the pipe. She fell with a splash into the water of the basin, relieved that her feet touched bottom and her hands were able to grasp the stones lining the sides. She hauled herself onto the muddy ground and lay there exhausted, but only for a moment. She had not wanted to drown in the *souterrain* or to perish in the drainage pipe, and she certainly was not going to be found dead lying outside the chateau. Struggling to her feet, she stumbled toward the chateau, shivering uncontrollably from the cold and the trauma she'd just been through. Both the front and the side doors of the chateau had been barred, and there were no lights on the inside. Thinking quickly, she ran to the orchards behind, found a ladder propped up on a now-barren apple tree, and dragged it over to the wall. Once on the other side, it was only a short walk to the shed where blousons and trousers for the workers still hung on their pegs. Slipping out of her wet garments and stuffing them in one of the sacks, she donned dry work clothes, wiped her shoes on the material of the bag, and then pushed open the rickety wooden door, which gave her entry to the pantry.

Noiselessly, Valéry hurried through the kitchens, the back hallway, and up the rear staircase until she reached her landing. Only then did she realize that she had locked her door, and the key now lay in the skirt she had left in the flooded tunnel. But just as the underground passageway had an alternate way to get aboveground, so too did the library offer another way into her room. It was a very tight squeeze to get through the back of the cupboard, but she did it and then piled books in the library side of the cupboard before replacing the back panel.

By now her body was so numb and she so exhausted that she sought only the warmth of her fire, which still burned well. She wrapped up in a blanket and sat on the hearth until the shaking stopped and feeling began to come back into her frozen limbs. The water in the big kettle which hung on the *crémaillère* was deliciously hot. After fixing herself some tea, she washed in her basin, dumped the dirty water along with the sack containing her wet clothes and shoes down the chute, and then sat by the fire to comb-dry her hair. Soon the effects of her ordeal overpowered her. Wrapping herself once again in the blanket and lying down before the fire, a thought ever-so-lightly crossed her mind before she slept. Someone had *lured* her into the *souterrain*, deliberately sealed the entrance, and had left her there to die. She did not for a minute think it was Régis. But who, then, wanted her dead?

Chapter Twenty-Three

When Valéry opened her eyes again, the room was still dark. Sitting up, she poked the live embers in the fireplace and then added a new batch of kindling. When that caught, she placed several larger branches on the wood. Soon the fire blazed nicely, lighting and heating the room.

Valéry washed and dressed herself, glad that her trip through the pipe had left only black and blue marks and not any broken skin. She took great care not to make noise that would be audible outside the walls of her room, and she left the curtains drawn and the shutters closed. Whoever had tried to trap her in the tunnel just might be watching and listening for any signs of life coming from her chamber. They would want to assure themselves that she had not gotten out of her tomb alive. The door to her room remained locked, and the only remaining key lay in the small casket on the fireplace mantel.

Outside, rain pelted the windowpanes and clattered on the pointed slate roof of the *échauguette* next to her room. Below her she could hear commotion as preparations for that evening's Twelfth Night banquet were in full swing. She imagined the sommelier rolling in enough wine barrels to supply a king's army and the hunters depositing their venison, *sangliers*, and other wild game on the thick planks of the kitchen tables. The baking ovens with their fires ablaze would be stuffed with breads and cakes and pies of every description, and Marthe would keep Lisette so busy she would not have time to bring her usual breakfast tray. In the great hall, the baron's servants as well as some townspeople would be squeezing in tables and benches all over the room, and setting the head table with the finest white linen, pewter plates, and goblets. Images of Marguerite's fêtes came back to her, and these happy memories lifted her spirits.

As she ate from the provisions stocked up in her room, she began to work out her plan. If all went well, by the end of the evening, she hoped to know the identity of her would-be killer or killers. She did have enemies in the chateau, but who hated her enough to want her dead? The banquet, where everyone would be present, provided an ideal opportunity to find out. Initially, her most obvious enemy, Odile, could have plotted with Marthe to steal the Bible, hoping to use it in some way which would result in Valéry's removal as librarian. But if this were true, why did they not want its absence discovered immediately and Valéry blamed for the theft? Furthermore, if they had written the note that lured her into the underground passage knowing that she would trust a message from Régis, whose help did they get to seal her into the *souterrain*? Bruno's light had been burning in the print shop when she first entered the tunnel. Earlier, when she had burst in on him unannounced, he had shown fear. In addition, when she returned the inflammatory tracts to him, his anger was unmistakable. Perhaps it was he who hid the Bible for the viscountess and the housekeeper somewhere in his quarters and then later certainly would have had the strength to slide the slab over the tunnel's entryway. She would watch all three of them very carefully when she made her entrance to the great hall this evening. If indeed they were the culprits, then certainly their surprise at seeing her would prove their guilt. The rest of the day was spent reading and resting. About midafternoon, she heard a sound in the library but dared not try to see who it was. Whatever they had wanted did not take long, for she heard the library door open, footsteps sound on the floor, and then the door shut again, all within a minute or two. Perhaps they had only returned a book to the library table. She held her breath when the footsteps paused by her door, but whoever it was did not knock, and soon she heard the steps fading away down the hallway.

As villagers began to arrive and the noise level in the courtyard and ground floors of the chateau rose, Valery got ready for the banquet. In the armoire, she pulled out her best dress, a claret-colored, richly embroidered gown Marguerite had given her before she left Nérac. She slipped into its soft folds, glad that none of the bruises she sustained the night before were visible. Standing before the mirror over the fireplace, she brushed her long black tresses, snatching them up with tiny tortoiseshell combs. Then she opened the casket on the mantle and withdrew the necklace, whose tiny gold hands clasped garnets the exact color of her gown. Surveying herself in the mirror, the décolletage of the bodice showed off well the exquisite piece of jewelry her mother had given her so long ago.

She waited until the noise in the courtyard had subsided and the voices from inside the chateau indicated that most of the guests were gathered by now. Then, unlocking her door, she headed down the marble staircase and into the great hall.

Villagers were seated at the dozens of long tables, helping themselves to the platters laden with food of all kinds and obviously having a good time. The noise was almost deafening. At the head table, which was placed on a dais, the baron sat in the middle, flanked by Odile to his right and Charles to his left. Philibert was seated next to the vacant chair by the viscount, which no doubt was intended for Valéry, and Sidonie looked happy as she talked with Régis, Lisette, and Lucien. Jules was next to his mother, with Marthe and Thomas Thibault just by him. *Père* Pierre and Bruno completed those seated at the master table. Although it would be hard for the priest not to be able to talk with his table companion, Valéry couldn't help but feel that it was a mercy since the two would certainly have had significant differences concerning the church.

As she mounted the platform, the baron rose to help her be seated. She smiled at Philibert as she slid into her place next to him but was startled when he suddenly let out a gasp, turned very pale, and then collapsed on the floor. Odile, who had leaned over to see what had happened, stared down at her husband's manservant and then looked up at Valéry. For a minute, the viscountess held her gaze, and then suddenly, she jumped up from her seat and, pointing at Valéry's necklace, began to scream. The baron and the viscount, who were leaning over Philibert, straightened up in time to see Odile lunge toward Valéry, her hands pulling at the necklace while she yelled, "That's what you stole from my room, you thieving peasant. That is my necklace." Then she turned toward the housekeeper, saying, "See, Marthe. You were there when we caught her going through my things. She has taken my necklace. Look, it matches exactly the earrings I am wearing."

To her amazement, Valéry looked at the garnets held by delicate gold hands dangling from the viscountess's ears. She was right, the earrings and the necklace were identical. Before she could even wonder why, Odile yanked so hard on the necklace that the clasp dug into Valéry's neck, drawing blood but refusing to give. Valéry cried out in pain and tried to loosen Odile's grip, but in vain. As she looked into the contorted face of the wild woman, she could not contain her own anger.

"You liar! This is my necklace, given to me many years ago by my mother. Queen Marguerite has seen me wear it, so I couldn't have taken it from your room." Valéry could not believe that it was her voice yelling back at the viscountess, for she had never raised it like that before.

By then, Philibert had recovered enough for the viscount to help him to his room, and the baron, with the aid of Jules, managed to separate the two women. While Jules tried to calm his overwrought mother, the baron had

Valéry sit down while he dipped his serviette into some water and dabbed at the wound on Valéry's neck until it stopped bleeding. Next, he turned his attentions to Jules, who had not been able to subdue his mother. She was screaming uncontrollably while pounding her son's chest with her fists. The baron instructed him to take her up to her apartments, and to Valéry, he suggested that she return to her room to minister to the cut on her neck.

"If you are not too hurt, Valéry, please come back so you can enjoy the rest of the evening. I would escort you myself, but I think it best not to leave my guests just now. They have been watching us with some degree of alarm and interest, I fear!"

As Valéry left, the baron rose and, in a loud voice, said, "Come, my friends, let us return to our feasting. This has been only a minor misunderstanding, and it is over now. I propose a toast to all those who have helped make my estate and our village prosper this past year. *Salut, salut!*"

At the baron's bidding, the crowd began to cheer, and soon the merriment and celebration continued as if nothing had happened.

Valéry climbed the marble staircase somewhat unsteadily, meeting the viscount on his way down.

"How is Philibert, monsieur?"

"I am afraid that all the excitement was just too much for him, Valéry. But he is lying down now and feels much better. It is you I am worried about, little one. My wife's actions are beyond my understanding. I have never seen her wear that necklace, and what caused her outburst is thus a mystery to me. I hope she has come to her senses by now."

"She was still very upset, so at the baron's suggestion, Jules has taken her up to your apartments," Valéry replied.

"And you too, little mademoiselle, have to return to your chamber to tend to your wound. I must go back to the banquet as I think the baron will have need of my presence in reassuring the gathering that all is well now."

Back in her own room, Valéry removed the necklace and, dipping a piece of cloth into the hot water in the cauldron, tried to clean the blood from her neck as well as from the clasp. She was just returning the jewelry to its casket when she heard steps outside her door.

"Who's there?" she called out. When nobody answered, she hurried to the door just as a slip of paper was passed under it. She grabbed it and hurriedly tucked it into her bodice while opening the door in hopes of catching the person. A figure retreated into the darkness, and then she heard a door close. She rushed down the shadowy corridor, pausing to knock softly on Philibert's door. There was no answer. Perhaps he had not heard the knock as he was growing quite deaf, but if he was resting, she did not want to disturb him either by knocking more loudly or even opening his door.

The adjacent room was Jules's, and the door stood open, revealing that it was empty. Perhaps he was in with his mother. Her heart pounded as she knocked on the massive doors of the Jean le Bon chamber. Then she pushed the doors open. It too was deserted.

This left the door which led to the spiral staircase in the north tower. It was possible that whoever had slipped the note under her door had retreated this way. Opening the door, she stepped through to the curving stairs, holding on to the newel post as she descended. As she rounded the first turn, she stopped in her tracks and screamed. Before her, the body of Odile lay sprawled facedown over the winding steps, a pool of blood coming from under her neck.

For a moment, Valéry stood transfixed, staring at the horrible scene. Then, not knowing what else to do, she grabbed the bell cord by the newel post and pulled as hard as she could. The bell sounded, and within minutes, Philibert appeared above her on the stairway, where no doubt he had just come from his room. Below her, the baron, viscount, and Jules rushed up the steps, having heard the unusual ringing from the great hall. It was the baron who bent over the still figure on the stairs and, with some effort, turned it over. Valéry gasped. Odile's sightless eyes were wide open, and a knife protruded from her neck. The handle was of ebony, decorated with tiny hearts and arrows. It was her mother's knife.

The baron gently closed Odile's eyes, removed the knife from her throat, and held it up for inspection. "It is my mother's knife! I left it in the library when I cut open the stitches on the Bible wrapping. I don't understand. Who could have done this?" Suddenly feeling faint, Valéry sat down on the stairs, tears streaming down her cheeks. While the viscount and his stepson removed the body, the baron turned to Valéry. In a very soft voice, he said that he would return with her to her room where she could lie down. Drawing her up, he put his arm around her waist until they reached her door.

"It is unlocked," she explained to the baron. "With everybody downstairs, I did not see any need to lock it."

The baron helped her inside and insisted that she lie down immediately. After covering her with a blanket, he sat down beside her and stroked her forehead.

"Valéry, I know that you could not possibly have committed this crime. Perhaps whoever did meant to place the blame on you by using your knife, but why anyone would believe that if you had done it, you would have been stupid enough to use your own knife is beyond me. I must return soon to the banquet, but I want to make sure that you will be safe. Where is the key to your room?"

"I had two keys, Paul, but one was lost in the *souterrain*. The only other one is in the little casket on top the mantel."

The baron opened the lid and reached in, fumbling at first with the necklace and then finding the key. As he walked to the door, he said he would lock Valéry in for her own safety, explaining that she might be tempted to open the door to someone she falsely trusted if she had the key. "But be sure you bar the door anyway," he added. Then, as Valéry rose from her bed, he paused and frowned.

"You said that the first key was lost in the *souterrain*. How did that happen?"

"Last night, someone placed a note on my bed, saying that there was a package on the last corbel in the tunnel and that it might be the missing Bible, and because the passageway was flooding, I needed to look there immediately. But I found no package, and when I tried to go back up the steps, someone had moved the stone slab over the exit. I would have drowned in the rising water if I hadn't been able to crawl through the drainage pipe into the basin at the other end. If you need proof of this, I think you will find my shawl and skirt, with the key in it, on the floor of the *souterrain* after the water recedes. I had to remove them as they were waterlogged." When the baron looked horrified, she pushed up her sleeves to reveal the bruises on her arms and again began to cry.

Very gently, the baron put his arms around her and drew her close. Then he pulled back to look her in the face. "You will be safe tonight, Valéry, because nobody can gain entry to your room. I will talk to you first thing tomorrow, but tonight I want you to sleep well."

He took her face in both his hands and kissed her very softly before closing and locking the door behind him. Valéry slipped the bar into its metal brackets and began to undress. As she did so, the note slipped earlier under her door fell from her bodice. Taking it over to her desk, she sat down and began to read:

> *Au profond de la cassette usée*
> *Un grand trésor y est caché*
> *Mais ne vous y trompez pas*
> *Sous filigrane, les réponses sont là.*

The person who had written the poem must have been in a hurry as the letters looked carelessly formed. The message itself was obscure. Who had written it, and what could it possibly mean? Very slowly, she reread the verse:

Deep within the casket worn
Treasure hides as bright as morn
But don't be fooled by what's inside
'Neath filigree the answers hide.

All of a sudden, Valéry began to shake uncontrollably. She finished undressing and sought comfort beneath the covers of her bed. The rain continued to pound against her shutters, and the noise of the crowd below lasted well into the early morning hours, but try as she may, she could not sleep. Long after her tremors stopped, her mind kept turning over and over the events that had taken place and the questions which she could not resolve.

The first puzzle centered around the missing Bible. Why was it taken, a substitute put in its place, and then, when the deception was discovered, used as bait to lure her into the underground passageway? Not for a minute did she suspect that Régis had actually written the note, but then who had? Furthermore, her plan to find out who her would-be killer was had just added to the mystery as the only persons who had reacted to her presence in the great hall were Philibert, who fainted, and Odile, who lunged at her necklace. In regard to the former, it was impossible to believe that the aged and loyal retainer of the viscount would be capable of such a nefarious act, and besides, what could be his motive? But why, then, had he turned pale and fainted? As for Odile, the viscountess certainly hated her, but it seemed that it was the necklace which evoked her violent behavior and not any discernible surprise at seeing Valéry alive.

And therein lay the second puzzle. How could one explain that Valéry's necklace matched Odile's earrings? Obviously, both of them knew that Valéry had not stolen it, but even so, Odile had become enraged the minute she saw Valéry wearing it. Had her violent outburst been triggered by some underlying fear—and if so, what was it? By far the most disturbing puzzle, though, was the death of Odile. Had someone who knew about her mother's knife used it deliberately so that the finger of guilt would point to her? But who would justify taking a human life just to implicate her? Perhaps the murderer had a double purpose in the killing, wanting to get rid of Odile and at the same time having the blame fall on the baron's librarian. Perhaps it was one and the same person or persons who stole the Bible, lured her into the *souterrain,* and killed Odile, all in an effort to eliminate her one way or another.

Valéry went over and over the possible suspects. The viscount certainly did not love his difficult and temperamental wife, but Valéry found it impossible to believe that he would be capable of killing her and then take such pains to implicate Valéry, to whom he had shown such affection. Jules certainly was kept squashed under his mother's controlling nature, but he had been friendly to Valéry, realistic about his future, and made a remarkable effort to break away from Odile by pursuing an apprenticeship with Monsieur Faguet. Sidonie was far too meek to attempt such an act, and Philibert too feeble. She couldn't imagine any others of the chateau capable of such a crime, and certainly it wasn't Marthe because she appeared to be the only person who actually liked Odile.

Her last thoughts were of the cryptic verse someone had slipped under her door. She would worry about that later. When she finally slept, the rain had abated, and the sun's first rays were peeping over the horizon.

Chapter Twenty-Four

It was with some effort that Valéry rose the next morning, for her head ached, and the short hours of sleep had not relieved her fatigue. She had just finished dressing when the baron's voice called to her through the door, and then she heard him put the key in the lock.

"I am afraid that you did not obey my instructions, *ma chérie*, for you do not look like you slept very well." The baron kissed both her cheeks and then stepped over to place the key in the casket.

"I will be bold enough to speak the truth and say that you look even worse, Paul."

"Do I conclude, then, that this is a contest, and I have lost?"

Valéry laughed and felt a little better just being in the baron's presence. "My lord, at least *I* slept a little, but you are wearing the same clothes as last night and do not look like you have had any rest."

"You are quite perceptive and also quite right," the baron replied, sitting down at the desk and motioning for Valéry to sit in the large chair by the fire.

"After the banquet was over, the viscount and I kept vigil over the viscountess's body the rest of the night, and we had a chance to talk, Valéry. It is the viscount's conclusion that Odile tripped accidentally on the stairs and fell on the knife she was holding. If this is what actually happened, then there was no murder involved."

Valéry considered that theory for a moment but then commented that it did not explain what Odile was doing descending the spiral stairs with her mother's knife.

"We considered that and decided that after Jules had taken his mother to her apartments and then returned to the great hall, Odile had gone to the library where she knew your knife had been left, and in her insane rage intended to return to the banquet to try to cut the necklace from your neck.

How she thought she could get away with that, we could not fathom, but as angry as she was, she certainly was not being rational."

"But from my room, the closest way to the great hall is the marble staircase just off the south keep, Paul. She was found on the stairs in the north keep."

"The viscount's theory is that after his wife emerged from the library with the knife, she intended to use the marble stairway but heard voices coming from below her on these steps. She would want to avoid at all cost the possibility of meeting anyone because she knew she would be stopped from returning to the great hall. Thus she rushed down the hall to the north tower and chose the spiral staircase as an alternate way to reach her intended destination."

"But," Valéry added, "those voices were the viscount's on his way down the stairs after coming from Philibert's room and mine as I went up to my chamber. Wouldn't the viscountess realize who it was who was talking and thus know that I was no longer in the great hall?"

"Charles thinks that his wife could not possibly have distinguished whose voices she heard but, in her distraught state, just wanted to avoid meeting anyone who would not let her continue on to the great hall."

Valéry rose from her chair and went over to sit on the floor beside the baron, resting her head in his lap. It was all so overwhelming, and she knew she had nothing in her background which could help her sort out the confusing events which had so recently transpired. The baron stroked her hair, his fingers lightly tracing the wound on her neck inflicted by Odile the night before.

"Does this hurt?" he asked.

"Only when I move my head," Valéry replied.

The two sat for a few moments in silence, watching the flames in the fireplace dance about, mesmerizing their audience. Finally, the baron spoke.

"Valéry, I am going to have to leave for about a fortnight. The viscount wishes to hold his wife's funeral Mass in Clairac and then take her body to Paris for burial in the tomb which belongs to her side of the family. He has asked me to accompany him."

It took a few minutes for the baron's words to sink in, and when they did, Valéry went cold all over. Just the thought of being left without the baron's protection was frightening, and she said so.

"I would not leave you if I thought that you would be in danger," he stated simply.

Valéry rose to her feet and went to sit by the fire again.

"Paul, have you forgotten that someone stole the Bible and then used it to lure me into the underground passageway?"

"Charles and I are of the opinion that Odile was behind both those acts, Valéry. From the very start, she was bent on getting rid of you and very persistent in the ways she thought would work. From Marthe, she no doubt learned that your position as librarian was far from secure—initially, at least. But after awhile, when I had not dismissed you, she decided that hiding the Bible might prompt me to suspect you of stealing it."

"But what possible motive could I have had to do that?"

"My naïve little love, if you were about to lose your source of livelihood here, you would realize a sizeable amount of money from selling the Bible after you left."

"I would never be capable of such deceit, Paul, and besides, Queen Marguerite would help me find another position. It is hard for me to believe that Odile had such an evil heart."

Again there was silence. The baron leaned forward in his chair, resting his face in his hands. Valéry stared into the fire, barely able to untangle the questions which persisted without answers. When she spoke again, it was to ask why Odile had taken the trouble to substitute a book in the place of the missing Bible, for it only served to delay the discovery.

"For one thing, she needed time to hide the Bible in a place where any possible search would not turn it up. Just where that is will have to be pursued after I return. Obviously though, she might still have held out hope that I would find you inadequate in your position and remove you as librarian. If that happened, she would simply return the Bible with no one the wiser, but if it didn't happen, she knew it would be discovered missing when Régis installed the new stand for it in the library. She was always looking for ways she could accomplish her goal."

It was beginning to make sense to Valéry as she tried to put herself in Odile's place. "She would know from Jules, who helped Régis bring up the stand, that we would discover the substitution," Valéry said. "Do you think that Odile's anger at finding me in her chambers was because she guessed I was searching there for the Bible?"

"That very well could be," the baron replied. "If you suspected her of the theft, she would feel very threatened. Remember that she and Marthe asked me to dismiss you right after that."

"And when I returned to my room, I found the note, ostensibly written by Régis, telling me that there was a package in the underground passageway which might be where the Bible had been hidden. Odile could have written it and then placed it on my bed while you were telling me how I had erred in my actions."

The baron drew Valéry from her chair and held her close. After a moment, he spoke, "You do not realize how deeply I regret my behavior. You also need to hear how much I love you. I hope that helps to heal the scars I have inflicted on your heart, *dame de mon coeur.*" His lips were warm, and the kiss lasted long enough for Valéry to believe the truth behind his words.

Pulling away from him, she asked how Odile could possibly have moved the stone over the entryway to the *souterrain* after she was sure Valéry was inside. "She would have had to elicit the help of someone else, such as Bruno, who perhaps did not know that you were down there."

Valéry returned to her chair and sat down with a sigh. "You are being very generous to Bruno and to your housekeeper, my lord. I wish I shared your trust of them, but I do not. You are going to be leaving me at their mercy, if indeed they have been guilty of any complicity against me."

"I have asked Jules to keep an eye on Bruno, Valéry. The pressman would never come into the chateau, and I want you to remain in your room or the library while I am gone, and just as a precaution, you should not under any circumstances walk around the grounds. But I do not suspect Bruno of wanting to harm you. As for my housekeeper, she helped us prepare the body last night. It was a difficult task for her, and I did not feel the time was right to ask her about any involvement with Odile's agenda against you. However, before I leave, I promise you that I will make it clear to her that while I am gone, she is to take very good care of you, seeing to it that you get your meals and ministering to any other needs you may have that are related to her duties."

"Oh my God, Paul!" Valéry sprang from her chair and looked at the baron in disbelief. "This is a woman who hates me, and I am sure that is even more intensified, now that Odile is dead. Do you really think she will honor your request? I want nothing to do with her. She scares me."

Paul regarded her without speaking. His eyes had become the same cold gray Valéry remembered when she first arrived and had met with his disapproval.

"She is the only mother I have ever known, Valéry. I am aware that she can be bossy and controlling, but you have no right to question her loyalty to me."

Valéry looked at Paul, tears welling up in her eyes. "I can only hope that you are right, Monsieur le Baron, for my life may depend on it," she replied softly. "As for Bruno, I discovered that he has been printing off tracts against the Church on your press. He was angry enough to do me harm, I can assure you. I imagine he has not told you about his clandestine activity." Valéry was aware as she spoke that she was betraying a promise she had made to Bruno not to tell the baron about the tracts, but if he had been angry enough to help Odile seal her into the *souterrain,* then the baron needed to know about the pamphlets.

Paul betrayed by his looks that he had known nothing about Bruno's tracts. To Valéry he said only that she would be protected from Bruno and that Marthe would obey his orders.

With that, he stood up and walked toward the door, pausing long enough to reach into his pocket and pull out the earrings and the knife. "The viscount wished me to give these to you" he said as he held out the earrings. "Obviously, they belong with the necklace, although neither of us can explain why they match. As for the knife, it should be returned to you. And now I need to prepare for the journey. I have asked Régis to accompany us as Jules insists he must remain here to welcome Monsieur Faguet when he returns. The viscount was upset about that, but he understands. Philibert has insisted on accompanying his master at least to Clairac, even though he is quite feeble, and the viscount has acquiesced. *Père* Pénicaut also will go with us as far as Clairac and then return after he has said the funeral Mass."

"What will become of Sidonie, and who will watch over Lucien and Lisette while their father is gone?" Valéry was mentally making note of those who would remain behind.

The baron came over to give her a reassuring pat on the shoulder. "I have taken Sidonie into my employ. It was the wish of Régis that she spend nights with his two children in Eauze, but all three of them will continue to work at the chateau during the days we are gone."

Valéry watched him as he left, her emotions in turmoil over his professed love for her but then his seemingly coldhearted dismissal of her concerns about Bruno and Marthe. It was several hours later when she saw the entourage leave the chateau, the five men on horseback, with two mules to pull the litter carrying the coffin. It was only then that she realized she had not told the baron about the cryptic verse that had been slipped under her door. It was no matter, though, for it did not seem threatening, and her love for the baron made her realize that he had been tired beyond belief and simply trying to manage as best he could a situation that was heartbreaking.

Chapter Twenty-Five

That evening, a tap on the door was followed by Sidonie's voice, saying she had brought Valéry's dinner. Far from looking distraught at the loss of her mistress, Sidonie had a smile on her face, and her eyes sparkled.

"You know, Mademoiselle Valéry, that my Régis has accompanied the viscount and the baron to Clairac, don't you?"

"Yes, the baron told me that before he left, Sidonie."

"I cannot pretend that I am sad over the viscountess's death," Sidonie continued. "In fact, I feel very relieved."

"And also quite happy, judging by the look on your face," Valéry observed, smiling.

"Well, I am not happy that she died the way she did, but oh, mademoiselle, something wonderful has happened because the baron has asked me to stay on in his employ. I can help here in the chateau and also be near Régis and to his children, whom I have come to love as my own."

Valéry gave her a hug and then took the food tray. "Did the housekeeper prepare this for me, Sidonie, or did she order you to do it? I am afraid she can be a very difficult woman, just like your former mistress."

"When she handed the tray to me, it was already dished up, so I guess she got the food from the meal the cooks had prepared. Her only instructions were that I was to bring it directly to you. As for her being difficult, I know from what Lisette has said that Madame Thibault seems to enjoy being bossy and controlling."

Valéry nodded at the maidservant, and added, "I think that Marthe Thibault as well as the viscountess had that in common. Theirs was a strange relationship, Sidonie, two strong-minded women united by their hatred of me.

Sidonie agreed adding that she hoped now that her mistress was out of the picture, Madame Thibault would act more agreeably toward both of them.

After the maidservant left, Valéry sat down to eat, but her fatigue, both emotional and physical, left her with little appetite. She picked at her food but then left the tray and got ready for bed. She fell asleep almost immediately but was awakened soon afterwards with terrible cramping in her stomach. Soon she was writhing in some degree of pain and spent a very uncomfortable night. By morning she felt a little better, so when Lisette brought her breakfast, she was able to eat most of it. After dressing, she decided to work on the cataloguing which still remained. The list was growing, but many of the manuscripts were quite old and often very hard to read, making categorizing difficult and her progress slow. About midmorning, she stood up and stretched, walking to the window to look down on the courtyard. All of a sudden, Bruno and Jules rushed out of the print shop and headed up the avenue of sycamores. Following their progress, she spotted someone riding toward them. As he drew closer, she recognized Arsène Faguet on his horse, which in turn pulled a small heavily loaded cart. The journeyman printer had returned.

Her first impulse was to rush down to greet him also, but then she remembered the admonishment of the baron not to walk on the grounds. The greeting between the men looked enthusiastic, and soon Lucien had taken Arsène's horse, and the three men pulled the cart through the *imprimerie* doors.

A night of sickness had left Valéry quite tired, and so she lay down for a nap before returning around midday to her library work. It was there that Jules found her bending over the parchment papers of her inventory.

"*Bonjour,* mademoiselle." He came over to sit across from Valéry at the library table. "I came to let you know that Monsieur Faguet has just returned and brought with him some elegant new font, a huge supply of paper, and much more. We have been finding places for it all and hearing about his journey."

"Yes, I saw him return," Valéry replied, studying the young man's face intently. If his mother's untimely death had had any effect on him at all, it did not show, for he looked well-rested and excited.

"I was surprised that you did not accompany your mother's body to the de Clairac chateau, Jules. The baron told me that your stepfather was disappointed but that he understood."

"Well, I needed to be here, didn't I, for the imminent return of Monsieur Faguet?" Jules replied, his voice rising as he spoke. After a slight pause in which he tried to compose himself, he added, "As you know, my mother was a thorn in my flesh, and my stepfather never did offer me the future she had wanted for me. What lies behind needs to be left there. I have broken with it and am concentrating on my new life as an apprentice."

He did not smile and was obviously annoyed and perhaps a little angry that Valéry had said anything about his failure to go with his stepfather to Clairac.

"I did not mean to judge you, Jules, or to put you on the defensive. I am sure the viscount has more than enough help from Philibert, Régis, and the baron, and I am glad that *Père* Pénicaut will be officiating at the funeral Mass." Then, sensing that the subject needed to be changed, she asked Jules about the plans which were being made now in the print shop.

"That is another reason why I have come. Monsieur Faguet wishes to look over the new inventory on which you are presently working." He pointed to the sheets of paper and asked if the baron had seen them yet.

"No," Valéry answered, "and I am afraid it will be some time before they will be completed. But I would be glad to send over what I have done so far as long as Arsène doesn't keep them too long. I will be spending the weeks during the baron's absence trying to get as much done on the inventory as I can."

Jules indicated that he would return them in a timely manner. Then he looked as though he wanted to say something else but instead just sat looking at her.

"Is there something the matter, Jules?" Valéry sensed some sort of discomfort in the handsome young man across from her.

"You may think me totally without propriety, Valéry, but since the baron is gone, this may be the only opportunity I have to say what I need to say to you."

"And what would that be, Jules?" Valéry felt a little tense but waited patiently for him to express himself.

"I had hoped that my interest in you would be reciprocated, and that there might be a future for us. You are, after all, of as low a station in society as I, but soon I hope to have a trade and a comfortable income in the printing business." He paused here and looked embarrassed but then continued. "However, I am not blind, and I know that the baron has his eyes on you. I don't know whether he will be willing to marry below his rank, but on the chance that he is not, then I want you to know how I feel."

Valéry was not so much surprised at his admission as she was caught off guard. Certainly, Jules had shown his attraction to her from their very first meeting, but for many weeks now, he had been spending time elsewhere and appeared to be totally absorbed with whatever assignments Arsène had given him. She replied that she was flattered at his interest in her, but that she was afraid she could not return his feeling and hoped he would understand and not hold it against her.

"I am really not surprised at your reaction," he said to her as he gathered up the inventory list and prepared to leave. "I ask only that you keep in mind what I have said."

Valéry returned to her room just as Lisette came down the hall with her food tray. "Sidonie and I are taking turns making sure that you are fed, Mademoiselle Valéry," the girl smiled brightly at her. "She is also seeing to it that Lucien and I are all right while Papa is away."

"Yes, I have heard that she will be living with you until your father returns," said Valéry. "You like her, don't you, Lisette?"

"Oh, mademoiselle, she is so nice to us, and I know that she and Papa like each other quite a lot. Lucien and I are hoping that they will get married and that we will have a mother again." Lisette covered the smile on her lips with her hand, looking at Valéry as though she hoped she hadn't said something she shouldn't have.

Valéry took the tray and set it down on the little table by her bed and then went over to hug the girl.

"I am not totally without eyes, Lisette, and we both have seen how Régis shows up after every class session to walk with Sidonie back to the chateau. It is wonderful to see them so happy, especially after your father spent years mourning the loss of your mother, and Sidonie suffered so much at the hands of the viscountess. I too am hoping that there will be a wedding."

"I miss those classes, mademoiselle. I know they had to be suspended when the Twelfth Night celebrations began, and now too since Père Pierre is gone with Papa to Clairac. But do you think that we can begin them again after our priest gets back?"

"I am sure we can, Lisette, and I too will look forward to it."

After the girl had left, Valéry sat down to eat her meal, but she was only partway through when the stomach pains began again. She could not imagine what was wrong. The food smelled just fine and was quite tasty. Perhaps she had caught some little illness due to all the upsetting events which the last days had brought. She pushed the tray away and went to lie down. She would be better again in the morning, but in the meantime, she dreaded the thought of another night of suffering.

Again, she slept only a little, but when she finally rose to a new day, she still felt quite sick. When Sidonie knocked announcing her breakfast, she had barely opened the door when she collapsed on the floor. Sidonie was alarmed, setting the tray down beside Valéry and bending over her in concern.

"I have been feeling ill these past two nights," she explained to the chambermaid. "I cannot imagine what is wrong, but my stomach pains seem to begin after I have eaten dinner."

"I will tell Madame Thibault right away, Mademoiselle Valéry, and she will surely send for the village doctor. Here, let me help you into bed, and I want you to promise me you will stay there until he comes."

Taking the untouched breakfast tray as well as the one from dinner the evening before, Sidonie left the room in a hurry. Valéry felt too weak to do anything other than moan with the cramps in her abdomen. She realized that she needed to lock her door or at least bar it but was afraid that she would fall again if she tried. What seemed like a very long time passed, and nobody came. Valéry began to have a hard time breathing, and this frightened her. Where was Sidonie? She fervently hoped that the doctor would arrive soon, but nobody came.

After awhile, her breathing became easier, and encouraged by that, she struggled out of bed and walked somewhat unsteadily to her little jars of various herbs and other provisions, searching for something which might ease her discomfort. What had her mother given her as a child? She seemed to remember crushed rosemary leaves and so poured some into a cup and added hot water from the pot in the fireplace. After a few minutes, she began to feel a little better but went back to bed just the same.

She must have slept, for when she opened her eyes again, it was dark outside. The smell of food prompted her to glance at the bedside table. Someone had placed her dinner tray there while she slept and thus must have entered through her unlocked door. Fighting dizziness and shivering from cold sweats, it was only through great effort that she got out of bed and went over to the casket to find the key. The necklace and earrings still lay nestled amid the folds of velvet, but the key was not there. Glancing toward her entryway, she noticed with alarm that the bar also was missing.

The fire by now had burned down to embers, but there was still enough wood for Valéry to coax it back to life. How she wished she could do the same for herself. Somehow, she would have to figure out a way to get some help. The only person she could think of who was close by and who she trusted was Jules. Perhaps he was still in the print shop with Arsène and Bruno. She looked out the window but saw no light coming from the *imprimerie*. Perhaps Jules had returned to his room down the hall. She didn't know if she had the strength to walk that far, but she wrapped herself in a shawl and went over to open the door. The handle turned, but the door did not give. Whoever had taken the key had locked her in.

Valéry tried not to panic. She had been through a dangerous time in the flooded *souterrain* and had survived by using her head. She would do the same now. Crawling back under the covers of her bed, she tried to control her shaking. The rosemary tea seemed to have helped her nausea, but she still felt horrible and very weak.

Suddenly she heard a key in her lock, and the door opened. Marthe Thibault stood over the bed, looking down at her. "You have not touched your meal," she commented in a cold voice. "You must eat, do you hear me?"

"I do not feel well enough to keep anything down, Madame Thibault. Sidonie told me that she would tell you that I was sick and have you send for a doctor."

"I sent Sidonie into Eauze to take care of Lucien and Lisette after I assured her that I would tend to you, and so I am. I am sure that there is nothing the matter with you that cannot be rectified by rest and good nourishment. The baron requested that I be the one to take care of you, and I am doing that. I demand that you sit up and eat the meal I have prepared for you."

"Madame Thibault, I am too ill to eat, and I insist that you send for a doctor immediately. I cannot understand why you did not do that earlier when Sidonie told you about me unless, of course, you want me to suffer. Do you realize that if you do not summon a doctor and something happens to me, Sidonie will tell the baron that she asked you to send for the doctor and you did not? The baron can easily check that by asking the doctor in Eauze if you asked him to come."

The housekeeper paused by the door and turned back to look at Valéry with a sneer.

"I will bring you your breakfast in the morning, mademoiselle, and assess then if you need a doctor or not."

"That very well may be too late," Valéry replied as firmly as she could muster, then adding, "and if you will not do as I ask, I shall have to go to Jules or even Monsieur Faguet for their help."

The housekeeper threw back her head and snorted, "And how do you think you will do that, locked in your room and as sick as you are? Besides, my husband has taken Jules, Bruno, and Arsène into Condom for several days as he knows some possible outlets there for books they might be publishing in the future."

Valéry fought a profound feeling of hopelessness rising up within her but made one last effort to win any ground she could in her favor.

"Then I must demand from you the key you stole from my jewelry box, madame. You have no right to make me a prisoner in my own room."

"I will lock you in for your own protection against yourself, you little fool. Obviously you must be prevented from taking any rash action that might come into your fevered mind. And *that*, mademoiselle, is what I will tell the baron."

With that, she stepped outside and locked the door behind her.

Chapter Twenty-Six

The night air was not as cold as Valéry had anticipated, and she was grateful for the clear skies, lit by a myriad of stars and a full moon. At least she could see the road ahead of her with no trouble, and she knew where she was going because she had traveled that way before, only in the opposite direction.

After Marthe left her locked in her room, she realized that remaining any longer at the mercy of the housekeeper would endanger her very life. That thought gave her an energy of which she did not know she was capable. Despite her illness, she had managed to dress warmly, place the cryptic poem and her mother's knife into the casket and then, tucking it into the pocket of her cape, crawl through the cupboard into the library. She did not waste precious energy replacing the back panel or any of the manuscripts which hid her secret exit, for it would be wasted effort. When Marthe discovered her room empty the next morning, she would know right away that Valéry had another means of getting out of her room and would discover soon enough how she had escaped.

Once in the stables, she put a bridle on her horse but knew she did not have the strength to saddle him. Instead she threw a blanket over his back and, standing on a stool, mounted without too much trouble. Once clear of the avenue of sycamores, she turned the horse down the road which led to Eauze. How she wished she knew which house belonged to the Maguis family, but she did not. Besides, it was late at night, and even if she knocked on doors, the chances were that nobody would dare answer.

Her chills and cramping threatened to overwhelm her, but she found that by bending forward over the horse's neck, she could relieve the pain a little and benefit from the warmth of the animal. Marguerite had said that it should be only a few hours' journey, barring any adverse events like the ones that had befallen Valéry and the guardsmen when they had traveled this route. If all went well, she should arrive at the priory about the time the nuns were rising for vigils. There she would find sanctuary. There also, she could get the aid of Marguerite, who would surely send for a doctor, and when she had recovered, return with her to the chateau to seek the justice she deserved.

The horse kept breaking into a gallop, and although Valéry knew it would shorten the time of travel, she had a hard time holding on so often had to press her mount to slow down. The sounds of night creatures seemed to fill the shadowy countryside with urgent messages—piercing screeches of *hiboux* and the explosion of flapping wings as flocks of *corbeaux* took flight from their tree branches as she passed by. From the river's banks came the guttural croaking of *grenouilles*, and out of the fields, she recognized the high-pitched barks of foxes in their noctural pursuit of prey. Through this cacophony she strained to hear any sound that would signal the presence of other travelers on the road. Marguerite had often warned her about the dangers inherent on the highways—brigands who would set upon any unprotected journeyers, robbing them of their possessions and sometimes of their very lives. She thought of the baron and felt an almost indescribable yearning for his presence and protection in the midst of her affliction and fear. All of a sudden, she spotted a fox standing in the middle of the road ahead of her, his fur tinged with silver in the pale light of the moon. He did not move until Valéry was almost upon him but then disappeared into the blackness of the brush, only to reappear a few moments later, this time with illuminated eyes staring at her through the enveloping darkness. To her feverish brain the apparition of the fox blended with the features of the Baron de Renard, giving her a strangely comforting feeling that Paul was indeed with her, and would see to it that she arrived safely at her destination.

The *auberge* she had stopped at for refreshment on her way to Eauze was dark and no sound issued from within. Sometime later, she crossed the Gélise river, its water partially frozen from the chill of winter. There was no danger of flooding now. By the time she reached the priory, the bell for vigils was sounding and candlelight shown from the windows. With some effort Valéry found the gate bell and pulled on the rope. From deep within the building she heard faint footsteps and within a few minutes, the heavy door to the priory was opened.

Valéry tried to speak, but her voice sounded like it came from a long ways away.

"*Ma soeur, je cherche la reine* Marguerite de Navarre."

The nun replied that Queen Marguerite was no longer there, having left about a week ago for Paris at the summons of her brother the king.

198

"Je suis malade, ma soeur, et j'ai besoin d'aide. Aidez-moi, je vous prie."

What happened next Valéry did not know, for when she came back to consciousness, she was lying in a narrow bed, with the prioress seated in a chair next to her, holding her hand.

"You have been delirious, *mon petit oiseau. Soeur* Scholastique fetched me when you collapsed off your horse, and I recognized you right away as the young woman who accompanied Queen Marguerite last fall."

"Merci infiniment, ma mère," Valéry replied weakly. "I am so sorry to put you to any trouble, but I was in desperate need of help and I did not know where else to come. I was so hoping that Queen Marguerite would still be here."

"Child, do not waste your strength trying to explain. We are happy to take you in. I have called for our doctor, and in the meantime, you need to rest. Do you wish for any refreshment?"

"A little water, perhaps, but I am still in great discomfort and dare not try to eat anything."

The prioress poured a cup of water for her from the pitcher on the bedside stand and then propped up her head so that Valéry could drink. Afterwards, she closed her eyes again, fatigued by even that small amount of effort. The next thing she heard was voices coming from the hall, and then her door opened.

"Mademoiselle, Dr. Duclos has just arrived."

Valéry looked up into the face of an older gentleman, who bent over her, looking into her eyes first and then feeling her forehead.

"You have a fever, child, and look to be in pain. Please tell me what has happened."

Valéry described the violent reaction she had after eating two evening meals at the chateau. The doctor examined her abdomen, poking his fingers gingerly in the area of her stomach and other internal organs, asking Valéry if this or that hurt. After several other questions, he covered her back up and sat down beside her on the bed.

"My child, you have all the signs that you have been poisoned. I do not know whether this was the simple result of eating food that had gone bad, but whatever the cause, your body is now struggling to rid itself of that which seeks to destroy it. I am amazed that you were able to ride all this distance, but it appears that the crisis will soon pass, and you will recover, given time."

Before he left, he prescribed some medications to the prioress and gave her instructions as to their administration.

"I will look in upon you in several days, mademoiselle, but in the meantime, you must follow the regime I have outlined for the prioress." Then, pausing a minute, he walked back over to her bed and patted her head. "It has been a terrible thing for you to go through, I am sure, but you are young and otherwise in good health. The poison could have killed you, but given the right care, I want to reassure you that eventually you will be fine."

Valéry tried to smile and in a barely audible voice, thanked him for his services. Then she fell asleep again, but with a sense of peace which helped to ease her aching body and quiet her anxious mind.

The days ahead were a blur when Valéry tried to look back on them. She remembered remaining in bed and acquiescing to the ministrations of various sisters who tended to her. By the third day, she was able to take a little nourishment along with her medications, and toward the end of the week, she felt well enough to get up. Dr. Duclos returned and was quite satisfied with the progress she had made. He was also curious about the possibility that someone might have deliberately put poison in her food. Valéry told him about the housekeeper at the chateau and added that when she returned there, she would be so grateful if Baron Paul de Renard could come to talk with him about his diagnosis. She did not put it past Marthe Thibault to try to twist the truth about how she had handled Valéry's illness, plus she knew that Paul trusted his housekeeper.

The doctor replied that he would be more than willing to give his diagnosis of poison if it was needed. He said that long ago, he had known Baron Guillaume de Renard and had even been called to treat him once. The doctor added that he had held Guillaume in high regard and felt sure his son, Paul, was equally as fine a human being.

One day as Valéry sat in her little cell, trying to keep warm by the fire, she remembered the casket she had hastily stuffed in her cape pocket, unwilling to leave it behind to the mercies of the housekeeper. Her warm woolen mantle hung on a corner *porte manteau*, and Valéry was relieved to find the jewelry case with its precious contents still there.

Opening the lid, she pulled out the verse and slowly reread it.

> Deep within the casket worn
> Treasure hides as bright as morn
> But don't be fooled by what's inside
> 'Neath filigree the answers hide.

Who had put that note under her door remained a mystery, but obviously they had a reason for casting their message in such a cryptic form. Perhaps they feared that coming out with a straight message might endanger them in some way, and yet they wanted Valéry to discover something. The first two verses were clear enough, obviously referring to the precious necklace. But the next verse seemed to infer that focusing on the necklace was not what needed to be uncovered. There was important information which lay hidden and would provide the answers to some questions.

Valéry traced the letters of her name on the lid, recalling how she had done so as a child with her mother looking on. These were tender memories, which brought tears to her eyes. Wiping them away, she touched the lines of the gold scrollwork decorating the rest of the lid. This must be what the verse referred to as the filigree. She had always wondered why her name was off center and found it curious that half the lid was covered with the netting of gold. Taking her mother's knife, she carefully wedged the blade under the metal and tried to pry it loose. At first, the delicate gold tracery held tight, but with patience, it began to loosen until the entire network pulled free of the lid. Valéry looked in astonishment at what lay underneath. Next to the name Valéry was the surname de Clairac, and underneath it a cypher of the entwined letters *VC* lay next to small crest bearing an open left palm and the Latin motto *Valere et clarere*. Valéry remembered talking about the de Clairac blazon with the viscount, commenting on how appropriate the motto was because he was indeed both strong and distinguished.

The fire cracked and a log dropped, sending sparks onto the hearth next to Valéry's shoes. She put them out with her leather soles, puzzling over what her new discovery could possibly mean. How did her father come to possess the valuable casket which bore not only the name Valéry, but the *VC* cypher and the coat of arms and motto of the de Clairac family? Examining the tiny gold hands of the necklace, she realized that they were all left hands which held the garnet stones. A further mystery was why Odile had the matching earrings and not the necklace but had reacted so violently when she saw it on Valéry.

Thinking back to the little wisps of information her mother had shared with her young daughter so many years before, Valéry remembered that Etienne Lefèvre d'Etaples, her father, had fought in the Battle of Marignano where he was killed. So too had Jules's father, who also perished there. Perhaps they had known each other, and even more intriguing, maybe they had met Charles de Clairac and his older brother, who fought in the same battle. Had the casket with the necklace been given as a gift to her father for some favor performed for the de Clairac family before they all went off to fight for King François? Perhaps her father had *Valéry* added to the jasper lid and then got an artisan to cover up the cypher and de Clairac coat of arms with the scrollwork so that the casket was personalized especially for his baby girl. Her mother never told her any of the details about how her husband had acquired the box and the necklace. As for the matching earrings, perhaps if Charles de Clairac wanted to give her father a gift in payment for some important service he had rendered, he had taken the casket and put the necklace in it, but then let his wife, Odile, keep the earrings to appease her loss of the more valuable piece of jewelry. If that were true, no wonder Odile had become so upset when she saw the necklace, for it had once rightfully belonged to her. But then Valéry remembered that the viscount had been baffled by his wife's outburst when she saw the necklace on Valery, saying that he'd never seen Odile wear it.

For the rest of the day, she puzzled over the problem, which included trying to figure out just who had written the cryptic poem. The viscount, whom she'd met coming down the marble staircase that fateful night, was headed for the great hall, so perhaps he had just slipped the note under her door after leaving his servant to recover in his room. After awhile, Valéry realized she simply did not have enough information to untangle the mysteries which still remained. When it was safe for her to return to the chateau, she would approach the viscount in hopes of getting some answers. The only thing which seemed clear at the moment was that she had been right to be fearful of the housekeeper. Paul became upset with her for even questioning the woman's loyalty to him, but someone had put the poison in her food, and Marthe was the logical suspect, for she had direct access to her meals and hated her. One way or another, the patchwork scraps of suspicion and guilt needed to be arranged in such a way that their pattern would be revealed, and she was more than ready to begin sewing those pieces together.

At the end of the second week, Valéry was feeling quite herself again. She said so to the prioress and discussed with her the possibility that she might be able to go back to the chateau soon. By now, Paul and his entourage should have returned from Paris, and it would once again be safe for her there.

The prioress wanted the doctor's approval before dismissing her charge and also expressed concern over Valéry traveling alone on the return trip. It was the doctor who not only pronounced her fit but also offered to accompany her to Eauze where he planned to restock his supply of medicines. Besides, he told her with a smile, it would be pleasant to make the acquaintance of Baron Guillaume's son, who had been but a small child at the time he knew Baron Guillaume.

Several days later, Valéry bid the nuns farewell, thanking them for nursing her back to health and in addition adding her gratefulness for the sanctuary they also had provided for her beloved Marguerite in her time of need.

The return journey was much more enjoyable than either of her other trips along that road. The doctor insisted that she stop and rest at the *auberge*, but after an hour, they continued along the way, reaching Eauze by midafternoon. Dr. Duclos knew the town doctor and said he would stay with him while he made the purchases he needed and then assured her that he would not leave before seeing the baron.

Valéry decided to drop in on Monsieur Guyot, who had been so nice to her when he replaced her lock and let her buy the other supplies. She found him at work over the forge.

"*Bonjour,* monsieur," she called out. "Do you remember me?"

"*Bien sûr,*" he replied, wiping his hands on the front of his apron and coming toward her with a smile. "How is the lock working?"

"It has done its job without any problems, monsieur," Valéry replied, thinking wryly that he would be surprised to know the ways in which it had figured into her life at the chateau.

"It has been awhile since I have seen you, mademoiselle. Is there something which I can help you with today?"

"I do not want to purchase anything right now, Monsieur Guyot, but I do need to ask you a question. Could you tell me where Régis Maguis and his children live? I would like to stop there before returning to the chateau, and I have never known which house is theirs."

"That is easily answered," the blacksmith replied, taking her outside to point down a road on her right. "Their house is the second one once you turn onto the next street."

Valéry thanked him and remounted her horse, a task made easier due to the pillion saddle the doctor had provided before they left the priory. She was anxious to find out for sure whether Paul was back, for if he was still gone, she would have to find somewhere else to lodge for the moment.

No one answered when she knocked on the door, and looking into the windows, the house appeared deserted. Most probably, if Régis were back, he and his children, plus Sidonie, would be working at the chateau.

Thinking quickly, she rode on until she reached St. Luperc, hoping at least to find *Père* Pierre. It was a huge relief to come upon him reading by the fire in the sacristy. He rose as she entered and immediately threw his arms in the air and rushed toward her.

"*Sainte mère de Dieu,*" he exclaimed, grabbing both her hands and giving her a look which exuded relief. "Valéry, where have you been? You cannot imagine how concerned the baron and the viscount were when they returned and found that you had disappeared. And I cannot begin to describe how little Lisette cried and cried, and Sidonie blamed herself for not making sure the doctor had come the night you were so ill."

"Is the baron in residence, then?" Valéry felt her heart pounding as she waited for his answer.

"Yes, and he has looked throughout the countryside for any clue as to what happened to you. The viscount even sent for more of his own personal guards from Clairac to help in the search. Right now, they are out looking for you, as are Régis and Lucien, but each evening they return for the night and then set out the next day to begin all over again."

"They would know, of course, that my horse was missing," Valéry said, sitting down by the fire and trying to warm her hands as she talked. "Have the men in the print shop helped them at all?"

"No, they have remained working in the *imprimerie,* but the baron was very angry with Thomas Thibault, Arsène Faguet, and Jules Machet for going to Condon and leaving you without any men in residence. Of course Bruno was still here, but the baron said he might be dangerous."

"And what about Marthe Thibault?" Valéry could not help but ask since she knew the housekeeper would have fabricated some story that would put herself in a favorable light."

"From what I understand, Madame Thibault said that when Sidonie told her you were ill, she went to see for herself, and you told her you were feeling better and wanted her to wait until morning to see if you needed the doctor. This she said she did, but when she went to your room with your breakfast, you were gone. She feared that you must have taken a turn for the worse during the night and in a fever wandered off, not knowing what you were doing."

The baron must have believed her story and that was why he organized a search for her in the countryside, Valéry thought to herself. To the priest she asked, "Is Madame Thibault in the chateau now?"

"I believe so, mademoiselle."

Outside the sun was setting, and a wind began to blow, scraping branches against the roof of the church and whistling as it lashed into the wooden window frames of the sacristy. Valéry realized that she would have to give the priest some explanation, but she decided against revealing more than was necessary.

"*Mon père,* I was poisoned by Marthe Thibault."

The priest looked incredulous and apparently was at a loss for words because he just stared at her, his mouth wide open.

"She put something into the dinners I ate which made me violently ill, and then she locked me in my room, refusing to call a doctor. I think her intent was to kill me."

The priest sucked in his breath.

Valéry continued. "After eating only part of my food that second night before falling violently ill again, I later managed to escape by opening up the back of a cupboard in my room, which led directly into the library on the other side. As sick as I was, I rode my horse as far as Notre Dame du Calvaire Priory where Queen Marguerite and I had stayed last fall en route from Nérac to Eauze. The good sisters called their doctor, and it was he who treated me. Today I was well enough to return here and grateful that this doctor could accompany me. He has said he will verify that I was poisoned."

There was silence for several minutes, and then the priest spoke.

"You must stay here, mademoiselle, until the baron and his party return this evening. I myself will go over to the chateau and wait there until the men arrive back. In the meantime, do not leave this room. I know you do not like to be locked in, but I am sure that this time you will not mind me securing the door. Do not open it to anyone."

Valéry nodded her acceptance, feeling a deep gratitude for the priest's concern and help. *Père* Pierre drew the curtains over the windows before he left and hurried off into the windy night.

The effects of the journey were catching up with her. Suddenly she felt very tired, and the pains in her stomach returned, only this time they were from hunger. She realized that she still was recovering from her bout with the poison and would have to be careful not to strain herself unduly in the days ahead. But how could she do that when a confrontation with the housekeeper seemed inevitable?

It was not hard to speculate what Marthe might have done after finding her gone. The key and door bar would be returned and the cupboard restored to its original state so that nothing would look suspicious. The housekeeper's explanation would sound very reasonable, and since there were no witnesses to what really happened, it would come down to Marthe's word against Valéry's. Already Paul had disregarded her concerns in favor of his housekeeper's assurance that she would take care of Valéry in his absence. Valéry held little hope that now Paul would believe his librarian's side of the story.

Valéry's head began to throb, so she closed her eyes and tried to think of something in her favor. It came without effort. Of course, Marthe Thibault did not yet know that Dr. Duclos would give his diagnosis that she had been poisoned, and thus the housekeeper would be the most obvious suspect. Still, in light of Paul's attachment to the woman who had raised him, what lay ahead could not possibly be anything other than extremely unpleasant, and in light of her precarious health, she was not at all sure she would have the strength to face it.

After what seemed like a long time, Valéry heard voices outside the door, and then the priest accompanied by Paul, Régis, and the viscount burst into the room. Valéry was enveloped by so many arms she could hardly breathe. Tears came easily as she realized she was safe, but still the battle had not yet been won. There would be many questions, accusations, and mysteries remaining to be solved. Valéry was afraid that living at the chateau would become untenable for her under such circumstances, and she was certain that, one way or another, this was exactly what Marthe hoped would happen.

Chapter Twenty-Seven

Little was said that evening beyond the expressions of relief that Valéry had returned safely. The baron and Régis rode off almost immediately to Eauze while the viscount accompanied Valéry to her room, acting much like a father concerned about the welfare of his child. Apparently the priest had shared her story with them, and Paul, expressing both shock and anger, said he would immediately seek out Dr. Duclos. He asked Charles to make sure that Valéry was protected in her room, and the viscount in turn appointed one of his guards to stand watch outside her door. He also ordered another guard to make sure that Thomas and Marthe Thibault did not leave their apartment at any time the rest of the evening.

Valéry lay awake long into the night, listening for the Paul's return but finally fell asleep in spite of her efforts to the contrary. The next morning, she dressed in a hurry and decided she would go to the kitchen for some breakfast, determined that she would never again eat meals in her room. A guard was still keeping watch outside her door. She thanked him for his vigilance, saying she was sorry that he had not gotten any sleep. He smiled and assured her that he'd replaced the original guard and that each of them had slept before going on duty. As he followed her down the hall, he explained that his orders were to not let her out of his sight.

Down in the kitchens, Sidonie and Lisette stood by one of the ovens, talking excitedly with each other. They stopped when they saw her enter, and both rushed towards her with their news.

"Mademoiselle Valéry, the baron, accompanied by the viscount, called Madame Thibault into his office first thing this morning, and they were there for some time."

"And did you try to listen through the door?" Valéry asked with interest.

"Well, maybe just a little," replied Lisette, blushing as she spoke. "Madame Thibault sounded like she was yelling at one point, but we couldn't make out her words, and we did not hear the voices of the baron or the viscount at all."

"Something must have happened, and it could not have been favorable for Madame Thibault," Sidonie said, looking very pleased.

"How do you know that, Sidonie?"

"Because the baron has just asked me to be the new housekeeper, mademoiselle. And when I asked him what that meant for his old housekeeper, he looked very grim and told me that I did not have to worry about that."

Valéry drank some fresh hot milk and ate a generous slice of buttered bread before asking the two servants if they knew where she might find the baron. When they said they had no idea, she turned to leave and saw the viscount coming toward her down the hall.

"There you are, child," he said with a look of relief in his eyes. "Paul has asked me to talk with you just as soon as possible so that you will be aware of what is happening."

"I was looking for him and hoping that I could talk to him myself, Viscount Charles. Does he not want to see me?"

The viscount suggested that they use the reception room Valéry knew from her initial introduction to the chateau. Its coffered ceiling and tapestry-hung walls, coupled with the huge fireplace, made it one of the most impressive areas of the entire chateau. It was also comfortably warm as the two settled themselves into the large chairs facing the fire.

"Valéry, Paul has made sure that you will be safe, but now he must attend to some serious business which only he can handle. It is not that he does not want to see you, little one. You should know better than that."

It was a mild rebuke, but in her weakened physical and emotional state, she could not stop the tears, which came all too readily.

"I thought that Paul and I were developing trust and respect for each other, monsieur," Valéry replied, wiping her eyes with her hand. "In truth though, before he left to accompany you to Clairac and Paris, he was less than receptive to my fears about Madame Thibault. It was *she* whom he trusted and not I, and I am hurt that he has made no effort to come to me personally to make amends."

The viscount handed her a *mouchoir* and then sat regarding her in silence for a few minutes before he spoke.

"*Ma petite* Valéry, his first thought has been of you. But now I need to ask that you try to understand Paul's actions from his point of view. It was Marthe Thibault who raised him after his mother died. He realizes her faults,

208

but if you want to talk about trust and respect, don't you think that these were a part of the relationship Paul had with her?"

Valéry wiped the tears from her eyes and looked over at the serious face of the gentleman by her side.

"My uncle had a name for people like me when they think only of themselves," she said in a contrite voice. "He called them *incurvatus in se,* and I am ashamed to admit that this now applies to me, my lord. Please forgive my selfish judgment. I want to understand better how I can be a help rather than a hindrance. I love Paul."

"I know you do, Valéry, and you need to trust his love for you but also respect the way he is handling what has turned out to be a highly complex situation."

"Sidonie just told me that Paul has asked her to be his new housekeeper, but he did not tell her what was to become of Marthe. She and Lisette said that you were with the baron when he talked with Madame Thibault earlier this morning. That meeting must have been very hard for him."

"Paul listened with amazing restraint as his housekeeper tried to explain how she had attempted to care for you after you became ill. She was sure that you were merely suffering some malaise due to the strain you had been under, and she insisted that she intended to call the doctor if you were not feeling better that next morning, but you had told her the night before that you were much improved. She told of her horror when she found you missing the next day and feared that you had taken a turn for the worse in the night, wandering off without knowing what you were doing."

"But when you and Paul returned from your trip, my lord, she must have told the baron the same thing that she did this morning."

"Indeed, it was the same story, Valéry, but Paul wanted to make sure that her explanation had not changed before he told her about Dr. Duclos's diagnosis. This piece of news threw Marthe into a panic. She turned very pale and then began to yell that Paul was trying to blame her for your illness."

Valéry buried her face in her hands, trying to control the wave of nerves which threatened to overcome her. The viscount gave her a minute and then continued.

"Paul just sat looking at this woman who had served his father and then himself for so many years. Then he asked her a direct question. 'Marthe, did you put poison in Valéry's food? If you lie to me now, I will have no recourse but to send for a magistrate to hear the evidence which will surely prove that you are guilty. Your punishment, I can assure you, will be severe. However, if you tell me the truth, I will show you mercy by simply dismissing you from your position here and sending you and Thomas back to Condom.'"

"What did she say, my lord?"

"She did not say anything at first, and I thought it odd that her face was so impassive. Then, without warning, she burst into tears and admitted, 'Yes, I put a substance in Valéry's dinner meals, but it was not supposed to kill her. I swear that all I wanted to do was to scare her enough so that she would leave while you were gone and never come back. You are my baby, the only child I ever had, and I did not want to share you with that usurper. I was ecstatic when I found that Valéry had left.'"

Valéry rose from her chair and walked over to study a giant tapestry on the adjacent wall. After a few minutes, she returned to her seat. "My lord, Marthe lied even then, for she locked me into my room and took the key with her. There is no mistaking that far from just wanting to scare me into leaving by using poison, she wanted me dead."

"Paul knows that, Valéry. The priest told him what you said about being locked in your room. He simply chose not to confront her with any further evidence of her betrayal. If you had died, it would have been much different, I can assure you, for he told me so."

"If I had died, Paul would have thought I came down with a natural illness which took my life, and he never would have been the wiser as to what really happened." Valéry looked somewhat defiantly at the viscount but when he said nothing, she asked, "Where is Paul now?"

"He is seeing to it that the Thibaults pack their things while Régis makes arrangements for a cart and some mules to carry them and their possessions back to Condom. They do not have much and so should be on their way before the end of the day. But, Valéry, this will not put an end to any danger. There is something which the baron and I need to share with you, but we are worried about placing too heavy a burden on you so soon after your life-threatening experience."

Valery gave the viscount a wan smile. "I suppose it is too much to expect that Madame Thibault also admitted to stealing the Bible and then luring me into the flooded *souterrain,* my lord."

"Paul asked her directly whether she had been involved in any way with those things, Valéry, and was satisfied when she said no. What we decided to share with you now is that while we were in Paris, we uncovered a surprising piece of the remaining puzzle. Within a few days, we will have company of some import who will be able to clear up at least one of the mysteries."

"And who will that be, my lord?"

"The baron does not wish to give you more information at the moment than is wise, for he knows your precarious state of health and does not want to cause you any additional stress. Here again, Valéry, I hope you can trust his judgment completely."

"I will try," replied Valéry, "but it might be easier on me if I felt I was helping in some way."

"Good! Then I would ask that you begin first by making sure the library is in a presentable condition. I can guarantee you that our company will be interested in it. Then, if you have extra time, perhaps you could ask Sidonie and Lisette if you can be of help to them. Do you feel strong enough to do that, my dear?"

"I feel new strength already and welcome the chance to be useful."

"One more caution," the viscount said as he opened the door to leave. "Make sure that no matter where you go, one of my guards is near you at all times. This is especially crucial, Valéry, if you are working in the library or walking on the grounds."

Valéry followed him to the door and then stood on her tiptoes to lightly kiss the cheek of her protector. She was surprised to see the viscount's eyes fill with tears before he turned to leave. "You are more precious to me, Valéry, than you know right now, and that involves another mystery which will be revealed soon, but only after the remaining danger is over." Then, with that intriguing remark, he disappeared down the hallway.

Chapter Twenty-Eight

The early February sun lent its pale yellow rays to the neatly ordered library shelves. Valéry had spent the last two days making sure that any inspection of her work would bring approbation from the expected company. In anticipation of such a visit, the baron returned Valéry's listing of the first inventory so that it could be seen easily by those who might be interested in its contents. The as-yet-unfinished portion of her work would now have to be addressed before she could give a complete accounting. She knew it would take many more weeks to accomplish that job, but in the meantime, she resolved to ask Jules's help with placing the rather large volume of unsorted manuscripts into cupboards where their untidy appearance would be hidden and to retrieve the unfinished listing she had loaned to Arsène at Jules's request before her flight to the priory.

With a guard in tow, she entered the print shop, where she found Jules, Arsène, and Bruno in the midst of another printing. Arsène looked up as she entered, giving the guard a curious glance.

"I have not had a chance to welcome you back, Monsieur Faguet," Valéry said as she approached the printer. "You have another assignment, I see! What is it you are running off next?"

To Valéry's surprise, the printer did not move from his task or take her proffered hand in greeting. However, he did reply.

"Yes, I have been put to work almost immediately upon the baron's return, for he wishes me to use the new font I purchased on my trip and run off more copies of the text we initially printed. The paper, also, will be of better quality. It is his hope that such an instruction text will find a ready market in some of the schools of learning which are proliferating in our region."

"And I hope that one of those schools will be my own, Monsieur Faguet. Did the baron say anything about that to you?" Valéry smiled at the rotund printer as she spoke but did not receive so much as one of his lopsided smiles back. Instead, he shook his head and then turned to take up once again what he had been working on.

Valéry stepped closer in order to address both Arsène and Jules with her request. "Before you continue with your work, messieurs, I would like to ask the help of you, Jules, to transfer some of the remaining unrecorded manuscripts into the lower cupboards of the library. They are a messy lot right now, so I want to conceal them before our company arrives. Also, I would like to display the newest listing which I have loaned you so it can be available for inspection." Valéry looked expectantly at Arsène and Jules as she spoke.

A frown crossed Arsène's face, but he nodded, and motioning to Jules, he handed Valéry the sheets of parchment. "I can only spare Monsieur Machet for a short time, mademoiselle, as we are very busy here also. The baron has given us a deadline to have the printing done by the time the company arrives and to be ready to show to whoever that is both the print shop and the results of our work."

Then, calling Jules aside, he spoke briefly to him before the two left. Once in the library, Valéry commented to Jules that Arsène was not his usual agreeable self and wondered aloud if his recent journey had not been as successful as he had hoped.

"From what Monsieur Faguet has said, his trip was very successful, but he is somewhat anxious about the anticipated company and what he perceives the expectations of the baron are for his print shop and staff," Jules replied. "In addition, he is not at all pleased at having to run off yet another printing of the same text as the first one, for he does not see that there is any money to be made from it."

"I have been aware that from the very beginning, there has been a basic disagreement between Monsieur Faguet and the baron about the purpose of the *imprimerie*," Valéry replied. "That is a shame because I am sure Arsène is being well paid for his efforts, so I think he needs to be willing to adjust his expectations to those of the man who employs him."

Jules shook his head, replying, "No, I do not think that is his only option, mademoiselle. He does not have to stay on when conditions are not to his liking. There are other opportunities to be pursued if one is as knowledgeable and enterprising as Monsieur Faguet."

Valéry said nothing as they began to transfer the stacks of materials from the open shelving into the cupboards below. Soon, there was no space left, and Jules suggested that he take the remaining manuscripts to the print shop where there was more storage space available. "Arsène has actually suggested that this might give him an opportunity to look through some of the compilations for possible future printings," he commented.

"That seems all right to me," Valéry replied, closing the last of the cupboard doors and surveying the room with satisfaction.

"Good then, I will return shortly with a small cart and take these out of your way," he said, sweeping his arm over the remaining stack of books and papers.

After he had left, Valéry went in search of Sidonie and Lisette. She found both of them working in the Jean le Bon room.

"Where has the viscount gone?" Valéry asked in some surprise. This apartment has been cleared of all his possessions, I see."

Sidonie pushed back a strand of hair which had fallen over her eyes and managed to smile.

"Mademoiselle Valéry, he has moved downstairs to the apartments adjacent to the baron's. We are now trying to ready this chamber for our expected company, who will be arriving at dusk. We are almost frantic trying to prepare everything, and I am sorry to have to admit this, but we almost wish Madame Thibault were still here!"

Valéry laughed and then offered her assistance. "You may place me wherever I am needed the most, and please do not hesitate, for the viscount himself has suggested that I contribute to these efforts, and I very much want to be useful."

"Then would you be willing to help in the kitchens? If you like to bake, the cooks are beside themselves trying to prepare for this evening's welcoming banquet." Sidonie gave Valéry an expectant look, and Lisette nodded in agreement.

Once in the kitchens, Valéry was glad to take instructions from the head cook, who put her to work immediately making *croûte de pâté* for the meat and fruit pies. Lamb, beef, and pork would make very presentable dishes for such a splendid occasion, and her specialty of *clafoutis* using dried cherries, although not as delicious as the fresh fruit, would still make for a delectable dessert.

Listening to the chatter of the servants, she learned that the great hall was being readied for the feast. Only the most elegant table service was to be used. Not since the days of the previous baron had such a gala occasion taken place, and of course they wondered aloud as to who such an extravagance would be honoring. There was much excitement in the air, mixed with an energy which enabled the chateau servants to work with gusto at their various assignments.

While Valéry's pies were baking, she went to the great hall, curious to see how it was being prepared. In contrast to the Twelfth Night banquet when the entire village was present and many tables filled the space, there was now only one long table, spread with a finely embroidered cloth and dotted with plates rimmed with gold beside jewel-encrusted goblets. The cutlery was of silver as were the tiny salt servers by each place setting. In the center of the table stood a magnificent saltcellar, a golden nautilus shell which doubled as the hull of a ship mounted on the flexed tail of a silver mermaid, with bowls of salt balanced on the fore and aft decks of the exquisite three-master sailing vessel. Valéry walked closer to study the complex rigging of the gold sails, marveling at the craftsmanship of the goldsmiths who had produced such a work of art.

As she was thus admiring the saltcellar, Régis along with several other men, entered the room carrying *caquetoire* armchairs, fitting them at each place along the length of the banquet table. Each had a narrow carved back, curved arms, and a wide seat. Valéry counted eleven in all, with a space left vacant at the center of the table. Smiling at Valéry, Régis motioned for two of his men to bring forward a massive wooden chair fashioned in throne form. It had simple but dignified pierced side panels and carved foliage in the pediment top, and it certainly dominated the entire table when put in its central place.

"This is truly impressive," Valéry commented to Regis. "Do you know who else the baron has invited and who our guest of honor is to be, Monsieur Maguis?"

"I know as much as you know, mademoiselle," he said with a little laugh, "but we shall all find out soon enough, won't we now?" As he turned to leave the hall, he said over his shoulder, "Whoever the company is, the baron has said that they will come with an entourage, so the stables and the guardsmen's lodgings and refectory need to be prepared! I must rush, but Sidonie, along with my children and I, has been invited, so I will look forward to seeing you tonight." Then, as an afterthought, he added, "Oh, and the baron also said that he had made a special point of inviting Arsène Faguet as he was gone when we had the Twelfth Night festivities."

That evening as Valéry dressed for dinner, she mused over the secrecy surrounding the expected company. What was it the viscount had told her? He and the baron had made a surprising discovery during their sojourn in Paris which would result in a special visit to the chateau that would clear up at least one of the remaining mysteries. It was the baron's judgment that to tell her any more would place an undue strain on her present state of health, and she had accepted that, but she could not help but be intrigued and also anxious at what would surely take place this night.

Her gown was the same frock she had worn to the fateful Twelfth Night fête, and she had just finished adding the necklace, along with the matching earrings, when a great commotion arose in the courtyard below. Looking down in the fading light of dusk, she saw a great group of mounted guards circling around a horse-drawn litter. With a start, she realized that she recognized that litter, and her heart began to beat rapidly. Just then there was a knock at her door, followed by the baron, who stood looking at her for a moment, his eyes shining with a warmth she had never seen before.

"I have come to escort you to the great hall, *ma chérie*, so that we may greet together our distinguished guest."

Valéry took his arm, and the two descended the wide marble stairs, arriving at the entry hall just as the massive front doors opened and Queen Marguerite stepped into the foyer. With a little cry, Valéry rushed to her beloved patroness, giving her a very unceremonious hug and then bursting into tears.

"There, there, my little Valy," said Marguerite as she stepped back to survey her protégée. "I have missed you too, my little one, and we will have time soon enough to share the events of these months we have been apart. But for right now, there are more important matters to which I must attend."

The viscount accompanied Marguerite into the great hall, seating her on the throne chair with a panache worthy of the nobleman he was. Then he took the place to her right, and after the baron helped Valéry to her seat, he settled himself next to her in the chair to the queen's left. Looking down the table to her right, she smiled at Philibert, who the viscount insisted must flank his master, and then on to Régis, Sidonie, Lucien, and Lisette. Glancing to her left, she nodded to Jules immediately beside her and then to Arsène and Bruno, the latter of whom did not meet her eyes. She was acutely aware of the armed guards standing behind them and also of another half-dozen guardsmen placed in the vicinity of the doorway, effectively barring any entrance or exit. Their caparison included both dagger and sword, and by the grim looks on their faces, they must have been alerted to some possible danger, but what exactly that might be eluded Valéry. Her heart soared as she offered a silent thanks to a loving God for the presence of her beloved Marguerite.

The banquet began, with platter after platter of resplendent courses placed up and down the length of the table. Wine stewards made sure that goblets were never empty, and by the time the sweets arrived, which included Valéry's *clafoutis,* the diners were thoroughly satisfied and obviously having a good time. Thus it was that what came next presented a stark contrast to the affability which had permeated the atmosphere.

Rising from her chair, Marguerite called for one of the guards to open the door. All eyes watched as a gentleman entered the room carrying a leather-bound chest in his arms. As he placed it on the table before Marguerite, Arsène gasped, a look of disbelief on his face. Marguerite glanced at him and then opened the coffer and without a word drew out the stolen Bible. *"Mon dieu, mon dieu, c'est La Bible qui manquait,"* Valéry managed to blurt out in amazement, but the baron took her hand under the table and whispered that she needed to watch in silence what would now unfold.

"This gentleman is my brother the king's agent, commissioned by him to make purchases for the royal library," Marguerite explained. Then addressing him, she asked, "Monsieur, do you recognize here the man who approached you about buying this Bible?"

The agent replied that he did and pointed to Arsène Faguet. The printer did not move, but his expression, far from the lopsided smile that had so endeared him to Valéry, was now a twisted grimace.

Marguerite continued. "I was visiting his majesty my brother, who was in residence at the Louvre, when this agent informed the king of the purchase of a rare manuscript Bible from a Monsieur Faguet. I recognized the name right away since both Paul and Valéry had spoken of him in their correspondence with me. So it was that on a subsequent evening when François had invited the viscount and the baron for a *soirée* while they were in Paris, I asked them about the sale of such a valuable manuscript. They informed me that the Bible had been found missing from the chateau's library collection."

As Marguerite paused, the viscount rose. "Since Monsieur Faguet had disappeared after getting his payment of 3,000 gold *écus*, we decided that he would probably return to the chateau in hopes of being able to steal more valuable manuscripts undetected as he knew that the master list which Mademoiselle Lefèvre was compiling was far from complete." The viscount paused here, and then looking very pained, he glanced at his stepson.

"The baron and I were quite aware that in order to get away with such deception, Monsieur Faguet would need the assistance of someone within the chateau, who would not be viewed with suspicion if he were to be discovered in the library. I am very sad to have to identify that insider as the son of my late wife, Jules Machet."

Up until this time, Jules had been sitting quietly at Valéry's side, but now he leapt to his feet, anger contorting his handsome features. "Yes, I removed the Bible from its wrappings and replaced it with a substitute, and I was happy to do it for Monsieur Faguet. You have offered me nothing, Viscount, and Arsène has promised me a real future. Kept in the library, that Bible would bring nothing to anyone, but sold, it would enable Monsieur Faguet, myself, and Bruno to set up our own printing enterprise, and we have begun to do just that, in Condom, with the help of Thomas Thibault."

Jules was breathing rapidly, flailing his arms and yelling, much like his mother had done at the Twelfth Night banquet. A guard tried to restrain him, but he fought him off and tried to escape from his place at the table, only to be stopped by several more guards, who knocked him to the floor, securing his arms behind his back. The viscount, with extraordinary calmness, asked his stepson to get up on his feet again, and when he did so, walked over to him, placing his hand on Jules's shoulder. "I am sorry for my failings, Jules, for I know that this has contributed to the action you have taken against the baron, our librarian, and myself. You will need to face the consequences of what you have done, though, and that will not be mine to choose."

Marguerite, who had remained standing, watching the proceedings, spoke with a note of authority Valéry had never heard before from her patroness. "As queen of these lands of Gascony, I order my guards to place all three of these men under lock in the ground floor room of the donjon, to be interrogated further." With that, Arsène, Jules, and Bruno were led from the room by the queen's men, leaving the rest of the banqueters stunned.

The viscount spoke first. "*Ma reine, vous êtes fatiguée, j'en suis sûr. Permettez-mois de vous escorter jusqu'à votre chambre.*" Marguerite rose and accompanied the viscount from the room, as the baron turned to those who remained and said, "There has been quite enough excitement for one evening, *mes amis,* with nothing more to be accomplished until the morrow. Thank you for your presence here, and now I bid you *bonne nuit.*" Taking Valéry by the elbow, the two left the room while the others followed, greatly subdued after such celebration and then shock. As Valéry unlocked her door, she looked searchingly into the baron's face.

"Paul, there are still questions to be answered before I will be able to put behind me what has taken place here. I want to know who lured me into the *souterrain* and why they wanted me dead. Added to this, I still feel uncertain about the circumstances surrounding the theft of my mother's knife and the viscountess's death. Finally, I am wondering about a cryptic poem placed under my door and the mystery surrounding a cypher I discovered on the lid of my jewelry casket as well as the question of the matching necklace and earrings."

Paul traced with his finger the tiny gold hands of Valéry's necklace, bending to kiss the soft skin next to the large garnet resting in the middle of her low-necked bodice.

"We are not yet done with the interrogation of Arsène, and that of Jules and Bruno as well, Valéry, for there is no doubt that they all have played a part in this whole deception. As for the mystery of these gems and their casket, on our trip to Clairac, Philibert confided an amazing story to his master, which in due order will be shared with you because you are the principal focus of the tale."

The baron drew Valéry into his arms and then kissed her before leaving. Valéry entered her room in a kind of daze. Nothing about the evening had seemed real. The lavish banquet had turned bizarre at the end. Arsène and Jules were not who she had judged them to be, and Bruno's part in enabling Arsène's scheme was still unclear. Marguerite's sudden presence evoked loving memories of old but now showed another side of her—that of judge according to her rank and position. Without a doubt, mysteries still remained which stubbornly refused to make sense to her overwrought brain. As she prepared for bed, she forced her mind off these unsettling thoughts and instead recalled the beautiful gardens Marguerite had created in Nérac and the long leisurely walks she used to take along the lazy waters of the Baïse. Thus it was that she finally was able to relax and fall asleep.

The next morning, Valéry was curious as to what was happening with the incarcerated print men. She had never explored the bottom room of the donjon and worried about what conditions the three men had endured overnight. The spiral staircase in the south keep ended on the *rez de chaussez,* but Valéry found a very low door in the wall which gave onto a steep, narrow flight of stone steps. Just as she began to descend, she heard a cry, followed by several loud groans, and then another cry. The coarse voices of the guards reached her ears, along with harsh questions from two voices she recognized.

"Did you write the note which lured Mademoiselle Lefèvre into the *souterrain?*" A rather high-pitched male voice yelled out, *"Non, non, non,"* and then came a horrible scream.

"Did you seal the *souterrain* with the stone slab after you were sure Mademoiselle Lefèvre was inside?" A crude expletive from a deep voice followed the question, accompanied by a guttural sound, perhaps made by Bruno.

"Did you murder your own mother?" Silence, and then the loud sound of a blow reverberated off the stone walls of the underground room. *"Arrête, arrête, pour l'amour de dieu."* Valéry froze on the stairs. That was Jules's voice crying for mercy. She burst into the room, looking at the horrible scene before her, but before she could say anything, the baron came to her immediately and with force pushed her back up the stairs.

Once through the small door, he shut it and turned to face the distraught librarian.

"Valéry, you have no business down there. This is what must be done to get to the truth of what has happened, and Marguerite has authorized it."

"But, Paul," Valéry was close to tears, "you are torturing those men. I cannot bear it. Surely there is a more humane way to elicit their confessions."

The baron's eyes were once again the color of steel, and his jaw clenched as he forced Valéry toward the winding staircase. "You are to obey me, mademoiselle. This is what must be done, and I will tolerate no protests from you. Stay away from here until you are sent for, and quit behaving like a weak, hysterical female!"

Valéry's mouth dropped open, and her eyes widened in disbelief. "You are cruel, monsieur, not only to those men but also to me. I am not a weak, hysterical female, but one who has both strength and a heart. Do what you must, but I reserve my right to do the same." With that, she hastened up the staircase and on to her room. She was shaking all over as she donned her cape and made her way out the main entrance of the chateau. How long she walked the extensive grounds of the estate, she did not know, although it must have been for hours as it was only when the thin rays of the winter sun gradually began to fade that she finally became aware of the passage of time.

Just where she was on the estate, she did not know, for the chateau was not visible, and the terrain looked unfamiliar. In the gray dusk of evening, she suddenly saw before her the outline of a mausoleum. Drawing closer, she realized that this was the burial ground for generations of de Renard barons. Richard was there, along with Antoine and Jean and finally Guillaume. One day, Paul also would lie in the vault, his name carved into the black marble of the tomb as he joined his forebears.

She sat down on the ledge circling the mausoleum and buried her head in her hands. It was then that she heard voices calling out her name. She did not answer but moved around to the back of the tomb so that she would not be seen if anyone came this far in their search. She did not want to have any encounters now, let alone to explain her behavior, for she knew she had to have the time and space to sort out her feelings about the torture of three men who she cared about, and even more, the hurt she felt at the baron's callous treatment of her.

Night enveloped the landscape, but the voices continued. Once one sounded quite close to her but never reached the burial vault. Then all was quiet. It was cold, and Valéry began to shiver with the night air, but still she remained where she was. She simply could not return to the chateau, knowing the suffering of the men in the donjon and the cruelty of the guards coupled with the two noblemen who led the interrogation. Curling up on the wide granite rim running around the circumference of the tomb, she wrapped her cape tightly around her body and pulled the vair-lined cap about her head. With her back against the marble wall of the monument, she fell asleep. When the eastern sky began to take on the pale hues of sunrise, she awoke, knowing that there would be decisions facing her this new day.

Sitting up and stretching her stiff limbs, she imagined what might happen if she returned to the chateau. There would be relief that she had been found, but also recriminations which would come mostly from the baron, for the viscount seemed incapable of being very stern with her. Marguerite, too, would have her say. "You have behaved immaturely," she would observe, and of course she would be right. But Valéry did not care. What disturbed her the most though was a recurring pattern of the baron, which seemed to involve a mean streak towards her, followed by an apology and an expression of tenderness. It was a pattern she did not want to have happen again, for she feared that she might have to face a lifetime of that, if there was to be a future at all for herself and Paul. The man simply did not like strong females, and she was certainly one. Her heart ached, for she loved him but knew that if she returned, she would be tempted once again to forgive and go on.

It was still early as Valéry sat contemplating her options. If she fled, she would have no place to go except back to the priory, and that would only be a temporary haven. Furthermore, any help which she might expect from Marguerite was highly unlikely if she did not return to the chateau. Soon, the realization that she was hungry led her to reconsider going back to the chateau, at least for now. Besides, she was curious about any confessions that had been elicited from the three prisoners and anxious to find answers to the puzzle of the casket cypher and the matching necklace and earrings. Her anger had dissipated along with the night's darkness, but the hurt remained. At last, mainly because of her feelings for the baron, she decided she owed it to herself as well as to Paul to be honest with him about what she thought to be his abusive treatment.

The servants were already busy in the kitchen and, hearing Valéry pound on the side door, opened it for her. Once inside, she went unhindered to her room where she washed and dressed in fresh clothes. When the breakfast bell sounded, she appeared in the *salle à manger* as if nothing had happened.

"I trust you had a restful night," the baron said, looking up as Valéry seated herself. Marguerite and Charles looked absorbed with their bowls of hot milk and freshly baked slices of bread. Valéry replied as politely as she could muster that she had slept very well. The rest of the meal was eaten in silence, and when the queen and the viscount had finished, they quietly rose and left the room. Valéry looked over at Paul, who met her gaze without wavering.

"Well?" he queried, pushing back from the table and continuing to look at her—with a touch of amusement, Valéry thought. "Did you enjoy your night in the company of my ancestors?"

Valéry had not expected this question and looked at the baron in surprise.

"How did you know where I was, my lord?"

"I continued to look for you until I found you, fast asleep on the stoop of the de Renard monument. I thought briefly of waking you and insisting you return with me to the warmth of the chateau but decided to let you be. We both needed to rethink what happened between us, Valéry."

Valéry looked down at some undefined spot on the floor and did not reply. After a few moments of silence, the baron asked for her thoughts.

"If I am weak and hysterical, what I am thinking could not possibly be important to you, monsieur."

"Of everything which is on my mind now, Valéry, what you are thinking is by far the most important." When Valéry gave him a dubious look, he continued. "I am not going to apologize for my behavior yesterday. The stakes were far too high for the viscount or myself to treat those pressmen with any leniency. I stand by my insistence yesterday that you needed to stay out of the methods by which we chose to interrogate them."

The room was very quiet as Valéry sat at the table, her downcast eyes hiding the hurt which she was feeling. After a few moments during which the baron waited patiently, she looked up at him.

"Your behavior toward me was harsh and unfeeling, and not altogether unlike other encounters I have had with you, Paul. And while I acknowledge that my own actions may have provoked you, I have a strong sense that whenever I act in ways which are indicative that I am not meek and without wits, you make me suffer for it." Valéry glanced at the baron then, conscious that he was not taking well what she was trying to express. At least he was listening, she thought to herself, and she knew she would need to continue despite the reaction she saw in the man across from her.

"You have professed to love me, Paul, and I have the same feelings for you. What a shame it is that there cannot possibly be any future for us if you continue to make me pay for the sins of your surrogate mother."

"I dismissed the woman who raised me. She is out of my life for good, and I am wondering why you now feel the need to accuse me of mistreating you because of her." The baron stood up then, and as he walked toward the door, he turned back and looked at Valéry from across the room. "And what makes you think, Mademoiselle Lefèvre, that I had in mind any future for us?"

"I had only hoped it might be so," Valéry replied with a broken voice. "But, Paul, it is for the best if that can never be, for I cannot continue to be the subject of your vitriol and then your affection."

The baron stared at her for a moment before replying. "Then you will not need to for very much longer. Later today the viscount will share with you what we have found out, and then you will be free to leave."

Long after the baron had left the room, Valéry sat at the table, her head resting on the hard oak plank, too stunned to move or even think. After some time, she rose and returned to her room. It did not take long to pack her belongings in the baggage she had brought with her. The books of her uncle would remain part of the chateau's library as she had already integrated them with the other contents of the shelving. Never in all her life had she felt so anguished. The memory of her months at the chateau, with all that had happened, held her in a strong emotional grip—as though she had just awakened from a terrible dream but could not shake the aftereffects.

A tap on her door was followed by the entrance of Marguerite, who came to sit beside her on the bed, patting her on the back and then wiping away the tears which welled up in her eyes.

"My little Valy, Paul has shared with me what has just transpired between you two. Child, I also have had heart-wrenching exchanges with the man I love. They are inevitable, I fear, when strong emotions are involved, but I am equally sure that this is not the final word between you and Paul."

Marguerite paused for a moment and then continued. "I have another purpose in coming to you now, Valéry. You need to accompany me to the reception room, for I think you must hear what the viscount has to tell you."

Valéry followed the queen down the stairs and entered the room where she had earlier encountered the baron. Marguerite did not follow her in but closed the door behind her as she left. The viscount was sitting by the fire, flanked by Philibert. The baron was not present. Looking up at her entrance, Charles motioned for her to take the empty chair beside him.

"You look so sad, Valéry. My heart is heavy too, but it is because of what Paul and I had to do to extract the truth from Arsène, Jules, and Bruno and what it is that we learned. As hard as this confession will be to share with you, nonetheless, you must hear it, for it answers who tried to kill you and who *did* kill my wife."

Valéry looked at the kindly gentleman and thought that he indeed looked grieved. She did not say anything but waited for him to continue.

"It was Arsène who instructed Jules to take the Bible, holding out to him the possibility of great riches and a bright future as his apprentice. When the journeyman printer left, he had in his saddlebags the valuable manuscript, along with others Jules had stolen, which he fully intended to sell at his own profit. Stating that he was going to Lyon, instead he headed for Paris where he knew he would find a ready market for his ill-gotten materials. There too he purchased printing supplies with Paul's money, and on his way back left some in Condom where he found a suitable place to set up his own print shop. He paid for the rental with the money he'd received from the king's agent for the Bible."

Valéry stared at the fire, thinking how gaily it danced about, reflecting warmth into the room. But Valéry felt chilled and numb as she tried to take in what the viscount was telling her.

His voice sounded like it was far off and totally disembodied from the man who sat just next to her.

"Valéry, do you hear me, child?"

She turned then to give the viscount a little smile and nod her head, trying to clear her mind for what she knew was coming.

"Monsieur Guyot, who Paul went to question in Eauze, said that two nights before the Twelfth Night fête, Arsène showed up at his atelier, requesting that the blacksmith re-shoe his horse and asking if he could leave his supply cart there for several days as he needed to make a quick trip to Condom before returning to the chateau to stay. Monsieur Guyot said that was fine and assumed that the printer would borrow another horse from the baron before he left again. But Arsène admitted that instead of going to Condom, he had sneaked back to the print shop late that night, prevailing upon Bruno to hide him in his room. Bruno agreed since Arsène had promised him a position in his new *imprimerie* in Condom as well as the freedom to continue printing up his religious tracts. Jules was let in on Arsène's presence the next day and agreed to help the printer carry out his next plan. Arsène knew that if he were to continue to be able to steal manuscripts from the library, he would have to get rid of you, Valéry, before you completed the final inventory, after which any missing materials could be identified."

It all made sense, Valéry thought to herself. That was why Arsène had shown such an interest in both her inventories. That she had never suspected him made her reproach herself for being so blind.

The viscount continued. "After Jules helped Régis carry the stand for the Bible to the library, he and the printer knew that you would now discover the valuable manuscript missing. It was then that Arsène had Jules check the state of the underground passageway, and when he reported to the printer that it was filling up rapidly, Arsène wrote the note which lured you into the *souterrain*. He signed it "Regis," knowing that you knew the steward checked the underground passageway, especially when it flooded, and thus such a note purportedly from him would be believable. He then sent Jules to place the message in your chamber while you were searching for the Bible in the occupied bedrooms. All the while, Arsène kept watch until he saw you enter the tunnel and then enlisted Bruno to help him move the stone over the mouth, feeling confident that, thus trapped, you would drown in the flooded chamber."

"Did Bruno know that he was helping to seal me in?" Valéry hoped against hope that the mute assistant was ignorant of Arsène's intent to kill her.

"Yes, Valéry, he did," came the terse answer.

After a few minutes, Valéry turned to the viscount and asked about the death of his wife.

"This is hardest of all for me to fathom," he replied. "Odile's son detested his mother, but I never imagined that he could murder her. He admitted that on the morning of the banquet, he took your knife from the library ledge where he knew you had left it, determined to look for an opportunity to kill his mother using the knife everyone would recognize as yours."

Valéry nodded, thinking back to the footsteps she heard entering the library when she was hiding quietly in her room the day of the fête. Jules had even stopped to listen outside her door before leaving the south keep.

The viscount went on. "Jules's opportunity came that evening at the banquet when Odile was so enraged at seeing you wearing the garnet necklace."

"But why did she react that way, Charles?" Valéry asked, reliving that horrible moment with all the alarm and anger she had felt when Odile attacked her.

"Let us leave that question until after I have finished with the matter of my wife's death, Valéry."

"I beg your pardon, Monsieur Charles. I know this must be terribly hard for you to talk about."

The viscount rubbed his hand over his eyes, a deep sigh escaping from his lips. "It was Jules who took his raging mother up to her room just after he saw you leaving, Valéry. He says that she fought him all the way up the stairs until they reached the door leading into the hallway, and it was then that he took out the knife and stabbed her. She fell headfirst down the steps, and Jules, satisfied that she was dead, returned to the great hall just as though nothing had happened."

"Did your stepson show any regret as he confessed this to you, my lord?"

"Not a shred, Valéry; not even a flicker of guilt or remorse. In fact, he said he would do it all over again, so great was his hatred of his mother."

During the silence which ensued, both Paul and Marguerite entered the room, drawing over chairs close to the other three occupants. Valéry felt like she would faint and must have turned very pale because the baron gently took her head and pushed it down over her knees. For a few minutes, Valéry sat thus and then straightened up again, feeling somewhat better.

"There is more, but we must not go on until you are quite ready to hear it," the baron said softly. Valèry had a strong urge to look him in the face but feared what she might find in his expression so decided against it. Instead, she assured everybody that she was quite recovered and urged the viscount to continue.

"It is not I who has any more to share, but Philibert, whose story he confessed to me when we were carrying the viscountess's body back to Clairac." Valéry looked in surprise at the aged manservant, not able to imagine what he possibly could have to say. Leaning over so he could speak directly into his manservant's ear, the viscount asked Philibert to give Valéry the information he had related to him. Philibert looked at Valéry and nodded.

"You will be interested to hear what I have to tell you, mademoiselle, but I am afraid that it will also bring you pain, for you are not who you think you are."

Again, Valéry could not imagine what he meant, but in a raised voice, so he could hear, urged him to go on, saying that if it cleared up the mystery surrounding the casket cypher and the matching necklace and earrings, then it would be worth any distress she might feel at the moment.

"I hope and pray that you are right," Philibert observed. "Mademoiselle, it was I who wrote the little verse and then placed it under your door. After Viscount Charles helped me back to my room following the fainting spell, I knew that I could no longer keep still. I alone had the answer to the mystery of why the necklace and the earrings matched and, furthermore, why the viscountess acted as she did. My fainting was the direct result of the shock I felt at seeing you wearing the necklace.

"Then it was you I saw hurrying down the hall and your door that I heard close," Valéry said. When Philibert nodded but remained silent, she added, "Well, for mercy's sake, don't prolong this drama, Monsieur Favard. Why were you so obscure in your message? I eventually pried off the gold filigree on the casket lid, but the de Clairac name, the entwined *VC* cypher, blazon, and motto just increased the mystery, so please continue with your story." The suspense she was feeling threatened to overwhelm her, and the baron's presence added to her anxiety, but Valéry struggled to control her reactions. The memory of Paul accusing her of being weak and hysterical was too fresh in her mind, and she did not want to give him the satisfaction now of proving him right!

"My message was veiled because I had not yet told my master what I should have told him many years ago but did not because of what I thought was a good reason," Philibert replied. "When I saw you wearing the necklace, I knew I had no choice but to reveal the truth to you both, but I knew it was only right that I tell the viscount first. So I wrote that coded verse, thinking it would give me time to speak with the viscount while you tried to figure out the poem's meaning."

In a voice which Valéry hoped sounded calm, she asked the obvious question. "And what exactly did the necklace mean to you, Philibert?"

The venerable manservant leaned forward in his chair, looking anxious to get on with his explanation but then appeared like he was having difficulty knowing exactly where to begin.

The viscount came to his rescue. "Philibert, it makes sense to start with my older brother, don't you think?"

"Oh yes, of course," the old retainer agreed. "My wife, Delphine, and I were the personal servants to the older brother of Monsieur Charles and his wife, Marie, at the de Clairac chateau. His name was Valéry, and as the older son, he had inherited the title of viscount and the estate which went with it.

"No wonder you said that was one of your favorite names," Valéry said to Charles with a smile. What a coincidence that this is my name also." The viscount returned her smile but remarked that it was no coincidence.

Philibert went on with his story. "Soon after the Viscountess Marie found she was with child, both Viscount Valéry and his younger brother Charles were called by King François to fight with him in his Italian campaigns. Not wanting to leave Marie alone with a baby coming, Viscount Valéry sent her to live with his brother Charles's wife, Odile, in their townhouse in Paris. Delphine and I accompanied Viscountess Marie but soon found that Odile was very jealous of Marie because she was going to have a child and she could not. When the terrible news was brought to us that Viscount Valéry had been killed, we grieved but were glad to hear that Charles was all right and would be returning to us soon. Just before he did, however, Marie went into labor and gave birth to a healthy baby, but sadly, Marie died soon after childbirth. Delphine, who had been the midwife, was inconsolable, but the worst was yet to come. Odile approached my wife and ordered her, mind you, to kill the baby."

Valéry grimaced but wondered silently what all this had to do with her. She found out in short order.

"She was almost like a madwoman, that Odile, saying to Delphine that now her husband Charles would become the viscount and she the viscountess, and her son Jules would be the rightful heir of the title and the lands. 'No child will take that away from my son,' she said, 'so do what I order you to, servant woman, and make sure the baby does not live.'"

Philibert stopped here, evidently overcome by his memories, but soon got enough control of his emotions to resume.

"When my wife protested, Odile threatened to kill the child herself and then dismiss both of us from her service. Furthermore, when her husband returned, she would explain to him that she had to let us go because Delphine had been responsible for the death both of Marie and of the baby."

The manservant threw a pleading look at those in the room. "You have to understand that my wife and I would have lost our means of livlihood if Odile carried out her threat to get rid of us, but still we could *not* take the life of a precious little innocent. We had to think quickly due to the immanence of the new viscount's return."

Charles rose from his chair and went to stand behind Philibert, placing his hands on the servant's hunched shoulders and reassuring him that everyone in the room understood the predicament. After a deep breath, Philibert continued.

"Vicountess Odile had helped herself to Marie's jewelry after her death, which included the casket with its necklace and earrings, a gift which I knew the Viscount Valéry had given his wife for their wedding. However, neither you, my lord, nor your wife were aware of that. The viscountess took to wearing the earrings all the time, but the necklace was too grand for ordinary days, so it remained in its box. It was I who wrapped the baby up in warm blankets, thinking to take her to the church of Saint Germain-des-Prés since it was near my father's house. We were sure a priest would find the baby there. Then, as payment for whoever this priest found to raise the infant, I also took the casket with its precious necklace along with me, stopping first at my father's goldsmith atelier where I had him cover up with gold filigree the viscount's surname, crest and cypher so that the baby's background could not be traced. We decided to leave uncovered the name Valéry, reasoning that the family who raised her would think that it was her name and thus her necklace."

Valéry sat in stunned silence for a few minutes as Philibert paused, almost as though he was waiting for the librarian to finish his story. She did not disappoint him.

"I was that baby, wasn't I? It must have been my uncle—that is, the man I always thought to be my uncle, to whom you gave me, for Saint Germain-des-Prés was his church then. He, in turn, must have asked his widowed sister if she would raise me."

Philibert nodded and then leaned toward the viscount. "You remember what happened after you returned from the Battle of Marignano. The viscountess told you that both Marie and the baby had died, and you never suspected otherwise because Delphine and I never revealed otherwise. At first, since we did not know you, my lord, we could not guess how you would react if we did tell you the truth. We reasoned that it would be our word against your wife's, and even if you did believe us and were able to bring the baby back, we feared the child would not be free from danger if she were raised under the same roof as the viscountess. Over the years, I think we assuaged our feelings of guilt by a conviction that you, Valéry, would be safer and perhaps happier wherever you were placed than with the Viscountess Odile. My precious wife kept this secret until her death, leaving only me now to beg your forgiveness, my lord."

The viscount put his hand on his servant's arm. "I will forgive you as many times as you ask, and more, my old and faithful friend, for in truth, I think that you did what seemed the only reasonable thing to do at the time. Sadly I also must admit that you were no doubt right about how my wife would have treated the little Valéry if I had found her and brought her back into my house. Let us leave the past where it belongs and rejoice at how miraculously things have turned out!"

Looking then at Valéry, Charles addressed her as his newly discovered niece, a true de Clairac and the eventual heir to his estates.

No wonder I saw something familiar in the viscount's face, Valéry thought to herself. *His expressions are much like my own, although I didn't realize that until now.* To the viscount she said, "I *must* be of the de Clairac line, *mon oncle*, because I bear one of the most distinguishing marks of the family!"

"And just what is that?" the viscount asked in surprise.

"I also am left-handed, uncle, and proud to know that I come by it naturally."

Everyone in the room laughed, which helped to release the tension they all were feeling. Valéry sat in silence for a few minutes, trying to think through the implications of what she had just learned. Her Uncle Jacques was not really her uncle, and her mother, Madeleine, whom everyone called Maddy, was not her true mother. Furthermore, they had both gone to their graves without telling her the truth. Perhaps they felt that revealing it would serve no purpose, but there had been at least one clue. Valéry remembered especially well the discomfort her mother had shown each time she recounted to Valéry the story of her supposed father and his gift of the casket with its necklace. It would take some time for her to accept the deception as well as to adjust to her new identity, but of one thing she was certain: For the rest of her life, she would continue to think of Jacques Lefèvre d'Etaples as her much-loved uncle and his rotund sister, Madeleine, as her dear mother.

"Did you know any of this, my queen?" Valéry asked, looking at Marguerite.

"No, Valy, your mother and your uncle never breathed a word of it to me, and of course, even if they had, they themselves did not know your real origins."

"There are still unanswered questions, Philibert," Valéry said, perhaps a shade too loudly as she turned from Marguerite to the manservant.

"You are quite right, mademoiselle, and I am not yet finished with what needs to be revealed." The aged retainer gave Valéry a thin smile and shifted nervously in his chair. "You see, there is the question of what we actually *told* the viscountess after we had taken you to the church. We simply could not lie, and so we were honest with her about what we had done."

Valéry could hardly believe what she had just heard. "I am almost afraid to ask you how the viscountess reacted to the news that you had not murdered me but left me as a foundling, along with the casket and necklace, at Saint Germain-des-Prés."

"Well," Philibert replied, "she exploded with rage at first, but we assured her that, although we had left the name Valéry on the lid of the casket, the de Clairac family identification had been covered up so that there would be no way the baby could be traced. She calmed down a bit then, but still lashed out at us for taking the valuable jewelry piece as payment for the care of the baby. Then she said she would let the matter drop if we swore to her that the viscount would never know. Under the circumstances, we promised for the reasons I have already explained to you."

Valéry remained perplexed. Leaning closer to Philibert, she asked the next obvious question. "I still do not understand why the viscountess made such a quick connection between the necklace and my true identity. Of course, she would recognize the necklace immediately, but couldn't she have thought that whoever raised the baby sold it for the money and thus I came by it through such a sale?"

"First, mademoiselle," Philibert said patiently, "the viscountess knew that the name Valéry had remained on the casket. In addition, when she met you, she must have wondered about your name coupled with something which was subtle but nonetheless there, and which I saw. You bear some resemblance to both your father, Valéry de Clairac, and to Master Charles. You may have wondered why I studied you so closely every time I had a chance and once I even asked you a question about your mother."

"Yes, I remember you looking closely at me once when we were in the library together, Monsieur Philibert, but I didn't make anything of it."

"Finally, Mademoiselle Valéry," Philibert appeared anxious to explain Odile's violent outburst at the banquet further, "she saw the reaction I had when I saw you wearing the necklace. I think that all these things served to alarm her that you were indeed that baby she had wanted killed but knew was still alive. She was not rational in her reaction, I admit, but she must have been both shocked and filled with fear as to what this would mean for her, especially with regard to her husband's reaction. The only thing she could think of doing was to accuse you of stealing the necklace, which she knew Marthe Thibault would back her up on, if necessary."

Long after the chateau went dark and its occupants slept, Valéry sat by her fire, going over and over all the answers to the mysteries with which she had been struggling. When sleep finally overtook her, it was while she sat there in her chair. She woke with a start when someone knocked on her door.

"You will have to open up from inside," the baron's voice announced, "as I have no key, and in addition, you have surely have put a bar across your door."

When she let him into her chamber, he looked immediately at her bed. "It has not been slept in," he observed, casting her a concerned look. "And yet," he continued, "you look amazingly rested, especially since you spent the night before, slumbering with my ancestors." He also glanced at her packed baggage but said nothing.

Valéry walked over to the mirror and tried to pull back the long tresses which hung about her face. The baron walked over to her and stayed her hands. "Leave it down as it is, for I have never seen it that way, and you look quite fetching thus."

When Valéry pulled away, he apologized. "I realize that I am once again following the pattern you accuse me of, Valéry—that of anger, apology, and then trying to make amends. I admit that it made me angry when you first pointed it out to me. Upon reflection, you were absolutely right. Whenever you showed that you had a mind of your own, I reacted negatively because Marthe also had a strong sense of self. But while she was bent on domination and intimidation and thus had destructive tendencies which I struggled against as a child, you had only good motives in mind, and the strength of will and character to achieve them."

Valéry turned to face him then, feeling far from sure of herself, but nonetheless unwilling to curb what she felt so deeply. If, once again, she provoked Paul's wrath, then she was afraid that she no longer had the resources to cope.

"Paul, I am so fortunate to have had a loving upbringing. The man I knew as my uncle loved me, and so did the sainted woman who mothered me. Marguerite too could not have been more of a blessing. I admit that I cannot even begin to understand what you had to endure from Marthe Thibault. But I do know from the viscount that your father and you had a very close and loving relationship, and your life has been one of privilege. Therefore, when you treat me badly and then try to make up for it, I have nothing in my upbringing which would help me handle that. You are what you are, but I too am who I am. I have thought deeply about this, and I remember all too well how you first received me as well as the number of times when you reacted heartlessly to what I did or said. It is a side of you which, if continued over time, would destroy me."

When the baron tried to say something, Valéry stopped him. "No, you must hear me out. This last time, you said that you were not sorry for how you treated me in the donjon, and when I pointed out that I could no longer take your recurring pattern of behavior, you said that I was free to go, which intimates that you are not willing to change. The final blow came when you questioned my assumption that you were contemplating a future with me."

The baron was silent for what seemed like an eternity to Valéry. He walked over to the window and looked down on the courtyard below and then out to the fields beyond the balustrade. When he did speak, it was with a broken voice.

"I am deeply in love with you, Valéry, and I had and still have the hope that you would agree to become my baroness. But I also realize my failings. I know they are a serious impediment to any committed relationship which marriage would certainly entail, and I cannot expect you to acquiesce to any behavior on my part which threatens to destroy you."

Valéry said nothing in response, and there was profound silence between them as each one realized the depth of the problem.

Before the baron left, he added only one thing. "I thought you would like to know that Régis and Sidonie are to be married next Saturday morning. Marguerite will need to leave before then, but the viscount has agreed to stay on until after the ceremony. I hope you will be willing to stay at least until then."

After he had left, Valéry could not hold back the tears. What she had been through these past months was difficult, and what she had so recently learned was even more of a shock. But it was nothing in comparison with the hurt and despair she now was feeling. The baron had not said that he would try to change, and under those circumstances, any possibility of a future together was a dream which had just died.

Chapter Twenty-Nine

Marguerite left several days later, but not before she and Valéry got a chance to talk.

"My precious Valy," she began after listening patiently to her protegée's concerns about Paul, "I understand perhaps better than you what cruelty from a man means. My marriages to both my first and second husbands were unions arranged by my brother, the king, and of course they were for political reasons. I was attracted to my present husband, Henri d'Albret, in spite of the fact that he is considerably younger than I, but I did not know that he would treat me badly at times until it actually began to happen. I think that he cares for me, and I love him, but he has had many dalliances with other women, and when he wants to, he can treat me with disrespect and even contempt. There are other times, though, when he is very solicitous of my feelings and a charming companion. Marriage is never between two perfect people, Valéry."

"I know that, my queen, but I cannot seem to accept it when Paul behaves in unfair and damaging ways towards me."

"You realize that you still have a choice, Valy. The baron truly loves you. All the time we were together in Paris, he talked of you in glowing terms. You have achieved a miraculous transformation in the library, for I spent some time in there the other day and marveled at the work and expertise it took to do what you have done. But the baron's appreciation of you goes far beyond that. You both share a love of the new learning and a desire to spread it beyond those who are privileged. Most importantly, you find joy in being with each other."

Valéry was silent, but her heart swelled with the praises of her patroness and the knowledge that the baron had spoken of her when she was not even there. Marguerite was right in her observations about the common values she and Paul shared and the happiness she felt when she was with him.

Marguerite continued. "I will be very serious with you, Valéry. You would be welcome at your uncle's chateau, for you are of the nobility and a de Clairac, Charles's closest living relative. Your future could lie there, but would your heart? However, you could also choose to marry Paul and then help him change through your patient and forgiving heart. He is still in the process of learning that there is more than one way to relate to a strong-minded and capable woman and is already aware that there is a huge difference between you and Marthe Thibault."

"How do you know that, my queen?"

"I have talked with him, Valéry. In fact, it was he who sought me out, and he was both forthright and honest as he poured out his love for you, his own struggles to change, and his fervent hope that you both could have a long and happy life together."

"I will think about it, my lady, I promise you that," Valéry replied.

"Good," said Marguerite, "and now I must prepare to leave. I will be returning to our chateau in Pau where I will rejoin my husband and all the duties which are mine as queen of Navarre and sister of the king of France."

As she rose from her chair, she stood looking down at Valéry for a minute and then added with a smile, "And when I get word that you and Paul are to be married, I will be there, Valéry."

The queen left early the next morning, choosing to ride on her own horse and let the mules pull her litter. Some of her guardsmen went with her, but the rest remained. It was the viscount who explained to her that they, along with himself and his own guards, would be escorting Jules, Arsène, and Bruno to Paris where they would have to appear before Parliament. Since their conspiracy over the Bible involved an offence against the king, their final judgment had to come from the king, who would also decree the manner of punishment.

"Uncle Charles, will Jules be sentenced to death?"

The viscount shrugged his shoulders. "I do not know, my little niece, but it seems likely."

"If you have any influence at all, my lord, would you be willing to plead for leniency for all three men?"

"I will do what I can, Valéry, and I think that considering what you have suffered at their hands, you are remarkably free of rancor. You are indeed an amazing young woman, and," he added looking kindly at her, "one whom I very much want to see marry the man I think of as my adopted nephew, for his father was like a brother to me, especially after my own brother was killed."

Saturday came, and with it the wedding of Régis and Sidonie. The entire village tried to cram into St. Luperc for *Père* Pierre's wedding Mass, and afterwards, the baron invited everyone to the chateau for a grand celebration. Looking at the happy couple and seeing the joy with which Lisette and Lucien welcomed their new mother, Valéry was profoundly touched. Somewhere in the midst of the crowd and the noise, she suddenly was overcome with emotion, and sought refuge from all the merrymaking by going back to her room. When she reached her door, she was surprised to see a large stack of newly printed textbooks by the wall. On top was a note. Unlocking her door, she lit candles and then sat down on her bed to read it.

My love,

I had Arsène run off these little grammars for you to use with your classes, which I am praying you will see fit to continue. But I have something else I am keeping in my supplications to God. I am hoping for a miracle, I know, but I am asking that our loving Father will enable me to be the husband you deserve, and that you will be willing to be my wife.

It was signed "Paul."

One month later, there was another wedding in the church of St. Luperc. Marguerite kept her promise, and much to the joy of both Paul and Valéry, she was accompanied by her husband, Henri d'Albret, king of Navarre, who gave his wife every consideration and was a true gentleman to Valéry. When the ceremony was over, and so many people, humble and exalted, had given the couple their congratulations, it was Marguerite who had the final word. Enfolding both Paul and Valéry in an expansive embrace, she said that in all her life, this was one of the few most purely happy moments she had ever experienced. With that blessing, the baron and baroness de Renard began their life together, and when their first children were born, a twin boy and girl, they named the boy Charles Guillaume Jacques de Renard, but for the baby girl, just two names would do! Their tiny daughter was christened Marguerite Madeleine, after the two women Valéry loved the most.

One evening, as the baron sat rocking his baby daughter and Valéry nursed their son, she looked over at her husband and asked a question which had long puzzled her.

"*Mon mari,* you never did tell me why you were so surprised when I told you that I had located that textbook you wanted me to find before I did anything else."

The baron chuckled. "It was something I intended to tell you as soon as our relationship got on a firmer footage, *ma chérie,* but then I was too embarrassed to confess. You see, I had just found the original text stuffed into the back of my armoire and was quite chagrined that I had totally forgotten I had put it there."

"Then where did you think I had found the duplicate text, may I ask?"

The baron leaned over and kissed his wife's cheek. "My precious, I thought you had used your magic powers to bring it into being."

When Valéry expressed doubt at this, the baron tilted his head to one side and gave her a wink. "Oh yes I did, because it was at that very moment that you cast your spell on me, and I fell deeply and irrevocably in love with my enchantress."

It was hard for Valéry to imagine that life could be any happier than it presently was. Paul had indeed changed, and there were now no episodes when he treated her unkindly. Furthermore, the enrollment in her classes had increased, with as many girls as there were boys. Best of all, three of the older students, including Lucien, excelled to the point where the baron offered to send them to a university if they wished to go, and underwrite their expenses.

The printing press experiment at the chateau had not worked out. After the loss of Arsène, Jules, and Bruno, the baron paid a visit to the fledgling establishment the journeyman printer had begun in the largest city of the area, Condom, transferring all the chateau's printing equipment and supplies to this much more central location. He paid the salaries of the new print men he hired, continued to supply them with manuscripts to be printed, and in return received a portion of the profits.

As for the baron's former printers, Arsène was handed a ten-year prison sentence in *La Conciergerie* in Paris. Jules also was imprisoned there, but thanks to the pleadings of the viscount for his stepson, he was not put to death but instead given a long sentence for the murder of his mother. Bruno, on the other hand, managed to escape while being escorted back to Paris by the viscount and the guards. Valéry suspected that Marguerite, a sympathizer with the cause of the reformers and who gave refuge to many of them, had something to do with arranging for his flight. Valéry was glad, for she had talked to Marguerite about him before the party left for Paris, asking if the sister of the king could lend her influence to aid Bruno. About a month after his escape, she received a letter from Geneva. It read:

Chère Mademoiselle Valéry,

Here I am able to work alongside other reformers of the church, including the Frenchman Jean Cauvin who is called John Calvin. He remembers your Uncle Jacques and has been kind to me. So were you, mademoiselle, and I regret my brutish behavior toward you. Please pray for our cause and for me, that God will forgive my past and bless the work I am now doing.

Humbly Yours,
Bruno